Subtractions

Subtractions

Guida Jackson

SUBTRACTIONS

iUniverse books may be ordered through booksellers or by contacting:

iUniverse
1663 Liberty Drive
Bloomington, IN 47403
www.iuniverse.com
1-800-Authors (1-800-288-4677)

ISBN: 978-1-4917-7797-8 (sc)
ISBN: 978-1-4917-7799-2 (hc)
ISBN: 978-1-4917-7798-5 (e)

Print information available on the last page.

iUniverse rev. date: 10/08/2015

Acknowledgments

This tale, written in 1982 when my own life was in flux, was titled *Subtractions* from a quote by French journalist and poet, Lucie Delarue Mardrus: "Life consists of subtractions: things you have to give up." To me, that described the situation contemporary corporate families face, specifically those in the petro-chemical industry of which we in Houston were most familiar; it was a metaphor for our disconnected modern condition.

But toward the middle of the story, a quote from a much earlier period of my life kept niggling as more appropriate for the second section: it's from an old translation of Lao Tzu: "The secret awaits the insight of eyes unclouded by longing./Those who are bound by desire see only the outer container." I realized that Nature does not tolerate a vacuum; that something rushes in to compensate for that which has been subtracted.

That ineffable *Something* is the subject of this book, whose characters and the circumstances are entirely fictitious.

Eventually I knew the title that best described the second part of the story is *Making Do*, a skill we eventually learn. The overall theme, as expressed by the main character, is: "Just because a thing is futile is no reason to give up on it."

Since this could be the last time I put pen to yellow pad, I feel the weight of acknowledging such a multitude who made its writing—and my life, really—possible. I owe much to my writing group: Phyllis Prokop, Carol Rowe Bennett, Sharon Boswell, Frances Chapman, Julia Gomez-Rivas, Joyce Hardy, Lynda Jackson Ida Luttrell, Olivia Orfield, Mary Schomaker, and Gloria Wahlen. To list a dozen slights so many others. I will just say, "Thank you, all, for a rich and rewarding life."

For Jeff, Andy, Tucker, Annabeth, and Richard

PART I

SUBTRACTIONS

1

The Big Deal

It first occurred to Quentin that he had more than once dreamed the whole nightmare as he made that long walk through the secretarial pool, forcing a bounce to his step. Secretaries knew to avert their eyes when someone returned from the store room with an empty box; bad news spread through the building like a tidal flood, washing into basement mail rooms and remote coffee nooks, so that by the time a poor schmuck learned he'd been canned, to the rest of the world it was old news.

Stunned by the summary firing, Quentin still felt the bristling neck hairs and accompanying cold chill as he maintained a pace brisk enough to avoid chatter with the secretaries. He couldn't bear to see their pity.

The exercise was pointless. They could smell blood. It didn't take a rocket scientist to figure it out. He had seen it happen to countless others: the gradual easing out, the horizontal transfers over several years tantamount to demotions, so degrading that the victim often left on his own, precluding the dispensing of a generous severance package. He had been so blind that it never occurred to him to quit. Considering all he had given to Llano Petroleum, he hadn't seen it coming. So he had sat there in that prick's office in slack-jawed paralysis, unable to swallow to relieve the awful dryness, as his superior clicked off his severance benefits in a dispassionate sing-song while an underling named Milt Walker lurked nearby.

His office would be easy to clear of personal effects; after many transfers he had learned to pare down the clutter. Milt would be waiting to oversee the packing, to make certain he took nothing belonging to Llano, to confiscate his keys, his memory stick—how he needed those contacts now! Why hadn't he made a copy for himself? Why hadn't he anticipated this? But no: he'd given his life and loyalty to Llano, believing he was set for life. He'd been more loyal to the Company than to his first wife. But that was an old story....

And there was that: he was no longer a young man, even though, with his second wife, he had three young children. Who would want him now?

He maintained a façade of geniality even for Milt, who was indeed waiting, perched on the corner of Quentin's desk, matching phony grin for phony grin. Milt was younger by a good ten years, headed on an upward track, already having passed him by. It galled Quentin to have to ask, but he had to know.

"What's really behind this, Milt?"

The younger man pretended ignorance. "Hey, how would I know? Don't make a federal case out of it. It's nothing personal, never is. It's a volatile business—it happens. They're downsizing the division, getting lean and mean. You know that."

"But why me? You know I've been shifted so far from Explorations— four lateral transfers—" He wasn't grinning anymore. He was sweating.

Milt Walker, that jerk, rose and took a pointed look at his watch, then began rattling keys in his pocket. "Hey, I know nothing about..."

"Oh I think you do." Quentin met him eye to eye, so close that he could smell Milt's fruity breath. "It's my wife's cousin, isn't it?" Or, he wondered, was it Faye herself, with her metaphysical affectations that must offend many of the conservative wives.

He had relived it often it often: that night five years ago at a company party when Faye, eyes bright from too many cocktails, had blurted out in president Masterson's presence, "We have connections with Texoil, you know: my cousin is married to Weldon Cadenhead, assistant vice president of Explorations." He had watched Masterson's face harden and had felt a chill.

Now Milt tried to shrug him off, but Quentin figured he had struck the right nerve. "I'm being squeezed out because of a vague connection to the competition. Ever since Masterson found out, I've been getting the stiff-arm. Do they really think I'd leak secrets to a rival?"

"It might be risky, see. Your kids might say something. There's big money in it."

"We haven't seen those people in years! Anyway, I never talk business at home." But he knew it was futile. Too late. He couldn't contain his outrage, his powerless, emasculating outrage.

"Masterson should know me well enough by now," he said through gritted teeth. He felt the heat brimming and slammed a picture of Faye and the kids into the box.

Milt, his tone casual, said, "Are we finished here?"

Quentin picked up the box and swept the office with one last look. It was little more than a cubicle, a far cry from his sumptuous one as Assistant Vice President of Explorations five years ago. He had managed to keep Faye from visiting, to keep her from knowing how far he had fallen. At least he had saved face with his family.

There would be no dodging this news. A knot of dread stuck in his throat. He could picture the faces of his children: analytical Arthur, mischievous Donnie, wiseacre Olivia, their expressions drained of all trust, all respect. He could imagine Faye, masking her devastation in front of the children—or worse: trying to say something to make him feel better. Faye had never taken their transfers gracefully--the kids either, for that matter.

But no, actually he could picture none of it. Pride would never allow him to admit to them that he had failed. Maybe he would be lucky enough to find a new job before she got wind of it; then he could claim he had an offer he couldn't turn down.

Milt relieved him of his keys and accompanied him down the hall and into the elevator, trying to make light conversation. He'd have to give Milt that: making it seem like a friendly send-off instead of a degrading security escort off the premises.

They were alone on the elevator, Milt, jiggling the new set of keys, rocked onto his toes, glancing at the ceiling with guarded interest. With staged nonchalance, he said, "Too bad about never seeing that cousin. He might've been able to help."

Quentin remembered the elevator was bugged: a surveillance camera was beamed at them from behind the overhead grill. So he was to star in one final test, to see if he might, at long last, reveal some connection to the rival company back during the days when he had security clearance, back before Faye shot off her pretty mouth. The speculation that perhaps his firing had nothing to do with his job performance both enraged and heartened him. The rage was now directed toward Faye.

The elevator doors opened onto the lobby. Milt didn't step out, but offered a damp hand and another phony smile. "Hey, don't be a stranger. Let us know when you get situated."

The doors closed with solid finality. Quentin turned to hand in his badge to the security guard when Van Lord, his old assistant from Explorations, sauntered off another elevator. There was no avoiding him, no hiding the tell-tale box. Van glanced at the box with eyebrows raised in mock-surprise, taking in the situation at once.

"Quent! On your way out?" He reached for the box. "Let me help you carry that to the car."

Quentin started to protest, but something about Van's hard, direct gaze stopped him. As the guard looked on, he handed the box to his old friend, feigning relief. "Thanks. It was getting cumbersome."

As they headed for the car, Van said something that stunned him. "I was hoping this gradually easing you out was just a bad rumor." He kept his tone low, as if the very air might be bugged.

The words hit him like a fist to the middle. So the news had been out for a while. It was falling into place: the last four transfers were indeed designed to remove him gradually from Exploration so that, by the time they let him go, he would have no access to documents. He would be undesirable, un-hirable, useless to Texoil, for instance.

Neither spoke again until they reached the car. As Van scanned the area, Quentin guessed that a distant devise could pick up their conversation. He opened the trunk and they both leaned in while Van lowered the box inside. Van growled, "Interested in revenge? Coffee shop on Tenth in ten minutes."

By now the melodrama didn't seem so absurd. Quentin made a show of shaking Van's hand, then got into the car and drove toward the coffee shop, heart pounding. His life, so predictable and steady only an hour ago, had rocketed out of control. It was Faye fault, he was sure.

He reached the coffee shop before Van and found a booth in a secluded area with a view of the door. He didn't have to wait long: his friend joined him in minutes, sweeping quick, furtive glances right and left.

"I can't stay long," Van said. "They've tried to render you useless to the industry."

The news, hardly unsuspected by this time, still left Quentin quivering. So it was deliberate: they meant to destroy him.

"It was too late to change course when Masterson discovered you had such a valuable connection. You could be very useful to him." Van leaned forward and whispered. "Now you're free to free-lance."

"Free-lance what?" He heard his own voice, dull and lifeless.

The answer was barely audible. "Maps. No questions asked."

His pulse quickened. Maps…of what? Indonesia? Burma? Wasn't exploration in the Far East forbidden, or had he been out of Explorations too long to know? Quentin could figure out who the prospective buyer might be. He said, "Let me guess: you want me to act as go-between with a certain relative of my wife's. How do you know he's interested?"

Van looked at his watch and drummed his nails on the table in agitation. "We shouldn't be seen together. Let's just be clear about one thing: you're unemployable in the industry. You've been neutralized. You may never find another job in your field. Don't believe me? Test the waters. This is your chance to do what they suspected you of doing all this time."

One part of Quentin still refused to accept Van's assessment. "In the first place, what you're proposing is illegal."

"Did I mention your commission would be fifty thousand?"

The words rang like gongs against his brain. So it *must* be the Far East, some secret explorations. What he couldn't imagine a moment before began to seem plausible. He was interested enough to ask, "How were you able to copy them? Some kind of micro camera?"

"It's just as well you don't know." Van stood abruptly, nervously glancing around. "Think about it. Get your feet wet in the job market. When you see what you're up against, give me a call. Tell me you want to borrow my fishing rod, in case my phone is bugged. When we have to meet, make it at the food court at the mall, the Chicky-Bite booth. Lotsa noise."

Quentin waited until Van had been gone a half-hour, then drove the hour's commute home in north Dallas, composing a speech for Faye about why he was there in the middle of the day. In his fantasy the whole family would be present, condemning him with large sad eyes. Faye would hold up well in front of the kids. But at night in bed, with her back to him, he would hear her snuffles. And in the odd moment for days afterward, he would catch them looking at him as if he were a pariah.

He would never tell them. There was more than his self-respect to consider. He had suffered their reactions to his every transfer. His children became vaguely hostile, glaring because their lives were being uprooted. He always had to convince them of how much better their lives would be in the new location. That wouldn't work this time.

He had to find another job on the sly. But with Faye and the kids underfoot, that would be like trying to hide an elephant in the closet. He would have to send them off someplace to keep them from finding out, so that he could get calls at the house. He just needed a decent job, that's all.

But a silken voice inside his head reminded him: fifty thousand…tax free…

Faye had just finished shampooing her hair when he banged into the patio room of their low-slung split-level. She stood in the sunlight by an open window rubbing her sandy hair with a towel; he often hoped to catch her violating her own low-tech philosophy by using a blow dryer. She looked up sharply and the inevitable dread clouded her face.

He rushed to answer her unasked question. "It's not what you think, I've got to be away for a few…days, maybe weeks."

"Doing what?"

He panicked and blurted out the first thing that came to mind. "Mapping a county." Drat! She could poke holes through that one in a minute.

"You're kidding! At your age? You haven't had to do that since the first year—"

"Let's just say this is something…classified. Fracking disposal wells. Don't ask anything else about it." He headed for the bedroom, hands shaking. The room smelled of the incense she always lit after he left for work. It was supposed to call in the muse, or some such drivel.

She followed close behind. "Does this mean our summer vacation is off? *Again?*"

Inspiration! As if some guardian angel—or devil—perched next to his ear, the perfect solution popped into his head. "Not at all! The boss thought, to make my assignment look more innocent, we could all go someplace for the summer. Then I could steal away and no one would be the wiser."

She sat on the bed, somewhat mollified, but twisting the towel as if she were wringing—something. "Where would we go?"

He thought fast. Maintaining a family at a resort for the summer would be astronomical at a time when they needed to conserve their small reserve. He thought of the Fromberg farm.

"There's a place near my work that's right down your alley, with your Mother Earth stuff. The kids will have a great time. How'd you like to spend the summer on a farm?"

Still wary and, he thought, weary, she said, "Such as?"

"There are some friends of my folks from years ago. I recall an extra cottage on their place that would be just right for—us." He reached for his phone. "I'm going to see if they'll rent it to us."

She went into the bathroom and closed the door. As he looked for the number, a happy thought dawned: maybe he could use the maps as leverage to get a job at Texoil. Maybe furnishing the maps would prove to cousin Weldon that he would be an asset to Weldon's company. Pride would never permit him to grovel before anyone, much less his wife's relatives. He preferred to be wooed. This might be his ace, in case he *was* an industry pariah. But his career, and saving face, came first, even before money.

No, Faye would never agree to such a thing, and keeping it from her might be almost impossible. Besides, if he approached Weldon and failed, or if Llano somehow found out—he didn't even want to think about the consequences.

Still, the silken voice urged, it would serve Masterson right. Placing priceless maps in the hands of Texoil could cost Llano billions down the line as soon as trade sanctions were lifted, and some sort of secret negotiations must already be in the works. Nobody had ever stuck it to Masterson; his dirty tricks easily managed to top everyone else's.

His mood lightened. His natural optimist resurfaced. Just the thought of revenge sent hot cleansing blood surging through his veins. By the time Old Lady Fromberg came on the line, he had worked out the details. It was a plan he was sure Faye would buy. He could even put this one past those three nosy kids. It was one time his home-grown rat-pack wouldn't be around to trip him up.

2

Qentin stopped at the vending machine near the north escalators and bought the biggest shopping bag available—visible proof that he had legitimate business in the mall. It was large enough to carry whatever Van had for him. All the maps he'd ever seen were much too long to be spirited out of the office undetected, much less out of a shopping mall in a shopping bag. But that was not his problem.

It hadn't taken twenty-four hours to decide to take Van up on his offer; he had lain awake most of the night planning how he would stick it to Masterson, hardly able to wait for morning to phone Van to tell him, "I want to borrow your fishing gear—soon!"

He looked at his watch: three-forty. Late enough to miss the mommies, scurrying home to beat the school buses, but early enough to catch noisy teenagers who would mask any attempt to record their conversation, in case Van had been followed. Van had thought it all out. Exhilaration pumped along his veins with a palpable heat.

This must be what the big boys feel: that surge of power that comes with control, being foxier than any board room strategist, stronger than any buy-out bid. There is no power in being a middle-man, he realized afresh, as if he hadn't been hit with the same epiphany dozens of times before, when he was much closer to the center of the action than he was now. There is only power at the top…

…and along the fringes. In the brush. Waiting for someone to trip the wire. The guerrilla's position was the only step above the power monger's at the top. The guerrilla occupied the throne where God used to be. No, he was better than God: he was God and Devil all in one, an unbeatable combination. His temples throbbed with the sweet warmth of vengeance.

He took the escalator to the second level and walked briskly to the food court. The Chicky-Bite booth was crowded with high schoolers. Two dusky-skinned teenagers in greasy red caps and aprons made slovenly passes across the counter with paper towels. The nearest eyed him with a glare that was anything but welcoming.

Quentin studied the menu and said, "I'll have an orange."

"What size?"

"Small."

The teenager turned to his companion and said, "One large orange."

Quentin interrupted. "No. Make that a *small*."

The boy's look of contempt telegraphed the message that he was dealing with a cretin. "Large *is* small."

Quentin felt like an idiot. The change in values had permeated every level of society, and he hadn't kept up. He took his drink to a table near the glass-brick wall in back and sat, glancing at his watch again. Van was late.

A man a few tables away lowered his newspaper and called a bit too loudly, "Quent! Is that you? Well I'll be darned!" Van got up with a great show of surprise, extending his hand. It was smooth, with carefully manicured nails, and his Princeton ring gleamed.

"How are you?" He pumped Quentin's hand with too much gusto. "Mind if I join you?" He went back to his table and retrieved his coffee and his paper napkin.

When he returned, Quentin grinned, lifting his drink in salute. "That was worthy of an Oscar."

Van's words did not match his jovial flash of porcelain caps. "There'll be a trial run to see how you handle yourself. But this is no game. You're in, I take it. So here's the deal: we'll help you arrange for a place close—but not so close as to look suspicious—to Texoil and Weldon."

Quentin winced. He hadn't realized the venture would entail another move. Faye would be livid when she found out.

Van went on. "Soon as you're settled, as soon as you can work it in naturally, contact him and make your pitch."

"Which is--?"

"Basically, it's a supermarket. After your trial run, he can have whatever we've got." He ducked his head, whispering, "Even Burma. Or the Amarillo Mountains."

Quentin harked back to his freshman geology to recall a range of granite mountains buried 100 million years ago under thousands of tons of sediment on the flat Texas panhandle. They are an extension of Oklahoma's Arbuckle and Ouachita Mountains that reach into Arkansas.

They were discovered, he recalled, by early oil drillers. But some peaks are 10,000 feet high, and you'd have to dig down 2,500 feet just to reach the top of the tallest peak. "Surely nobody's desperate enough to drill all the way…"

Van's frown was enough to silence him. Van lifted his cup to his lips and spoke from behind it. "Don't ask me why, but there's a new level of interest since the frackers hit the scene."

Quentin had noticed no briefcase, not even a shopping bag. "So where's the merchandise? How am I supposed to know what we have?"

"You'll get a menu, plus a sample, in about four seconds. Also the number of your contact from here on. This will be our last meeting." As he leaned forward, the heavy scent of Giorgio settled between them. Quentin focused on his face. Not a single hair was out of place, not a stray eyebrow hair unclipped. The brows closed in a frown. "I should warn you there'll be tests along the way. You understand the need for absolute discretion. Not even Faye---"

Quentin cleared his throat to hide his discomfort. "Understood. No problem there." He shifted on the narrow chair. He couldn't put it off much longer, couldn't keep avoiding her. She was going to find out sooner or later about losing his job. If only he could only get them out of town before she found out, then he could break the news in a letter. Then he wouldn't have to put up with her guff. Or see the look on her face when she found out they were moving again.

Van got up as he spoke, raising his voice again. "I've got to run. Good to see you again. Say hello to Faye and the kids."

Quentin half rose, looking around, expecting to find—but Van was turning away. As if in afterthought, he hissed over his shoulder, "Check the napkin." Then he hurried off, whistling.

Quentin's gaze riveted on the paper napkin, which appeared thicker than normal. With nonchalance he slid it toward it, wadding it slightly, bringing it to his lips, feeling two stiff squares inside. Ordinary slides, they must be. Slides that Weldon could examine on a viewer in the safety of Quentin's study. Not sensitive material, surely, which would probably be on microchip.

He stuck the napkin into his pocket in what he hoped was an absent-minded gesture and, abandoning the shopping bag, left the food court at a saunter, with a fresh surge of adrenaline propelling each step. He was alive as he had never been before!

He should have been an explorer, or a test pilot. Now he understood why men dared to do foolhardy things, why they take risks. Risking made everything stand out in sharp relief.

Then there was the promise of tangible rewards, big time.

Oh yes, and the one he'd probably have to miss and could only imagine: the look on Masterson's face when he found out he'd been bested.

He hurried, whistling, to his car and locked himself inside before he dared to draw the napkin from his pocket. Sure enough, two slides were wrapped in its folds. But the sight of the name and number scratched on the napkin brought an involuntary rush and changed everything in a split second. He let out an audible, "Oh my God!"

It was Betts's number; *she* was to be his contact! But Betts was Masterson's stooge, his private secretary!

3

The day after classes dismissed, the Aherns packed up for a summer on the farm, which, Momma said, was so they could be close to Daddy while he did something Important for The Company, something to further his Career. Olivia had shot Donnie a "here we go again" look. After all, it was hard to ignore the gradual lateral drift of Daddy's famous Career, but somehow Momma managed to remain blind. Even Olivia at six and Donnie at seven could see that Daddy was slipping sideways.

Olivia sensed something fishy even before the others, even though Arthur was supposed to be the one who tested out at near-genius level. "Am I the only one who thinks this is weird?" she asked as they climbed out of the van. "Haven't you ever wondered why we don't just visit Grandma like other kids?"

Donnie bopped her on the arm. "Because other people's grandparents *speak* to them, yogurt-brain. Because they go to a different church, or something. So we're like dog doo to them."

"Convenient," Arthur said. "Fewer people Dad has to explain to." Arthur, from his vantage of his almost twelve years, was particularly put-upon by having to leave for the summer and added, "I doubt anybody bothers to write down our address in ink anymore."

"Like your public's going to care where you are," Donnie said, referring to the fact that Arthur set great store by the number sixteen, when his life would magically begin.

Even though Daddy helped with the move this time, it was still an exhausting job, because the North Texas sun remains high overhead for hours during June. And despite a great pile-up of cumulous battlements on the horizon, the merciless heat boiled down on Olivia's head all afternoon with no let-up. They took only necessities for their three-month stay in the country; still, it was later afternoon before they finished unloading.

Afterwards, Olivia and family stood out beside Daddy's car, mopping off the sweat and fanning to get dry.

Momma stared out across the road through the shimmering heat at a field of buffalo grass, flat as a landing strip, comparing the place to East Texas. "I'll miss the trees, miss their sentience. You can hug a tree and draw strength. But—" Optimism surfaced in spite of herself. "The sky is stunning! Like back where I grew up." Then she began wondering aloud why Llano would want to send Daddy back to map a *county*, for goodness sake! It was a point that had puzzled Olivia as well.

"Surely every company on earth has already done it. Why would Llano do it again?"

By then they all knew that Daddy set more store by Llano Petroleum than it did by him, but Arthur had explained that there was a lot of fat in the whole industry, and so long as a man was only mildly inept, it was safer to keep him on the payroll: after a few years, he knew too much to risk letting him go. It was Arthur's certainty of their secure situation despite all evidence to the contrary which once led Olivia to pop off, "If Livvie is short for Olivia, Arthur must be short for Authority!"

Too, Arthur had explained the night before, the oil business had a brotherhood that took care of one another. At Llano the winning combination was being ex-football from A&M or else being Kappa Sig from LSU like Mr. Masterson, which thank goodness, Daddy was, too, before he went off to study religion but ended up becoming a petroleum nerd for some reason. Olivia and Donnie had to concede that Arthur was generally right. Surely he wasn't old enough to remember first-hand all he knew, but he caught onto things by listening and thinking about what he overheard. Arthur thought deeply about things, all things. He spent his time reading and thinking and preparing for his life, his wonderful life, which would begin on his sixteenth birthday.

Even Olivia recognized that Daddy had many trap doors his mind disappeared through, the first being that Llano would take care of them forever so that they would never have to wake up. He had illusions about how he was moving up the ladder, how all their lived revolved around his career, which was the case only when he was around. Most of the time Daddy governed from afar. Olivia and her brothers saw themselves as holding down the home front for one of the absentee fathers engaged in a different sort of campaign than the wars that had kept other generations of fathers away. This campaign had no end that she could see.

They suspected that Daddy's illusions kept him alive. Daddy ("Old Profit and Loss," Arthur called him) believed what he wanted, and then Momma ("Old Ebb and Flow," Donnie rebutted), grudgingly joined in. So the prevailing illusion was that every transfer was to a better job, regardless of all indications to the contrary, and despite what Momma heatedly called "flagrant corporate contractual slippages and infringements."

Anyway, even if they had learned the truth, it wouldn't have stayed uncovered for long. But they sensed the truth anyhow. "Truth is a lot like cat poop," Arthur told them. "You can't cover it up enough to keep it from being found."

In their numerous relocations they had slipped gradually from the well-pruned upper middle class oil patch neighborhoods to gimcrack suburbs of close-pressed houses, and sometimes to shabby little towns choking in honeysuckle where nobody forgets you're a newcomer. It worked to their advantage, particularly with teachers. Momma, who had a natural need for solitude, insisted that she preferred small places: "In a city, you forget what freedom is like. Besides, everything's human scale and people's identities go down deep, back generations."

But Momma, on one of her tirades, falling easily into what Arthur called her "college days vocabulary," would claim with great fervor, her beige cheeks showing hints of pink, that the country had fallen all the way back to Defoe's time, into a "binary clad conflict," in which small towns were unwittingly losing ground. Although Olivia could only guess at what it meant, she often thought of it in the tub, as her bath water was gurgling down the drain.

The transient tenor of their lives was hard on Momma: the Aherns never knew the comfort of abandoning pretense. They lived in constant tension due to their contrived stance of affluence and stability. But since no one outside Llano ever knew them very long or very well, they got by. Olivia and Donnie, prodigal seedlings, had learned to settle in quickly and bluff it out when against the snootiest gangs, even those in their current community just out of the city limits north of Dallas.

Now they found themselves miles from home, having lugged their boxes into a cramped little gray stucco house that Momma, finally reaching the end of her endurance, openly called a sharecropper's house, a new low, even for them. When they first saw it, Donnie had whispered, "So this is the great family vacation paradise."

"Sea World it's not," Olivia had snorted, electing not to call specific attention to the whipping dust or the crumbling red paint on the trim of the tiny box of a house. Peeling paint always worried Momma; she was sure it was full of lead and they would all be poisoned immediately from eating it. The front porch floor was covered in green Astroturf, because the last occupant had been Mr. Fromberg's mother, who was afraid of slipping. Even the porch steps were carpeted with Astroturf. Momma called it "Tammy Fay-ish," but Olivia liked its prickle against her bare feet.

Daddy usually bragged about his assignments, but he'd barely said two words about this one. Olivia wondered if Momma, gullible Momma, had her suspicions as well. Even if she did, she wouldn't get a straight answer out of him, no matter how much she pried. He only said, more than once, in a peevish bark, "Typical of Frank. Always has to do things his own way."

It irked Daddy how Frank could wheel and deal and get his name in the papers. Daddy called him "Frank" behind his back, as if they were on the verge of sleeping in the same bet, but if they ever talked by phone—in the old days—it was "Yes *sir*, Mr. Masterson!" Kissy-face talk, Arthur called it.

Now, Olivia and Momma and Daddy stood beside the car as Daddy prepared to leave, and Momma returned to the subject, as if she might at long last wheedle some explanation from him. "But such a waste of talent! A third-year geology student could map a county."

For once Daddy didn't argue. He looked down at Olivia and said, "Yes, in the old days, even Livvie could do it."

Olivia colored at the casual sideswipe and a pain, quick as a snake, darted in her chest. He liked her better before she got so gawky. Why couldn't she be dimply, instead of all shoulder blades and elbows, sharp edges? Sweat trickled from her temples, and she wished her hair wouldn't stick to her head in mousey strings.

"I wish you wouldn't call her that," Momma snapped, in a lashing tone that would fillet a catfish, which caused Olivia to glance up quickly at her suddenly dark eyes. "Can't you ever just call things by their right names?"

Her outrage seemed all out of proportion. Olivia recalled Arthur's telling them that their parents never talk about what they're really talking about. Arthur had heard Momma tell Daddy he always had a hidden agenda, as if it were an accusation.

Momma's voice petered out. She and Olivia held their breaths and watched Daddy stiffen, then shrink. He looked at his watch and said,

"Guess I'd better go if I'm going to make it back before night." Right before their eyes he had taken on the sapped look of a vagrant, or a whipped little boy.

Like quicksilver, Momma perked up and began to smile and spring around, trying to divert him from his gloom. Probably sorry she'd popped off, Olivia figured, having observed that females can't bear for anybody to be mad at them and seem compelled to make up even if they're in the right. Momma cleared her throat very business-like and said, "I sure don't want you to be out on the road after dark. Not on those old worn-out tires!"

Momma had a hard time with his leaving, and as usual she began batting her eyelids fast and swallowing out loud. Her tears seemed to galvanize him out of his funk and into overdrive. He fairly spat out his words. "For crying out loud, Faye, do we have to go through this every single time?"

"I'm sorry," she said, but Olivia could tell that she couldn't help herself. She might, in fact, get worse.

"You live in a world of pure Kitsch, Faye! You not only worship it, you worship your worship of it. Give me a break this time, for God's sake! I'm trying to make a living—" Daddy was in his attack mode: his best defense out of every tight spot.

"I'm sorry." Her valiant effort not to tear up again was awful to watch.

For something to do, Olivia yelled at the others, who had drifted to the side yard playing fifty rounds of grab-ass. Arthur had the dog looped around his neck like a fur collar with two stiff white stumps: she had two broken legs set in home-made casts. Donnie was trying to coax her to him, galloping circles around Arthur.

"Daddy's about to leave," Olivia hollered. Both boys stopped, and she could see the pleasure drain out of their faces. They shambled over and everyone stood there lapping up Daddy, getting him fixed in their minds. Things were never the same when he was gone; he left them malnourished, at least for the first few weeks until they had practically forgotten him.

They weren't so blinded by his shortcomings as not to appreciate his talk-show-host good looks: the tanning salon leanness and the patches of gray at his temples. He kept his hair styled and perfect; with overheated self-concern, he stood in front of the bathroom mirror for hours, trimming little hairs out of his nose and going over and over his face with the razor, feeling and smoothing his cheeks between each swipe, keeping everybody waiting while he prepared to meet his public. Often he quoted somebody who said a good exterior is a silent recommendation. So he had an excellent recommendation, for all the good it did. Arthur groused more than once, "He wouldn't worry so much about what people think about him if he knew how seldom people think about him." His polish extended to the gray silk suits and Italian shoes—the children weren't to touch him when he was dressed for fear of marring his impeccability.

Their father had been all over the world, the children often told their cohorts with pride. Llano had sent him to Dubai, Libya, Colombia, Scotland; Olivia couldn't remember where else. He could keep them entertained with tales he'd heard from roustabouts during his nights of well-sitting years ago when he was just starting out.

Or he could ignore them as if they didn't exist, which particularly devastated Arthur. Donnie and Olivia, having each other, never felt totally deprived, and Momma seemed to fare all right after the first few hours. But he had a way of minimalizing their emotional poverty, particularly just before he left them alone to wallow in it.

Daddy said Momma was "charged with moral fervor left over from college days." Whatever it was, Momma used it to hold them together, growing more beige by stages, to match her fading hair. A hint of jowl was noticeable along her jaw when she wasn't smiling, when she thought no one was looking. Although she maintained face for all their sakes, even Olivia sensed that the family was being sucked by degrees ever closer toward what Uncle Cas called "a growing pool of permanent sleaze class," and they only just kept above it by her frantic and unceasing treading. What mystified Olivia was why they were sliding so badly. They didn't fit the pattern of any other oil family.

Daddy bent and nipped Olivia's cheek a little too hard, his bright blue eyes crinkling at the corners the way she liked. "Let's see a smile. You'll have so many things to do this summer, you won't even miss me. You'll be begging your brothers to let you help them pick Mrs. Fromberg's peaches." He slipped this in so fast they hardly noticed it, then pointed off toward the river, whose sandy path was marked by a line of cottonwoods, and hurried on. "I've heard there are thousands of fossils in those banks. Maybe you can dig up a whole dinosaur."

Arthur snorted. "Some vacation this is going to be for me! They'll wander off and Mom'll start worrying about rattlesnakes, and I'll have to stop every ten minutes and go look for them."

"Dodo, you're the one who'll end up getting lost," Donnie shot back, and Olivia nodded. Some people can't come out of a mall and find the car in the parking lot. They invariably come out the wrong door and end up thinking their car's been stolen. Arthur was like that, or would be, when he got old enough to drive.

Momma told them to quit bickering. "Can't we all put on a pleasant face for your father just this once?" As if it was the absolute only time he had ever left them, or ever would, and as if hers wasn't the longest face of all. Arthur looked miffed that he didn't get to make a snarky come-back. What sacrifices they all made for Daddy.

But Momma had picked up on the bomb. "What's this about peaches? What have you neglected to tell us? Are the children expected to do chores for our keep, like share-croppers?"

They all turned to him expectantly. Even the dog had caught the mood and was quiet, waiting. Not that it was going to do any good, Olivia and Donnie agreed with a look between them. Daddy could wiggle out of any cross-examination by pretending something was too trivial for comment.

They were used to surprises by now, except Momma. Why she didn't catch on that things were always this way, Olivia couldn't figure. After he left there would be some fresh outrage, an unpaid bill, or something broken that he left unfixed for them to find out about when they needed it. Momma would promise this would be their final move; that Daddy was at least settled in a Big Important Position and they would be able to join Scouts or take dancing lessons. Then she would fling across the bed, snuffling in the dark, before she started packing and making a new round of excuses—because invariably she had taken root despite her best intentions not to. Olivia would hide her own distress even from Donnie. But Daddy took moves as opportunities, leading to better things. Arthur often groused that if Daddy pitched in with the actual work of moving, reality might sink in.

Now Daddy waved off her question about the peaches as if it were a gnat, smoothed his shirt and climbed into the car. Regally. You'd think he was off to assume a throne. Olivia half expected him to give the royal wave. He rolled down the window and unpinned Momma's hair so that it fell onto her shoulders: a sudden tender gesture that caused Olivia to swallow hard. Momma gasped, caught off guard.

"You can wear it this way all summer, like you used to, be a budding anarchist again, and who's to care?" he said with tenderness. When he spoke like that, Olivia began to feel left out.

Momma snorted to hide her pleasure. "Don't be too sure! Mrs. Fromberg is no Dr. Zim."

Donnie curled his lower lip. "Dorky! Who's Dr. Zim?"

"Somebody from our flower-child days: a philosophy guru and fellow crypto-anarchist," Momma said in a drifty voice. Her hand closed around a wad of her shirt front, as if clutching some precious, happier memory.

To keep from having to watch, Olivia made a circle in the dust with her bare toe and placed five dots inside, naming them Momma, Daddy, Arthur, Donnie, Livvie. She wondered how she could fix it so that they would finally all be together in one spot all the time.

Daddy turned on the motor and revved it to a roar. The wind from the exhaust obliterated her circle. It was a hot car: a Porsche, granted, with old bald tires, but tasteful. Daddy justified the expense because it was good for his image. Momma got to keep the van, the Brown Mud-Hen.

"Mind your mother," he called as he pulled away.

"Write!" Momma yelled into the wind, but he didn't hear.

Olivia looked up sharply. Momma sounded much more frantic than usual, and she wondered if there was a reason.

4

Faye and the children stood in the yard and watched until the Porsche turned onto the highway and the pluming dust had sifted to white haze. Then Donnie began dancing around, poking at Arthur, wanting to get back to their game. But Faye's mood seemed to have communicated itself to Arthur, and even the puppy Ramona began to fret. With effort, Faye relaxed her clenched jaw and tried to smile. Still, she wondered what all this was really about. She couldn't put it out of her mind that Quentin was up to something. But once again, he had left her out of his life.

Eventually even Donnie subsided and they all headed back to the little house, scuffing up the dirt as they dragged their feet. Inside, Faye wrinkled her nose at the smell of mothballs and camphor. How could they bear this place for three whole months, with its sluggish ceiling fan, green Naugahyde couch and two mustard vinyl recliners separated by a dark particle-board table topped by a lava lamp? The only picture on the water-stained flowered wall depicted Jesus, holding what looked like a heart in his hands.

Arthur stood before it and jabbed a forefinger to his tongue. "Double barfo!"

She examined the bent metal slats of the grimy blinds and said, "These'll look better up. At least we don't have to worry about prowlers out here. How about some fresh air?" She raised the blinds, sending a cloud of dust motes tumbling in the shaft of afternoon light. The room looked, if anything, worse. She tugged at the window sash, but it was stuck tight.

Donnie plopped down on the sofa, which made a wheeze that sent Olivia into storms of laughter. Arthur grimaced and said, "Oh barf! It's a smarmy snake pit!"

Secretly, Faye agreed, but she said, "Well, who says we have to stay inside on a nice afternoon? We can sit on the porch...Just think! A whole summer to sit and look at the huge sky. I love to put my feet up and watch the clouds. And at night we can watch for shooting stars."

They scuffed behind her back out to the porch. Donnie and Olivia rushed to capture the big swing, while Faye and Arthur sat on the top step. Arthur turned to them and said, "You dorks should let Momma have the swing. She wanted to put her feet up."

"She can't put her feet up here," Donnie said. "Out, maybe, but not up."

Faye patted Arthur's knee; her champion, he generally stood up for her, no matter what. "It's okay. There are very few places left anymore where you can put your feet up." She felt the Astroturf and added, "You know, I gave up my dream of being a bag lady because I wouldn't have been able to put my feet up." She looked off wistfully across the prairie, now growing pale and bare in the slanting light. "It's funny how dreams die over trifles."

She must not allow herself to grow melancholy, must not feel abandoned. She could read, she could meditate, listen to music. She was free, at least, from Quentin's disapproving eye.

A lone bird squawked high overhead, probably lost from its flock. She strained to see it, but the light was changing rapidly. "Might be a goose, looking for its leader." She turned to Arthur. "Want to be the lead goose this summer?"

She often told them about the lead goose: how one goose must fly harder to slice the wind for the ones in the vee behind, and how the geese took turns, the leader dropping back to float on the air currents of the others while a rested one took its place in the lead. Now Arthur didn't answer. Her question didn't seem to call for an answer, anyway.

Sitting there in the fading light amid awakening chirps of night creatures, surrounded by the familiar shapes of those closest to her, Faye needn't worry about who would be lead goose. She felt safe, comforted by the presence of her three very bright children. Whatever happened, whoever led, her flock would cling together until Quentin returned from his mysterious trip.

Probably out of boredom, Donnie said, as if it weren't a name they'd lived with all their lives, "Who is Frank, anyway?" Donnie wasn't as clueless as he pretended. Faye remembered her own childhood, when most of the information she gleaned came by affecting a naiveté she had long ago left behind. Her children's cunning was second nature. They were inured to sudden change, with handy answers for embarrassing questions.

It wasn't only to salve their own egos; it was partly to protect her, she knew, and she was touched by their concern.

"You know very well Frank is the President," she said, pretending to be cross. "He and Daddy went to the same school, and he thinks very highly of your father. Ever since Daddy was moved from Explorations to Acquisitions, Frank has been looking for the best position so that Daddy's talents wouldn't be wasted."

The children had heard it often enough to be able to recite Quentin's whole history: "Next it was to Main Personnel, but after all the jealousies there, he went into Distribution. Next he was in Sales, which is Very Important." They recited it in high nasal unison.

Faye ignored the sarcasm. "But Daddy's much too brilliant to be happy in Sales for long, so he took over the In-house Organ."

Olivia and Donnie exchanged glances. Olivia clamped both hands over her mouth. They invariably broke up at the mention of In-house Organ. Faye frowned at Olivia and hurried on. "Daddy could have edited the In-house Organ blindfolded, and that's probably the real reason that Frank Masterson has decided to send him out on this hush-hush assignment—for the challenge."

Arthur sniffed and muttered, "Baloney."

Arthur: Faye studied him sitting on the top step with his oversized feet planted on the second, hunched over so that his knees almost hid his profile. The pooch sprawled beside him, splinted legs askew. It was a challenge keeping up with such a brilliant boy.

But what else could she say about him? Not that he epitomized the fresh-faced, clear-eyed promise of youth, because he never had. She remembered one spring when he had come close, when he had become pitcher for his team, and he spent hours practicing into a pillow in the back yard as if he were on fire. But then Llano transferred them, and it was too late to play ball in the new place. Arthur took up reading astronomy and went back to looking the way he always had: he went around open-mouthed, as if he were gasping. As if he were starving for a drink, or starving for something. His eyes stayed moist with a faraway hopeless longing. Like the dog. Ramona had the same kind of needy look. Arthur and Ramona: what a perfect pair.

She often thought Arthur could have come out of the mind of Aristotle: almost too smart for his own good. It was frightening to have the responsibility of rearing such a son. She recalled the time he looked up from his book and said to nobody, "If the universe is in chaos and there's no order, anybody who invents a survival technique is actually smart, not stupid like we thought."

Faye had come to, startled. "What do you mean by that?"

"We live in a time of shaken convictions," he intoned, like an old man, stealing a glance down at his book to be sure he got the words right. "We have to cling to something. We're not all evolving at the same rate, see. People at a certain stage invent religion to get through the chaos with less discomfort. It's their hot water bottle. I think Blaise Pascal must've said that."

He promptly went back to his book while Faye stared at him and marveled that he was older than the oceans. Later, after she had had time to think about it, she told him, "If you deprive people of their religion, you defeat them. Just remember that, when you grow up."

The children claimed that Daddy's Career was his religion, although nominally he always chose an upscale Episcopalian church for the family to attend. Even the children knew it was strictly for making business connections. Faye held onto backwater virtues, her "Aristotle words" which she required the children to memorize: sweetness, tolerance, prudence (wisdom being too lofty), and fortitude—to give her dictum authority, she attributed them to great sages.

Too, she had an affinity for Mother Earth and Nature and animals and trees, which Quentin complained was turning into a religion. Faye reminded her family that druids worshiped trees and she, being part Welsh, must be part druid.

When Olivia asked, "What *do* you believe, Momma?" Faye had answered after some hesitation, "We are compelled to believe in grace, most certainly."

"Who's grace?"

"Grace is that in the universe which assents to our being."

She knew she hadn't answered adequately. "But it takes more grace to be happy than some people can muster. Anyway, don't squeeze the life out of every single mystery. Great revelations are lost on the literal-minded." She couldn't forget her own strict childhood training.

As a girl, Faye had sung in the church choir, but she rationalized that, being a Llewellyn, she loved to sing, and besides, her father had directed the choir—"a case of the bland leading the bland," she said. Often when Quentin was gone, she would drag out the auto-harp and put the children through the ordeal of singing old hymns and folk songs, even though they never got the hang of harmony. Still, no matter how they sounded, she took them doggedly to the end; that partly satisfied some deep need in her parched soul, and she was grateful that they humored her.

When they had mangled every tune in sight, Faye was content for a while and nostalgic about her own upbringing, which, now that she was removed from it, seemed chock full of music. ("And therefore far superior to our own pitiable carefree state," Arthur would opine with sarcasm.) She often told them, "You poor, poor little waifs are coming up without a bit of training!"

To please her they would try to look appropriately deprived, but Arthur really meant it. "Someday I'm going to take up an instrument," he'd say grandly, and Donnie would lean over to Olivia and say, "Maybe it'll be his In-house Organ."

Faye usually ignored their irreverence, but the evening of their move to the farm, sitting out on the porch in the cool of sundown, watching for the first firefly, she said suddenly. "I know exactly what we can do this summer!"

Donnie and Olivia popped up, ready for adventure. Arthur didn't move. Faye said, "I've neglected your musical training long enough. There's no reason we have to wait until we can afford lessons. I can teach you what I know, and as soon as Daddy gets on his feet, we'll insist on a piano."

Donnie and Olivia sank back and exchanged nudges and looks of resignation. As if on cue, they broke into a gradually escalating whine, which they had down to a fine art.

But Faye cut them off. "None of that. You'll want to be in the band when you get into junior high, and you'll need at least the rudiments of music theory before you try out." She never asked. She just made statements like, "You'll want to be in the band." Generally the children accept these as unquestionable Truths that they just hadn't encountered yet.

Donnie caught the bait and jumped out of the swing, marching around as if he was in a band, with his sandy curls like brambles flopping into his eyes. Olivia pulled at his shirt and said, "Sit down. You look like a Chia pet."

"I'm going to play a horn! Can I have a trumpet? What'll Livvie play? Can she be a baton twirler?"

Despite herself, Faye shuddered. "Goodness no! Twirling's not music! I think the flute is the instrument for Olivia. And don't call her Livvie."

Arthur couldn't lower himself to join in Donnie's march, but he had lifted his head and was snapping his fingers—out of sync, of course. "What'll I play? A clarinet?"

That stumped Faye. Finally, with more tact than the others probably thought necessary, she told him, "I think you will be a percussionist of some sort."

That was impressive enough to mollify Arthur, but Donnie muttered, "Whatever that is, it won't be melodious."

When Arthur harmonized, he was always plus or minus about a half-tone. At times he wandered all over the scale, and Faye would have him sing Pom Pom Pom so that he didn't interfere too greatly with the melody. Arthur didn't have a clue about how tone deaf he was. It mystified the rest of them how he could sing so lustily without any clue of how wretched he sounded.

Several months ago Arthur had come into the room holding an old broom as if he were strumming it and announced, "When I'm sixteen I'm going to buy a guitar and form a band."

Donnie and Olivia rolled off the couch, convulsed with laughter. Even Faye had difficulty suppressing a smile. After all, ambition, if it were to be taken seriously, much less achieved, had to be rooted in possibility. But Quentin had jerked both youngsters to their feet and barked, "Enough of that!" Faye had never heard him so angry. He was almost tender toward Arthur as he told him, "Pay no attention to them, son. Don't ever let anybody steal your dreams." A quick pain stabbed her spirit.

So began Arthur's delusion toward stardom. Fortunately for them all, he was never going to scrape together enough to buy even a cheap guitar, so at least they were spared the twanging. But after that he went around air-guitaring and yowling, under the impression that he was singing. Strange thing: although Olivia and Donnie considered Arthur their natural enemy, about his aspirations they became protective, apparently enduring his noise out of pity. Faye figured they were buoyed by the secret knowledge that in this one area, they were his superiors.

Quentin's tenderness toward Arthur wasn't just because he was the first-born. It had to do with his looks: Arthur favored Quentin, while Donnie and Olivia looked like Faye. Arthur was already tall for his age and slender, and except for the usual adolescent blemishes, he was a nice-looking boy. Quentin often compared Arthur to himself at that age. Faye sighed. The others had plenty of reason to despise Arthur, all right. Who would want to resemble her? She was bland.

Then there was the instance of the dog. The night Quentin brought her home, shortly before their latest move, he had presented her to Faye as a gift. An injured dog, yet. With two broken legs. Some present. He went to work splinting her two legs, which he claimed were broken by a hit and run driver just after he'd paid good money for her. Or so he'd said. Faye didn't take the gift in the spirit in which it was offered, thinking about another mouth to feed and one more thing to look after. Quentin's rationale was that they would need a watch dog while he was gone, although Donnie pointed out, "A puppy in leg casts isn't exactly a high quality watch dog." But Arthur grabbed her and hugged her so fiercely that Quentin laughed and said, "All right, son. She can be your dog, then." The others must have felt a sting of favoritism.

Faye noted that secretly they began to woo Ramona. Since she could barely stump around, she had to be carried everywhere, an added inconvenience as they tried to pack. Olivia and Donnie fought over the privilege, yanking her until she yelped. Arthur scooped in with a venomous, "Get your nasty paws off my dog!"

During the long drive to the farm, Ramona's good-natured presence had kept the children diverted. They took turns nursing her, whom Arthur named Ramona after a girl who used to be in his class. He tried to convince them ("as if we're morons," Olivia said) that he'd forgotten all about any girl by that name. Donnie struck a blow by agreeing that Ramona was a good name because "that girl you used to like was a real dog!" But Arthur looked so crestfallen that the others were immediately sorry. Even when he was The Enemy, he was first of all their big brother.

She didn't forget the promise of music lessons. As soon as supper was over that first night at the farm, she called them in from chasing fireflies to begin what Arthur termed "post-druidic torture." Olivia was first, to her dismay: "By Arthur's turn, you'll be pooped out and ready to quit." Faye, cheeks warm with anticipation, sat Olivia down at the auto-harp with an old songbook she found, and watched Olivia's expression turn to disbelief as it dawned on her that she was to decipher those notes. But Faye had a way of bending the children to her will, and somehow Olivia began to read. The process obviously wasn't unpleasant, especially when Faye sang along in her high crystal voice. Soon Olivia was joining in, sure that hers was as pleasing as Momma's.

By bedtime, suspicions about Quentin's activities subsided. The children squabbled over who was to sleep where. Faye decreed that the two boys would have the front bedroom while she and Olivia shared the dismal back one. She boosted Olivia into the high narrow bed to sink into the strange wool mattress that, despite Faye's crisp clean linens, smelled of liniment and rancid urine.

Down the short hall they could hear Arthur and Donnie biffing one another and bickering about who would sleep next to the wall. A window air conditioner switched on, drowning out all other sound and filling the air with a musty smell. Olivia pulled the sheet under her chin and let out one last pitiful whine. "But I *need* to sleep with Donnie, or I won't be able to sleep at all!"

Arthur's voice belled down the hall, above the air conditioner's whir. "Give it up, Liv. Not going to happen. It's futile."

Olivia yelled back stubbornly, "Just because something's futile is no reason to give up on it, snot-head!"

Faye gasped with delight. "Why Olivia! That's absolutely brilliant!" She leaned down and kissed her forehead. "You know, don't you, that even a drowning person doesn't quit calling for help. The reason you're so wise is that you're so recently arrived from Mother Earth's womb. You haven't forgotten her wisdom yet. Optimism still clings to you like amnion!"

Olivia grinned with pleasure, folded her hands and said her prayers as Faye listened. When she had finished, Faye kissed her again and said, "Sometimes you sound exactly like Marjorie Jo."

"Who's Marjorie Jo?"

"A favorite cousin I haven't seen in a long time. Maybe someday we'll drive over to Richardson and you'll get to meet her."

Olivia kicked off the sheet and flipped her pillow over, grumbling about finding a cool spot for her cheek. Faye sat on the edge of the bed, staring out the cramped little window at the gradually sweetening sky, missing Quentin.

How different life might have been if she had stayed in Abilene and married Alton, who turned out to be a preacher. Father would have been so pleased.

But at the thought of her father, bitter memories of his displeasure and harsh punishment pushed all regret from her mind. She berated herself for even thinking such thoughts. Quentin was a good husband, and he would be fine when this mysterious assignment was over. Then he would be home more, she reasoned as she watched a plummeting star with only a smidgeon of foreboding.

5

Momma was distressed to learn that the farm sat in a dead spot where cell phone reception was nonexistent. So there would be no text messages, even. They would have to depend on the U.S. mail for word from Daddy.

The children had intended to spend time every day looking for fossils in the nearby sandy river bank, each anxious to surprise Daddy with a large collection by summer's end. But in the lazy drifts of shapeless days, they were drawn more and more often to helping out in the garden patch which lay between their house and the Frombergs' larger house. Once she got over her depression, Momma even tried to pitch in, although it appeared the Frombergs didn't quite know how to take her.

Olivia had noticed that Momma often had that effect on people. Momma came out with strange little remarks that baffled them, like referring to the river as a "shy little thing." Once she wandered upon Mrs. Fromberg pulling radishes in the garden. She watched for a few minutes and then said solemnly, "They are children of the Earth, those feisty little salubrious radishes? Just like every one of us. And it seems out here on the plains that Mother Earth lets out her belt, and we all increase in stature along with her."

She threw out her gauzy arms and called into the wind, "I love you, Mother Earth!" By way of explanation, she knelt beside an alarmed Mrs. Fromberg and said, "Sometimes I think the Earth has feelings of her own, don't you? Maybe ours are only reflections of hers. Sometimes she seems to breathe. Maybe the whole universe breathes!" The old woman moved quickly away, saying something about leaving a burner on in the kitchen.

As the days wore on into July and even the hot blanching wind gave up, Momma began to grow quiet again. She was cross during the children's music lessons, but she didn't hound them to practice. She seemed to forget about them for long stretches of time, and she quit tidying up the world.

"What do you think is wrong?" Olivia asked Donnie.

"I don't think Daddy has written."

Olivia knew that. She also knew the rest of them never expected him to, because he never did. It seemed to her that Momma should know this by now, but Momma was always freshly shocked by his neglect, as if it were something new. It also seemed that Momma made entirely too much of it, because after all, Daddy was Daddy.

Something else was bothering Olivia this time, because this time felt different somehow. "Do you think he'll come back for us?" she asked Donnie.

She expected him to laugh away her fears; instead, he looked grave and considered for a long moment before he said, "I think the odds are pretty good he probably will." They were growing up, she saw, and coming to grips with the hubristic impermanence of their Daddy's life and of their own. At least that's how Arthur put it.

"But what if he didn't? What would we do then?"

Donnie snickered. "We could go to Hollywood with Arthur."

Olivia's fears returned whenever she caught a glimpse of Momma when she thought no one was looking. She put on a pasty smile in front of the Frombergs and pulled out a stock remark, "Lovely day, isn't it?" Which was enough right there to make them doubt her sanity, since they were in the midst of a terrible searing drought. The wind gathered up very early every morning bringing dervishes of dust across the prairie into their houses, their eyes, their noses. By midday, when any breeze would be welcome, the wind vanished completely, leaving them at the mercy of the stick, unrelenting heat.

One oppressive dust-overcast afternoon about mail time, Momma went out to sit on a stump beside the mailbox. Mrs. Fromberg started out to feed the chickens, but she caught sight of Momma and scurried back inside. Olivia figured Mrs. Fromberg had come to the point that she didn't want to put Momma through the hypocrisy of saying "Lovely day" another single time.

Olivia felt a great responsibility, if not for Momma's unhappiness, at least for the resolution of it. She followed Momma and knelt beside the stump. Overhead, the electric wires twanged in the wind like a mournful prairie harp, and the Fromberg windmill scraped and groaned like human keening. She laid her head in Momma's lap and told her with wan assurance, "Don't worry if you don't get a letter. You know how the mails are."

"Momma patted her head. "I know. But we'll probably get one today."
She disentangled herself, wiping her eyes, claiming the sand was stinging
them. Olivia felt miserable and helpless.

She saw Donnie trotting toward them, holding his ears and pretending
to be in anguish. "Arthur is practicing again. He sounds like a turkey
squawking...with the auto-harp! He's murdering the dang thing!"

Momma jumped up almost as if she were grateful for the interruption.
"Oh good lord! He'll get it out of tune and never know the difference!"
She streaked across the field to the house. Donnie and Olivia shook hands
in congratulations: maybe now Arthur would be forbidden to touch the
harp—after all, he was absolutely hopeless and always would be.

But the sun shines on the deserving and undeserving alike; in this case,
Mrs. Fromberg finally decided to come out and feed the chickens and she
waved the children over with some purpose and said, "Your brother is quite
a singer." Obviously, Olivia thought, casting a look of shock at Donnie,
the woman's hearing was as bad as her eyesight.

Full of devilment, Donnie said, "Yes ma'am. He's going to be a great
singer on TV when he grows up," and Olivia had to hold herself to keep
from wetting herself. But the old woman shot her a disapproving look and
Olivia straightened up and looked appropriately grave.

"Good for him! Tomorrow's his birthday, I hear." Again the children
looked at each other, surprised. Momma hadn't reminded them.

"I want you to come into the house with me and wrap some tissue
paper around Papa's old guitar—my hands are too crippled with arthritis.
Papa'll never play again, and Arthur needs encouragement. If you two
would practice as much as he does, you could get to be as good as he is."

They were too outraged to do anything but follow her mutely. She
went on, fishing, they could tell. "Arthur must be such a comfort to your
poor mother, with your daddy gone all the time."

At once they closed ranks, an exercise they had perfected. Olivia piped
up first. "Oh, Daddy's never been away before."

"Except to a convention once, to get an award," Donnie put in. He
was by far the cleverest, Olivia thought.

"Is that so! It's a wonder, then, that he hasn't eased her mind by
writing." She was watching them with sharp little eyes.

"Oh he writes a lot. Every day. But he forgets to mail them," Olivia
said.

"He's used to having his secretary take care of it," Donnie said. "He's a busy executive and doesn't have time to buy stamps and stuff." He made his cherub-blue eyes round and innocent.

Olivia felt he left the whole matter hanging, and besides, she had caught the spirit of the game. "He has to write lots of other things all the time. They make him a whole lot of money."

"What sort of other things?"

"Music," she said at the same time that Donnie said, "Mysteries!" Olivia caught his eye and nudged him; his sounded better than hers. But they could both see disbelief on Mrs. Fromberg's face, so Donnie began to fall back and regroup.

"Well, mostly he writes technical stuff for the Company. But in his spare time he writes—musical mysteries," he said lamely.

"I don't think I ever read anything by Quentin Ahern," Mrs. Fromberg said, as if she made a habit of dropping in at the corner bookshop every other day.

They entered the house in her wake, assailed at once by the sour smell of old age and feeling ignobly defeated in Round One. But they determined to be more believable in Round Two.

Mrs. Fromberg led them into her bedroom and pointed to a seedy-looking guitar leaning against the wall. The varnish was worn away below the frets, due, Olivia supposed, to years of the old man's strumming. Mrs. Fromberg picked it up with caution and said, "Mr. Fromberg doesn't know yet that we're giving Arthur his guitar, and this is going to be our little secret, hear? Papa keeps thinking someday his arthritis will get better and he'll be able to play again. Not that he was ever any good, anyhow. He never thinks about this old thing—it was up in the attic until I thought to bring it down for Arthur. So we'll just wrap it up and carry it out of here before he comes in for supper, hear?"

Donnie stroked the musty-smelling guitar with reverence after she left. "First Ramona, now a guitar," he said. Olivia nodded. They could have killed Arthur right then, before he ever reached thirteen, much less the magnificent sixteen.

They had just finished wrapping the hated thing when Mrs. Fromberg came back inside with the mail. She handed one letter to Donnie, who didn't bat an eye but said with the greatest calmness, "Oh, a letter from Daddy." But Olivia saw his pupils grow and turn his pale eyes black.

In a fizz of elation Olivia forgot her part and began jumping up and down. "Open it quick! Read it out loud! Does it have any money in it?"

Mrs. Fromberg laid a firm hand on her shoulder. "Hold your horses, girl. Wouldn't be right to open your momma's mail."

Ashamed about what her outburst might have revealed, Olivia stepped quickly back into her role. Donnie frowned at her and said, "Olivia didn't mean money, exactly. She meant a check for Arthur's birthday. Daddy never forgets our birthdays. He's a very generous man."

"He's always giving to the poor," Olivia said, in an effort to redeem herself.

They picked up the guitar, thanked Mrs. Fromberg properly and marched out, careful not to rush. They continued across the chicken yard at this pace, not even trying to conceal the package, in case Arthur was watching out the window. It was only Mrs. Fromberg's impression that they worried about; Arthur could go hang, for all they cared. Except it *was* his birthday.

As they made they made their painfully measured way home, Olivia said, "Do you think Daddy remembered Arthur's birthday?"

Donnie, walking in front, said, "Do you think even Momma did?"

In the kitchen Momma was lecturing Arthur about the proper way to treat an auto-harp while he stood there with his arms folded across his chest as if he could hardly endure to listen. Olivia shoved the guitar into the broom closet while Donnie dropped the letter on the auto-harp strings.

Momma stopped playing and sat looking at the letter as if she dreaded reading it. But Olivia had stood the suspense as long as she could. She jumped up and down and hollered, "Read it! See? It says 'Quentin Ahern' up in the corner."

"So it does," Momma said. She pulled the flap aside cautiously and after reading a line or two, she began to grin, showing all her large white teeth clear to the back of her mouth. It was the grin that always made Olivia feel warm.

"He's found us a house, a great house—in Garland, of all places!" Then abruptly the grin faded. Lines appeared at the corners or her mouthy as she pursed it tighter and tighter. The children stood quietly waiting. Olivia could tell that whatever it was, it was bad, bad. Momma seemed to shiver and let the letter flutter down, unfinished, while the children were motionless, mute and watchful as deer.

"So what else does he say?" Arthur asked finally.

Momma's voice, small and weak, caught in the middle of the sentence. "He's—lost his job." She batted her eyes and looked up quickly. Her voice changed to brassy bright, the way it had been a hundred times before when they had received a sudden shock. "But we have a great severance bonus and a nice house, with room to play with your new friends—"

Arthur snorted. "What friends?"

It occurred to Olivia that moving must be tougher on Arthur, because she and Donnie always had each other. It was harder on Arthur to make friends, anyhow, because he was such a turd. Now he walked over and picked up Ramona, careful not to touch her splinted legs, and held her to his cheek. There were moody blue hollows under his eyes. He looked very much alone.

Well, she decided, maybe it wasn't so bad for Ramona to be his dog.

6

As the days wore on with no further word from Daddy, Momma began building up her courage. One hot morning in August she pinned back her sun-streaked hair and took out across the field to use the Fromberg's phone. She had decided after much soul-searching to call The Company—not to talk to Daddy, she assured the children. He had warned her never to call him at the office, but now it shouldn't matter, since he no longer worked there. She decided to risk his displeasure by speaking to his former secretary.

Later she came running back, flush-faced and panting, bursting to tell them the great news. "Eugenia not only knew the address of our new house, but she also told me that Mr. Masterson *himself* had arranged for it! Now doesn't that show how much he thinks of Daddy?"

Arthur looked up from his book with an air of open disdain. "Let me get this straight: the man gives Dad the shaft and then goes out himself and finds us a new house to live in? Get real!"

But Momma saw the news as a hopeful sign. That Frank Masterson was so well-disposed toward them tipped the balance: maybe Mr. Masterson had found a new niche for Daddy, after all. Anyway, she knew other men who were terminated, relieved of their keys and ushered out of the building. Surely they hadn't done that to Daddy, or he would have come home to them long ago.

The news galvanized her into action. There was no need to wait on Daddy to make moving arrangements. Sometimes he forgot about details until the last minute. Since she now had an address, she could make a trip back home to contact a moving company herself. Even the children, who were inured to sudden changes, were taken off guard.

"There's no need to wait another day. Olivia will go with me tomorrow, and you boys will stay overnight with the Frombergs. Take Ramona with you. I've already spoken to Mrs. Fromberg about it," she said.

The next day, as if to herald their adventure, the first hint of autumn-scented air streamed down across the plains, swept all the way from the Rockies, Momma said. The weather change brought an unexpectedly sweet evocation of school days as Momma and Olivia got into the van and headed for East Texas. As they pulled away, Olivia turned and waved at the trio on the porch: Arthur pale and somber, clutching that infernal guitar, Ramona, still in casts, lying at his feet, and Donnie, blue eyes wistful, looking lost without his sister. With a sudden ache she realized they had never been separated before, but someday they could actually be parted for good. She pressed her head against the window and watched Donnie until the road curved and took him out of view.

She had been too excited to sleep the night before, so she burrowed into a ball and slept most of the way. She woke only when they pulled to a stop, feeling only momentarily cramped but rejuvenated—too much so for Momma, who was stiff and weary from the long ride. For reasons which Olivia assumed might have to do with bill collectors or nosy neighbors, Momma parked around the corner two blocks away. They walked the rest of the way to their house.

Here, in the depths of the piney woods, it was still deep summer. Olivia sniffed the familiar dampness of dense foliage steaming up from mossy bogs as she bounded along the sycamore-lined street, skipping back to meet Momma every few paces, happy to be home. They passed Eisenhower School, and Olivia swallowed a lump. To think: they had often passed Old DDT the previous summer with the greatest contempt.

Except Arthur, who often began to pine, actually *pine* for school along about July, because he was usually teacher's pet. Grownups seemed compelled to do nice things for him. Olivia refused to admit that probably Arthur was especially smart; she figured he was just needy. One thing about Arthur, he was doubtless quiet in class, not because he meant to be good, but because he was shy. He was seldom in one school long enough to make any friends, because it took him such a long time to build up to it. Olivia suspected that Arthur walked around about half-depressed most of the time. Teachers mistake depression for being a model student, she figured. Arthur was probably only a model of depression.

As they neared their pleasant sprawling ranch-style house, that Momma labeled "woefully out of date" when they'd moved in less than a year before, they spotted Mr. Thibodeaux next door adjusting his sprinkler system. He was retired from Shell and had plenty of time to fiddle with things that were supposed to be automatic. They increased their speed up the walk, pretending not to see him. Momma worked frantically to get the door opened, saying under her breath, "A lovely man. We must remember to send the Thibodeaux's a box of fruit at Christmas."

But she wasn't quick enough. He yelled and came hobbling on over and said, loud enough to be heard in Canada, "Say, Faye, sure was sorry about Quentin losing his job."

"My!" Momma said with a hard bright edge to her voice. "Bad news travels fast around here."

"Not too fast. I read it in the 'Petroleum News' back in June, I think it was."

Olivia glanced up sharply at Momma. So the whole world knew about Daddy's job at least a month before his family did. Momma's hand fluttered to the buttons on her blouse and she grinned and began rattling on about Daddy's great new employment prospects. For a minute Olivia hoped she had just forgotten to tell them. But when Momma waved him away and shut the door behind them, she leaned against it as tears ran down her cheeks. She quoted a Dickinson line she'd used before: "Home is a holy thing—nothing of doubt or distrust can enter its blessed portals."

She remembered Olivia and dried her eyes. "It's not your daddy's fault. It's The Company. They bled us dry, completely dry. Ate our flesh and sucked the marrow right out of our bones. Then they threw us away. Shucked him off like a dirty sock. How he must have dreaded to tell us!"

Olivia followed her through the house as she talked to herself about how he had been trying to protect them. Daddy did a lousy job of protecting them, Olivia wanted to tell her, but she never would. Momma's survival depended on maintaining a mythic image of Daddy as their Savior.

In an attempt to console her, Olivia leaned against Momma and pronounced with great solemnity and confidence, "I'll always protect you, Momma," denying that she would be powerless if ever the time came.

7

The Ahern family's move to Garland introduced new elements of secrecy: that Mr. Masterson himself had chosen their house was a puzzle which they all intended to confront Daddy about as soon as they had the chance. Even Olivia could not understand why a former employer would go to trouble to find even a fine man like Daddy a house after firing him.

But they did not get the chance to ask Daddy immediately, because he didn't come back to the farm for them as he had promised. Instead, he sent word that he was tied up, and that they should come on their own and ship the remaining things to Garland. Even with Ramona out of casts, they would have an overloaded van, but maybe Daddy hadn't thought of that. They understood his familiar pattern: he was putting off facing them a little while longer.

In fairness to him, this wasn't the only move he had missed. Except for the move to the farm, Olivia couldn't remember Daddy ever being around for the packing, as if packing was beneath him. So the whole family concluded that, indeed, it was.

The new house sat on a patch of unmown lawn, shaggy with crab grass and dandelions that would have to be dug out by hand. Momma noted, as soon as they drove up, that the railroad tracks ran only a couple of blocks away. On either side of the front walk, like enormous guarding deities, stood ancient pecans shading the whole yard. The structure itself was a big shambly wooden place with one dormer shutter handing by a hinge. But it had possibilities: there was a fine porch and two concrete lions stood on either side of the steps, which Momma labeled tacky but much too heavy to remove. Olivia liked it at once, and she thought she read relief on Momma's face.

Although there was no sign of Daddy, the movers had already placed their furniture and boxes inside, so they knew he must have overseen them. They had just stepped inside the foyer when they heard his car in the drive. The children dashed out to meet him, but Momma hung back on the porch while they dragged him up to her. Olivia looked from Arthur to Donnie and knew they were all thinking the same thing: how handsome Daddy was. In three months she had almost forgotten.

He stopped in front of Momma, looked her up and down and said, "My God! You're thin as a stick!" He gave her a peck and hugged her until he appeared to become uneasy and let her go. The children dragged him inside leaving Momma to straggle in a few paces behind.

He threw out his arms. "You like it? After a lot of looking, I discovered just the right place."

Olivia tugged at Momma and said in a mock whisper, "I thought you said Mr. Masterson found it for us."

A pall settled over them. They looked from Momma to Daddy. Olivia had forgiven him for whatever he had done the minute she saw him again, but she could tell Momma needed answers.

"What's going on, Quentin? Is Frank trying to salve his conscience with this house? How can we afford it?"

Daddy was uncharacteristically abrupt. "As the one who has always provided the living, I believe that's for me to decide." The biting words stunned them, but he appeared not to notice. He was immediately cheery again. "Now! Do you want a tour? I hope you like how the furniture is arranged. If not, we can change it, can't we, Arthur?"

To Olivia, it was truly a grand house; not as modern as the place in Sands' Point on Long Island, where they lived for less than a year before Olivia was born and which she knew only from photographs, and not as elegant the one they had in England that even had its own name. But to her, it was a monster of a place with all sorts of crannies for hiding out. As they wondered through the oversized rooms and out onto the long pack porch, she watched the color rise in Momma's cheeks and drive away the pallor. Even Arthur conceded, "It's fairly decent."

Daddy indicated a closed door at the rear of the house near the kitchen which he had already designated as his study.

"This room will contain my important papers. It is off limits to everyone, understand? Even for cleaning." He was looking pointedly at Momma.

His mood lightened and he led them down a short back hallway, taking Momma's arm and indicating a room. "This sunny little room would make a fine hobby room for you. I had them put your sewing table here."

Olivia did her best not to turn around and look for Donnie, because she was sure he had hung back to try the old-fashioned glass knob on the forbidden study door. When he caught up with her, he shrugged and mouthed the word, "Locked."

They climbed up to the two dormer bedrooms, the larger of which Donnie and Arthur would share, and the smaller Olivia would occupy. Then and there she made the resolution to win Ramona's affections from Arthur so the dog would sleep with her up in that lonely room.

The two other doors off the upstairs hallway led to the only bath and an unfinished attic room, which Daddy promised to convert into a special playroom one of these days. Olivia's elation died as she heard Donnie mutter, "Oh sure!"

They trooped back downstairs into the dining room, so cavernous that it made their long table look insignificant. Daddy went over to the bay windows, saying, "There are identical bays in my study—and look!" He raised the lid on the window seat, something the children had never seen before. Even then Olivia felt a strange portent as she and Donnie leaned cautiously over to peer inside, as if they expected to see goblins lurking in the depths. A sweet fusty odor rose. She took a quick daring peek, then drew back, not having seen the bottom, remembering the bottomless pool in Carlsbad Caverns, where an unreasoning fear had seized her that she might somehow flop over the guard rail, tumble into the water and keep sinking forever. A wave of nausea welled up and threatened to overwhelm her.

"Radical!" Donnie's voice echoed from inside the box. His upper body had disappeared, leaving his upturned seat a tempting target asking to be swatted. But Olivia, occupied with her gut-rumblings, resisted the temptation. Apparently he did not share her shiver of augury.

8

After a meal of Thai takeout, Momma sent Arthur to the back porch to reassemble the glider, and she put Donnie and Olivia to work in the kitchen unpacking a box of cooking utensils. "Meanwhile, I'm going to locate the Lares and Penates," she said, referring to an assortment of household gods she had collected over the years in which she professed to put great store.

As soon as she had left the room, Donnie dragged the box over near the screen door so he could talk to Arthur. He began nonchalantly. "So, Arthur: How do you figure it?"

Olivia knew why the caution. Arthur could, if irritated, turn sarcastic and treat them like a couple of dweebs. You had to give him the prima donna treatment with just the right mix of groveling and indifference if you wanted results. He was getting to be almost as hard to handle as a grown-up.

Arthur was receptive this time, and more talkative than he had been for days. "You mean why Garland? Oil town, I suspect. Close to Dallas. He probably expects to get on with another company. What doesn't compute is why Masterson would have arranged for this house. I'm not sure I believe that. Why would he want to help?"

"Fat chance of that, huh?" Donnie said. They waited. No answer. So Donnie changed directions. "Naw, I don't mean why Garland. I mean why the whole firing thing."

Arthur gave the glider an unnecessary whack with the hammer. Olivia hoped to God he didn't break it; she loved that glider. He handed Olivia a wad of paper with a pan inside, which she dutifully unwrapped. She always got the easy stuff.

"They wanted to boot him out without giving him a chance for retaliation," Mr. Know-It-All said, obviously enjoying the spotlight.

Olivia stopped unwrapping. "What's retaliation?"

"Like burning the place down to get even," Donnie said, handing her another wad of paper. Olivia noticed he wasn't doing much actual unpacking.

"No, rabbit-balls, like making off with some company secrets," Arthur growled.

Olivia figured they couldn't be very interesting secrets. "What kind of secrets have they got?"

"All kinds of crap. Like where the oil is. Or what kind of dirty tricks the competition is up to." There was a pause, then, "Uh-oh. Trouble from next door."

They looked out to see a large woman at the side gate, carrying a pitcher. Arthur opened the screen door and stepped inside. "I'm outa here," he said. Olivia and Donnie would have left, too, but the woman had spotted them and was waving from across the yard.

They bowed to the inevitable. They knew the routine. They had to become "established." Besides, Momma said they needed all the allies they could get, just in case. They'd been though the routine before. Donnie grabbed Olivia and pulled her out the back door. "We'd better head 'er off before she gets her fat ass in the house."

The two set their customary bland smiles and waited on the back steps for the woman to reach them. She galumphed across the lawn like a camel, grinning so big that Olivia could see the insides of her cheeks. She had big healthy hippo teeth, like Momma's except for a crazy crooked one. Her glut of hair was reddish and frizzy. Several grasping tentacles were plastered to the sweat on her forehead. Olivia decided she liked her: harmless-looking, and much livelier than their last one.

"Hi, kids! Your mom home?" She stuck out the pitcher. "I brought iced tea. Thought you might be thirsty, all that unpacking...."

A look passed between them that said, *You go, I'll stay.* But Olivia knew Donnie would be better at fielding questions than she. He obviously thought so too, for he hitched up Arthur's cast-off Cub Scout shorts, picked up the screw driver and attacked the glider as if to say, *I'm busy here.*

Olivia didn't race through the house calling for Momma; nothing was ever learned by announcing your presence beforehand. She wasn't sure where to look, so she stopped in the back hall to listen. She could hear her parents' voices probably coming from their bedroom. She hurried up the hallway and saw Arthur already posted just outside their door crouched over like a gangly crawdad. He motioned for her to keep quiet. It was Momma talking.

"When someone is let go, he's escorted to his desk to collect his stuff and escorted out of the building that very minute. He isn't kept around for the rest of the summer."

Daddy's barking laugh cut her short. "To steal company secrets? They'd already made sure I couldn't do that, hadn't they? Transferred me so far away from anything sensitive—" He ripped open a box with a loud pop. "They'd already relegated me to a position of so little importance that I was no threat to anyone. I think somebody was jealous."

Momma persisted. "Mr. Thibodeaux said he read about it in the 'Petroleum News' a month before you told me."

"Thibodeaux's getting senile. Probably read about somebody else." He sounded irritated. "What is it with you, Faye? Aren't things bad enough without my own wife ragging my ass?"

"I didn't mean…" Momma's tone became apologetic. "Eugenia did tell me that your boss arranged for this house."

"No. No. No way! You misunderstood her. Why were you talking to Eugenia, anyway? I thought I told you never to."

"You hadn't written, except to say you'd lost your job. I needed to know where we were going. I didn't know anybody else to ask but Eugenia. She told me about your boss getting us a house. I thought that was awfully nice. But I wondered, why on earth?"

"You see? That's why I told you never to call the office! You got facts all tangled up. Just stay out of things that don't concern you."

She tried again on a different subject. "I had a thought about why they might have…let you go. You know how your tongue gets a little loose when you've had a few—"

"My God, get off it! We've been over this a thousand times before! I know better than to discuss company business. Okay, you want to know what *was* holding me back? I'll tell you: It was my lack of ruthlessness."

Olivia looked at Arthur and mouthed the question, "*Ruthlessness?*" He motioned for her to shut up.

Daddy was saying, "You have to know when to look the other way, when to avoid asking questions, when to screw your best friend."

Packing dust was getting to Olivia. Without thinking, she snuffled out loud. Arthur frowned menacingly at her to be quiet, but it was too late. Momma called, "Olivia?"

Arthur shot her a dirty look as she entered the bedroom, panting as if she'd just run in from outside. Her parents stood over a box of linens eyeing her with suspicion. Olivia said, gasping and wheezing, "Lady out on the back porch…brought you some iced tea." She flopped over onto the mattress, panting with exhaustion, until she wondered if she might be overdoing it.

Momma said, "Oh lord," and went to see. Olivia looked at Daddy, dressed not surprisingly in his good jacket and slacks, and felt uncomfortable being alone with him. So she popped up to follow Momma out to the porch.

The neighbor lady was bent over the glider, giving a screw one final turn while Donnie watched. "There!" she said with satisfaction, straightening as Momma and Olivia came onto the porch. She broke into her crooked-toothed grin and stuck out her hand. "Mrs. Ahern? I'm Twyla Pruitt from next door. Donnie and I have just assembled your glider!" She motioned to the pitcher on the wide porch railing. "I brought you some tea. Thought you might be ready for a break."

Momma hesitated only a second before she wiped her hand across her tee-shirt and took the woman's hand. Olivia watched her muster enthusiasm, saw her force a smile. "Oh, it's just the thing! Call me Faye." Olivia could see Momma's mind working, trying to figure out how to keep from inviting Twyla Pruitt inside.

She motioned behind her. "There are packing boxes piled everywhere! Why don't we try out the glider?" She turned to Donnie. "See if you can find some paper cups in the kitchen."

Twyla eased onto the glider, cautiously at first. When it emitted only a slight creak, she grinned again and motioned for Momma to join her. But Momma didn't like getting too close to people, so she dropped quickly to the step and leaned against the post, turning to face them.

"Olivia's been dying to try out that glider. Sit down, sweetie."

Much as she would have preferred to escape. Olivia reluctantly climbed up next to Twyla Pruitt, moving over when she brushed against Twyla's damp arm. Donnie returned with paper cups, then slid down with his back against the wall. Arthur, no doubt, was stationed just inside the screen door. Past experience had taught the children to rally around Momma to offer interruptions when the conversation became too personal.

Twyla rocked the glider, watched Momma pour the tea, and said, "Your kids seem like such good kids."

"If they're good, I hope it's reluctantly!" Momma said. "Being good with reluctance is the best kind. Much better than being good because you don't know any better."

Twyla looked puzzled. She cleared her throat and tried again. "Donnie tells me your husband's in the oil business."

"Um hmm," Momma said vaguely, busy handing around tea. She was quick to change the subject. "What does your husband do?"

"He's an environmental engineer."

The trick was to keep the visitor talking. On cue, Olivia piped up. "What's that?"

Twyla chuckled. "Beats me, sugar. All I know is, it gets him out of the house for weeks at a time." She turned back to Momma. "Which company is your husband with?"

But Momma had raised the cup to her lips to take a long sip. She flicked her eyes toward Donnie in a signal meaning, *It's your turn*. Without a bobble, Donnie, with phony enthusiasm, blurted, "No, *really*, we wanna know: what *is* an environmental engineer?"

The woman sighed, gave the glider a squeaky push, and went into a rambling description of her husband's occupation while Momma's eyes glazed over and Olivia, stifling a yawn, pretended rapt attention. Donnie, that fart-head, had closed his eyes, but he continued nodding with a little frown that said he was concentrating on every word. At length Twyla Pruitt came to an end of her monologue by announcing, "I've been thinking of going back to work myself."

"So have I," Momma said suddenly, out of nowhere, with a defiant lift of her chin.

"Oh? What's your field?"

Momma's laugh sounded bitter. "Oh, I'm in great demand! Art history." She looked fragile and pitifully beige. Olivia was puzzled; she had presumed that Momma was just making conversation, but now she wasn't sure.

"There might be an opening in the schools," Twyla said brightly.

"Don't confuse me with someone with a degree. I don't know how to do anything. Never even took a typing course, much less a computer course. I got married and quit school when…uh…"

"Well, there must be something. What on earth could you do?"

Olivia lost track of the conversation after she heard the forbidden words "on earth." Momma said the problem with the world was that people got their prepositions mixed up, and it affected their politics and their religion. She told them often: "We are *of* the Earth, not *on* the earth."

Olivia opened her mouth to correct Twyla, but Donnie shot her a look that said, *Don't bother.*

Twyla was rattling on. "I'm thinking of taking up ceramics."

"Mmm," Momma said. "Working with Gaia. Could be very visceral. Still, a denatured version of art, condoned…"

Twyla sat upright. Momma had gone too far again. Beginning to sound like a nut case. But Donnie knew what to do. He grabbed the pitcher and began refilling Twyla's cup until it overflowed.

Twyla squealed and leaped up, brushing the cold liquid from her jeans.

Donnie said, "Oops! Sorry!" while Olivia crossed her legs to keep from peeing.

Momma got to her feet and started to the kitchen. "I'll get a towel."

But Twyla reacted in the predictable fashion, like others before her. "No, no harm done. Anyhow, I've got to get home to start supper. Say! Do you two play bridge?"

The woman just did not give up! Olivia could see panic rise and flush Momma's cheeks an ugly red. But Arthur brilliantly intervened with the save by calling from the kitchen, "Mom, somebody's here. I think it's the telephone man. Where do you want the phones?"

Momma had already established the fact that Daddy had forgotten to contact the phone company yet. Score one for Arthur.

Momma excused herself, promising to return the pitcher soon, and hurried inside, barely able to conceal her relief. Twyla turned to go but called back to the children, "By the way, what oil company did you say your daddy is with?"

Olivia hopped out of the swing as she hadn't heard and said, "Is that Momma calling?" while Donnie spread his arms out wide and said with grave innocence, "It's a *real big* name, something with *Corporation* in it." Olivia tugged his arm and he allowed himself to be dragged inside.

A flawless performance. They mustn't, after all, antagonize the woman; she might come in handy one day. They usually did.

9

The following Saturday over dinner Daddy announced that it was high time they got themselves to the Episcopal Church. "…Begin making contacts," he said aside to Momma, as if the rest of them were nowhere around. Momma made a straight line of her mouth and swept a glance right and left to remind him of Little Pitchers.

Arthur, misreading her meaning, grimaced and spoke around a mouthful of peas. "Don't worry, Mom. We won't let this experience taint us." The closer he got to sixteen, the more insufferable.

Just to be noticed, Olivia piped up. "What's taint? Like paint?"

"Just about," Momma said as she dumped a helping of salad on Donnie's plate. "I think you overlooked your greens."

Donnie emulated his brother's caustic tone. "Oh yeah. Got to eat something from Mother Earth!"

Momma folded her hands on the table in a signal that always meant *Pay attention.* "It is impossible to put anything into your mouth that is *not* from Mother Earth, Donald Eugene."

Daddy looked pained. He turned to Arthur. "Be sure your shirt's pressed. I don't want any last-minute malingering tomorrow morning."

"Remind me to check the length of your trousers," Momma told Arthur, then promptly forgot.

They woke early the next morning, ate a brief breakfast, and dutifully dressed for church. Olivia looked longingly out the window at the brilliant September morning and wondered how many Sundays would be wasted like this before Daddy lost interest.

Daddy got out the whisk broom and brushed the flood mats while Momma fed Ramona and ordered her to guard the house. It was discovered that Arthur had outgrown his good trousers, Olivia's sox didn't match, and Donnie wasn't wearing any underwear, deficiencies Momma hurriedly addressed while Daddy sat in the car revving the engine.

Olivia sniffed the morning air and dawdled on the porch until the others were in the car. The three children, elbowing each other with jabs, crowded into the back of Daddy's Porsche, despite that there was barely room for two. Arthur, crammed behind Momma with his knees pressed to one side, grumbled, "God forbid that the Brown Mud Hen should be seen in the parking lot of the Episcopal Church! That glorified Chamber of Commerce!"

Daddy said, "Sarcasm will not save you, Arthur."

"Neither will the Episcopal Church," Arthur muttered.

As usual, Olivia ended up in the middle with no window. To see out, she stood and held onto the seat backs until Daddy told her to sit down. "I look in the rearview mirror and all I see is a face."

Olivia plopped down and whined. "I like to know where I'm going."

"To hell," Donnie said, smiling sweetly. He smelled strongly of the toothpaste he had eaten so Momma would think he brushed.

Arthur nudged her over. "I don't know why you're so eager to get there. They're all a bunch of snotty shits." He wrinkled his nose and his voice rose in imitation. "And where do *you* go to school, little girl? *What? Surely* not *public* school! What a miserable little wretch!"

Olivia clammed up. Secretly, she didn't mind she didn't mind so much going to church, pretending to be part of them, because Daddy said they ran the world. But they appeared to be a cheerless lot, as though the burden must bring them no pleasure. She recalled once or twice when they had wandered among Presbyterians instead, that they also were cool and aloof and lacking in any degree of good humor toward children, as though shepherding a dour flock were a special kind of punishment reserved for the most severely damned.

Arthur preferred to pick on Episcopalians, calling the ministers a godless crew with complexions the color of chicken skin. But Donnie said their faces were usually half red, where their golf caps didn't shade them while they were on the course.

Once, when their parents stood at the parish door shaking hands with the minister, she had deliberately danced upon his shiny shoe, to see what would happen. The action was met with such a withering glare as to leave no doubt that if the minister had his way, all children would burn in hell.

As they reached the new church and Arthur began to unfold his long legs from the back seat, he groused, "I can't fit in here anymore. This is bloody ridiculous!"

Momma turned to Daddy. "Why don't we just fold him up in the trunk next time? Zip him up in a body bag."

"I probably should start thinking about getting a Mercedes," Daddy said.

She snorted. "You're talking Mercedes when Arthur's pants are an inch too short, even after I let them out."

"Who sees them but his teachers?" Daddy studied Arthur's trouser legs, riding precariously close to the tops of his socks. "My God, son, what's happened to you over the summer?"

"I'm going to get a job," Momma murmured as they closed ranks near the church entrance and put on their careful Christian smiles.

"Now just how would that look at this point?" Daddy said. "Think about it."

Olivia and Donnie had learned to avoid hassles in Sunday School by appearing to be overcome by shyness. They would linger in the back of the room with heads tucked low until eventually the teacher would decide to leave them alone. Then they would make spit-balls of their lesson folders and flip them at the necks of the kids on the next row. The hour passed relatively painless that way. They managed to escape a full five minutes before Arthur and went to wait on the gray stone portico outside the sanctuary doors. Olivia could hear the loathsome organ whipping the worshippers up to a fevered pitch to escape with something wildly jubilant from Hayden.

Even when the doors opened and the congregants streamed out, their parents did not immediately appear. Donnie groaned. "Guess Dad's in there kissing up. Man! I'm about to starve!"

From the other direction, Arthur pushed through the crowd, face flushed with excitement. "Somebody's leaning against our car—looks like Uncle Cas!"

The children galloped out through the leaf-litter to the car, where their uncle lounged against its side. They threw themselves wildly upon him. Faint beads of sweat dotted his tanned forehead, but he was still the handsomest man in the world. He was taller than Daddy, and younger, and always laughing. Anyway, he used to like Olivia in a special way, which she couldn't quite remember about anymore. He laughed now and swept her up into his arms. His shirt felt damp against her leg.

"Careful!" she said. "I'm full of water."

Their parents soon appeared. Momma rushed ahead of Daddy and kissed Caswell with obvious pleasure. "Cas, you're drenched! What are you doing here? And how did you find us?"

He leaned past her to tousle the boys' heads and to clutch his brother's hand, while Olivia clung onto his neck and wrapped her legs around his chest so he wouldn't put her down. His voice was deeper than Daddy's, and musical.

"You're not too hard to track down. I called your sister, Faye; hope you don't mind. Figured if you'd written anybody, it'd be her. I didn't have a current cell number, and when I couldn't reach you by land line—"

"We don't have one yet," Arthur said, rolling his eyes.

"Like somebody's just *dying* to call *you*, bone bag!" Donnie jeered.

Cas went on. "I drove over from Fort Worth and found your new place. When you weren't home…Sunday morning…I figured it out. Just Googled the nearest Episcopal Church. Then I cruised around to spot the Porsche." His grin waned and he looked somberly into his brother's face.

Momma saw the look and took a breath. "Oh no. Is it your dad again?"

Caswell still fixed his gaze on Daddy. "Mom called from the hospital. They can't keep him going much longer."

"And they shouldn't." Momma stopped short and looked at Daddy. She touched his arm, and Olivia saw her fingers tighten. "You have to go."

Daddy's mouth was pressed into a hard white line. Cas rushed on as if he were apologizing. "We have to think about Mom now. She's stressed to the limit, and she needs us all." He looked at Momma, anticipating her question. "Faye, I think you and the kids would just be in the way. Frannie and Kathleen and all the kids are there, and I think Mom would just like to be with her immediate family and not feel strained to—get to know new people right now. No offense." Olivia was trying to remember who those people were until Donnie mouthed, "Aunts."

Momma covered her relief well. "And Margaret Mary?"

"Maybe even Margaret Mary, if she can swallow her pride. It'll break Mom's heart if she doesn't come. It's time for healing, if it's ever going to happen."

Momma hesitated. "And how's…" She searched for the name. "…D-Dorothy?"

Uncle Cas appeared to be embarrassed for a second, but his grin quickly returned. "Barb. You're one wife behind. Barb's fine, but I convinced her that now's not the time to break in a new wife on the family. Besides, there'll be a real bed crisis at the house."

Momma was still doing her best to hide her relief and doing a pitiful job of it. She turned to Daddy again and said, "Why don't you ride back to the house with Cas so you can talk? I'll stop by and pick up chicken for lunch."

Arthur let out a derisive laugh. "You expect Dad to let you behind the wheel of his precious Porsche?"

"Take mine." With no reluctance Cas handed over his keys and pointed to a dark BMW.

"Thanks. Arthur can come with me. I'll need somebody to help me carry," she said.

Olivia and Donnie delighted in Arthur's crestfallen face. Arthur loved Uncle Cas more than either of them, and now he was stuck carrying chicken for Momma. Donnie called out, "Don't drop the chicken, Arrthurr!" and ignored Arthur's finger stuck up behind him as they walked away.

Olivia said, "He'll probably spit in the gravy, just for that."

She and Donnie climbed into the back of the Porsche, vying for the spot behind Uncle Cas, but Donnie won. Anyway, she could see Uncle Cas's profile, while Donnie could see only the back of his head. She could smell his cologne, but for some reason the odor evoked a sense of something unpleasant...guilt?

Uncle Cas ignored them once they were headed for home. He said to Daddy, "Tough luck about your job. Anything else lined up yet?"

Daddy made a lot of noise shifting gears. "I'm looking at several things."

"I wouldn't take it personally. Look at it from Llano's standpoint: they can hire a kid fresh out of school for a fraction of what you were making."

"But without my years of expertise."

"That's what consultants are for. Figure the savings to them in benefits. Seniority is like shark bait anymore. It just makes you vulnerable."

Olivia was set to pipe up just to get noticed, but Donnie knotted his fist and held it threateningly close to her nose. Daddy appeared to have forgotten they were in the back seat.

He said, "Goddam rules have all changed in our lifetime."

Caswell was silent for a while before he asked. "So are you coming with me?"

Daddy was quiet. Olivia strained to hear. Finally he said, "Does Dad know about...Llano?"

"That you've been terminated? You don't understand how sick he is. He doesn't know anything about anything. He may not even know us when we get there...if we make it in time."

Olivia leaned over to Donnie and whispered, "Is this our granddaddy in Abilene?"

He shook his head. "The other one. In Galveston, I think."

"We know Margaret Mary. She's the one Uncle Cas calls the Collapsed Catholic."

Cas was saying, "I didn't tell Mom. She has enough to worry about. Nobody knows."

Daddy said, "I don't want the whole goddam bunch picking over my bones. If the man were conscious at all, he'd be gloating, saying he told me so."

"Quit thinking about yourself. It's not going to happen. He's out of it. Besides, some fathers *push* their sons into corporate careers. Some people might envy you because yours didn't."

"It wasn't that he minded; he was never so set on the priesthood. It was changing course that he objected to. To him, it was a sign of weakness."

"Weakness of the flesh was what he objected to," Cas said.

"Enough!" Daddy said sharply. Nobody said anything more until they neared the house, then he said, "What time does your flight leave?"

Cas looked at his watch. "Three-ten. You have time to grab a bite and pack a bag."

Daddy turned in and drove on back to the garage. Olivia knew what that meant, and a piercing little pang struck her, the way it always did when he was about to leave them. He flicked off the engine and gave a weary, resigned sigh. "I presume you've already booked me a seat."

10

Momma phoned Daddy in Galveston the next morning. No matter how much he had protested that he didn't want them to come if Granddaddy died, it was clear that, if there was to be a funeral, Momma meant to attend.

It was school registration day, but to the children's relief, Momma said there was no need to bother with school until she found out about Granddaddy. With the new excitement, both school and the loss of Daddy's job had been all but forgotten.

They were assembled around the kitchen table for a late breakfast. Momma hushed them with a frantic wave and stopped her ear so she could hear. "Frannie? Oh, Kathleen. It's Faye. How's--?" She got up abruptly and took the phone into the pantry. From the tone and drag of strung-out words, Olivia could tell Granddaddy was dead.

Arthur said, "Oh great. He's dead and we never even got to see what he looked like."

Olivia thought it was odd that someone she knew would die, but Donnie voiced it for her. "I've never been to a funeral before."

Olivia's spirits lifted. This was at least an experience to record in her diary. She said, "Do they put the dead person in the room with you?"

"What do you think, pea-brain?" Arthur said, meaning he didn't have a clue but was about to expound anyway. He dug his finger into the peanut butter jar and brought out a glob, then sat with his finger poised in mid-air, dripping oil onto the placemat. "They embalm 'em and then you look at 'em lying in a casket."

"So we *will* get so see what he looks like, dead, at least," Donnie said.

Things moved swiftly once Momma got off the phone. She hustled in and took up their plates so quickly that Arthur had to rescue his toast as she swept his away. "The rosary's tonight. Mass is tomorrow. I don't know what all that is, but if we're not going to miss everything, we've got to get moving!"

She sent the children upstairs to finish packing while she ran next door with a bag of dogfood to ask Twyla Pruitt to feed Ramona for the next couple of nights. During the previous afternoon, she had packed their Sunday clothes, in case of a funeral. Olivia tried to understand the connection between Sunday School and funerals. Momma sighed and said she guessed she hadn't civilized them enough, hadn't taught them about the unavoidable ceremonies of life.

After they had loaded the Mud Hen and said goodbye to Ramona, Arthur got in the front beside Momma and grumbled, "Looks like Daddy left us to do all the work, as usual."

"I just hope he checked the fluids," Momma said absently, because Daddy was In Charge of Car Maintenance. "He was in such a hurry to get there before your granddaddy died."

Donnie leaned over from the back seat. "What for, if he was going to die anyway?"

"To tell him that he loved him." Momma unfolded the road map and handed it to Arthur. "You're my head navigator. Get us to Galveston." Before Arthur could complain that theirs was the only car left on earth that didn't have GPS, she turned to the two in the back seat. "And no whining for bathroom breaks. We have a seven-hour trip, and we've got to get there in time to change for the wake. It starts at eight o'clock."

Arthur looked at his watch. "Piece of cake, if Livvie's bladder holds."

But an hour down the highway, the engine began to overheat. Momma pulled off the highway and stopped at a service station outside of Ennis. When she turned off the motor, they could see steam pouring out.

After the attendant and Momma had peered under the hood, she leaned into the window, face flushed with exasperation. "It's only a hose, but they don't have one to fit. So we'll have to wait a while. Besides, he spotted a belt that's almost worn in two. It would've broken while we were miles from anyplace, most likely. The car won't be ready until mid-afternoon."

"Thank you, Mr. Ahern," Arthur muttered bitterly.

Olivia swatted the back of his head. "You blame everything on Daddy!"

They unloaded their bags and Momma cajoled the attendant into driving them to the nearest motel. She had decided that they would dress for the wake. If the car was ready soon enough, they might barely make the rosary. If not, they would drive into the night.

Arthur, with a dogged grip on the practical, said, "What's the use of driving all night is the wake is already over?"

"Because there's still a mass to get through in the morning, and then graveside services. It all begins tomorrow morning at ten."

"Man!" Donnie said. "How come it's so strung out?"

"It gives the family time to adjust," Momma said. "I used to think it was silly, but people have been doing it forever, so it must satisfy some deep need in the psyche."

Momma phoned Daddy from the motel and let them all speak to him. When it was Olivia's turn she asked, "Daddy, are you sad?"

His voice sounded far away, as if he were in Dubai again. "I'm sad because you are having so much trouble getting here, little Liv."

"But I thought you didn't want us to come."

"Not at all. I need you in the worst way."

"Daddy? I'm sad, too. Do you want to know why? Because I might miss the only funeral I'll ever get to go to."

He snorted. "That's only if you plan to die tomorrow."

"I don't ever plan to die!" She felt uneasy and handed the phone back to Momma. What made Daddy say such a thing? She had never even considered dying!

Despite their best resolve, the children fell asleep in the darkened room. Momma must have made only a half-hearted attempt to wake them when the car was delivered. Olivia stirred several times but, hearing the even breathing of her mother beside her, fell asleep again. But she was wide awake instantly when Momma turned on the light and said, "Good lord! It's three in the morning! What have I done?"

They scrambled into their Sunday clothes while she barked breathless orders. "You'll have to try not to get wrinkled or eat anything messy. We'll get something at a drive-in and drive straight through to the church." She skinned off her polo and pulled her black dress over her head. Her unusual lack of modesty only emphasized the great urgency.

Once they had eaten a dry breakfast of biscuits and yogurt, Olivia lay looking out the window at the sky, half-listening to Momma talk to Arthur about the stars. Arthur was leaning toward Momma, intent on hearing what she was saying above the engine's hum.

"We are made of star dust, literally. The iron and calcium of our bodies were formed from the explosion of a super-nova long before our universe came into being. Much later, Earth was impregnated by comets, sperm of the stars, which caused life. All creativity is like that: caused by invasion from without. Think about it."

No matter how many times she heard Momma speak of the stars, Olivia was always freshly troubled. She could almost hear the whistling galaxies; she felt sucked into a fearful howling wonder of nothingness by Momma's words, particularly so this time, with their grandfather lying cold in his coffin.

Momma was still talking. "Primitive tribes all over the world worship Father Sky and Mother Earth, the creators. They instinctively knew how life came to be."

Olivia tried to keep her eyes open, tried to focus on a star and feel the kinship with it that Momma felt. It seemed to her that she had spent great segments of her life riding in this car with Donnie and Arthur and Momma, driving somewhere hours away to meet Daddy, listening to Momma talk about the stars and Mother Earth.

At daybreak she woke. Donnie was already awake. They entertained themselves wrestling and punching each other, taking care not to get too wrinkled. Arthur still held the map stiffly in front of him as if he was on constant duty, but he didn't say much. Arthur usually got carsick if he had to eat and ride.

They arrived in Galveston shortly before ten and drove past miles of esplanade grown up in oleander and wind-wracked palms before Momma stopped at a service station to ask directions to the church. By the time they reached the cathedral on squealing tires, the service was set to begin.

The building was large and somber with castle-like turrets. The inside was a wax museum, with statues everywhere, except for the candles burning with no one to watch them. The organ echoed through the sparsely-filled auditorium like something from "The Addams Family." As the usher led them down the aisle to the second row, Donnie whispered, "Is this weird, or what?"

Olivia punched him and pointed to the flower-draped coffin at the front. "That must be it! Isn't that it? Isn't that where the dead body is?"

Momma shushed them as they reached their seats. The women on the front row turned and whispered greetings. One of them pinched Olivia's knee. Must be The Aunts, she decided. Momma leaned over and kissed the cheek of one white-haired woman who didn't turn around. From out of nowhere, Daddy slipped in next to Arthur. The corners of Daddy's nose were red.

The service lasted forever with much kneeling and getting up, and singing dull songs with no beat. In between, words, words. Olivia's stomach growled. She lost interest in the casket, which wasn't open the way they always were on TV—the way Arthur had promised—and began to study the colored glass windows. She wondered if Camelot had been like this. When she got the fidgets, Momma laid a firm hand on her knee and looked meaningfully at her watch as if to say, *Not much longer...*

After the choir finished bellowing about "And I will lift him up..." with what to Olivia seemed like entirely too much pleasure, the priest offered Communion. When the usher stood at the first aisle, one of The Aunts, the one in a dress of bright winking fabric, did not rise and follow the others to the altar. Olivia recognized The Aunt as Margaret Mary, the Collapsed Catholic with the long crinkly blond hair and clanking ear hardware who had once come to visit. The ushers moved to the second row, and Arthur rose to go to the altar, but Daddy pulled him down. The rest of the family sat and watched as the people on the rows behind them went up to the altar to be offered a sip from the cup and a little wafer on their tongue.

Arthur, his face a mortified red, was having a whispered argument with Daddy about why he couldn't go to the altar. Olivia understood that she and Donnie were not old enough, but Arthur had had his first Communion in their old Episcopal Church, and he was incensed that he was not allowed to go up now. Probably starving to death, she figured. Momma leaned over and whispered, "Only Catholics are allowed to go."

Margaret Mary suddenly rose, leaned over so that Olivia could see down the front of her orange dress, said something to Daddy, and left. Olivia could smell her perfume as she swept by, stilettos hammering up the aisle.

Olivia meant to ask Daddy about the priest, who had made a great to-do of waving a smoking container over the casket. Olivia thought the grown-ups ought to be alarmed, but no one seemed to pay him any mind.

When the service was over, Daddy hustled them out a side door and toward a strange car, explaining, "There isn't enough room for all of us in the lead limo. Margaret Mary wants us to join her in her car." It was a four-door Honda. Olivia had to sit up front on Daddy's lap. Margaret

Mary was combing through her wild raging frizz with long silver nails and puffing hard on a cigarette. But she ground it out as they got in.

Daddy said, "Why did you leave before it was over?"

Margaret Mary took a tissue from her bag and mopped her neck underneath the long frizzy hair. It was only mid-morning in early September, but it was very warm. "Couldn't take the arrogance," she said. "Withholding the body and blood from all but the Chosen. What a crocking farce!"

Donnie asked Arthur in a loud whisper, "Wasn't the dead body in the casket?"

Margaret Mary exploded with laughter, setting her earrings jangling. "Yes, lord! In the casket at last! God forgive me for what I'm thinking."

Olivia was the only one who could see Daddy's grin. "'Yes lord'? 'God forgive'? Old habits die hard."

"If at all," Margaret Mary said. She drummed on the steering wheel some more with her long bright nails. Olivia wondered if her aunt was in the entertainment business. She looked around to see why they weren't leaving yet and decided they must be waiting for someone to load the casket into the long black hearse parked by the side door.

Margaret Mary was still talking. "Just like you and your job. We keep on trusting the system we were taught to trust, even when it screws us."

Olivia felt the jolt of Daddy's body tightening. Momma and the boys sat in the back not making a sound. It was a long time before he said, "Cas said he didn't tell anyone about my job. I should have known better."

"Far as I know, he didn't. Who do you think tried to call you to tell you about Dad? When I found your phone had been disconnected, I called Llano to get your address. They're the ones who told me you weren't with the company anymore. So I called Cas and told him to track you down. What's the big deal? So you got laid off! Get a grip on the ego. We're just your family. Don't be so damn touchy!"

"I'm not touchy. I had hoped my first visit home in fifteen years might not be likened to the return of the prodigal son, that's all." He opened the car door and plopped Olivia onto the curb, motioning for Momma and the boys to climb out.

He snapped to Momma, "Get the car. I'm going to say goodbye to Mom."

"But..." Momma caught his look and stopped, smiling an apology toward Margaret Mary, who looked as if she had been slapped.

"What's going on?" Margaret Mary's painted eyes were open wide, shifting from Daddy to Momma.

Daddy was smooth as pudding. "We have to get back home tonight. I'm due to catch a plane out for Dubai tomorrow morning."

In the awkward silence the children looked from one parent to the other, trying to figure it out. Daddy said, "I didn't know about it until Faye got here. She brought me the message."

Momma recovered, except that Olivia could see how hard she was gripping her purse. "They…phoned just before we left Garland."

"Oh." Margaret Mary appeared to be doing her best to sound as if she bought it. "So…guess I just…jumped the gun about your job." She didn't sound convinced.

Daddy didn't answer directly. He only said, "Take care, Sis," and sprinted off to the side of the limo parked behind the hearse. Momma took a step after him and then faltered.

Margaret Mary leaned over and stuck her hand out the window, closing her long silver talons around Momma's hand. There was a dark part down the top of Margaret Mary's head. "Nice to see you again, Faye. Guess I blew it in spades."

Momma pushed the children forward to say goodbye and murmured something about having to fetch the car. Olivia felt tremendously cheated, not getting to go to the cemetery and see them put her grandfather in a hole, and she planned to let Daddy have it when they got into their own car. Donnie was squeezing her arm hard, as if she didn't have enough sense not to say anything wrong in front of an outsider.

Arthur pulled them both toward the car, as Daddy crossed the drive at a trot to meet them, pulling at his suitcoat and straightening his tie as he came—as if he were off to see someone important. Olivia had planned to whine at him, but the hard look in his eyes stopped her. The three children crawled into the back, amid the warm organic smells of long close habitation, and Arthur said under his breath, "Shit!"

Daddy slid into the passenger seat and issue clipped orders. "I have to pick up my bag at the house. I'll show you where to turn."

Momma didn't say a word. She put the car into gear and drove away with both hands clamped on the wheel. Olivia, sitting in the middle behind them, could see Momma's jaw working. Daddy's jaw was working, too, for once. Olivia did a little bounce on the seat, but Donnie swatted her and she stopped. She examined Donnie's face. It was damp and flushed, and his freckles stood out. He wouldn't look at her, but glared straight ahead at the back of Daddy's head. His arms were folded across his chest and his bottom lip stuck out.

They drove up to a large yellow wooden house with scalloped white trim. They parked at the curb under a huge oak tree whose roots, bigger than Daddy's leg, were growing on top of the ground and buckling the sidewalk. Daddy got out and told Momma, "I'll be back in half a second. Move over. I'll drive."

Olivia couldn't restrain her outrage any longer. "You mean we don't even get to go inside? I'm about to starve to death!"

Daddy was already halfway up the walk. Momma, her face pasty and set, changed seats without a word. Olivia looked at her brothers, but she could see from their glum faces that she would get no support from them. So she whined the ultimate threat, "And I need to go to the bathroom!"

Momma still didn't weaken, didn't answer. Olivia was stunned into silence. She studied the house and noticed that it had a hollow-eyed look and was in need of paint. It was here that Daddy had grown up. She tried to imagine Daddy's parents sitting on the porch swing sipping lemonade on a summer evening, watching the children play kick-ball in the quiet tree-lined street. The trees must have met over the middle of the street even in Daddy's day. Why would he leave such a grand old house and never come back?

Arthur finally let out a protracted sigh. "We've been in this car half our lives."

But there was no goading Momma into a response.

Donnie said, "You mean we're going clear back home? Now?"

The enormity of that possibility struck Olivia like a rock. Surely they were not going to spend another seven hours in the smelly old car!

Daddy came hurrying back down the walk, looking much more buoyant than Olivia though necessary. As soon as he had tossed his case into the back and climbed into the driver's seat, she decided to try again.

"I need to tinkle in the worse way! I mean it!"

Daddy switched on the ignition. "We'll stop for gas on the way out. You can go then." He made the tires shriek as he gunned away from the curb, ram-head thrust forward. Olivia was thrown back against the seat. She snorted and deliberately scuffed the back of the seat in front of her with her dirty shoe sole.

Momma finally said something, but Olivia had to strain to hear above the grind of gears. "We're exhausted. We haven't eaten…" She sat stalk-straight, never looking aside.

Daddy must not have heard. He sped down the street, white knuckles gripping the wheel, barely gliding through a traffic light before it changed to red

Momma said louder, "We've been up since three o'clock."

Daddy cut her off. "You can sleep on the way home. Now just shut up, all of you! I don't know why the hell you had to show up anyway! I told you not to come in the first place."

Olivia sucked in her breath. She hated it when he talked hard to Momma. She looked over at Arthur, who was clenching and unclenching his fists. Arthur's hands had begun to grow over the summer until they were so big, they didn't look as if they belonged to him at all. They looked like fists that could do some damage if they were to connect with something.

11

They picked up Chinese take-out on the outskirts of Garland just as the last of the sun faded, leaving the sky a certain pickled blue that always made Olivia sigh. It was at last the end of a long, clamp-jawed, miserable day, maybe the most miserable day of her life. They had stopped only twice for gas and bathroom and a few snacks from the machine. Their Sunday clothes would never be the same.

Plus, she'd never even gotten to see the dead body.

She and Donnie carried the food into the house while Daddy handled the bags and Arthur tended to a leaping and joyous Ramona. Momma lingered in the back yard, bending to finger the dirt in the flower bed by the gate. Momma frequently played in the dirt when she was upset; she called it getting grounded or reconnecting with Mother Earth. It was an activity the children had learned to tolerate, if for no other reason than to counteract Daddy's contempt. They did not speak openly of it, but her very act signaled that at best only an uneasy truce was in effect between their parents.

The children lost no time in ripping open the sacks and opening the cartons of egg rolls, chow mein and pot stickers. Olivia found paper plates in the pantry while Donnie sent a handful of silverware clattering across the table. Arthur and Momma came in. He went to the fridge for the milk jug while Momma got glasses from the cabinet. While her back was turned, Daddy came in and put a large brown envelope into the trash basket before he sat down. Donnie wrinkled his freckle-peppered nose and cut his eyes in a meaningful command to Olivia, who understood her assignment at once. She began to plan how to carry it out.

Midway through the subdued meal, while both parents kept downcast eyes on their plates, Olivia tilted her glass and sloshed milk onto the table. In a sudden show of fastidiousness, Donnie yelled out, "Milk slob!

Milk slob!" while Arthur pointed in outrage. "You did that on purpose! I saw you!"

"Did not! Did not!" She got up to fetch the paper towels.

She sopped up the mess and before she threw the towel into the trash, feigned great surprise and grabbed the envelope out of the basket. "Hey, what's this? It says, 'Photos. Save for Quentin.'" Before Daddy could protest, she upended the envelope and spilled pictures onto the table. Momma shot a questioning glance at Daddy as the children grabbed for the pictures.

Arthur held up a snapshot of a teenage boy wearing a track uniform. "Hey Dad, is this you? Gaw, check out the weird hair!"

Daddy said to Momma, "My mom had been cleaning closets. She had divided pictures for all of us to take home."

"But you threw them away?" Momma seemed to have forgotten about being angry.

He shrugged. "No use touring the ruins."

Donnie picked up a family portrait and pointed to a man who looked something like Daddy. "Is this the dead guy, Daddy? Which one is you?"

Daddy took the picture and studied it. Olivia watched with dismay as he began to blink very fast. Momma laid down her fork and waited; she appeared to be holding her breath. Olivia glanced at her brothers, who looked on in alarm. The whole family seemed stunned by the possibility that Daddy might be about to cry. But after a minute he gave a long broken sigh and chuckled. "We thought we were such a special brood back then."

Like us, Olivia thought. *We are a special family.*

He went on. "Special kids, every one of us. We thought we were so outstanding. We were going to amount to something..."

"And you have!" Momma's last word rose with a bit too much enthusiasm.

Olivia felt an uneasy prophetic shadow fall across tem, as if a stray guest had suddenly risen from the table and was standing between them and the light. She dismissed the sensation as unworthy, because her family really was different.

"There's Margaret Mary: left her order, married twice about three months apart and now...."

Arthur leaned forward with an eager face. "Now what?" It was something they all wanted to know. But Daddy's voice tunneled on through him.

"And the other girls: given the best educations at Sacred Heart. And both ended up married to ordinary men, mothering ordinary kids, living ordinary, congealed, insular lives."

Olivia opened her mouth to ask what congealed meant, but it occurred to her that Daddy might stop talking if she did. She squirmed in her chair because first he said they were special, then that they weren't. She didn't want to think about it.

Momma said, "But to have had a happy childhood is worth….It gave you a bedrock…"

"It was so long ago," he said. "Yet the time in between seems to have collapsed like a balloon. Time has accordioned." He studied the photo again and continued. "And Cas, the baby, the one we all coddled. Now he's the existential gadfly. My God, he's no deeper than a pane of glass, with his phallic cars and his string of check-out-stand silicone bimbos."

Momma said, "I don't even know how he manages, what he does for a living."

Daddy was in control again, but the curl of his mouth made his tone thin and bitter. "At least the bastard has a job."

Momma didn't even correct his language. She reached across the table and patted his arm, a signal to the children that the danger was past. "I know, babe. It isn't fair."

Daddy seemed to have forgotten they were there. He stared down into his plate as if he could see a long way beyond it, down deep into a hole. "Corporate loyalty is out the window like the evening slops. I believe I've just had one of Joyce's epiphanies."

Momma picked through the pictures idly. "It's painful to find out we're only incidental music to fill the frame."

"We promised ourselves to be great," he said stubbornly. "Nothing is so sacred as a promise made to yourself. If you don't keep it, something inside you tries to do you in."

"Maybe great isn't important," she said, and Olivia fidgeted with a fresh feeling of unease.

"There's no corporate security," he said as if he hadn't heard her. "No more twenty-year watches. You take whatever you can get. In the end, you end up groveling just for a decent severance package."

"What's a severance package?" Arthur asked, but he was ignored.

"A man with a family has no bargaining power. He has to accept any humiliating offer, has to settle for any crumb that includes hospitalization. Has to make any deal he can."

Momma stammered. "Oh gee. I hadn't realized."

He glared, almost accusingly. "Then realize it, Faye. Men like me are a glut on the market. We have too much experience and too many obligations to work cheap." He seemed to remember the others and cut off abruptly.

But the children were quick to show that they were paying no attention. Arthur wadded his paper napkin and flipped it across at Donnie at the same moment that Olivia began wiggling and humming and gawking up at the ceiling. But Momma was not as easily put off as Daddy, and she dismissed them with, "If you're all through eating, go up and take your baths."

Olivia noticed that Donnie sat still as a rock. Only Arthur rose reluctantly. Donnie said, in answer to Momma's glare, "Well, what do you want? We can't all take a bath at the same time. Unless we're Japanese."

"Then go up and unpack your bags and decide what you're going to wear tomorrow. We have to register you for school bright and early."

They muttered protest, but Donnie and Arthur were soon arguing over who would be first in the shower. As they bounded off down the hall and up the stairs, Olivia scooped up the forgotten pictures and replaced them in the envelope, which she carried away unnoticed. She lingered outside the kitchen door, still vaguely troubled by Daddy's comment about his family's specialness. And uneasy, too, about the deep rumble of rage she detected in his voice. Surely he was not still angry with Momma. It must be something else.

She could hear Daddy's chair leg scraping and Momma's sharp tone of alarm. "Where are you going?"

"Out. To clear my head."

Momma sounded trembly and frantic. "Please don't go now, Quentin. Don't run away. Let's face it together."

They had apparently moved to the back door. With heart pounding, Olivia crept closer and peered around the doorway. Momma had her hand over Daddy's, which was closed over the doorknob. As she talked, she gradually moved between him and the door, with her back against it. Small splotches of pink stood out in her cheeks. Her wax-colored hair stuck up in a funny hump in the back, where she'd leaned against the car seat for seven hours.

"Let's face it together," she said again. "Change doesn't have to mean anarchy. Let's make a plan. Together."

Daddy's bitter rage boiled up again. "Together? What do you think you can do? The company holds all the cards." He pulled away and turned so quickly that Olivia scarcely had time to duck out of sight. She backed into the shadows and Daddy stalked past her and headed for the bedroom. Momma came hurrying after him.

"There are other jobs, Quentin, other companies. It isn't the end of the world."

"You don't have the remotest idea how bad they jerked me around, Faye." He had wheeled to face her just outside the bedroom door. "They gradually separated me from my specialty, gradually removed me so far from Explorations that my resume looks like a goddam hodgepodge. They planned this for months—maybe years! They didn't *want* me to be employable!"

"But why?"

"Because they don't want company secrets leaked. And because they wanted to put me in the position that I'd be willing....Never mind." He slammed into the bedroom.

Momma followed him, sounding indignant. "As if you'd stoop to anything like selling secrets!"

Olivia tiptoed closer to their door, but even so, his voice had dropped so that she caught only snatches of what he said.

"Don't ascribe to me any special virtues, Faye...Nothing would give me greater satisfaction than to screw Masterson as royally as he's screwed me. I'd do it for nothing. I'd almost *pay* someone to let me...."

Daddy was through talking about his mysterious special family, and Olivia could take only so much of his grousing before her stomach got upset. She turned her attention to the shouts of her brothers upstairs. They were both special, even Arthur. And she was the most special of all.

Great things were going to happen to them someday. They were going to be famous and rich. They would be the biggest and the most—whatever. Maybe even Arthur, turd-ball that he was.

Later, when Momma came up to tuck them in, Olivia gave her a little tug so that she would sit down on the side of her bed. She said, "We *are* a special family, right?"

Momma chuckled and kissed her forehead. "Sure we are! Why? Was it what Daddy said?"

Olivia thought about it. "So we get being special from your side, right?"

The moonlight struck Momma's face at an angle that made it look stricken. Momma never talked about her childhood or about Aunt Thelma, who was a great deal older and lived in Tulsa. Now she looked off toward the windows where the light streamed in white across her. She gave a little shake of her head. "No." Her tiny tight voice was hard to hear at first until she seemed to gain strength.

"No, we never thought we were special, Thelma and I. I think your Grandfather Llewellyn was very disappointed that he never had a son."

That seemed peculiar to Olivia, girls being obviously superior to boys. "But he loved you, right?"

"Oh, fiercely! But he was scared to death we'd—get into trouble. He was very strict." She shook her head. "Sister was a good girl and married a Baptist preacher. But I'm afraid I was a great trial...

"But yes, in a way, I must have believed I was special in spite of everything! Else I wouldn't have tried to save myself."

"Save yourself from what? Bears or something?"

Momma laughed softly. "Something *did* have me by the throat. I used to have spells, especially in junior high and high school, when I thought I was choking. My throat would close off, and I would get panicky.

"One day my cousin Marjorie Jo told me—her daddy was a psychiatrist—that I had hysteria because my parents were so strict. So the day I was to begin college right there in Abilene, I ran away to San Francisco."

Olivia sat up. "Gaw! You never told me that!"

"Oh, it wasn't a big dramatic thing. Three of us girls left together. I don't think we'd have had the courage if it hadn't been for something that happened up in New York when we were freshmen. It was a "happening" called Woodstock, where thousands of kids got together for a rock concert and discovered there were jillions like them who felt like rebelling. It became sort of a defining moment for kids everywhere. It gave everybody permission to break free."

Olivia waited, scarcely breathing, trying to imagine Momma ever being rebellious.

"But we girls weren't very adventuresome or rebellious, really. After we got to San Francisco, two of us enrolled in college anyway. My father continued to pay my tuition. We worked hard. Had jobs on the side. For a long, long time I still had choking spells, but they finally went away."

She bent and hugged Olivia hard. "I met your daddy and lived happily ever after! And I promised myself that when I had children, I wouldn't be strict. I would be very, very lenient."

Olivia lay back. It didn't sound very special to her. "But didn't you ever want to be famous?"

Momma thought about it. "I don't believe I ever had time to consider. I was too busy trying not to choke."

She tucked the cover around Olivia's chin and gave her another peck. "No more questions, now. I'm onto you! Tomorrow's a school day."

After Momma left, Olivia flopped onto her side and groaned. Another new school Another bunch of kids to break in. She found herself gritting her teeth.

12

As the family settled into a new weekly routine, Arthur voiced the opinion to Olivia and Donnie that they had slipped another cog. The children set out for school on foot each morning while Daddy headed off to the city for "job interviews." During the first week, Momma put an ad on the grocery store bulletin board offering tutoring in grammar, and after only a few days had signed two students for Wednesdays after school.

"Not much of a contribution to the budget, but it beats cranking out situation manifestos for nothing," she admitted, to which Daddy frowned and answered nothing at all.

After the first disastrous week, no one asked Daddy how his job searches went. In fact, after several weeks, Arthur offered the private opinion to Olivia and Donnie that surely Daddy had run out of places to apply by now, but no one challenged Daddy as to how he actually spent his days. Arthur, however, said he smelled a rat.

One afternoon the children came home to find Momma perched by the counter on a kitchen stool, making coils of clay from a large blob of terra cotta. Her face was flushed with pleasure as she brushed hair from her forehead with the back of a muddy hand. Obviously the influence of Twyla Pruitt had reared its head.

"This is wonderful stuff!" Momma said. "I think maybe I can cure it with only oven heat."

Donnie poked a finger into the clay. "What're you doing here?"

"Making a pot. Out of Mother Earth herself. A very feminine symbol, the pot." She pounded the clay happily before pinching off another piece and rolling it with the flat of her palm. "A Chinese legend says that the goddess Nu Kua made people out of yellow clay, so this red clay must've been used to make American Indians."

The children wandered off, excusing her eccentricity. Anything for tranquility. Of late Momma's voice frequently rang with a steely edge, and only the evening before, Olivia had seen her cut her eyes with a bitter glint toward Daddy while he was bragging about something of no importance. Momma appeared to have come to some new personal resolve about her life that Olivia didn't want to think about, for they would all learn how they would be affected soon enough.

That evening Daddy was late for dinner, but Momma kept firmly to their six o'clock schedule and served the meal without him. They had almost finished eating when they heard the Porsche roar into the drive. Daddy banged through the back screen and burst into the kitchen almost breathless, blue eyes flashing with, Olivia thought, phony enthusiasm. It was easy to tell about Daddy by now, although Momma could still be fooled. At least it was best to remain wary and not get any hopes up.

"Faye, pack a bag! This might be it!"

Momma pushed back from the table only slightly with a chary, "Oh?"

"We're going to Pittsburgh! I've got a meeting tomorrow afternoon with Freemont Oil, and then they'll meet you in the evening over dinner. I've made plane reservations—"

"Meet me? Whatever for?" She said it with great calm, but Arthur shot Donnie and Olivia a warning glance. They could all tell that Momma was not asking a question requiring an answer.

Daddy was too caught up in his own excitement to notice. Still, Olivia could see impatience building up like a cloudbank across his face. He was loosening his tie and unbuttoning his shirt on the way to the bedroom as he called over his shoulder, "To check us out. You know the routine." He disappeared down the hall, but Momma didn't get up to follow.

Instead, she cave the clay an extra pounding and said in a voice loud with sarcasm, "I think you're mistaken. Nobody's offered *me* a job in Pittsburgh."

He pushed open the door and glared down at her. "What's that supposed to mean?" Olivia could feel his deflation, and she put her forehead down against the table and stared at the floor.

"I'm not going anywhere, that's what! What would we do? Hang the kids on a nail until we got back? This is our home. We just got here. I'm through going. I'm tired."

He stood there seething down at her until Momma rose and began clearing the table, never looking at him. Olivia had moved her head slightly so that she could watch her daddy's disbelieving expression. He turned to the children and gave a curt command. "Go to your rooms." It was his first acknowledgment of their presence.

Olivia got up with a heavy heart and followed her brothers as they filed past Daddy and went down the hall toward the stairs. Their parents remained silent until the children stomped up the steps, a signal they seemed all to have agreed upon without discussion. This time no one made an attempt to eavesdrop. Olivia knew exactly what Momma was going to say because she, too, was fed up with moving, fed up with fake dinner parties and putting on a company face. Fed up fudging to the neighbors and fed up with kiss-ass talk. They'd been doing it for years and what had it gotten them?

She wandered into the boys' room, expecting them to agree with her. But to her surprise, Arthur was flung face down across his bed grumbling, "She ought to go. She's going to queer everything. *If* there's anything to queer, which I doubt."

"But then we'd have to move to Pittsburgh!" Donnie called from the bathroom.

Arthur rolled over and stared at the ceiling. "Maybe not. That's just their headquarters. They might send us anyplace, just like Llano did. Maybe they'd let us stay right here. *If* there's *really* a job and *if* he's really hired. But he could be making the whole thing up."

"What would be the point of that?" Olivia plopped down on Donnie's bed and waited for him to come out. She would know how to feel about all this after she heard from Donnie. He walked in and frowned at her for sitting on his bed, then dropped beside her and biffed her until she moved out of range.

Finally he said, "I don't think Momma plans to move, no matter what."

"That's what it sounded like," Arthur said.

Olivia said, "If Daddy gets a job in Pittsburgh and Momma won't move, what's going to happen?"

"Nothing," Donnie said. "Nothing's going to happen." He looked toward Arthur. "Right?"

But Arthur was still gazing at the ceiling, his thin fingers clasped across his chest and his Adam's apple sticking up as if it might burst through the skin of his scrawny neck. At once it seemed vital to Olivia to know what Arthur thought, so she said, "Right, Arthur?"

He leaned up on one elbow and glared. The rims of his eyes looked red. "Nothing's going to happen because he's not going to get a job, turd-balls.

And it's going to be all Mom's fault. The wife is supposed to support the husband."

Olivia grabbed a pillow and flung it at him. "You always blame everything on Momma!"

He caught the pillow easily and got up and rammed it into her face until Donnie kicked him away. He went over to the dresser and began carefully combing his hair back into place: neat hair had become a recent priority for Arthur. He scowled slightly into the mirror, as if Olivia's accusation might actually trouble him. He said, "If you think about it, I actually usually blame everything on Dad."

Donnie nodded his agreement, and Olivia knew it was the truth. Donnie slid off the bed onto the floor and sat there morosely staring at the wall. "Arthur's right. Momma ought to go. *Somebody* has to help him or we'll all starve to death. God knows he can't do it by himself."

Arthur let the comb clatter to the dresser top. "Like you never heard of food stamps! Nobody ever actually starves, buzzard-breath. Even street people eat."

"You never see a fat one," Donnie said stubbornly.

"I do!" Arthur insisted. "I see fat ones all the time!"

"Anyway," Olivia said with a faint-hearted show of optimism, "it's all going to work out fine."

But when no one came upstairs later to tuck them in, she began to wonder. And when they woke the next morning to find Daddy already gone, she felt an ominous sense of foreboding, certain that Daddy had no idea whatsoever of how to get a job without Momma. If that was indeed what this was all about.

13

Daddy returned in a couple of days and nothing more was said about his trip. But instead of the resumption of a state of "peace without harmony"—Arthur's description, Daddy became particularly solicitous toward Momma, arousing the children's immediate suspicions. They never for a moment thought Daddy was trying to make up. He could easily forget all about the past as if it had never happened.

Daddy had never been keen on relatives, but to everyone's surprise and Momma's delight, he suggested that since Momma was so lonely, she should call Marjorie Jo and invite the Cadenheads for a visit. Momma had often talked about Marjorie Jo, her closest pal when they were growing up. She was really Momma's cousin, but they were more like sisters. She had married a geologist named Weldon Cadenhead, and they lived in the next town. They had a daughter about Donnie's age, named Fayedell after Momma.

Olivia was faintly irritated that some other girl would bear her mother's name, and she told Momma, "Don't invite 'Faye' on my account."

"I won't," Momma assured her. "It will be on my account. I've always wondered what my namesake looks like." Momma never liked her name; she said only a hardshell Baptist would saddle a daughter with a name like Faye, after an early star named Faye Dunaway. Momma thought it was the height of tackiness to be named after a movie star.

Arthur suspected that Daddy had ulterior motives, like maybe hitting Weldon Cadenhead up for a job at Texoil—although Daddy had cautioned them not to mention to Weldon that he had lost his job at Llano. Whatever his real reasons, Arthur was sure they weren't what they seemed. Donnie, however, with an unusual show of perception, took Olivia aside and explained that Daddy probably figured Momma was lonely. After all, Momma was an outgoing soul with no one except Daddy, who was never around, and beefy old Twyla. So if she wanted to bum out a weekend with relatives, they'd live. No matter how gross this kid Fayedell turned out to be, they could stand her at least once.

When Momma could find no number listed for the Cadenheads, she wrote to Marjorie Jo and waited to hear. To keep herself occupied in the days that followed, she busied them all with chores, getting the place fixed up for company. She had Arthur climb out onto the roof and reattach the shutter, which made a big difference in the looks of the house. She professed a great love for yard work and put them all to work weeding and pruning. Almost overnight the place took on a whole new personality, ready for anticipated guests.

Two things broke the rhythm before long: the first, only the following week. Momma stopped getting up to fix their breakfast, even on school days. She would call out from the bedroom for Arthur to pour them some cereal. The children took this new deprivation as a matter of course, not necessarily expecting that things would ever return to the old way again. Usually when they lost something, it was lost to them for good.

But in a few days she was up scrambling their eggs as usual. They did notice peculiar new mood swings: she would be morose one minute and ecstatic the next. But Olivia and Donnie were too young to guess what Arthur was too dense to figure out.

They learned about Momma's condition as a result of the other thing that broke the rhythm. A man carrying a large suitcase knocked on the door the next Saturday afternoon and asked if Daddy was home, and when Momma said no, he said, "I'm sorry to bother your rest at this hour, Faye. I didn't know that you're expecting."

He looked so downcast that the children anticipated the worst. Momma asked him in and sent the children up to do homework. He kept his voice low, but once Momma's voice rose with, "I had no idea!" It was all they were able to hear.

When they heard the front door close, the children rushed to the dormer window and watched Momma walk the man to his car. He was no longer carrying the suitcase, but he was smiling and once patted her on the shoulder. She nodded and turned back toward the house. The children didn't duck soon enough, but although she was looking directly at them, she seemed not to see. Her face was grim and set. Olivia wondered if it was because of the suitcase, or because they were expecting.

"Arthur, what are we expecting?"

"The bill collectors, probably," he said, and then a light came into his eyes. "Or…it might be a baby."

That could explain why she had missed their music lessons all week and had dismissed her two Wednesday afternoon tutoring students. It might also explain her stricken look, but Olivia had the uneasy sense that the look had to do with the man's visit. She quickly put it from her mind and returned to thoughts of a baby. The children had developed a habit of leaving those things that were bound to happen anyway to run their course without their attention until it was absolutely required. They pushed his visit so far from their thoughts that by suppertime they could scarcely remember it had happened. In that way they convinced themselves that nothing might come of it.

But they soon learned, when Daddy came in, that this was somehow different from past troubles. Outwardly, nothing appeared to change, except Momma's cold furor. But something more was happening, and it began late that night. Momma maintained her peace until the children were in bed, and then smoldering unanswered questions erupted in angry muted voices that gradually rose to such a pitch that, even if the children had been asleep, they would have been awakened. Olivia thought it was pathetically decent of their parents to want to hide their feud; Momma must have known how Olivia's stomach churned when there was conflict in the house.

Arthur discovered they could hear what was being said in their parents' bedroom through the vent in the boys' room. The argument had to do with something Daddy—or possibly the man who had come to visit—wanted Momma to do that she was against doing. She accused Daddy of using her, just as Masterson had used him, and asked where was it going to end. Daddy kept telling her not to be selfish, that everything he did was for the family and now it was her turn to do a little something for a change. Olivia couldn't listen long, because her stomach was turning every which way.

But by morning, Momma had apparently regained her good humor, and after the family returned from church, attention shifted to Arthur, who suddenly professed to be in pain because of his own aspirations. Over and over, all afternoon long, he complained in a loud nasal whine that drove them all batty, "How am I ever going to get anyplace with this old acoustic guitar?"

`No one paid him any more attention than was absolutely necessary, figuring it was a case of Sunday afternoon boredom that he would get over eventually. But on Monday afternoon after school, without asking anyone's permission, he went down to the grocery store and got a job as a sacker, even though he didn't look anywhere near the legal age. The whole episode so astonished their parents that they allowed him to keep the job.

Momma could feel nothing but joy that Arthur would have money to spend on himself, and even complimented him on his good old Yankee ingenuity. But Olivia observed that Daddy suddenly began to look upon Arthur as a rival of sorts, and he got red-faced every time the subject of Arthur and his job came up. He would point a finger in Arthur's face and say, "I'll tell you one thing, young man: you'd better never keep your mother waiting supper on you." ("Imagine Daddy, of all people, saying that," Donnie said.)

Olivia decided it was because of Daddy's intimidation over Arthur's job that he insisted that Momma find some household help. Behind closed bedroom doors, Arthur said it was ridiculous for somebody in their outward financial distress to hire a maid, but there was no puzzling Daddy out. Donnie figured that by now Momma and Daddy had privately thrashed out their true status.

"To my way of thinking," Olivia said, "Momma probably figures Daddy owes her a maid."

Donnie snickered. "Maybe he's hoping we'll get another bare-assed au pair." When neither of them laughed along with him, he squirmed and fell silent.

Olivia wondered if either of them had ever come across Daddy and Inge, as she had once at about age four. She had heard noises in the laundry room and became suspicious because the door was closed. She quietly inched it open and saw Inge bent over the dryer, and Daddy standing behind her, pressed against her rump. She closed the door quickly and never told anyone. But after that, she began noticing little things about Inge, like the way she always sat across the room from Daddy, and if Momma went out of the room, Inge would spread her knees and give Daddy a meaningful look. Again, Olivia could never bring herself to mention it, even to Donnie. The situation was soon resolved when Daddy was transferred and the family left Inge behind.

Anyway, an au pair was no good by herself. If they could have only one household helper, it wouldn't be an au pair, who had been good primarily for "baby sitting" when Momma and Daddy had to be away on Company trips. Inge would've been a complete fizzle at helping with a *real* baby.

This pregnancy was bound to be hard on Momma. Arthur said, "Maybe Mom doesn't feel up to starting all over again with another baby. Gaw, she's so *old!*"

Momma soon found the right woman: it was a time of rampant unemployment and they could have had their pick of a half-dozen. But Momma had no trouble choosing the best. Her name was Josephine, and Olivia heard Momma tell Daddy that Josephine wasn't much more than a girl herself. She had a slightly off-beat puckish air that Momma couldn't possibly have resisted. She was a warm-skinned little person no taller than Arthur, and she won the children over in the first half-hour with her quick and ready smile that crinkled her warm eyes, dark as wine. At once she filled their rooms with a comforting placid quality of deliberate monotony that they needed so desperately.

Her real name was Willow Flower, she told them. She was a full-blood Coushatta who had left the reservation in East Texas to earn more money. "Which says something about earning power on the reservation," Momma commented.

There was something else about Josephine that Momma didn't mention to them, details of which Arthur eventually uncovered on his own. Olivia figured Momma chose Josephine because she was Native American and thus closer to nature. "You are one with Mother Earth," Momma told her in wonder. Josephine smiled uncertainly, and the children were afraid Josephine would be scared off before she discovered what an amazing person their mother was.

Daddy seemed proud to have Josephine because she appreciated good music, and there was a certain status to having a housekeeper with culture. This part worried Momma, who whispered to him, "Oh dear. Do you think she'll quit when she hears Arthur sing?"

"I doubt it," he said. "She'll never recognize it as music, so it won't offend her."

As it happened, Josephine appeared to relish all music, all food, any entertainment. She loved games and took apparent genuine pleasure in playing with the children. She smiled constantly and often burst into singing, the same as Momma, except that Josephine's nasal tremolo had to be listened to with a great deal of tolerance. Still, the family began to feel very prosperous and contented.

Part of her salary was to be her room and board. She moved temporarily into the small room nearest to Daddy's study that he had earlier designated as Momma's sewing room. If they remained in that house for long, he promised to have the bare room upstairs finished out for her. Meantime, he made it clear in tones entirely too sharp and menacing that she was never to enter his study to clean, never. Josephine's dark eyes widened in distress as he spoke and she nodded over and over, wringing her plump little hands all the while.

Thus in all the new excitement, the visit by the man with the suitcase, and Momma's overheard comment, "I had no idea!" slipped from their minds.

14

The day after Josephine came to live with them, all the family, except Daddy, attended Open House night at Arthur's school: Momma in a new navy maternity top, Josephine in her good rayon jumpsuit of splendid deep reds and golds, Donnie and Olivia with cowlick and bangs freshly tamed for the occasion, and Arthur with a splotchy red face from spending an hour in front of the bathroom mirror popping zits. It was the onset of his preening period, Donnie explained to Josephine in a stage whisper.

It wasn't until they entered the gym to hear the band perform that Momma gasped and said, "Oh my gosh! I forgot all about it! You were all going to be in the band!"

With one voice the children assured her that Donnie and Olivia were too young and that there was always next year for Arthur. But like a little wet bee, she wouldn't let go of it. "A whole year of his life wasted? How could I let this happen?"

She marched right up after the band numbers to speak to the band instructor. The others watched the helpless director squirm and turn to look at Arthur while Momma talked—and talked, never taking a breath. Finally she motioned for Arthur to come; Donnie and Olivia kept their distance with Josephine even though they were in no immediate danger. After Momma and Arthur rejoined them, Momma said, "So! That's better! And just wait, Arthur, you'll love the drum much better than the guitar."

Arthur set his jaw in adamant defiance. "I'll never quit playing the guitar! I'm not quitting my job until I earn enough to buy one, either."

"Lucky for us he's short a bass drummer," she went on happily as if he hadn't said a word. "The school furnishes that instrument."

"But it's so heavy," Arthur said. He looked dismal.

Olivia and Donnie clutched their mouths to keep from exploding. Arthur was going to have to lug a huge drum all over the football field at every game. And the rhythm section would forever be fouled up and the band out of step from then on into eternity.

The detail about Josephine that Momma had neglected to mention was that she was on probation with the law. Her probation officer, a woman named Hart, had come around the first day, only Momma never said a word about it, and the children only found out about it as a result of Arthur's vent snooping.

Olivia figured that Momma took one look at Josephine and knew she couldn't possibly have committed any crime. Wasn't she of the Earth? By the time the rest of the family found out, Josephine had made herself indispensable, and Momma was too far along in her pregnancy to break in a new housekeeper.

The day after the school Open House, Momma announced that, since Marjorie Jo hadn't come to see them, now that they had Josephine to look after the house, she was going to drive over to see Marjorie Jo before the baby came, and of course Olivia would want to go along to meet her cousin Fayedell. ("What a wretched name! She's doomed for ever getting into a sorority!" Momma said without thinking.)

Had Olivia been asked if she would like to go, she probably would have begged not to be parted from Donnie. She still didn't appreciate some upstart having her mother's name. But Momma had yet to make a single friend besides Twyla—and now Josephine, and Olivia felt tremendous compassion for her.

It was a three hours' drive to Marjorie Jo's place. Olivia passed the time in quiet agony while Momma horsewhipped herself for being so wrapped up in her own problems that she'd forgotten about the band for Arthur, who needed all the help he could get. Olivia tried to console her by reminding her, "Arthur's a big boy now, Mom."

"It's part of my duty to encourage you," Momma said. "Praise and encourage, that's a mother's job. The rest of the world will take care of the criticism. And now look what I've done! You can never undo the harm you do to your own children. And I was going to do such a good job!"

She did, finally, hit upon a solution that mollified her. "Well, I can't undo the past, but I can at least bless you every morning, and maybe Mother Earth will take care of what I forget." Momma was forever tormented by duty, forever wracked by guilt over one thing or another, it seemed.

The Cadenhead house was one of the smaller homes on the block in a typical hotbed of oil patchers: the kind of neighborhood the Aherns had so recently fallen from. Momma was nervous about going in; she fiddled around doing things to her hair and face before getting out of the car. Then the front door flew open and a broad little blur in a billowing tent top sailed out with her arms thrown wide shrieking. "Faye! My stars, just *look* at you!" Olivia stayed behind while the two fell into each other's arms.

Finally Momma turned and pulled Olivia forward. "Olivia, say hello to cousin Marjorie Jo."

Marjorie Jo shot Momma a look. "It's been just Marge for years, Faye!" Then with a brutish arm lock, she enveloped Olivia in the folds of her tent, strong with cigarette smoke and musky cologne, and gushed, "What a little angel! Olivia! Just another little Faye!" She began to bellow for Fayedell, and Olivia pulled away sullenly instead of cooperating like the little lady Momma had warned her to impersonate.

They were maneuvered inside amid explanations about why Marjorie Jo hadn't answered Momma's letter yet; how she hated to have Momma see her like that, all fat; how it had gotten to the point where she hardly ever went anyplace because she didn't fit into any of her clothes. "I'm thinking of hiring out as a balloon in the Thanksgiving Parade. Either that or offering to give Mr. Goodyear a hand," she said, howling at her own witticism. The overfed outie of her navel showed through the filmy top.

Still no sign of Fayedell, which was all right with Olivia. Marjorie Jo said, "Olivia honey, go on out yonder in the back and see if you can't find her. I don't know where that girl got off to."

At that moment Olivia detested not only Fayedell but Marjorie Jo too. Marjorie Jo dragged her through the den and thrust her out the patio door and yelled at the scrawny girl who sat out by the pool, dangling her feet in the water, getting the legs of her jeans wet. "Fayedell, where's your manners? This is your cousin Olivia. Be nice to her, now."

The girl with Momma's name didn't give Olivia more than a fleeting glance. Olivia stood on the patio and surveyed the yard. Beyond the pool. beside the garage, stood a hutch on legs. Olivia made for it while the girl ignored her with great talent. Inside the hutch were two large rabbits. Niggled by a burr of contrariness, Olivia opened the top and reached inside.

"Don't do that, estupido!" Fayedell said sharply.

Olivia ignored her and grabbed for the largest one. He hopped easily out of her grasp. Fayedell dashed over and slammed the top of the hutch down hard against her fingers. She waggled her wild crackly hair and said, "I said don't, butt-brain!"

Olivia yelped with pain. "Godammit, you mashed my fingers!"

"You'd think mashed if that rabbit got ahold of you! He'd take a hunk out of your hand like you wouldn't believe. I oughta let him, just for that! And watch your language, butterball. I know all about your weirdo family and your mom's weirdo hog-slop ideas about kid-raising."

Olivia had no idea what she was talking about, but this was no time to stop and find out. She pushed Fayedell aside, yelling, "Stingybutt!" and the two wrestled back and forth against the hutch until they tipped it off its wobbly legs and it fell over, breaking one side loose. The rabbits jumped out and scampered across the yard.

"Now look what you've done, shithead!" Fayedell screamed. She ran after one and then veered off to try to catch the other. Then she let out a howl, "Maamaa!" and from inside the house they heard, "Be nice to company now, hear? You all take turns."

Fayedell eyed Olivia with loathing. She clenched her fists and edged closer until the two were almost nose to nose. Except that Fayedell was about two inches taller. "Now you're really going to get it, you sorry shit!"

Olivia, haughty as she could manage, pulled herself up to her full height and said, "I'll buy you a new hutch."

"Hah!" Fayedell spat out, "That's a laugh! Everybody knows your daddy lost his job and you're poor as Job's turkey, turdball!"

With the mention of Daddy, Olivia almost boiled over. But it wouldn't do to fight. Better to rise above it all, especially since she couldn't afford to replace the hutch or the rabbits or anything else. So she shot Fayedell the bird and stomped back into the house.

Momma and Marjorie Jo were at the breakfast table drinking coffee. Marjorie Jo was puffing on a cigarette and Momma was saying with great animation, "The whole economy's built on nothing but vulgar seductions." Despite that her eye sockets were slightly green from the smoke, her face was flushed with pleasure until she saw Olivia's, and the pleasure drained away.

Olivia felt like a dirty dog. She walked past them, ignoring Marjorie Jo's. "Honey, would you like a cool drink?" and went into the den and plopped down in front of the TV.

Marjorie Jo called, "Now what in the world's the matter, hon? Did Fayedell run you off?" The chair legs grated against the tile and Olivia knew Marjorie Jo was going after Fayedell, so she said, "I've got a stomach ache, is all. Can't somebody have a stomach ache in peace?" She lay down and curled her knees up.

The two women bustled in and Momma felt Olivia's forehead. For some reason that she couldn't understand, Olivia began to cry. Momma's face got blotchy and she said she guessed they'd better go. Olivia felt more miserable than ever.

There were more hugging and promises to get together soon all the way out the door and down the sidewalk. Momma had a few tears, and she ran back and they hugged one more time, and all the time Marjorie Jo was shrieking over her shoulder for Fayedell to come on and say goodbye.

Olivia slipped into the rear seat and lay down. Momma reached back and patted her leg and said they should never have come in the first place. She drove away in silence. Olivia was pretty certain they both cried all the way back. It was a fitting beginning for what waited for them at home.

15

Before they turned onto their street they could see the flashing lights reflected off the low-lying clouds. Momma wove the car slowly though the vehicles and people milling around in the street. When a fire truck pulled away down the block, they knew. Olivia, heart thumping, dared not warn Momma to expect the house to be gone. But as they drew nearer, although it was hard to see in the dark, their home appeared to be intact. When she heard Donnie call out, "Here's Momma!" she jumped out as soon as the car rolled to a stop.

Donnie's words tumbled out as he galloped up, looking wild-eyed and uncharacteristically close to tears. "The house caught on fire! Wait till you see! It burned the whole back...Josephine's room is all black! It's a godawful mess!"

Momma had joined them just as Arthur and Josephine, clutching her rosary, ran up. Josephine was near hysteria, making strange high-pitched keening noises through her nose. Momma hugged her close and asked if she was hurt, but Josephine couldn't answer for choking and crying. Momma turned to Arthur, "What happened?"

"Don't ask me," he said, about a half-octave higher than usual. Arthur invariably assumed a defensive mantle of guilt for any disaster. "I'd just come home and was lying on my bed. Donnie was watching TV. We thought we smelled smoke, and then Daddy yelled at us to get out because the house was on fire. We could hear Josephine screaming, only we thought it was a radio."

Momma's voice sounded so stringy that Olivia strained in the dim light to get a look at her face, to see whether she was angry or sad. "Where's your father now?"

The boys looked at each other and said, "Where'd he go?"

Momma got Josephine by the arm and led her toward the house, trying to soothe her. "Don't worry, dear. Whatever you lost, we'll replace."

But Josephine pulled away. "I have to go back home," she said between shudders, her round little chest heaving up and down.

"It'll be all right. We'll fix up another room for you."

Josephine stopped in her tracks on the front porch and began to shriek, her little fists clutched and shaking in front of her. "I won't go back in! I have to leave this place tonight!"

Momma, who could get tough when she had to, snapped, "That's enough! You know very well your probation officer won't let you just leave on a whim. You're expected to stay here, and that's exactly what you're going to do! Besides, you know very well what she'd think if you left."

Josephine hesitated, then resumed her pleading. In the dusk Olivia could see water streaming down the mounds of her plump little cheeks. "Please, *please* don't make me stay, Mrs. Ahern."

Momma told the children to go inside, but they left the door ajar so they could hear her whisper, "Whatever he did, it won't happen again, we'll all see to that. You can sleep with Olivia tonight, and we'll clean out the extra attic room tomorrow and make you a find room just across the hall from the boys."

She finally coaxed Josephine inside. Olivia took her by the hand and led her upstairs while Momma went to the back to look at the ruins. Donnie had exaggerated the extent of the fire damage, which was confined to one wall in Josephine's room and to smoke in the kitchen and back hall.

Soon after they had settled down for the night, Olivia heard Arthur say, "The dog! What happened to Ramona?"

They all got up and met in the hall. The boys tried to think when they'd seen her last. They all hurried downstairs to tell Momma—Daddy still hadn't appeared—and she convinced them not to worry. "The fire truck and all the noise probably scared her. She's hiding out under some bushes, no doubt. She'll be back by morning."

They went back to bed reassured but when Olivia climbed in beside Josephine, the housekeeper snuffled and said, "The dog is gone for good. I just know it. That dog has good sense."

Josephine slept fitfully, as did Olivia. She tried praying to God and Mother Earth to bring Ramona home safe, and figured if she fell asleep and quit praying, the prayer wouldn't come true.

If Daddy came home at all, they weren't aware of it; he was gone when they got up the next morning. Momma was already at work cleaning up the rubble, having phoned the insurance claims department as soon as it opened.

As soon as they had eaten, she put them to work: she and Arthur cleaned the attic room while Olivia and Donnie helped Josephine move her things. Every so often, as thunder began like biblical tramping on the roof, they would stop and go outside to call Ramona.

Toward evening, when rain hit all at once like furious pummeling fists, the dog appeared, wagging her tail as if she'd just been out for a stroll. But when Daddy finally appeared, she whimpered and scampered up the stairs ahead of Josephine, who lifted her long skirt and took them two at a time. It was a habit they both continued as long as they remained with the family.

Momma, always strong during a crisis, fell apart immediately afterward. The trip to see Marjorie Jo, the fire, the exertion of cleaning up, and whatever dark suspicions she had about Daddy, all had their effect. The next morning she told Josephine to call the doctor. She stayed in bed all day.

When Daddy hadn't come home by evening, she had Josephine phone Twyla Pruitt, but Twyla was out of town. So Momma asked Josephine to call the only other person she knew to ask for help, Marjorie Jo.

The next morning Marjorie Jo showed up very early, minus Fayedell. She and Josephine bundled Momma into Marjorie Jo's car and took her off to the emergency room.

As they were leaving, little Momma, eyes sunken and stark, shook a stern finger at the children and mustered a reasonably strong tone. "Go on to school as usual, hear? And no monkey business while I'm gone, hear?" Her hand looked unusually thin, and Olivia wondered why she hadn't noticed before.

They didn't know from that if Momma would be gone an hour or a week. It was a long and miserable day, and twice the teacher reprimanded Olivia for not paying attention.

But when they got home from school, Momma was back in her bed and Marjorie Jo had gone. As soon as they had kissed Momma, Josephine scooted them out of the bedroom with the warning, "The doctor said the next few days will be critical and that your momma isn't to lift her head off the pillow. If she does, she might lose the baby."

Olivia thought about this. She had never been positive that she wanted another kid. Maybe it would be best if no baby came after all. But if anyone died, Momma would be miserable, which would cause them all more grief than anything else in the world.

The children did as they were told and behaved as model offspring for one whole day. But on the second day Arthur banged into the house, threw down his books, got his grocery store name badge and started out the door again.

Momma called from her bed, "What's all that racket?"

Arthur poked his head into the bedroom, glaring. "Nobody told me we'd have band practice every day after school! The band director wouldn't let me leave, even though I told him I had to go to work. Now I'm late! I'm quitting that goddam band tomorrow!"

Momma answered quietly. "You'll do no such thing. You have only this one opportunity to get free musical training beyond what I can give you, and you are going to take every advantage of it. You'll just have to quit your job."

Arthur stared as if he couldn't believe such sabotage. His eyes grew wild, and he began screaming, something Arthur never did. "No! You can't do this! You can't ruin this for me, I won't let you!"

No one ever spoke to their parents like that. Donnie and Olivia, waiting a few paces out in the hall, moved closer to each other, thinking that somebody ought to bean stupid old Arthur. Momma raised her head off the pillow, as if she couldn't believe what she was hearing. Then she lay back and pursed her lips, but her words came out much too kind. "Arthur, it's time to face up to reality. Being a singer is no career for someone with your fine mind. You need to channel your energies into more constructive things."

"And you think marching around a dusty field banging a bass drum is constructive?" Arthur was still screaming, and the backs of his ears were a blistering red. "Oh no you don't! You don't suck me in with that crap again. You've fed us all this shit about how we were so special!" He held his arms out from his sides. He appeared even more long and stringy than usual. "Look at me! Look at all of us!"

To Olivia and Donnie's surprise, he rushed over and polled them into the room by their shirt fronts. "Have you ever seen tackier kids in your life? Take the blinders off, Mom. Look at Olivia! I don't know how she makes it through the day. Everybody laughs at the way she dresses. No, Mom, I'm not giving up my job. I'm going to buy a guitar, and I'll start singing—"

Donnie broke in, "Dodo, you can't sing worth diddly spit!"

Arthur turned, sneering. "How would you know, you little turkey snot?" He stalked out of the room trembling, almost ricocheting off the door jamb. He stomped out of the house, banging the door in a way that would've earned him a swat if Daddy had been home.

Donnie and Olivia lowered their eyes to they wouldn't have to look at Momma's distress. They backed out of the room and went slowly upstairs. Olivia stole a glance at Donnie: he did look pretty groty, in Arthur's old flannel shirt that drooped off the shoulders, his sandy curls frizzing every which way.

Olivia didn't want to see what she looked like. She knew she didn't dress well, because kids her age need a lot of overseeing in the best of circumstances, but she didn't think anybody else noticed. At times the kids at school treated them rotten, but she and Donnie usually figured it was because they were new, or because of something they had heard about their family. They seldom took it personally. Olivia purely hated old Arthur for talking like that.

It was later in the evening, after Arthur had come home from work, that they heard Daddy's car pull in. Donnie, Olivia, and Josephine were sitting at the kitchen table playing Scrabble, but Josephine jumped up and scurried upstairs before Daddy came in. The children, always thrilled to see him, were even more so now, with Momma lying in bed so helpless. They ran outside, ignoring that he was dressed in his good suit, and threw themselves on him, loving him and forgiving him as always for being gone so long. They led him to Momma and then ran upstairs to let Arthur know he was home. As they passed Josephine's new room, Olivia saw her slumped on the side of her bed looking forlorn, and she felt sorry that Josephine was scared of their dear Daddy.

"We'll go on with our game in your room, okay?" Olivia said.

Josephine raised grateful eyes and nodded.

They finished their game in uncomfortable silence in the middle of Josephine's bed, unable to ignore the voices of their parents, which gradually grew louder. Josephine kept clucking her tongue as if to say that Daddy shouldn't upset Momma like that. Finally, dragging in misery, the children scuffed off to bed, while the harangue downstairs went on, muffled but audible. Olivia hid under her covers and tried to block it out.

Hours later, Donnie came in and said, "You've got to hear this, Liv." He led her across the hall to his room. Arthur was sitting up in bed eating a sandwich. Donnie said, "Tell her."

Olivia watched Arthur's Adam's apple as he swallowed more than once, so superior, keeping them in suspense. Finally, when he was good and ready, he said, "Did you ever wonder what Josephine was convicted of?"

They had never thought about it; part of their self-preservation lay in ignoring the dark deeds of grown-ups. Arthur had been listening at the register again and heard their parents talking about Josephine. Olivia wondered with alarm if Josephine could hear them through her vent, too.

"Daddy told Momma she ought to fire Josephine," Arthur said in a hushed voice so Josephine wouldn't overhear. "Momma started crying and said if the probation officer found out that Josephine had been fired, she'd have to go back to jail, and if Daddy fired her, it would be over the dead body of her and the baby. Daddy said she would even try to whitewash the devil."

Donnie and Olivia exchanged glances, weak and sick to think of Momma down there crying and begging. Donnie said miserably, "Why'd he have to act like that when she's so sick?"

"Maybe he thinks it's best for us," Arthur said. He leaned close to Donnie's face and leered eye to eye, then drew up just for dramatic effect, and whispered to Olivia, "Know why Josephine was in jail? Because she was convicted of arson."

16

It came as a surprise to no one that Momma went into terrible labor that night and lost the baby. It would have been another girl. Olivia wondered if Arthur or Daddy felt guilty about upsetting Momma that day. The lost cast an awful pall upon the household; bad news seemed to be coming more and more frequently.

While the children waited on the front steps for some word about Momma, Josephine, with a set, forced smile, kept coming to the door and offering them popcorn or cookies. But they all felt ill at ease around her and declined politely. It wasn't that they didn't trust her; it was just that they decided they didn't know her so well after all. There was apparently a dark side to her nature that they hadn't come across.

After a time, Donnie said in a low voice, "Do you think Momma was worried about having to put Josephine upstairs with us?"

Olivia shook her head hard, to push away any doubt. "Momma trusts Josephine. Josephine loves us. She wouldn't do anything that might hurt us."

"Then why did she set the fire?"

"Maybe she didn't." Olivia didn't feel much conviction.

Arthur was sitting a little apart from them on the steps, but now he joined in. "Maybe she had good reason to."

"Now what's that supposed to mean?" Donnie whirled around and stuck out his jaw as if challenging his brother to a fight.

Arthur shrugged, closing his eyes, looking smug. "You figure it out. Maybe Dad—you-know—tried something."

Olivia knew exactly what that ugly-minded turd ball was getting at. For a brief flash the image of the voluptuous Inge rose in her mind, but she dismissed that thought as unworthy. She jumped up and rammed her fist down hard on the top of his greasy old head. "You know damn well

91

our Daddy wouldn't do anything like that, you--" She couldn't think of anything to call him that was bad enough.

Donnie stood and led her away, saying they didn't have to stay there and listen to that twisted mind. They decided to go in and keep Josephine company just to show that those dark insinuations were impossible for two such fine people as their dear Daddy and their dear Josephine. For all of Daddy's faults, for all he had done to make their life one long flight, still he was more handsome and more charming than anyone else they knew. All things considered, they had the best daddy in the world.

Daddy telephoned Josephine with the bad news and said he had better stay at the hospital with Momma. After the children heard about the baby, Arthur came into the kitchen and stood in the doorway, waiting until he had everyone's attention.

"I've decided something tonight," he said in a sort of tragic croak. "I'm going to ask the store manager if I can work in the evening and on Saturdays when we don't have a game I have to march in." Something dawned on him; Olivia saw it coming in his pale eyes like a wisp of candle light, flickering for just a minute. But he went on as if he had thought it all out days before. "And after I've earned enough to buy a guitar, I'll keep working and give my salary to Mom, to do whatever she wants."

It sounded too wonderful for words. Olivia wished she could do something so noble, but she couldn't think of anything right off-hand. While she gazed at Arthur worshipfully, Donnie, who wasn't so easily taken in, said, "Oh sure. I just bet you will!"

Arthur glared. "Wait and see, frog bait. But I'll just see to it she never spends a penny of it on you!"

Olivia saw it as sacrilege to bicker when Momma was lying up in a hospital, maybe wondering how they were going to pay the bill and pining for the dead baby. Olivia felt tremendously burdened and knew there was no way to prevent what was about to happen: tears sprang up in her eyes. It occurred to her that now that there would be no baby, they wouldn't need Josephine anymore, either. She left them squabbling and went on up to bed, but her heavy thoughts kept her awake.

Finally, in a hazy state of half-sleep, she drifted back to a time she could barely remember. She seemed to be a toddler, following Daddy as he entered a half-open door where a dark-skinned woman waited wearing a robe. Daddy lifted the robe from behind, revealing dark fleshy buttocks.

But no, Inge's rump had been white and firm, and she hadn't worn a robe. It must only have been a dream. Both times.

Next day when Daddy came home, Olivia, still troubled by the dream, and chafing with a raw sense of personal slight, had worked up a good case of mad at him. She blamed him for upsetting Momma so she lost the baby, and for wanting Josephine to leave. But mainly she blamed him for not loving his own daughter properly.

Lately he had taken to baiting Arthur, challenging him, daring him to stand up to him, as if they were in competition. As if he were showing off for Arthur. And as if to display his special disaffection for Arthur, he would grab Donnie and box him around and wrestle and laugh. But Olivia, he ignored. She had ceased to exist for him. She couldn't remember when it had happened that she became a nobody to Daddy.

That afternoon he asked the children if they would like to go to visit Momma, but Olivia decided that no matter how nice he was to them, she was going to remain aloof to him for the rest of her life. She worked hard to look pretty, so that he would be sorry he hadn't noticed her. Josephine saw her struggling with her scraggly hair and came in and brushed away the tangles and put one of her own colored bows in it. But when the children got into the car, did Daddy raise his eyebrows and say how nice Olivia looked? No, he hardly noticed her. She was relegated to the back seat with Donnie while Arthur hogged the front.

At the hospital the nurse wouldn't let them all go in to see Momma at once. She took the boys together, leaving Olivia to wait outside with Daddy. She felt so bereft that a tear slid down her cheek. Daddy wiped it away with his thumb. "Hey, is that any way for an Ahern to behave? Come on let's go look at the courtyard."

He took her by the hand and led her away, actually took her by the hand. Her whole being warmed to him despite her best intentions. As they walked along the white corridor, he reached into his pocket. "I almost forgot. I brought you something; a pocketful of days."

It was a small calendar like insurance men give away. She gazed up into his handsome face, into those blue eyes that were so much like Arthur's, and she couldn't hide her delight.

"A pocketful of days?" It sounded so poetic, like something King Arthur might say. Her heart swelled with pride.

"A whole year's worth. Be careful to spend them wisely."

She held the little calendar and stared at its simulated leather frame in reverence. "I will keep this forever."

Olivia knew she would always look upon this incident as a great and shining moment with her father. If such intimacy had ever occurred before, it had been lost in the mists of her infancy. She would take this memory out and polish it from time to time and admire it for the rare and wonderful thing that it was.

When it was her turn to go into Momma's room, she was almost reluctant to share the company of her dear Daddy even with Momma. But when she saw Momma's face light up, when she heard Momma say, "How pretty my baby looks!" all her reluctance vanished. Olivia fell upon her and kissed the circles under her eyes—she couldn't bear those dark circles. She hadn't really seen Momma's face for a long time. She wanted to tell Momma that she didn't look like Momma, but she was too overcome.

"I miss you, Momma," she said, blubbering like a stupid baby. She hated herself for being so weak, but Momma didn't seem to mind. She held Olivia close and stroked her hair and said how nice it was to be missed.

Then Daddy said in a husky voice, "We've all missed you," and they smiled at each other over Olivia's head. She began to feel left out, so she hugged Momma harder until Daddy lifted her off and said they should go. Olivia whined while Momma laughed and said, "That sounds more like home." Daddy dragged her out of the room while she frantically blew kisses. Then she remembered the calendar, still clutched in one hand. She held it up waving wildly. "I forgot to show Momma my calendar. Let me go!"

"I see it," Momma called just as the door closed. Well, anyway, Olivia would show it to the boys, and they would be wildly jealous.

When they got back to the car, Daddy reached into his pocket and brought out two more calendars. He handed them to the boys, saying in a loud cheerful voice that sounded phony as the devil, "I got these especially for you, boys. It's a pocketful of days, a whole year's worth. Be sure to spend them wisely."

Olivia sank lower into the back seat. She wanted to throw her hated calendar out the window.

17

Momma came home the next day but was confined to bed, which meant the children would have Josephine with them a while longer. Olivia chided herself for not being deliriously happy, but something didn't feel quite right. Daddy was particularly attentive to Momma all week, but she didn't respond the way Olivia expected; she seemed cool and distant, and nothing any of them could do would bring a smile to her face.

On the weekend there was another revolting development: Marjorie Jo drove over with Fayedell and her gross rowdy dad, Weldon. He and Daddy were complete opposites, and the children were sure Daddy would make some excuse and disappear. But to their surprise the men seemed to hit it off immediately, to the extent that almost as soon as they arrived, Weldon was invited into Daddy's holy of holies, the study.

Donnie and Olivia were assigned to entertain Fayedell. Arthur was off sacking groceries but even after he came home, he shut himself up with his old guitar and had nothing to do with anybody, except to take one look at Marjorie Jo and hiss to Olivia in passing, "Talk about needing your own area code!"

By mid-afternoon the younger children had run out of anything to do and were bored listening to the grownups who by then were gathered around Momma's bed telling "remember back when" stories.

They wandered into the kitchen to get a snack, and Olivia looked Fayedell over critically as they ate. She was even more sandy-haired than Donnie, and the same freckles straddled her pudgy nose. She wasn't at all pretty; except for her coloring and her skinniness, she looked too much like Weldon. Olivia didn't like her any better than she had the first time. Fayedell glared at her occasionally but spent most of her time talking to Donnie.

Fayedell stuffed her mouth with cookies and went out into the hall and pointed to the study door. "What's in there?" blowing cookie crumbs everywhere through a gap where a permanent tooth was coming in.

Olivia said, "Don't open it. You're not allowed."

"Who says, jackass? What's in there?" She tried the door, but it was locked. Donnie and Olivia both gasped at her audacity. Fayedell faced them with her hands on her hips. "So where's the key, hockey pucks?"

Donnie looked at Olivia and she blinked assent; Fayedell had given them reckless courage. A ring of keys hung on a hook in the kitchen. He tiptoed in and took it down with both hands, to muffle the clanking so as not to alert Josephine.

Olivia was fidgeting and dancing around. "Hurry it up, Donnie!" When she got nervous, she needed to go to the bathroom, and she didn't want to miss out.

Fayedell grabbed the keys and pushed him aside. "Let me do that, scum-ball." Since she didn't bother to mask the noise, she was able after only a couple of tries to find the right key and turn the lock. The drapes were always drawn in Daddy's study, ever since Olivia and Donnie had tried to peer into the bay window from the side porch. Now the three crept into the darkened room and felt along the wall for a switch.

Fayedell spied the window box and rushed over to it. "Hey cool! Does it open up?"

Then they were scared out of their socks as from behind them Josephine hissed, "Get out of there! Do you want to get us all killed?"

It occurred to the two younger Ahern children later that they must be dull-witted without a glimmer of curiosity or else terribly well disciplined. Up until the appearance of Fayedell, they had never once questioned why they weren't allowed into Daddy's room, any more than they questioned why they mustn't go out in cold weather without their coats. Their parents trusted them to mind and left the keys hanging in the kitchen, knowing that the children would never steal them, any more than they would steal money from Momma's purse. If Josephine had turned them in, they would have been unable to beg for mercy because they would have felt they deserved whatever punishment Daddy cared to give them.

But she didn't rat on them; instead, she directed Donnie to put the keys back on the hook and tell no one. The children went away to their rooms in shame, which Fayedell found mystifying. Olivia and Donnie were both shocked when she said, "Wait until Josephine comes upstairs and we can try again."

Olivia stared at her as if she were a raving idiot. "What's the matter with you, numbskull? If we'd been caught, Daddy would've killed us good, and Momma would've died of a broken heart."

But Fayedell only broke into a murderous cackle. "So? Bone-diddly-do to you!"

Donnie, apparently ashamed of his cowardice in front of company, said, "Shut up, Livvie!" Olivia couldn't believe her ears.

That moment was the beginning of their estrangement. Olivia stomped into the bathroom, slamming the door. But she could still hear them, and she leaned against the door to listen. The others were congregated in the boys' room.

"Want to know what I think?" Fayedell was saying. "I think our dads are up to something together."

"What makes you think that?" Donnie said.

"Parents are so stupid! They think you're deaf. I heard my dad tell Mom if this works out he could became a vice president or maybe quit entirely and never have to work again. Mom said if that happens, she wants a sauna room built onto the house. Then dad said to hell with building on, he'd buy her a whole bigger house."

While Donnie explained how that couldn't be so, Olivia stood there thinking how their Daddy never discussed business with their Momma, and she felt a new wave of jealousy. Maybe Donnie was thinking the same thing: suddenly he became strangely quiet. Then Fayedell scared her almost into wetting her pants by banging on the bathroom door. Olivia jumped back and hid as if Fayedell could see through it.

"I know you're listening, skuz-breath I could see your feet under the door. What're you afraid of, Lily-livered Livvie?"

Donnie cackled, "Aw haw! Lily-livered Livvie!"

Stung, Olivia screamed back, "Stupid idiot shits!" which was the best she could think of. As soon as they had clattered downstairs trailing storms of laughter, she ran to her bedroom and buried her face into her pillow to stifle her sobs of rage. Donnie was a traitor, and Fayedell was a temptress. They must have turned against her because, as Arthur had pointed out, she was tacky. That's what he had called her.

Her misery was so acute that, long after the Cadenheads had gone home and the boys and Josephine had turned out their lights, she still lay grinding her teeth. Outside of Momma, she had only one friend to turn to: Ramona. Because the pup had grown to be mammoth-sized, she had been banished to the back yard. Besides, since the fire, the dog seemed to prefer to stay outside. Olivia stole downstairs and stopped outside her parents' door when she heard Daddy's voice.

"She's about the homeliest child I ever saw."

Olivia sank down against the door, weak with grief.

Momma said, "Oh, I don't know. She has nice cheekbones. She may be striking when she gets older and fills out some. At least she has decent clothes; they don't have to pretend poverty. What chance do our children have? These are important years for them."

Olivia perked up. They were talking about The Enemy!

"What chance? Why, every chance! They're intelligent, talented, nice looking...."

Momma's tragic voice rose. "Oh dear God, Quentin, look at your children once in a while! See what other people see! They're deprived—sometimes they look like street urchins!"

Daddy didn't say anything, so Momma went on in a softer voice. "What's happened to us? We used to want to reform the world, together. You used to care about what I thought. Now you finish my sentences for me."

Daddy's impatience returned. "Oh good grief, Faye, not this again! I'll be damned if I can figure out what in the hell you want!"

Momma was quiet for so long that Olivia decided to leave, but as she crept away, she heard Momma's wistful voice. "Maybe I just want my back buttons buttoned...."

Olivia wandered off to look for Ramona, finding it hard to swallow. They must be the most desolate of families, for some reason that she couldn't fathom.

And when had the game plan changed? She had thought they were pretending to be prosperous. But Momma had said they were pretending poverty. Olivia didn't know whether they were rich or poor. Maybe in her uneasy state she had misunderstood.

She found Ramona bedded down on an old blanket on the porch. The dog was undone with ecstasy to see her and covered her face with sloppy kisses, tail thumping noisily against the wall. Grateful for the warm welcome, Olivia settled down against the dog's warm side and slept.

But fitful clouds flitted across the full moon all during the night; the flashes of brassy moonlight were like beams from a warning sign. The intermittent light invaded her dreams like a railroad crossing signal blazing off and on: *Caution! Caution!* as over on the nearby tracks less than five blocks away, a freight train clacked through the night, its whistle turning mournful as it faded.

18

When the Cadenheads showed up again the next Saturday, Olivia thought she detected a certain reticence in Momma's welcome, although Daddy, surprisingly, seemed delighted to see them. He and Weldon went off for a round of golf, and Momma and Marjorie Jo piled up in the middle of Momma's bed with the family albums. Arthur went to work at the grocery store, and Donnie and Olivia were stuck with putrid old Fayedell again.

But Donnie had become openly worshipful, even imitating Fayedell's brittle comebacks, and then howling at his own cleverness. Fayedell in turn encouraged his stupidity by cracking up at every dumbass word he uttered. Olivia thought she would puke. In addition, Fayedell had come up with a brilliant plan—"I've been hatching out a scheme all week"—which shocked Olivia but to which Donnie immediately agreed.

"I figure after our dads get home they'll shut themselves up in the study again," Fayedell said. "We can hide out in the window seat and find out what's going on."

"Cool!" Donnie said.

"Stupid!" Olivia said. "Daddy would notice the door had been unlocked—"

Fayedell interrupted with a sneer. "Why don't you shut up till I'm finished, cheese-brain? See, one of us will lock the door after the other two are inside, hang the keys back on the hook, stand watch outside, and after our dads come out, get the keys again and unlock the door and let us out!"

"Perfect!" Donnie said, and even Olivia had to admit grudgingly that it might work. Then something dawned on her.

With certain apprehension, she said, "So you've already decided who's going in and who's staying out, I guess."

Fayedell grinned wickedly, marched to the kitchen and got the keys, unlocked the door, and handed the keys to Olivia. Without another word, but with more than a few snickers, Donnie and Fayedell scurried into the study and closed the door. Olivia heard Donnie hiss, "Lock the door, Miss Sour-Puss."

Fayedell said, loud enough for her to hear, "She's got her tail in a crack 'cause she can't come. But she's too yellow not to panic: old Lily-livered Livvie."

Donnie laughed appreciatively and Olivia, feeling completely betrayed, didn't know what to do. She gave the key a twist in the lock and went into the kitchen to hang the key back on its peg. Josephine had a sandwich tray all laid out on the table, and Olivia decided she would keep Donnie and Fayedell locked up all through lunch. In fact, maybe she would pack herself a lunch, go down to the park, and let them stay in that window seat all day! She felt better already.

She dawdled for a long time, tiptoeing back to the study door several times to listen to the children's giggles, hoping that maybe they might change their minds and invite her in. Finally, hearing Daddy's car in the drive, she grabbed up her lunch and slipped out the back door. She set off for the park by way of the back alley.

But it was no fun eating lunch alone in the park. She sat on a bench tucked away by itself and listened to the shrieks of happy children drifting on the wind like small colorful kites. She shuddered in deep despair, scorched by the thought of Donnie's betrayal and Fayedell's wisecracks. She was never going back until Donnie saw the error of his ways and came to find her.

Anyway, she couldn't bear to go home and have to explain to Momma and fat old Marjorie Jo what they would never be able to understand. She thought about slipping back and hiding in Josephine's room until the Cadenheads left, but she decided instead that she would just run away, since nobody cared about her anyway. For *sure* not Daddy. Not Arthur. Maybe not even Josephine. And now not even Donnie. And Momma was too weak. With sick longing she remembered Momma telling Daddy she wanted her back buttons buttoned. Who would button Olivia's buttons now?

She left the park in the opposite direction from home, veered onto a side street and kept her head high as two of her classmates ran out of one of the houses ahead. She had often heard them talking about sleeping over and wearing each other's sweaters. A sudden empty yearning washed over her for such a friend. She had never had a girlfriend like that.

She crossed to the other side of the street and began to run, as if she had somewhere important to go. The wind brought tears to her eyes. She didn't know how long she went on, turning down circular streets leading deeper and deeper into a much better neighborhood. When she tired of running, she slowed to a pace that she could keep up without panting, but she would never turn back. She couldn't turn back. Several hours must have passed while the sun had moved completely across the sky.

She should have become hungry, but so acute was her state of despair that she hardly noticed twilight settling in. By now she had taken so many turns that she had no notion where she was. So it was fate that now she was truly lost. Now let them worry. Let them come looking; maybe she would be dead by then.

She sank down beneath a ligustrum hedge that hid a tall iron fence surrounding a large house. As she prodded the base of the hedge to find a soft spot to bed down, she didn't realize she had invaded the territory of two large Dobermans confined behind the fence. The smaller one poked his hot snout between the bars and tore at her leg half-heartedly. She screamed in terror and rolled out of reach, holding her throbbing leg.

Their snarling barks and her shriek of pain brought a houseman running from the big house. But she decided that either she or the dogs had set off an alarm, because a patrol car sped up with its lights flashing even before the houseman reached her.

"Down, Heinz!" the man said. He bent over and sucked in his breath. "My God, it's just a little girl!"

The man examined the ugly laceration on her leg. The blood was spurting, spreading out dark red on the ground beneath her, and the sight of it made her weak. She was clutching her leg and screaming for Momma, sure she was about to die, when the policeman leaped out of his patrol car and twisted his handkerchief tight around her leg.

"He got an artery," the policeman said. "She'll have to go to the ER."

They scooped her up and put her into the back of the patrol car. Frightened and in shock, Olivia still had presence enough to realize that hospitals cost money and that the Aherns were probably really very poor.

The patrolman gave her shoulder a gingerly pat, as if he hardly knew what to do. "What's your name, little girl? Where do you live?"

Momma had once taught them a story in Spanish about a rabbit and a hedgehog. The children memorized it and used it often on telephone salesmen and door-to-door Jehovah's Witnesses who came to warn them about the end of the world.

"El erizo se levanto gritando 'Aqui estoy.'" She said it very fast, in case either man spoke real Spanish.

"My God, she's a little gypsy!" the patrolman said.

"But don't take her to the charity hospital," the houseman said. "Her people will sue for all they can get if they find out it was the Formby's dog. Take her to the Formby Wing of Drexel General and don't say a word to anybody. I'll phone ahead and make sure she gets the best treatment. Then we'll figure out how to get her back to her people."

Olivia lay back and tried to remember how the rest of the hedgehog story went in Spanish, in case she needed it at bill-paying time. And thus she was spared the first few hours of the nightmare going on at home, where nobody had even missed her.

19

Olivia's deep wound required surgery, and her identity had already been discovered by the time she came out of anesthesia. She must also have blathered about being afraid of the size of the hospital bill, because when she came to, the nurse assured her that someone named Mrs. Formby-Herself had already taken care of it.

The pain in her leg stopped her from moving. A television was suspended on the wall in front of her. The nurse turned it on to a children's program and placed the remote control under her pillow.

"Did you call my mother?" Olivia asked. The nurse nudged her glasses up, straightened the covers, and nodded gravely.

"Is she coming?"

The nurse locked steamy eyes onto the TV and took a long breath. She smelled like Lysol mixed with Crabtree and Evelyn, and she wore a stiff hat with a gold pin on it that no self-respecting doctor would be caught dead in. With steely composure, she said, "Your mother isn't feeling very well. I don't think she can come this afternoon. Someone will be here for you tomorrow when the doctor dismisses you, or else the Formby's chauffeur will take you home."

Olivia tried to imagine what they would all say when she rode up in a fancy chauffeur-driven car. She hoped it wouldn't be during school so that Donnie would burn with envy. Quickly she drifted off to sleep on that thought.

It was the last peaceful rest she would have for years. She dreamed, or maybe she remembered, Daddy's admonishment, "I don't care what you decide to do in this life, just be the best at it that there is." She shifted in half-sleep, trying to escape those troubling words, burdened because she was a disappointment to him by not being the best at *anything*. She wasn't any good at competition; she decided maybe that was why she lost out with

Donnie and Fayedell. She covered her head with her sheet, trying to blot out the thought of Fayedell, who had stolen Donnie from her.

There were great gaps in her memory of the next few hours, even days. She was mystified the next day when Marjorie Jo came for her, wearing dark glasses, even inside the building. Some strangling dread had finally communicated itself to Olivia. She was afraid to ask why Momma hadn't come.

A nurse wheeled her out to the car in a regular wheel chair. Well, that was something to tell Donnie about. And they gave her a pair of crutches to take home with her. He would be wild with envy!

When they were in the car heading home, Marjorie Jo reached over and patted her leg and began in a voice dry as the wind. "I know you're wondering why I'm picking you up, hon. It's because something has happened. Your daddy is going to expect me to tell you about it before we get home—" With that she began to sob, and she pulled the car over and put her head against the steering wheel, wailing, "Oh dear lord!" again and again. Olivia's alarm catapulted out of control, and she began to moan along with Marjorie Jo.

Is my Momma dead?" she finally brought herself to ask.

Marjorie Jo pulled her close and held her, causing Olivia to wince in pain. "No, my oor baby; is that what you think? No, your mother is all right. Well, she's very ill because of what's happened, and the doctor has her heavily sedated because she was so hysterical."

Olivia knew then that Daddy had only been acting up again. She didn't know what it was, but her relief was so great that she didn't care. The children could handle whatever it was, as they always had. They never took these things as hard as Momma did. Olivia felt she should console Marjorie Jo, who seemed to be crying on her behalf, so she stroked Marjorie Jo's arm and said, "That's okay. You don't have to tell me. I'll ask Donnie when we get home."

With that Marjorie let out a wail and clutched Olivia to her even harder, sending a stab of pain down Olivia's wounded leg. "Oh my poor lamb! You can't ask Donnie ever again. Little Donnie is—God love him—he's dead!"

20

Of course Marjorie Jo had to be mistaken. Donnie was Olivia's one constant. Olivia pushed her away and cried out, "No! Take me home!" Her fury at such an outrageous statement carried her through. She supposed they must have moved up the street in an orderly fashion, otherwise she didn't know how she got to the door of Momma's room, having pushed past grasping fingers of sympathetic strangers gathered in the somber dark of the front room. She burst in, hobbled to the bed and threw herself onto Momma, shaking her awake.

Momma reached out eagerly and drew her close, moaning, "Donnie? Donnie?"

Olivia was sobbing, heaving, blubbering all over her, kissing her cheeks, trying to get her to open her eyes. "It's me, Livvie. Where's Donnie, Momma? What's happened to him?"

Momma squinted against the pain with wild, screaming eyes, hugged her tighter and shuddered. "He's gone, dear God! He can't be gone!" The two lay wrapped in disbelief for no telling how long. Arthur came in and knelt beside the bed and rested against them, his forehead cold as a cadaver. Then Daddy came in and said, as gently as he could, "You mustn't tire Momma."

But Momma pushed aside the covers and struggled to sit up. "No, no. I should get up. Let Livvie lie here, poor baby. Nobody's even asked how she feels. How's your leg, baby?"

Olivia didn't care about the leg. She closed her eyes against them all. Donnie was not dead. She hated them all for saying it. She dared not think beyond a certain point. She longed to know how it came about, because she still supposed that he wasn't totally *dead* dead, beyond some kind of recall. They left her there in the big bed to take what comfort she could from its warmth and familiar smells. Sleep became her instant protection from the unwilling memory that she had left Donnie, angry.

Later she heard someone whisper, "Let her sleep. She wouldn't eat anyway." She dozed off again, just as the painful awareness of the horror crept in again. All through her sleep the doorbell and telephone kept ringing, and people continued to tiptoe in. She could hear the hushed voices and covered her head to blot them out. By that time her dreams became vivid and jarring. She dreamed of crashing in an airplane. There were wild chase dreams where she and Donnie were fleeing something. Always with Donnie, ever-agreeable Donnie. She dreamed they were hiding, terrified, as menacing footsteps drew closer and closer. She woke up screaming more than once.

She couldn't remember if she stayed there all day, if she spent the night in that bed or in her own. As time wore on she became aware of the voices of Marjorie Jo and Fayedell. She hadn't yet missed Josephine.

But on the morning of the funeral, as Marjorie Jo bathed her in the upstairs lavatory so as not to dampen her bandage in the tub, it occurred to Olivia that Josephine should help her with her bath.

"Where's Josephine?" she asked, but Marjorie Jo shook her head as if Olivia shouldn't ask. It struck her then that Josephine might also be dead. "Did she die, too?"

'Fayedell, who was in the adjoining bedroom, stuck her head in. "Don't you know? Josephine's in jail. Josephine did it."

"Hush up, loudmouth!" Marjorie Jo said. "We don't know that at all. She only confessed to setting the fire." She scrubbed Olivia harder, as if trying to erase Fayedell's words.

Olivia's tongue felt like stone. She had to ask, but she wasn't sure she wanted to know. "Did someone *kill* Donnie?"

Marjorie Jo stopped and hugged her tight. Olivia took it as an insincere gesture to keep from having to tell her anything. She wriggled free and turned to Fayedell, who had a ready answer.

"What do you think? Doesn't anybody that dies get killed, except old people?"

Olivia could see that Fayedell was pale, even trembling. Marjorie Jo put a hand on Olivia's shoulder, trying to protect her from whatever Fayedell might say next.

"Josephine killed Donnie. She hit him and broke his neck. Then she hid him away in the window seat," Fayedell said.

The words kept resonating, echoing down a long dark passage of her brain as she went blindly through the ritual of getting ready for the funeral.

She had locked Donnie in that room. She had left him to his fate, unable to escape. Had Josephine already been inside the room, or had she taken the keys from the peg later? She considered almost shyly asking Momma for assurance that Fayedell's monstrous story was false, but it had the ring of a truth too terrible to have been made up. The ringing persisted as they dragged through the next hours.

Momma's face frightened Olivia more than her own thoughts; she wasn't prepared for Momma's deterioration: she was a grey, hollow-eyed specter, a whisper of a person, but not their beautiful Momma. Yet in one sense, loss had sweetened Momma's voice so that the simplest utterance sounded like angel chimes: almost too sweet to bear.

But it was Daddy's face, the hue of a caliche road, eroded with washes and gullies, that brought her beloved brother's death irrevocably home. Never in all their years, through whatever catastrophe or hardship, had his demeanor ever faltered. Now his face, usually immaculate, was unshaven. His shirt was grey and rumpled, and he'd combed his fingers through his hair so many times that it stood up in ridges. His cheeks, drawn and ravaged, looked as if they had been raked by the talons of death itself. His once dancing blue eyes had died, and behind them was a hot mountain of grief so monumental that she couldn't stand to look.

Olivia sank into the car seat beside Arthur, whom she hardly noticed, and reconstructed fast disintegrating memories of Donnie, her lifelong other half. Now she couldn't even remember what he looked like. She could almost hear his voice, but she couldn't conjure up his face. Swelling panic filled her chest. She had been angry when she left him. She had locked him inside and deserted him. The knowledge was too awful to bear.

A placid insipid man met them at the funeral home. Through a set, saccharin smile, he said, "Would you like to step in and have a few minutes along with Donald before the service?"

"No," Daddy said quickly. "We don't want the casket opened."

Olivia tugged at Momma's sleeve. "I want to see Donnie."

Daddy heard her. "No, Livvie!" His sharp tone brought tears to her eyes. So she did what she did best: she bawled. Deafeningly.

"Open the casket," Momma told the man. It was an abrupt, harsh command. Olivia looked up quickly, not even recognizing the voice as Momma's. Daddy seemed too numbed to argue.

The family waited until the man motioned them into the room where the big box stood, banked by flowers so sweet Olivia almost gagged. The thick carpet sucked at them. Momma held her up so that she could see; she was surprised at Momma's sudden strength.

No strong emotion swept over her as she strained to look. She stared dumbly into the casket at the wooden figure wearing Donnie's Sunday suit. She saw nothing else of her beloved brother in the white waxy form. The mouth was an unnatural flat slit; Donnie's mouth was never like that. The pasty hands folded across the chest were not his. Relieved, she squirmed to be put down. She said nothing to the others, but in her heart a secret faith had planted itself. Since Donnie was not in that box, maybe he wasn't dead after all. Maybe she hadn't killed him.

Still, as Momma lowered her to the floor and she glanced at the others, the shock of mortality showed on all their faces, except that of the funeral man. She decided that he had somehow managed to sustain his ignorance of the fact.

She hadn't thought much about Arthur during all this, but she had the impression that he, too, had peered down into the casket. Later, as she hobbled on her crutches to their pew, she noticed how Arthur tottered stiff-legged in front of her. Arthur looked like a stick, a zombie.

And from that day onward, he never played his guitar again.

21

After a steely-skied service under a graveside tent whipping in the stinging wind, Weldon insisted on taking Marjorie Jo and Fayedell home directly from the cemetery. Marjorie Jo protested that Momma needed her, but Weldon smelled of booze and wouldn't listen. Olivia suspected that his rheumy eyes had little to do with crying.

While Marjorie Jo hugged Momma and Daddy and even Olivia and Arthur for the hundredth time, Weldon stood off under a skeletal Chinese elm and picked his teeth. Olivia decided he was leaning against the tree to keep from passing out. Finally he got into the car and sat like a stolid unyielding mass behind the wheel, occasionally giving the horn a discrete tap until the others came. Olivia maintained a face of unruffled dignity, although she was relieved to see them go. She couldn't pretend nonchalance much longer, but she wouldn't give Fayedell the satisfaction of seeing her cry.

The family, along with Twyla Pruitt, drove home in the limousine in silence, leaving the small coffin hovering on straps above a deep, fake grass-lined hole, its blanket of flowers wind-buffeted and already fraying. The limousine windows were tinted, giving a grey caste to everything both inside and out. Daddy sat in front beside the driver. The back of his head looked scruffy and lopsided because he'd forgotten to comb his hair again.

Twyla held Momma's hand and from time to time tried to say something comforting, like how pretty the flowers were, but Momma only shuddered. Once she murmured bitterly, "Beckett was right: mothers may as well give birth astride the grave."

Arthur and Olivia sat in the rear and didn't speak. Arthur had folded his funeral program into a fan; Olivia kept smoothing hers out in her lap, thinking about where she should keep it.

When they reached home, Daddy sent the children upstairs and instructed Twyla to put Momma to bed while he prepared trays to serve everyone meals in their rooms. But Olivia, by suspending all thought, fell into an exhausted sleep before her tray arrived.

She presumed that Daddy would stay close-by for a few days. When he was nowhere to be found the next morning, she chided herself for not having expected him to disappear. Arthur did anticipate this, or so he said, in the only statement he made all day—not to her. Arthur seldom talked to her anymore. "He always escapes when the going gets tough. Crawls away like a snake."

Arthur had withdrawn more than ever, but she couldn't allow him that luxury. Starved for comfort, she couldn't leave him alone. She followed him everywhere, just like Ramona. When he retreated to his room and locked the door, she squatted down against it and waited him out. Sometimes she slept there. Maybe it irritated him, but he was too beaten to protest.

The household was invaded by outsiders, the most unexpected being police investigators. From her bed, Momma instructed Arthur to keep Olivia upstairs out of sight, so she watched from the dormer window and stairwell. She watched when Parole Officer Hart came for Josephine's things, later learning from Arthur that Josephine was probably being returned to prison. But it had nothing to do with Donnie's death, for which she had been exonerated when Fayedell broke down and admitted she had lied about Josephine's involvement. But while the authorities were questioning Josephine about Donnie, she had blurted out that she had set fire to her own room after Daddy chewed her out for unlocking the door of his study. Josephine had a habit of setting fires whenever she got upset, Momma was forced to explain. The children pretended that was the first they'd heard of it.

The investigators made several trips to their house, calling in Momma and Arthur separately, wringing them almost senseless with the same questions about how Donnie happened to be in the window box and how he got hurt. Once they even called in Olivia, but Momma insisted on being present, so the interview was conducted in Momma's bedroom, where she still stayed most of the time, hot eyes closed against this unspeakable intrusion.

Olivia sat on the bed and swung her feet and tried to act nonchalant. Without Donnie, she might not be so sharp, but she could handle it. One of the men squatted down and smiled. Olivia pretended to smile back.

"Tell me, Olivia, who do you think hit your brother?"

Momma reared up, clamping her hands over Olivia's ears, protesting, "This is monstrous! He fell! Can't you believe what they all said?"

Olivia could have given some bland answer, but if it was going to upset Momma, she couldn't participate in this farce.

"Nobody did," she said.

"Nobody?"

She shook her head and pursed her lips. No more. She was through.

He took her hand, and when she tried to withdraw, his grip became firm. "No Olivia, we both know that Donnie didn't break his own neck and then climb into that window box—"

Momma shrieked and pulled Olivia to her, covering her daughter's ears. Olivia disentangled herself and patted Momma. She said to the man, "Donnie might if he wanted to, but he didn't."

"He didn't? How do you know?"

"Because he isn't dead," she said with stubborn conviction. She let herself down from the bed and left the room with her head held high.

He followed her into the hall and said, "Show me the room your dad keeps locked, where your brother was when he fell."

Olivia's heart was bounding. "I'm not allowed to go in, and you better not either. That's Daddy's private study, where he does important work." She was afraid the policeman would ask who locked Donnie in that room, and she would have to admit her guilt. Besides, although she had not seen Daddy come home, she was fairly certain he had returned and was lurking in his study waiting for them to leave. She ran upstairs and bounded onto Arthur's bed. She could hear Momma threatening to call the policeman's superior, warrant or no warrant.

Arthur was sitting on the edge of the bed, facing the wall. Momma's voice reached them, shrill and hysterical, and the children knew what the man had done. They jumped off the bed and ran to the head of the stairs and heard him say, "Hey Marvin. Take a gander at this."

Olivia wanted to see, too, but she and Arthur were held in place by dread. The men came out of the study with Daddy by the arm. The man called Marvin said, "Mr. Ahern, you'll have to come down to the station." To the first policeman, he said, "This is classified information, property of Llano Petroleum, Says so on each roll."

The investigator secured a strip of yellow tape across the study door. He turned to Momma, holding up a key. "I'm going to take this key along to protect what may be evidence. In case you have another key, I advise you not to tamper with anything in that room. You could be charged with obstruction of justice if you do. Regardless of whether your son's death was an accident, it appears that a felony may have been committed here. I know a bit about the oil business, myself."

Their father had remained silent. Olivia could see that he looked even worse than before. The gaunt dark circles under his eyes were even more pronounced. He had lost whatever it was that had once made him Daddy. He didn't protest, didn't even say goodbye to Momma, who burst out screaming and sank to the floor as they left.

Momma never liked to see anything restrained. Olivia remembered how she once startled old Mr. Fromberg, when he was proudly displaying his flock of Dominicker chickens: "Isn't it a pity that they're penned behind that fence." So it would have been no surprise to either Olivia or Arthur if she had taken Daddy's incarceration hard.

The wonder of it was that Daddy's arrest had the opposite effect. Over Donnie's death she was powerless, but Daddy's plight was something she could fight, and it gave her new spark. By suppertime she sat across the table and watched them through mere slits in her puffy lids, but from them glinted fresh fire. The children ate obediently, nourished as much by the sudden attention as by the food.

She said, "You mustn't feel bad toward Josephine. Some people learn inappropriate ways to make themselves feel better. When she feels really bad, she sets a fire. It's cruel to lock her up in prison for that. I hope I can talk her probation officer out of such a drastic move."

Olivia and Arthur both nodded, stunned that Momma didn't mention Daddy. Momma was thoughtful over each word, tiptoeing between them with great care. "Some people don't have the advantage of good upbringing. They haven't had freedom of expression. They're never taught to sing, for one thing. Singing is very important to health. Don't ever forget that." Olivia remembered Momma used to say that about poor Daddy, too: that he was raised Catholic and never taught to sing in church.

She went on, as if nothing else on earth were on her mind, "Nothing important, down in their soul, ever gets said. So it begins to get acted out, pushing its way up just like a seedling through a crack, only in peculiar forms, sometimes. Just like a plant is sometimes crooked if it has to grow through a crack."

Olivia waited for Arthur to ask the obvious, but he had sunken back into a morose silence, so it was up to her. "But what about Daddy?"

"I'll tell you what about: I'm just going to gather myself up and locate Mr. Masterson in the morning if I have to drive all the way to Dallas to do it! Mr. Masterson will straighten out all this business about stolen property in no time."

This announcement had an immediate emollient effect on Olivia, although she couldn't figure why Mr. Masterson should be disposed to help. She went up to bed feeling so buoyed that she didn't sink into a heap outside Arthur's door as usual, but climbed into her own bed. Before she turned out her light, she opened the drawer on her night stand and took out Donnie's funeral program to read once more. The dull pain throbbed against her insides all over again. She felt guilty for having forgotten about Donnie, even for a moment. She examined the program, but nothing was there except the phony name: Donald Eugene Ahern. She replaced the program, turned out the light and stared up into the dark, wondering where Donnie was. Suspecting he had become a worm in her brain

Momma left early the next morning for Dallas and came back in the evening in part—she never actually returned to them again all of a piece.

When the children asked if she had seen Mr. Masterson, she gave a phony smile. With forced enthusiasm, she said, "I saw his secretary. He was in a conference. I wrote him a long note explaining everything and told her to see that he got it the minute he was through. Oh, he'll act, all right!"

She took to talking to herself out loud in a low voice that was toneless, mutterings that were not at all like Momma: "It always takes me a while to digest how things are…There is no control, no control over anything… It's a joke, to think we can influence events." She would cover her face and make queer gurgling noises. Her distress was too private and ugly for them to witness.

That night Momma came into Olivia's room and called Arthur to join them for a conference. Olivia lay on her side with her back to them, but she watched them through the dresser mirror. Momma, appearing pitifully shrunken and wan, sat on the bed and patted her shoulder, then made Arthur sit beside her. The room was in shadows, but she left it that way. It was hard for Olivia to see the subtle changes in Momma's expression. Olivia studied the wallpaper. It had pink flowers that had turned brown in a circle under the window where rain had leaked in. It was ugly paper. It was an ugly room. It was the ugliest house they had ever lived in.

"I know you've been trying to make sense out of this," Momma began after a big sigh her chin quivering in spite of a valiant attempt at a smile. "I know I have."

Olivia felt great relief. She knew somebody would explain it to her eventually. She rolled over and held her breath, sure that soon she would understand it. Her longing for Donnie had sucked her down like an undertow.

"We all come from the Earth, you know," Momma said.

"Oh Jeez!" Arthur said, while Olivia thought, *Not that again.* She felt a tremendous let-down.

"Everything we see if part of the Earth: the trees, houses, food—all that had no place to come from but the Earth. Donnie—" and here Momma's voice cracked and her eyes batted furiously, but she rushed on, "—is still of the Earth, just as he's always been. He has returned to Mother Earth's womb."

Olivia frowned a command to Arthur but he ignored her. It was always up to her to ask, "What will happen to him now?"

Momma thought for a minute, then said, "Tomorrow I'll show you... yes, I *should* show you." At last. With a rush of relief, Olivia fell asleep at once, even before Momma and Arthur left the room.

22

The next morning Momma called them early and told them to dress warmly and grab their breakfast to eat on the way; she didn't want to be away from the phone long in case Mr. Masterson should call. She must have been awake for hours, Olivia decided: there were egg burritos and still-warm oatmeal muffins, along with two large mugs of fresh-squeezed orange juice. Olivia ate heartily, feeling warm and cherished, but she noticed that Arthur only picked at his food.

After breakfast they drove to the cemetery, and as they passed through the iron gate, Momma shook her head and clucked her tongue. "Fencing death in. That's all wrong. That doesn't encourage life; it only preserves death longer."

She stopped in an older part of the cemetery, before they reached Donnie's grave. Here, the deep green of huge old cedars contrasted with the winter grey of brittle grass and the occasional urn of artificial flowers. Overhead, the quiet sky was swept clean, but to the northwest, a new winter front hovered on the horizon. They stepped into the dormant air and followed her as she wove between time-pocked leaning stones until she found what she was looking for. She knelt beside a small grave and said, "This one will do. Come here."

She put her palm lightly on the dry sprigs sprouting near the headstone. "A boy named Richard was buried her a long time ago, probably in a pine box. Maybe he wasn't even embalmed."

"What's that?" Olivia asked as Arthur said in a strained voice, "God! Can we go now?"

"They drain out the blood and put in a preservative. Isn't that silly? They did that to Donnie, then flushed his blood away, It has returned to Mother Earth. She's recycling it already. Death is a very active state to be in, you see."

Arthur had taken several steps away but Momma called him back. "Come here. Feel this grass, both of you." The hairs stood on the back of Olivia's neck as she touched the prickly dead grass on the boy's grave. Arthur put a tentative hand next to hers.

"Here is Richard, here in this grass," Momma said. "Mother Earth has claimed him and set him to work again."

Arthur snorted. "Even if that was so, he's only grass. And it isn't even green grass. It's dead!"

"Ah, but if they didn't pen him away, those cows over there..." she pointed to the adjacent meadow..."could come over and eat the grass, which is only sleeping. But all the same, the wind will carry seed to the pasture. After the cow eats it, it might become milk. Some woman will drink the cow's milk, and the child in her womb will develop from the stuff that Richard used to be."

Momma seemed satisfied with all this. Olivia sat very still and waited for Momma to say something sensible, but Arthur grunted in disgust and started back toward the car. Olivia thought about it for a minute, then followed his lead and said, as if to undo it, "I don't like this."

"We are all of the Earth, Olivia; you may as well accept it. She holds us all our lives, and she holds us even closer after we die. But we lost our link with the past with 'perpetual care' cemeteries. Now a stranger will tend Donnie's grave."

We. She had said "we die." So Momma and Daddy would die, too. What was the point? When was somebody going to tell her the point? Why did it have to be a big secret?

As Momma rose to go, she suggested they stop by Donnie's grave, but Arthur reminded her that Mr. Masterson might call. She lingered on a moment, looking about the quiet graveyard with an air of reluctance. A meadowlark tweedled overhead and she sighed. "Everything that is sweet is tinged with sorrow, and sorrowful things have a profound sweetness."

She turned to them and said, "That's why the first of your Aristotle words is sweetness." Then she allowed them to lead her back to the car like a blind woman.

Once they reached home, Momma phoned Dallas and learned that Mr. Masterson had received her message and would contact her. The news brightened all their spirits, even Arthur's. Momma rammed around with purpose, bustling to fix a huge meal, saying Daddy would be starved for some home cooking when he got home, just as if she'd been doing it every single night.

She cooked, and they waited. They waited all day, through noon, long past suppertime. She sat stolidly in the front room and waited until the house grew dark and Olivia finally had to ask her to turn on some lights. Still nobody came.

The children had already gone upstairs to bed when Mr. Masterson drove up, alone. They tiptoed to the landing and took up their listening post. They could hear, but not see, the great man who was to be Daddy's savior. Olivia longed to get a glimpse of the person whom she pictured as nine ways greater than God. His voice, strangely familiar, rumbled unnaturally loud, like a truck full of watermelons.

He was a smooth as a well-oiled hand-tooled machine. "I haven't seen him. Didn't think it would look right. But at your request, I've made inquiries. My secretary called and learned that he has pleaded destitution and will have a court-appointed attorney. He has that right, you see, being unemployed. You understand, Faye, that from now on Llano can have nothing to do with this, officially. He has refused bond."

Momma gave what sounded like a shriek of disbelief. *"Refused?"*

"Quentin doesn't want to get out. He's swamped with guilt. He thinks he's where he belongs. And under the circumstances, I agree, but for different reasons. He has sent word to tell you not to interfere, to forget anything he might have confided to you, for the sake of your future and his. I would like to add my warning to that: forget anything you might even suspect."

Momma made some protest, and he said, "Quentin may have lunged at Donnie, causing the boy to fall against the corner of the window box. That's my take on it, and that's what is eating him up. And of course, he has admitted taking the maps. I thought you knew. Our legal department had no recourse but to file charges. He plans to plead guilty at the hearing, and he'll be handed over for arraignment on that charge, I feel quite certain. Of course, we'll accept a plea bargain to close the matter as expeditiously as possible. Obviously, under the circumstances, Quentin's usefulness as a go-between with Texoil is probably at an end, regardless of the family connection."

"But, but..." Momma said.

"As for the matter of the boy, given the testimony of the other two witnesses, I feel certain he will be no-billed, regardless of how much he wants to punish himself. Quentin was clearly not at fault. It was an accident that could happen to anyone. The boy stumbled backward and fell, that's all. End of story."

She didn't make a sound that Olivia could hear. He moved across the opening into the hall so that Olivia and Arthur could see: it was the same sorrowful man with the suitcase who had come before, from whom they first heard that Momma was expecting. He reached into his breast pocket for something. "You'll want to make eventual plans to move, I expect. I have a check to tide you over until you or he can find employment. We have a heart; that's why I'm delivering this to you personally. We don't forget our own, although now that Quentin's usefulness is minimized, monthly stipends are out of the question. I hope we can count on your discretion in exchange for this check."

The other night, in her own bed, where frail Momma had somehow carried her after she fell asleep against Arthur's door, Olivia had been caught in a whirling nightmare from which she woke with echoes of her own cries in her ears. She lay in a knot of sweaty covers. She longed to rush down to Momma's bed, but superstition restrained her: Daddy might not come back home if she were to take his place. If she left it vacant, he might soon slip and restore them to some normalcy.

But after Mr. Masterson left that night, she knew the game, whatever it was, was over. Nothing was ever going to be the same again. Although she hated to leave Arthur upstairs alone, she tiptoed downstairs and climbed into Momma's bed. She slept there almost every night from then on until Momma went to the hospital.

23

From her classroom window, which abutted the end of the street where she lived, Olivia saw a dark BMW turn into her drive and, remembering Momma's fierce-eyed optimism at breakfast, knew without a doubt that it was Uncle Cas. She got up quickly and headed toward the door, barely slowing when the teacher said, "Olivia, it's only ten minutes until recess. Can't you wait?"

"I'm about to throw up," she said without turning around, using her Fail-Safe Excuse. Anyhow, to her disgust, the teacher had been too lenient and condescending since learning of Donnie's death. Olivia grabbed her jacket from her locker and made a dash outside. She ran the three blocks home, buoyed by the sight of the familiar car in the drive.

It had always been a house she longed for during spells of great loneliness. But not this house with its disarming shabby gentility, as Momma termed it; no more. Not this street shaded by mammoth pecan trees whose roots had dislodged the walk as if by accident instead of deliberate design. Olivia remembered hearing—and marveled that she hadn't heeded—that the larger the house, the smaller the heart. Then this big old shambly house that had beckoned them so cozily was in fact a monster that had already devoured their happiness. Josephine had known all along. Josephine had tried to destroy the monster by burning it to the ground. If only she had.

She arrived breathless with a stitch in her side but managed to bound up the steps and throw open the front door so hard that the doorstop twanged. At once she realized her error and closed it silently behind her, waiting against it for a few minutes to see if she had been detected, forcing her breath to come slow and deep, hearing the thump of her heart until it gradually slowed to normal.

When sufficient time had passed and no one appeared, she tiptoed through the darkened house with its close-pulled drapes toward the sound of murmuring voices. They led her to Uncle Cas and Momma in the sunny breakfast room off the kitchen.

Olivia stopped in the dining room and slid down near the register. She bent and peered through and saw her uncle's mocs and his bare ankles. He was sitting across the table from Momma, whose feet she couldn't see, but whose high-pitched hysteria had become all too familiar. Olivia recognized the same story Momma had told last night over the phone—maybe even to Uncle Cas—about how Daddy had refused to post bond and come home; how he was going to plead guilty for...something. Olivia had yet to figure out exactly what. She had tried to question Arthur, but something was wrong with Arthur. He never heard her anymore.

Olivia crept to the door and peeked in. Momma got up from the table and turned her back, moving to the windows that looked out onto the drive and Twyla's house beyond. There was nothing to look at, Olivia knew. Momma shrugged deeper into her ever-present bathrobe and blew her nose, trying valiantly not to cry anymore.

Uncle Cas stood, as if he meant to comfort her, but apparently he had a change of mind. He said, "Nevertheless, you should've called us when Donnie died. We would've been here for you, all of us. You needed support then. God, even a drowning man never stops calling for help!"

Momma didn't turn around. Her words came out in choked spasms. "That's just it. Quentin...He always comes up looking like the black sheep..."

Cas exploded. "My God! Couldn't he at least set aside his ego for the death of his son?"

"You see?" Momma whirled, tears forgotten, and countered with outrage, her thin hands balled into sharp fists. "That's always the way it is with this family! Judgment and blame, judgment and blame!"

But Cas was not backing down. He rapped his knuckles against the tabletop for emphasis. "Hell, don't fall into that Freudian trap with me— that somebody in the family has to get the blame!" He moved closer to her and laid a hand on her shoulder. Olivia watched as Momma went rigid and half pulled away.

But Uncle Cas went on. "Let's start over, Faye. The last thing I want to do is blame anybody. Contrary to what you may believe, we have always been a typically strong Catholic family. Up until this generation, I don't think it ever occurred to us that would *not* get along with each other, that we would *not* honor our parents, no matter what. Those simply weren't options. Our family stood together against the world."

Momma had relaxed as Cas released his touch on her shoulder. She went back and sank into her chair at the table, looking up at him with wistful tragic longing, traces of moisture still shining on her cheekbones. "It was that way for us, too. Family was family for life. You're right: I should have called about Donnie. I didn't call my folks, either....What's happened to us? Why are we so cut off, so miserably alone? We used to be the haves; now we're outsiders."

He shrugged and returned to his seat opposite her. "Don't be too hard on yourself. I'm as bad as you; Margaret Mary too. Medics who view everything as pathology sure didn't help our attitudes. But moving every year or so left you dangling and disconnected, with no support. It's splintering. My God, in my checkered career, I've transferred, prostituted myself for corporate interests, just like Quentin."

She sipped her coffee and shook her head. "That can't be it. We should have kept in touch. Think about the pioneers who struck out—maybe they never got to see their families again. But they still kept in touch."

"That's Hollywood's version. Pioneer wagon trains weren't a hodgepodge of strangers. They were usually great clans. The whole tribe, in-laws, neighbors, would move together. People took their identities with them. Now you lose yours every time you move. I don't think Quentin even knows who he is anymore."

Momma added, "We have no ancient and venerable mentors anymore, either." She was quiet for a while, and when she spoke again, Olivia winced at the bitterness that kept creeping in until it had gutted everything else. "Llano kept us constantly off balance. We never knew what to expect next."

She looked up at him pleadingly and said with stubborn insistence, "Something isn't right. Quentin would never 'lunge' at Donnie. Never! And he didn't take the maps. I can testify to that. They were delivered here in a suitcase by the Great Man himself. Why would he dirty his hands? So there'd be no other witness!"

Olivia felt a small thrill because Uncle Cas sounded reassuring, like Daddy. "Sure. Everyone knows nobody gets that close to a corporate president. Did you actually see the maps?"

Momma fumbled. "N-no. But that's what they were."

"Masterson told you that?"

"No, but Quentin did, reluctantly. I was furious to find out he was working undercover and hadn't even told us. It was like they blackmailed him into doing it. First they fired him, and then when he was desperate enough, they could use him to do their dirty work."

"Masterson would deny it, of course. What I can't fathom is why a man of his stature, the CEO of a prosperous independent oil company, would be interested in running a rival out of business."

"Didn't you know? It's personal with him. Masterson and Sims, Texoil's president, were fraternity brothers. When Masterson was first starting out, he offered Sims a chance to come in with him, but Sims probably wanted to be his own boss. Now Texoil has a greater net worth than Llano. It's eating Masterson's lunch, so Quentin says," she said.

Cas chuckled. "The guy's so rich he can afford to play million-dollar practical jokes! Even if it backfires, he doesn't lose a thing."

She broke down in sobs again and blew her nose. "I don't understand it. Even Quentin denies the whole thing! Masterson kissed us off with a very big check and a warning that I was to keep my mouth shut."

Cas remained quiet until Momma quit sniffing. The legs of his chair scraped, and Olivia shrank farther into the shadows. "It must be part of the deal. If Quentin gets caught, he takes the fall alone. Would a jury believe him, or the president of Llano Petroleum?"

"What would possess a man—a family man—to confess to stealing something he didn't steal? How could he put us through this?" Momma threatened to erupt into tears all over again, and Olivia felt overwhelmed anew by the dull weight of so much grief.

Cas had moved across the room out of sight. His voice came from the direction of the kitchen door. "I don't know. Maybe it was for the very big check. Maybe it was because of the accident. That's a terrible burden to have on your conscience: being angry at your son for eavesdropping, just before he dies. But you can ask him yourself. I'm going downtown to hire a good lawyer who'll spring him whether he wants sprung or not."

Momma sounded afraid to hope, which brought a rise of anger in Olivia. "What can a lawyer do without Quentin's consent?"

"No judge in his right mind will hold a man who's posted bond when jails are overflowing with violent felons." The back screen door squeaked and he paused and called back, "Anyway, now that I think about it, we both know the real reason he's still in jail."

"What's that?"

"He lied to you. He'll avoid facing you till the cows come home, if he can."

She said with resignation, "He does it every time."

"He's been doing it since we were kids," Cas said, and slammed the screen door behind him.

24

Olivia and Arthur both stayed home the next day with croupy coughs; they were often ill lately. Josephine would have accused them of playing sick, if she'd been there. This time they had both somehow managed to develop a genuine low-grade fever, but Josephine would have sniffed and dismissed it as "excitement fever" because maybe Uncle Cas would bring Daddy home.

They missed Josephine; Olivia asked about her every day. Even Arthur, showing a hint of genuine concern that morning when Momma came in to take their temperatures, had wondered if she would be locked up in a real prison for starting the fire.

"She'll go into therapy," Momma said, tucking covers around him just as if he weren't almost fourteen going on sixteen.

"Same thing," Arthur said wryly, flinging them off again.

Momma was much too weak to climb the stairs to nurse them, so she had placed them in her bed with a protective pile of pillows between them. "To keep me from catching dweeb germs," Arthur said, groaning like a sick cow. Olivia saw this only as a good development, because they would be able to see Daddy all the sooner.

But when they heard Uncle Cas's car in the drive, Momma rushed into the bedroom and ordered them upstairs. Olivia leaped up to peek through the curtains. She could see two heads in the front seat. She squealed, "But he's got Daddy! Daddy's home!"

Momma grasped her firmly by the shoulders and aimed her toward the door. Her tone, sharp and commanding and oddly cold, left no room for argument. "I said run! This minute, hear? You can see him later."

Atypically, Arthur did not protest, but left immediately and called to Olivia from the stairs. "Come on, runt. Get your skinny butt up here."

She followed with great reluctance, turning once to catch Momma wringing her hands as she returned to the bedroom, of all things. A cold dread brought an involuntary shiver that Olivia knew was not caused by fever. Arthur grabbed the sleeve of her pajamas and pulled her the rest of the way upstairs. Without further communication, the two rushed to the vent in Arthur's room to listen.

There was no jumble of voices when the two men came in; in fact, she couldn't hear her parents at all. Instead, Uncle Cas was telling them both goodbye! Olivia stared up at Arthur, wide-eyed. "He's leaving!" She said it too loudly, and Arthur clamped a hand over her mouth.

How could Uncle Cas go back to Fort Worth without telling her goodbye? She had always been very special to him; he rewarded her with extra attention. She fought off Arthur's hand with the grudging unspoken promise to be quiet.

Momma walked Uncle Cas to the front door, murmuring polite things. Daddy must be in the front hallway, too, but he wasn't saying anything. Not a word. They had yet to hear Daddy speak, although they heard pants pocket change jangling.

When the front door closed, Momma's heels sounded on the hallway floor. Olivia turned questioning eyes toward Arthur. Where was Daddy? Arthur thought for an instant, then got up and left the room. Olivia gasped as he quietly opened Josephine's door. No one was allowed to go in when Josephine wasn't there! Even though she was gone, it was still her room. If they violated her sanctuary, as if it weren't hers any longer, as if they no longer had faith, maybe she would *never* come back.

Still, she followed him, to scold him, before she saw him crouched beside the vent. From there, sounds from Daddy's study were much plainer.

She knelt beside him and heard Momma talking to Daddy in low, sporadic, loaded words. Daddy's answers, short and mumbled, were lost in the rustle of papers.

Then Momma's voice rose enough to hear the sob in her throat. "You've left me completely out of this. If only you *cared* about us, I think I could bear it. The power of caring is strong enough to heal, but the power of *not* caring is stronger. I feel cut off at the knees."

"Nonsense," he said.

"Your indifference has paralyzed me. Everything I think of to say is left unsaid when I remember, 'What's the use?'"

"I care," he said, so absently that Olivia wondered if he were riffling through the mail.

There was an audible hiss of exasperation, and Momma became bitter. "I rest my case."

Daddy sounded indignant. "Look here, Faye. If there was ever time when I don't need this—You know, I've done my damnedest to keep things on an even keel, to maintain peace ever since you found out."

"We've had peace, if you want to call it that, without harmony. Life on earth is about harmony."

"Oh for God's sake! Here comes a goddam sermon! Pontificating doesn't become you, Faye."

"This is your old tactic learned in business: go on the attack instead of facing things. I ought to be used to it by now."

Silence. The air was charged.

Daddy's voice: "We both know what this is really about, don't we?"

Silence. Like the pendulum-pause on a very slow clock.

They moved closer to the register. Daddy went on in a quiet voice.

"It's not about me and Llano. It's about Donnie, isn't it?" Even Daddy's voice broke.

Momma's bitter tragic sigh tore at Olivia's spirit. "Why don't you just leave?"

Arthur stood abruptly and left the room, while hot tears coursed down Olivia's cheeks. She sat before the vent hugging her knees against her chest. But her parents had moved to another part of the house. After a short while she heard the back door slam, heard Daddy's car roar out of the drive. Still she sat hunched in a ball on Josephine's floor, scarcely able to breathe.

Some time later she heard the back door slam again. She jerked up—she must have fallen asleep against the side of Josephine's bed—to listen for Daddy's voice. But it was Momma, calling Ramona for supper. She kept calling for a long time.

Arthur, hollow-eyed and stricken, reappeared. "Ramon's run away, I bet, like last time, when Daddy yelled at Josephine for going into his study. Ramona can't stand yelling." He peered out the dormer window, shaking his head.

"But Ramona came back pretty soon." Her tears welled again. She followed him into the hall, still insisting, "She came back, didn't she? This is just the same as last time, isn't it?"

Arthur scuffed into his room without answering, and Olivia knew that this was like no other time in their lives.

25

Subtle changes in Momma did not go unnoticed. If Olivia missed them, Arthur called them to her attention: the way Momma's clothes hung loose, as if they belonged to Josephine; the fire of Momma's rage lit by purple depths beneath her grey eyes; that gaunt hollows below her cheekbones that in shadows looked like gashes; the little knobs on her elbows; the slump of her shoulders; the listlessness of her unkempt hair, now noticeably streaked.

Their days were peppered with unsettling incidents, testaments to their ongoing tumult: Momma's pleading calls to Josephine's parole officer, couching her own desperation in halting arguments about Josephine's return "for her own good."

There were overheard snippets of her parents' abortive attempts and reconciliation on the days when he returned to get clothes. Momma would try to hide her pleasure and relief. At least twice he spent the night, and once he stayed for several days, during which Olivia happily returned to her own room upstairs.

But there was no easy peace; frequently Olivia walked in on the tag end of a quarrel.

Often Momma was the accuser, but once Olivia heard Daddy's scorching indictment: "You've never supported me. I've had to scratch my way up by myself!"

Momma struck back. "You deserted me. Deserted our dreams. We had seen a man land on the moon; there was nothing we couldn't do. We were going to be different, cure the world's ills...or have you forgotten?"

With more sarcasm than Olivia thought necessary, Daddy said, "There were practicalities. Even herb tea costs money. And no sector can insulate itself from the rest."

"But you sold out! There's a difference between dropping out and selling out. This hasn't ever been about money. It's about power. You became a power junkie. All the things you used to hate, you've become."

Once she and Arthur overheard Momma accuse Daddy, "You even lied about that job offer in Pittsburgh…I wonder what you were really doing then?"

Arthur nodded gravely and muttered, "I thought there was something fishy about that."

But Daddy insisted, "I didn't lie. I actually interviewed. We had to keep up appearances that I was looking for work. Who knows? If they'd offered me a better job, I might have told Masterson to stuff it. Do you think I *liked* what I was having to do? But they asked too many questions. Frank told me to back off and concentrate on Weldon."

"Appearances!" she shrieked. "Our whole life has been nothing but appearances! There's been no substance to our marriage. And don't tell me you *had* to do it; nobody twisted your arm."

Momma went on. "I tried to invent substance for the children's sake and especially for mine. I lied to myself. I supposed that's even worse than your lying to me."

Daddy was posturing; Olivia could picture him dismissing Momma with a wave of his hand. It was his favorite defense. "As usual, you're blowing everything out of proportion. I did it all for your good."

"No, for *your* good! Just what else did Masterson promise you for this little stunt?"

Whenever Momma used demeaning words like that, Daddy would grind his teeth and look away, as if were looking for the nearest exit. But Momma kept hammering away.

"You *used* me, used my relatives!"

He blurted out, "If you must know, when this was over, I was to be reinstated and oversee Aberdeen Development: a posh assignment."

Arthur sat back on his haunches and slapped his forehead. "Jesus! So we were supposed to pack up and move to Scotland and eat haggis for the rest of our lives?"

Olivia thought probably not. In the past Daddy had left them behind when he had an assignment overseas. She remembered the long months without him when she would almost forget what he looked like. Even now after only a three weeks' absence, she was surprised at how haggard he looked. His hair appeared sparser: she could see patches of shining scalp underneath. Still, he dressed in the same impeccable style. The formerly greying hair at his temples was now as dark as the rest, and Arthur remarked that "the hair salon from hell" had gotten hold of him.

The main difference was something in Daddy's eyes. Even when they confronted him face to face, he looked past them vacantly, as if he had already left for Aberdeen and forgotten about them.

During one of her parents' last conversations, Olivia heard the word she had been dreading. She heard Momma quote Twyla that divorce is worse than death because everyone you know takes sides and assigns blame, to which Daddy snapped, "I don't believe in divorce. My faith forbids it."

Momma snorted. "A strange time to trot out faith! But it doesn't matter. I would never marry again, now that I know what marriage is *really* about."

When Daddy left that day, Olivia and Arthur went out to the landing and waited as Momma climbed the stairs. Momma breathed heavily, exhausted by the effort, and sat down to rest on the hall bench. Olivia sat beside her while Arthur leaned against the wall as if, by not being part of the group, he could avoid having to face what she had come to tell them.

Momma turned and motioned to him. "Come over here where I can see you."

Arthur moved to her other side and leaned over the railing, studying the floor below. Olivia noted again with a start how much he had begun to look like Daddy, particularly now that Daddy frequently appeared tired and dejected. Arthur was in a perpetual state of dejection.

Momma took a deep, determined breath and plunged in. But as usual when she had something important to tell them, what she said made little sense. "I've come to believe that our fate is not chosen at all. Instead, it comes to meet us. It washes over us like a tidal wave."

She turned her faded gaze from Olivia to Arthur, seeming to address only him. "Do you understand what I'm telling you?"

He nodded, stood erect and walked stiffly to his room, closing the door. Momma sighed and slipped her arm around Olivia, who snuggled gratefully against Momma's thin chest, ignoring the sour sick odor. She asked, "What's that supposed to mean?"

Momma had difficulty answering. At last she said, "Basically, it means that we'll soon be moving again." She cradled Olivia against her and kissed the top of her head. "I wonder how people with no children get through crises like this. It must be unbearable."

When Momma went downstairs, Olivia thought about asking Arthur how, if they were to move, Daddy would be able to find them. But his door was closed, and besides, that was not what really concerned her. What she secretly wondered was how Donnie would be able to find them. Because Donnie was bound to come back someday.

In the days that followed, Momma was sick constantly. The dull weight that had settled in Olivia's stomach when Donnie died would not go away so long as Momma was sick, regardless of whether Daddy came home or not.

There was tacit agreement between Olivia and Arthur not to mention their father unless Momma brought him up. Momma seldom mentioned him anymore, even when Twyla was there. They often found Twyla in the kitchen preparing their meal or cleaning up, when they got home from school. Once or twice Marjorie Jo was there, but without Fayedell.

One afternoon while Olivia and Arthur were polishing off the snack Twyla left for them, they overheard Momma pleading on the telephone and concluded that she was making yet another attempt at convincing Josephine's parole officer to let her come back. They heard her weak exasperation: "We don't want someone else. We *need* Josephine. She knows the children."

Arthur muttered close to his sister's ear, "Notice she said 'we' like Dad was still here. Could be that's important, so if the parole officer ever shows up, don't give it away."

When Momma finished her call, the children entered her room. Olivia noted how hard Momma worked to muster a smile. Their mother had forgotten to pull her hair back, and it fell in straight oily strands, closing in on both sides of her wan face and almost touching under her chin. She brushed it away and gave a triumphant toss of her head. "Good news! We may eventually get Josephine back again!" Olivia gave a whoop of delight and bounded up onto the bed beside Momma.

"But not right away, I take it." Arthur, looking glum, lingered near the door, as if by distancing himself he could remain detached.

Momma's smile faded. "No, not right away." She held out a blue-veined hand, beckoning him to come closer. He shuffled forward as if reluctant to abandon his post. But she reached for his arm and drew him to the bedside.

Olivia moved over, in case he should sit, but he remained stiffly upright, chin elevated, eyes on the window.

There was something different about Momma, a new urgency in her papery voice. She continued to grip Arthur's arm while her words came out like dry steam. "It's your turn to be the lead goose. Can you handle it till Josephine comes back?"

Sometimes when Daddy had spoken sharply to Arthur, he looked as if he had been struck in the stomach, like he looked now. He pulled away from her grasp, thrust his hands deep into his pockets and said with gruff finality. "I don't want to!" Olivia felt like bopping him herself.

Momma waited while Arthur frowned at the floor and while Olivia framed the words she was going to bless him out with when they were alone. He shook himself to attention and seemed to make a manful effort to face Momma squarely for the first time. "Why don't we go on a vacation, like you always wanted to do?"

Momma chuckled, or so Olivia hoped; it was hard to tell. "Where would we go? We've got no one to visit."

He shrugged. "You've always liked the Pacific Northwest. We could go to Costa del Weirdica, like we planned."

Momma sank back into her pillow and stared up at the ceiling. "I've long since given up wanting to go someplace else, just so I could view the moon from a different angle. Eventually you have to give up wandering. You have to settle down and nurture your own soul." She plumped the pillow so that she could sit up a bit again, as if what she was about to impart would be taken more seriously if she were erect.

"I would probably be healthier now if I'd made a more determined effort to nurture my spirit all along. Maybe we'd all be healthier now."

Olivia scooted up to lean against Momma's pillow, even though Momma never smelled sweet anymore. In the old days, Momma's remark would have called for a wisecrack, but now Olivia could only manage, "Is your spirit hungry, Momma?"

Momma folded her hands across her chest like a supplicant. "All I ever really wanted was to have a comfortable pack of kin to flop with under the porch, like an old dog." She patted the bed, indicating that Arthur should sit. Olivia was not surprised when he obeyed, because she, too, was caught up in the renewal of Momma's spirit. Momma's psyche gained strength and animation as she went on.

"But once in a while I've wanted to be a smart-mouthed savior of the world." She turned to Olivia in great earnest, eyes awash like gleaming glass. "Don't ever stand back in the crowd and allow yourself to be overlooked. Don't let clerks wait on the tall people and ignore you. Speak up for yourself! Remember that to Mother Earth, tall people may not be so important."

"Maybe trees, or hedgehogs, or frogs are more important, right?" Olivia, having heard it all before, finished it for her.

Momma gave her arm a squeeze and turned to Arthur. "Remember how your father once told you not to let anybody steal your dream?" She caressed his back with exaggerated gentle strokes.

He shifted away. "Why are you going on like this, for corn's sake?"

"I'm telling you both the same things again and again because Plato said that oral discourse is written on the soul. That makes it handy, doesn't it? Like a reference book we always carry with us. So regardless of what misinformation the world feeds us, we always have the *truth* written on our soul. It weighs on us, it natters at us, refusing to be ignores."

Arthur had become increasingly agitated and fidgety. He stood up and glared down fiercely at his mother, but his voice betrayed him by trembling. "I'm not going to listen to you talk as if you were dying!"

Momma laughed softly and shook her head. "Is that what you think? I have no intention of dying! I've always aspired to reach what my grandmother called the time of consent."

"What's that?" Olivia asked.

"Old age," Momma said. "Anyway. I have something written on my soul that Olivia once said—about just because a thing is futile is no reason to give up on it." She smiled at a perplexed Olivia, who was trying to remember saying such a thing.

"You see how wise you are?" Again Momma pulled a noticeably relieved Arthur down beside her and looked from one to the other of them. "But there will soon be great changes for us, so we may as well accept them. We'll have to move, and I'll be gone a great deal—"

"Where are you going?" they both asked almost in unison.

Momma squared her shoulders. "Initially, to the hospital, for surgery. And ultimately, when I get well, I'll need to get a job, because we no longer have hospitalization insurance. So we need to find a cheaper place...."

"But we saw Mr. Masterson give you a big fat check!" Olivia blurted.

Momma looked stunned, and not amused. "Why you sneaks! You were eavesdropping!" Still, she recovered her good humor and said, "That check will probably be consumed by medical costs. I hate to use it for myself, instead of for your future, but on the other hand, I want to be around to *see* your future."

She closed her eyes and said faintly, "I just don't see how I'll find the energy to locate a place and get us moved."

Olivia shot a meaningful assignment to Arthur, appointing him instant lead goose. He accepted the challenge and brightened. "What's the matter with asking Twyla? Hell, she's always underfoot anyway."

"Oh, but I couldn't ask her to do that much," Momma said.

Arthur grinned. "You won't have to. We'll sic the famous Ahern secret weapon on her: our world class puler!"

Olivia's black mood lifted. She knew exactly what to do.

26

By the time Olivia and Arthur acknowledged the seriousness of Momma's illness, they had moved out of the house into a one-bedroom garage apartment behind the constable's home. Arthur had to sleep on the living room couch, which posed a problem when Momma had to find someone to stay with them while she went to the hospital. Prior to the first hospital trip, Momma had been forced by the new landlord to give Ramona to Twyla Pruitt, devastating them further and precipitating Momma's collapse.

Momma hadn't missed a day being at Daddy's trial and had brought home optimistic reports nightly about how well the trial was going. She had held up until the verdict and the sentencing: five years for corporate theft. Even though she assured the children that the verdict would be appealed, and that it would take years for anything to come of it, she soon lost all stamina and fell prey, as she put it, to Rene Thom's catastrophe theory.

A parade of dark-skinned women climbed the stairs to the apartment, sniffed and left. Marjorie Jo, who had grown even larger since they saw her last, eliminated herself from the competition, saying, "I couldn't take this, Faye, even for you. I'd drop dead of a heart attack the first week, climbing all those stairs."

The first, Lupita Espinosa, didn't like having to sleep with Olivia, who was not part of the package she'd signed on for. So the second time Momma went to the hospital and a new live-in appeared, Olivia slept on a pallet in the living room, as close to Arthur's couch as she could get. The third time, and last, Arthur slept on the floor and gave her the sofa. Only she kept rolling off and eventually just slept on the floor beside Arthur. He never acknowledged her, huddled up in a ball against his back, except occasionally to complain, "Gaw! Your knees are like razor blades!" His gruff words were an immense comfort to her.

As more responsibility fell to her, delegated by reluctant live-ins, Olivia often thought, if only she could be sweet instead of having sharp edges, then she wouldn't have to *do* anything.

Finally, when it appeared that Momma would be in the hospital forever, the probation officer took pity on them and allowed Josephine to return. But Arthur grumbled that it didn't seem right for Josephine to be sleeping in Momma's bed.

Arthur, who was by then fourteen, seemed to have decided where all this was heading. He was failing several courses: Arthur, the family brain! Until Josephine's arrival, the two had been more or less raising themselves, and Arthur had become even more withdrawn than usual. Even Josephine was too preoccupied to do more than keep the household afloat, all the while shaking her head and sighing aloud.

One day when they got home from school, Josephine was nowhere in sight. Instead, Marjorie Jo and Fayedell were waiting in the front room with an old woman with stiff-sprayed hair and luminous blue eye shadow whom Marjorie Jo introduced to them as Grandmother. Fayedell was incredulous. "Gaw, Livvie, don't you know your own grandmother?"

After Josephine, who had been skulking outside the back door, made a discreet appearance, Marjorie Jo left to take their new relative to visit Momma. Arthur went to work, leaving Olivia to deal with Fayedell. She noted that Fayedell, who must be eleven, had grown fat on the chest and butt, and Olivia began remembering that her own knees were too pointy.

Fayedell followed her into the kitchen, while Josephine scurried back out onto the back stoop. Olivia poured a glass of milk without offering Fayedell any. In retaliation, Fayedell said, "Your mom's got cancer. Mom told your grandma to be prepared for a shock, says she looks terrible."

Unspeakable pain scraped across Olivia's heart, but she contained herself and pretended she knew all about it. She nodded and shrugged as if it was no big deal, left the house and stayed outside until Marjorie Jo brought Grandmother back. But she didn't go around back to find Josephine, who had betrayed her by not telling her about Momma.

Grandmother's stiff poochy hair was all mashed in on one side and the blue eyeshadow was smudged. Marjorie Jo had a ball of tissue in her chubby fist and she was wearing her dark glasses again. Olivia could tell they had both been crying.

Grandmother said, "I should have come sooner. You should have let me know." She appeared not even to see Olivia.

Olivia followed them inside, ignoring Fayedell, who sat somberly on the couch watching television. Grandmother motioned for her to turn down the sound as she picked up the phone. She called somebody named Hank and started crying again. "You'd better come right on so you can see her while she still knows you," she said, holding the phone with both trembling hands.

Arthur came home early and went straight into the kitchen to talk to Marjorie Jo. His face had gone unnaturally white, even for Arthur. Olivia tagged along behind him, anxious to tell him about the phone conversation still going on at that moment. But Arthur didn't appear to know she was there, either; she was invisible to everybody, paddling along in a gully-wash of grief.

He was shaking and blubbering, not at all like old stoic Arthur. He stalked up to Marjorie Jo with fists clenched and croaked, "I want to see my mom and you can't stop me!"

There was a quality in Arthur's voice that cut down through time, too sharp and pervasive to die out, as if were alive on its own and would continue to be years later or years *before*, always off somewhere in the other room. Olivia thought that the sound came from somewhere deep in the earth, beyond the earth, in Hades, maybe. It was a primal rumble that could not ever be ignored. It was as if she heard Arthur's voice, and exactly two or three octaves lower, she heard another voice just like his, only terrible, so terrible that anyone would recognize it as agony even if they had never heard what agony sounds like before. And the two voices made a chorus like the Devil's voice that chilled her to her core.

Grandmother hung up the phone and came into the kitchen. She tried to put her arms around Arthur, cooing like a sick cow. Lipstick had run into the lines around her mouth and moisture clung in the crevices around her old eyes. "Honey, you don't want to see your mother this way," she said.

Even though Olivia never doubted the authority of the diabolic voice that was Arthur's, she could see that he needed her support, because she was the family expert at loud eternal whining. She ran around the small kitchen, circling the table, beating on its surface, then on the countertop, yelling to the top of her voice, "We want to see Momma! Take us to see Momma!"

Resigned, Marjorie Jo said over their heads, "Let them go, Mable. They have a right to go."

So after supper they left Fayedell with Josephine and drove up to the hospital. They sat under the glaring lights in the waiting room while Marjorie Jo went to argue with the nurse. The nurse came over, frowning under that phony stiff hat, and said, "Children are not allowed in ICU at any time whatsoever, and only one visitor is allowed at a time." She hesitated. "If the doctor finds out about this, it will be too bad. So make it fast."

The double doors opened and the horde of people who had been waiting swarmed in and hovered around the little sheet-draped cubicles. Olivia and her family were led to the first bed.

Would she ever blot out the memory of that thin colorless body strung with tubes, eye sockets purple with pain, pale hair dark and stingy with sweat? With unearthly rattles the slack-jawed mouthy let out the foul smell of death. Olivia pressed Arthur's hand and whispered, "Is that Momma?"

The eyelids on the body fluttered and a boney hand, to which a tube was taped, lifted a scant inch off the sheet. Olivia saw a glimmer in the eyes and recognized it as Momma's glimmer. *Maybe the soul is a glimmer*, she thought. Momma tried to moisten her lips, but there was a tube taped to her mouth. She was trying to say something. Olivia could tell Momma wanted to touch them. She wasn't sure she wanted Momma to, but the glimmer was commanding, so she let go of Arthur's hand and timidly touched Momma's. Arthur hung back, looking as if he was going to croak. Momma's blackened hand was death cold, and so small and sharp.

Momma gave the barest tug, meaning for her to bend over so she could hear Momma's raspy whisper. At first she thought it was a question, but then she decided that it was a command: "Remember how we used to sing."

Their grandfather didn't make it in time; Momma went very quickly the next day while they were in school. She went peacefully, Olivia heard them say; such a blessing she's gone, such a blessing she got to see her children while she was still lucid. Too bad her father didn't get here a day sooner, they said. Hadn't set eyes on her in nearly fifteen years, not since she ran off to become a hippie with that Catholic. Pregnant.

Olivia couldn't believe, much as Momma hated fencing off death, they had put her in a bronze box behind a fence. At least they buried her beside Donnie so the two of them would become grass about the same time.

She became aware that their future was being discussed, and in the coming weeks her greatest regret was that she didn't spend more time with

Arthur while she had the chance. There were too many people in too little space saying too many meaningless things and being too sorry too late.

Sometime during those first hours Olivia heard Marjorie Jo tell Josephine that she would have to go. "There just isn't room, and besides, the children's father—"

Josephine nodded. "I know how he feels about me!" She left very quickly, not even waiting for Arthur to come home to say goodbye. Olivia could not forgive her for abandoning them so easily, adding to their already intolerable grief.

Their grandfather had arrived the day that Momma died. His name was Hank Llewellyn. Olivia overheard him, with saccharin heartiness, tell the visiting pastor from the Episcopal Church, that he was minister of music at Redemption Baptist Church in Abilene. He had the large deep-chested look of a singer: he had generous full lips and reddish hair out of a bottle. His springy grey eyebrows didn't match his hair and looked as though they might take flight. To her, they made him look puckish and untrustworthy.

He pulled Olivia onto his knee even though her feet still dragged the floor. He smelled of after shave, reminding her of Daddy—why hadn't Daddy come?—and bringing fresh tears to her eyes, rendering her mashed flat, heel-ground.

"If you aren't the image of your momma," he said, shifting her over so he could get his handkerchief and blow his nose. Just like a rag doll, she let him flop her whichever way. It hardly mattered what he did to her; her life was over anyway.

She didn't know where Arthur was. If he was in the apartment, he could hear them saying, "The boy, though. There's too much of his daddy in him."

"No matter. We couldn't afford to keep them both, anyhow. But the girl: it'll be like starting over with Faye, having a second chance at a family."

"Has anybody contacted Quentin's people?"

"Someone must've. A sister showed up at the funeral, according to the guest book. There's his mother—Peggy?—in Galveston. That's probably where you-know-who's hiding out."

"Galveston's a hotbed of Catholics. Good place for him."

The upshot of the discussion was that two days after a funeral through which the two of them had walked like robots, refusing to acknowledge that they were burying their mother, Arthur was put on a bus for Galveston, and Olivia went back to Abilene with their new grandparents. It was almost a casual goodbye that she said to her brother, because the import of all that was happening was too great to sink in. If Arthur hadn't withdrawn so much at the end, she might have waked and fought to keep him, she decided after he was gone. She thought about it often, about how it all happened too fast, how they weren't given time to think, how Josephine could have helped them.

They might have taken different actions at this juncture. The two of them could have run away together, if neither grandparent would take them both. They were versatile; they had developed skills, although the absence of Donnie had diminished those skills. If Arthur and Olivia had stayed together, they could have preserved at least some of what Momma was, what she taught them, particularly since Momma persisted: a shadow-glide glimpsed in her mind's periphery. On that much alone, they could have survived. Or so she often thought in later weeks.

One moment in that day, when Olivia lost Arthur, played itself over during the succeeding months: as the bus pulled away, she saw Arthur, who had stoically avoided looking at her and had said only a curt goodbye, press his forehead against the window and follow her with great sad eyes until the bus turned the corner. She recognized what she hadn't known before: Arthur cared for her just as she had cared for Donnie back when she and Momma had left them standing on the farm porch that summer so long ago. And she knew she couldn't live without Arthur.

Just as the bus disappeared, she waved wildly and screamed, "Write!" and knew he was too much like Daddy to do it.

27

They came upon Abilene from the east, arriving at mid-afternoon. The severe stark drama of the vista all but took her breath away. The city, which lay lower than the interstate, sprawled against a crown of high mesquite and cedar-dotted mesas to the west and south, and gently rolling hills to the north, and over all was the enormous sky, studded with towering flat-bottomed thunderheads. One vast cell, swaddling the tallest butte, unraveled great sheets of blue rain, and from its black belly shot slender scars of unending lightning: demonic bristlings of a new unknown Baptist god. Olivia shivered with awe. Still, this subtly beckoning land was miles from where Momma and Donnie lay side by side, safe in Mother Earth.

Overhead, military planes crisscrossed the wide sky. Granddaddy pointed with pride to a strange-shaped black plane and announced, "That's a secret plane the Air Force is testing here." To which Olivia popped off, "Some secret! With the whole town watching?"

Granddaddy said, "The people here know how to keep a secret." He added aside to Grandmother, as if Olivia were nowhere about, "A mouth just like her mother's."

Once in Abilene, Olivia was given little time to be alone. Her grandparents, intent upon molding her into a little lady, enrolled her in Sunday School, Training Union, Girls' Auxiliary, and Girls' Chorus.

"It takes a whole church to bring up a child," Grandmother said, rebutting her frequent complaints, and Granddaddy would add, "The child is mother to the woman."

On nights when he didn't have choir practice, Granddaddy, doling out hymnals like medicine, insisted that she and Grandmother join him around the upright after supper. His favorites were not the dry Episcopalian hymns Olivia had heard, but light-hearted songs about being saved which had more melody and schmaltz. But he always ended with a grisly shocker: "There is a fountain filled with blood/ drawn from Immanuel's veins,/ and sinners plunged beneath that flood/ lose all their guilty stain." He often teared up when he sang it, and she would cry along with him.

After they finished, she would go off and cry alone, freshly dazed with the awareness, *I'm in a nightmare!* She was caught in a never-ending frenzy: a war between good and evil, with devils disguised as angels.

Life centered on the church. Members often expressed regret that she was an "orphan" but assured her that it was God's will that had brought her to their bosom. Apparently her grandparents hadn't told them that her daddy was perhaps by now in prison, but certainly not dead. Too disheartened to set them straight, she put on her best public face and responded to their overtures with saucy but tolerably good manners, allowing them to maintain their delusions.

Olivia considered them unbearably jolly, pretending everything was wonderful just because they'd been saved. One woman squatted before her and told her with a wide damp smile that she should be happy that, since Momma had been baptized when she wasn't much older than Olivia, she was now with the Lord. Unable to let this outrage pass unchallenged, Olivia shocked the woman with the ardent news, "Momma's not with any Lord; she's with Donnie in Mother Earth making grass!"

She tried to talk to Grandmother about what the woman said, but Grandmother, with her fierce propriety, admonished her, "Accept! Don't ask questions. You'll destroy the mystery."

The statement recalled something similar Momma had once said. But her particular beliefs had not saved her; better if she had retreated to the church of her childhood. Olivia drank in the promises of her new church like a parched wayfarer. The temptation was strong to abandon Momma's beliefs, which were at best ephemeral as shadows on a cave wall. Her grandparents' god would take care of her: *Ask and it will be given; seek and you will find; knock and it will be opened.* Mother Earth held out no such hope.

She wrote to Arthur several times, long agonized pleadings for him to come for her. She received a letter saying he had a job in a hardware store. "Dad's mom also works there, in the office. Her name is Peggy. She doesn't want to be called Grandmother. She's afraid she'll be fired for being old. The worst part of this place is having to go to Mass once a week, or sometimes more. Mom would have a horse if she could see what they make you do. A lot of it is like our old church, except the priest has brown eyes! Also, he's not a fruit."

Then he added news that stunned her: "I haven't seen Dad, but I've been studying Benjamin's concept of constellation of ideas trying to understand our situation. What has happened to us is the result of a constellation, so I'm not surprised about anything."

There was a P.S.: "I found out Dad was going to be a priest before he met Mom." She heard from him once or twice more. It was a long time before she found out why he quit writing. She wondered if he was too depressed to write. Arthur became immobile when he got depressed. Eventually she became too dejected by no response to continue writing to him. Although Grandmother Llewellyn hadn't encouraged their correspondence, she did give Olivia money to buy him a Christmas present that first year.

She didn't hear from him at Christmas, not even a card. Nor from Daddy She was sure he had remembered her, but it had been years since he'd had a secretary to take care of such things.

During the holidays of her second Christmas Marjorie Jo and Weldon and Fayedell came for an overnight stay; Marjorie Jo was wearing dark glasses as usual. Fayedell was probably eleven, Olivia reckoned. Weldon and Marjorie Jo were wallowing in Olivia's bed like two pregnant whales, while she and Fayedell slept on the den sofa bed. In all her life nobody had ever asked Olivia to sleep over. Now she had better clothes than before, and she took piano lessons and had even submitted to the ordeal of Sword Drills—a game involving locating scripture—just to get some peace, but still she was never asked to sleep over by anymore. She had come to realize there was a stigma attached to being an orphan. She considered having Fayedell sleep over a Major Event, a chance to find out what was the big deal.

They smuggled cheese crackers under the covers and giggled for hours about school and boys. Then abruptly Fayedell said, "Do you ever hear from your daddy? Or can't prisoners write letters?"

Olivia felt a stab of incredible pain by the by such casual mention of someone her grandparents refused to mention. Besides, she no longer considered the possibility of his writing. "He isn't in prison, stupid yutz! His lawyers are appealing stuff, and that takes years. Don't you know *anything* about court stuff? He's a very busy man, or he would've been writing all along."

"Maybe. Maybe not." Fayedell sounded smugly all-knowing.

Olivia didn't want to discuss it, for fear the oozing grief would break loose again. But she decided that when Fayedell was gone, she would ask

Grandmother about Daddy's case. Maybe he *was* in prison: that would explain why she hadn't heard from him. She flopped over onto her side and groused, "I'm getting sleepy. Finish the crackers if you want to."

Fayedell didn't speak for a while, and then she whispered, "Did your daddy ever whip you so hard it jarred your teeth loose?"

Olivia snorted at the absurdity: Daddy hardly ever touched them, hardly came near them at all. "Of course not! He wouldn't do that!" Sometimes she had wished he *would* spank her, even. Anything. Sometimes he had almost dared him to.

"If your mom thought he was innocent, she wouldn't have got sick and died. So that proves he was guilty. That's what my dad said."

Olivia recalled what Arthur had written in the P.S. She turned back to Fayedell, hot with outrage. "A lot you know! It just so happens that my daddy was a priest once. Priests don't steal stuff, even if they *are* Catholics!"

Fayedell was almost stunned into silence. Finally she said, "Bullshit! We'll just see about that in the morning!"

But Fayedell had communicated more than she'd intended. It was a full ten minutes before Olivia could figure out how to broach the subject without desecrating Donnie's memory. She leaned up on one elbow. "What did you all hear in Daddy's study that day?"

Fayedell wasn't asleep; Olivia figured she'd been waiting. "What do you care?"

Olivia thought of something else. "Did your dad ever hit you?"

Pay dirt. Fayedell's words cut through the dark like a hot knife. "My dad's a sonofabitch! He gave Mom a black eye again: I guess you saw it though the sun glasses. Usually he tries to hit her where it doesn't show. We've both got bruises all over. I hate them both! I'm going to get married soon and leave home for good!"

Now Olivia knew. "I bet he said he'd beat you if you told anybody what you heard that day. That's why you tried to blame everything on Josephine."

Fayedell kicked her hard. "Why don't you shut up! Get over and quit hogging the cover! Just for that, I'm going to find out what a liar you are, saying your dad was a priest!"

"I bet Weldon stole the maps, didn't he?"

"He never! Anyway, your dad even said it was all his fault. Ask him yourself, if you don't believe me."

Ask him! As if she knew how to contact him. If he was really in prison by now, she supposed that he was lost to her forever.

28

True to her threat, the next morning Fayedell brought up the subject of Daddy while Grandmother and Marjorie in flowery muumuus, scurried around the kitchen like large colorful mollusks, preparing breakfast.

"Livvie says her daddy was a priest, Aunt Mable."

Grandmother's perm had escaped its lacquered bonds so that it stuck out like an abandoned jaybird's nest and hid her face when she bent over. She made an excessive amount of noise setting the table but her sharp piety sliced through it. "We'll not discuss—him in this house."

Fayedell was not easily put off. "I thought Catholic priests couldn't get married."

"Fayedell, did you hear what Aunt Mable said?" Marjorie Jo glared at her daughter through her sun glasses. "Now just shut up about it, hear?"

Fayedell pinched the corner of a straw place mat so hard, it cracked. Olivia could tell she didn't plan ever to let go of the subject. "Unless they *have* to get married."

Marjorie Jo dropped her spatula with a loud clatter. "Now that's enough out of you, missy. What's done is done. Can't you see you're grieving your poor Great-Aunt to death, harping on it?"

She whipped around to Olivia. "And you! You ought to have more respect for your grandmother than to keep parading your dirty linen in her house. She's taken you in and started all over with the burden of raising another child when she ought by rights to be able to relax. Can't you think about her for a change?"

Somehow, Olivia expected that. In her experience children frequently had to bear responsibility for adults. Without a word she left the kitchen and retreated to the piano, which had assumed a magical quality with power to make her dance during the syncopated fervor of Grandfather's more raucous gospel songs. Sometimes, when he struck an unexpected dominant seventh, its poignancy sent her fleeing to her room to hide the tears.

As she played, she pondered this new image of Priest-Daddy, wondering if she ever knew him. She recalled his early admonition to "be the best" which she had pretended to resist. Maybe under the surface it was working its spell on her, while Momma's Aristotle words were too lofty to apply. She struggled to remember them: sweetness—or was it virtue? tolerance, prudence, fortitude—as if to forget them would be to forget Momma. But no: she was tied to Momma by a chain of homilies, potent as DNA.

Daddy's admonishments, issued almost as warnings, even threats, were easier to recall. Maybe she couldn't help but abide by his little dictums. Maybe he couldn't, either. She saw how unfit he was for competition. They had watched him struggle valiantly to stay in the game, all the while slipping farther behind. Maybe he was also struggling against teachings that didn't fit him.

As soon as Marjorie Jo and her family left, the focus returned to Olivia's shortcomings. The matter of her baptism had become a major concern to both her grandparents. Perhaps they had made a New Year's resolution to see that her soul was saved.

Their responsibility weighed heavily on Granddaddy, who was suspicious of all change, seeing it as an ominous sign of the hand of Satan. Maybe he guessed at the rising hormones which she wouldn't have noticed if Fayedell hadn't warned her that someday they would both have Periods which would turn them into sexpots like Madonna.

Granddaddy must have known about Periods, for he harped on the importance of being saved. "You can't put it off too long, Olivia. You must surrender to Jesus before you reach the age of accountability. It would be a terrible thing for something to happen that would cause you to have to spend eternity on the wrong side of the river Jordan."

Olivia would hear Grandmother murmuring to him at night after they were all in bed. "Don't push her, Hank. She's had such a long way to come. She's a good girl. She'll come forward one of these Sundays when we least expect it."

"But Mable. You and I both know what likely has already happened. All those Catholic baptize their babies."

"What difference does that make? A little sprinkling doesn't make a Christian. You worry too much. She'll come around."

But Olivia lay on her back in the dark in Momma's old bed, stiff with resolve never to give in.

By her tenth birthday, a few weeks after the Cadenheads' visit, she could no longer conceal new rounder proportions that appeared almost overnight. Her grandparents' agitation about her graceless state intensified. Sunday after Sunday they prodded her before they all left for Sunday School, which was the last time they could approach her until after the preaching service had ended, what with Granddaddy leading the choir and Grandmother singing in it. Olivia usually sat in the balcony with classmates, passing notes, making crude jokes about the size of various body parts of the nearest boys.

Each Sunday her grandparents would pointedly suggest that she sit on the lower level, in case she was moved by the Spirit to come forward when the preacher gave the call. At times she was tempted, she had to admit, when the choir had wrung out the fourth verse of "Just As I Am" with the preacher, arms raised in supplication, promising, "He means you, my friend. Whatever your sins, He is ready to forgive. He has borne it all for your sake. Won't you come?" Sometimes she would feel herself turning to jelly, swept up in the emotion of the moment. If Momma had trusted Jesus instead of Mother Earth, maybe He wouldn't have let her die.

At those times, in spite of her resolve, she longed to go forward, if only to please the preacher, who pleaded so pathetically but at the same time appeared so virile and almost out of control, like a rock star.

But she could not. It would be a betrayal of her poor dead mother, and of Donnie. Maybe of Daddy and Arthur as well.

One Sunday in late January as they were leaving for church, Granddaddy looked her over and ordered, "Olivia, go back and change that dress!" He sounded like Moses pronouncing the Commandments. He didn't so much speak as intone, in the rich rumble of a professional baritone, so that all his commands had the quality of granite-chiseled authority.

Grandmother took up the protest for her. "Really, Hank. All the girls are wearing them that length these days."

"Take it off, you hear me, young lady? And I don't want to see you wearing it again!" His face had turned a dirty red. The sprigging eyebrows made him look like a wild sand crab on attack. Olivia sensed his anger was directed as much toward Grandmother for defying him, as toward her.

When she looked to Grandmother for some sign of support, Grandmother only lowered her powdery blue eyelids. She spun around and stalked off to her room, sensing that his volatility had to do with her new roundness and being secretly pleased. Just for spite, she swayed her hips in an exaggerated manner, hoping to send the old toad into apoplexy.

In breathy outrage, he told Grandmother, "I can't wait any longer for her to make herself decent." He boomed at Olivia, "You'll have to walk, young lady, and don't you be late! See that you sit on the lower level at the preaching, hear? And when that call comes, just you bear in mind that the preacher is talking to *you*, understand? To *you*!"

She would not be spoken to in that way. She made up her mind that she wouldn't go at all. She flounced onto her bed, trying to think how she could get even. After she heard them drive away, she got up and marched into their room, where she was never invited.

She pulled open a drawer and began idly picking through its contest, fired only by revenge. Maybe she would find something she wanted and just take it. She would ignore Momma's niggling definition of virtue as "doing the right thing even when nobody's looking." She would think about Daddy instead.

But she must be doing the right thing! Maybe it wasn't coincidence that led her to that drawer. Maybe Grandmother had unwittingly communicated that this was forbidden territory. It seemed improbable that by merest chance she would have chosen the one drawer containing the answers to her unformed questions, for it was Grandmother's memento drawer. She could tell by the packet, fastened with a lace garter, of old yellowed letters bearing Grandfather's handwriting. And by the withered corsage, shedding powdery petals onto everything. She pushed them aside and saw a smaller bundle tied with twine, letters in Momma's handwriting using her maiden name and bearing the postmark of San Francisco.

She felt such a rush of grief at being confronted by something Momma had once touched that she jerked back and stared at it them through sudden tears. Cautiously, in case the paid might prove too much, she eased out one of the letters. It contained a note and a small snapshot.

"Since you haven't answered, you must still be angry. I love you, but I still choke when I think about coming home. I have to work for the causes I believe in, and one of the inequities is that, if you are rich enough, the rules don't apply. That isn't just. This generation, working together, will build a new fair world of peace and love.

"I have met a wonderful boy. He encouraged me to try writing you again, to make you understand. You would like him. His name is Quentin Ahern. Enclosed is a photo."

The snapshot showed two people whom she wouldn't have recognized but for the letter: Daddy's youthful face was hidden by a scraggly black beard; his dark hair hung to his shoulders. Momma, too, wore her hair long. In those days it had been almost blond, She had been quite pretty, not the faded wretch she had become toward the end of her life.

She heard the car in the driveway: Grandfather must have come back for her. With careless haste she returned the things to their envelope. As she replaced them in the drawer, her gaze fell upon another envelope tucked beneath the two stacks. It was addressed to her in Daddy's handwriting, and the return address showed that it was recent. Following his name was a string of numbers. The address was Texas Department of Corrections, Huntsville, Texas.

There was no time to make a decision about taking the letter; Grandmother was coming in the front door. She shut the drawer and rushed out of the room where she met Grandmother in the hallway. Grandmother frowned, looking past her toward the bedroom; Olivia could fancy that she was looking at the drawer. Her gaze returned to Olivia's face, searching.

To cover her panic, Olivia caught Grandmother's arm and blurted, "I've decided to go forward today and be saved. Will you sit with me instead of singing in the choir?"

Forgotten were Grandmother's suspicions. She broke into a smile and gave a pathetic little gulping sob as she drew Olivia against her. Olivia sucked in the odor of lavender sachet and body sweat, then held her breath. So little it took to please them. Yet Olivia cursed herself for playing her only ace, selling her soul, to keep Grandmother mollified. If not for that diversion, Grandmother might very well destroy Daddy's letter before Olivia got to read it.

As it happened, she did anyway, or at least she moved it: the next time Olivia had an opportunity to steal into their room, it was gone. Her sacrifice and betrayal of Momma's faith was for nothing. But Momma's Aristotle word prudence stayed her from confronting Grandmother as to why she had hidden Daddy's letter from her. Maybe there had been other letters before this. Maybe even a Christmas present or a birthday present, back before he was sent to prison.

Maybe Arthur had written as well.

She had learned enough about Grandmother's treachery to know never to trust her again. Grandmother didn't want the Ahern family reunited, that was plain. But no matter; she would find a way to get them back together on her own.

In the meantime, she could survive on burning resentment alone.

29

Toward the end of the church service, while the congregation sang "Precious Lord, Take My Hand," Olivia, her head buzzing, left Grandmother's side in the second pew and went forward to the altar to shake the preacher's cool sticky hand. He flashed dazzling teeth and put an arm around her shoulder, drawing her close until his lips touched her ear and she could hear him above the singing. It wasn't an unpleasant experience.

"Do you accept Jesus Christ as your Lord and Savior, honey?" He smelled good, like Daddy, and he spoke with Daddy's kind tones, unlike Grandfather's gruff and accusing ones.

She felt tears spring into her eyes. She nodded and at once wanted desperately to please the preacher and be saved by Jesus. She leaned against him as he squeezed her tight. She had forgotten about the bellowing sea of faces before them.

He said, "Come back to my study after the benediction." He released her and raised his arms again, calling out above the chorus, "Won't you come? Jesus is calling, my friend." In dismay, she realized he had already forgotten about her.

She had never noticed the preacher before. Now she watched him with admiration. His great head of perfectly styled dark hair, with its searing swath of gray at the temples, was much more dramatic than Daddy's. His face was more expressive than Daddy's ever was: It was almost rubbery with emotion. Olivia could seldom ever read anything by searching Daddy's expression, but she watched in fascination as a wide succession of disturbances crossed the preacher's face, like restless clouds flitting across the sky. He was like a fine actor. She could hardly wait for the benediction.

When the service was over, she hurried off to the pastor's study, still exulting in the miracle of her newfound salvation, happened upon so by accident. The seven verses of "Precious Lord" still rang in her ears. She entered the somber room and sat down in a deep leather chair opposite his desk, waiting for him to appear. The walls of the room were a deep rich brown, like the paneling in Marjorie Jo's den.

Framed diplomas hung behind the desk, like in a doctor's office. She squinted to read the name; she had not paid much attention when her grandparents spoke of the preacher. Now she couldn't even remember it.

She got up and went around behind the desk so she could get a better look at the diplomas. Raymond Wesley Conklin, they read. Dr. Conklin is what Grandfather called him.

The study door opened and in a rush of guilt she whirled to face him, embarrassed to be caught behind his desk. But his ready smile infused her with courage. She appropriated Donnie's bravado, pointed to the wall and said, "Pretty impressive, all these diplomas."

He chuckled and came to stand behind her, studying them. "Yes, honey, those pieces of paper represent years of study and hard work." He put his arm around her shoulder again. "You're a crusty little thing aren't you, honey—what's your name again? Olivia? That's a mighty pretty name."

She leaned into him, hungry to be cherished and flooded with warmth. No one had hugged her for a very long time. "Olivia Louise Ahern," she said, glad that she had such a fine name.

He sat in his great leather chair, pulling her down onto his lap, still regarding her with a tender smile. His war breath smelled like cinnamon. "Well Olivia, honey, you're a pretty little lady. Now before we talk about your baptism, why don't you tell me about yourself? What do you like to do?"

She wanted desperately to say something that would interest this great man. But to her dismay, her eyes suddenly filled with tears again, and she blurted out, "I like to think about my momma and my brother because they both died, and my daddy is—gone!"

He drew her close as she sobbed and heaved. "Precious lamb! Cry it out, little angel, God love you." He pulled out a handkerchief and daubed at her eyes, murmuring, "Like a lost, starved puppy."

She took a shuddery breath and blubbered, "And my other grandmother took my other brother to Galveston to live and didn't take me, and now I'm all alone." She fell against him, burrowing into his chest.

His large warm hands made circular caresses on her shoulders and back as he whispered over and over, "Cry it out, precious lamb...Little orphan with no one to love."

It seemed natural that his lips should brush her forehead. It was moments before she realized that he had kissed her. His hand came to rest lightly on her leg; she warmed to the sensation of his touch. It seemed natural and comfortable, like Daddy's. He liked her, really liked her, she could tell.

Suddenly she felt uneasy and pushed to her feet, straightening the stupid dress that Grandfather made her wear. Donnie would give her the devil if he could see her being such a weenie.

"There!" He spoke easily. He sounded as bland as warm cream. "You feel better, don't you, sweetheart? Jesus is going to heal your pain and replace it with joy. Remember the Lord said, 'Let not your heart be troubled; nether let it be afraid.' Now! Let's talk about next Sunday night."

When she looked puzzled, he said, "Your baptism."

He explained that she should come early to the evening service and go directly to the dressing area behind the baptistery. There she would change into a robe—"Bring some dry underclothes to wear afterward."—and wait at the entrance to the baptismal tank until she saw him beckon to her from the water.

"I'll be standing down in the tank, and after the scripture reading, I'll hold out my hand like this—" He reached out for her, but she backed a step out of his reach. It was an automatic reflex that she regretted immediately, as soon as she saw disappointment cloud his dark eyes.

But he smiled and went on. "You'll come down the steps and take my hand. Be sure to hold onto the handrail so as not to slip."

He described how he would hold her and dip her backward under the water, and how in that instant, her old sinful self would die and Jesus's blood would wash away all her sins. Then he would pull her upright and she would rise, born again, cleansed and forever saved. Olivia had the uncomfortable sense that she harbored certain new guilty thoughts that she hoped Jesus didn't find out about.

She left the preacher's office and tried to remember Momma's four Aristotle words, wondering if she could by any stretch of exaggeration still be adhering to them.

The following Sunday evening an overjoyed Grandmother led a dry-mouthed Olivia to the dressing rooms. She carried a small tote holding a towel and carefully chosen underpants for Olivia to wear after her baptism.

"No socks?" Olivia said, peering in the bag.

Grandmother gave a rare laugh. She was in a festive mood. "You don't wear your shoes into the water, silly."

Olivia thought about Dr. Conklin's shiny black shoes. Of course he wouldn't wear them into the water. But she couldn't imagine him standing in the water in his bare feet.

There were weights sewn into the hem of the robe, "so it won't float up around your neck," Grandmother explained. Olivia squeezed her eyes tight to block out the image of the preacher's robe floating up around his neck so that his underwear showed. *Jesus, hurry up and save me*, she thought.

The preacher tapped on the door and opened it a crack, talking to them with his profile discretely turned. Olivia pulled the robe tight around her with one last delicious sense of sinful danger as Grandmother gushed on to Dr. Conklin about how thrilled she was.

He interrupted her. "After the baptism, I want a few minutes alone with Olivia." By the change in his tone, she knew the next words were for her. "So dear, I'll come back here before you change into your street clothes and join your grandmother out front for the sermon."

Grandmother beamed, kissed Olivia on the forehead, and went out front to watch the baptism with the congregation. Olivia followed Dr. Conklin toward the back of the baptistery. She noticed that he wore shower shoes below his robe, and that his feet and ankles were a disappointing white instead of tan like Daddy's. His ankles were crosshatched with tiny red veins. He left her with a pat on the back and went around by way of a back hall to the opposite entrance to the tank.

She gripped both handrails and heard her heart pounding in her ears as the organ music diminished and the lights dimmed. Suddenly the music swelled as the beam from a single spotlight fell upon the bowed head of Dr. Conklin, who stood in the tank. Olivia gasped. He had appeared in the water like magic.

She couldn't concentrate on his words, which she recognized as being from the Bible. She was going to be baptized. In only a few minutes she would be completely transformed. Maybe she would be able to work miracles. She began to breathe rapidly as the music rose again and Dr. Conklin looked her way and extended her hand toward her.

She forced herself down the steps on rubbery legs into the tepid water and reached out for his hand. He grasped her and pulled her to him. Her feet left the bottom so that she felt herself drifting. Panicky, she realized that she could not right herself; her feet were in danger of rising to the surface. But he held her securely with both hands, setting her firmly erect.

His voice boomed out, "Olivia Louise Ahern, I baptize thee in the name of the Father, and of the Son, and of the Holy Spirit!" With that, he pressed her backward, one strong hand in the middle of her back and one on her chest. She held her breath, waiting for the magic, for what seemed an eternity as the water closed over her head in symbolic death. Then he lifted her out, resurrected, as the spotlight streamed against her wet lashes and the triumphant music reverberated in her ears. She sputtered and wiped the water from her nose, trying not to snort.

Well, that's it. Now I'm saved. For better or worse, it was something she didn't have to worry about anymore. Anyway, now maybe God would pay more attention to her.

"Let us pray." He held her against him while he gave an interminable prayer of thanks for her salvation. She began to tremble slightly. For a moment she had the terrible thought that she might pee in the water. But she chided herself for such a thought: God wouldn't let such a thing happen.

He guided her to the steps and handrail, then returned to the center of the tank and announced. "We will turn to page three-sixty-seven and sing all four verses of "Love Lifted Me."

She could hear her grandfather's lusty baritone ring out above the choir: "I was sinking deep in sin,/ far from the peaceful shore,/ very deeply stained within,/ sinking to rise no more..."

She padded back to the dressing room and sat down on the stool, quaking not so much from chill as from excitement. Water splatted from her robe and disappeared into the blotter-like floor covering, some sort of paper thing that must be replaced after every use. She dug the towel out of the bag and wiped her face, reluctant to acknowledge a niggling disappointment. She didn't detect any great difference in her state of grace, but that attitude was unworthy of her now. When she got home, she would try out her new powers in privacy.

The preacher, with a large towel draped over his arm, came into the tiny room and shut the door behind him. She stiffened and tried to return his smile through chattering teeth, feeling awkward in his presence. Other than his dripping robe, he was as well turned-out as ever: not a hair was out of place. Just like Daddy. He walked behind her and took the ends of her hair between his fingers.

"You're not an orphan anymore, honey. You're a member of the family of God now." He began to dry her hair as he talked, massaging her head. She began to relax, but her teeth continued to chatter.

"You have a family who loves you. Jesus loves you, and I love you."

The kneading hands moved to her shoulders and to the back of her neck. She yielded in great relief. It was as if he was protecting her from danger. His voice lent to the soothing sensation of Peace and Arrival.

"Now that you are a member of the church, you'll want to give back to the Lord for all he has given you. When you grow older and have an income, you'll want to give ten per cent of it for His work. Until then, you'll want to serve the Lord with gladness. You can serve right here, by working in the church. Would you like that?" She nodded eagerly. "Would you like to come here on Monday after school and work for me?"

She was sure she was special to him. She felt very blessed. She put aside the shame-filled uneasy thoughts and wallowed in this new sense of belonging and of being cherished.

"I'll be here,' she said. For the first time in months, her chest welled with happiness.

30

Olivia's announcement that she planned to work at the church on Monday afternoons met with Grandmother's enthusiastic approval and Granddaddy's grudging admission, muttered when she was supposedly out of earshot, that maybe things were turning around with that child, thanks to the Lord.

She slept enveloped in the knowledge of her salvation, of being safely wrapped within the sheltering arms of Jesus, indistinguishable during sleep from Daddy's arms. She dreamed of sitting on Daddy's lap, of Daddy kissing her forehead, drying her hair, rubbing her back and shoulders. She woke feeling warm and cherished, until the awful crashing memory of her separation from her family swamped her again. She sat up on the side of the bed, trying to shake off the terrible heaviness, trying to recall what Momma had said about fortitude. Surely now that she'd gotten herself saved, God would hurry up and help her. In fact, she ought to call the whole matter to His attention.

She slid to the floor on her knees and folded her hands on the bed. It wasn't the first time she'd resorted to prayer, sometimes to Momma, but up until now, both Momma and God had ignored her. She began softly, so her grandparents wouldn't hear, and as politely as she could manage:

"Dear Jesus, if you didn't notice, I'm baptized now..." The sunlight touched her shoulder. She was sure it was a sign. "...and as you know, I've been all by myself here." She choked back the tears and then decided she'd been patient long enough. She gave vent to her outrage, still keeping her tone in check.

"Anyway, if you're so good at miracles and bringing dead people back to life, what about Momma and Donnie?" She slapped angrily at the tears spilling down her cheeks, striking herself so hard that it hurt. She wanted it to hurt. She gulped and shuddered, then went on.

"Besides that, I'm even going to work at the church every Monday." For the first time she thought of Dr. Conklin and her spirits lifted. He liked her. "...because the *preacher* asked me to! So will you please hurry up and get our family put back together?" She waited to let this sink in on Jesus, then pronounced a firm no-nonsense, "A-men!"

She slogged through the school day with the sure knowledge that she was doing all she could possibly do to make things turn out right. Now it was up to Jesus. She recalled that once long ago, when she had said that just because a thing is futile is no reason to give up on it, Momma had called her wise. Maybe Momma would nag Jesus until he got busy.

When the dismissal bell rang, she walked the three blocks to the church with great dignity and purpose, holding her head at a proud tilt, looking to neither side, as if she had her eye on some Vision Glorious. She had no time for classmates anymore.

The church was strangely quiet, but she let herself in the side door and tiptoed down the long cool hall toward the preacher's study. A woman sitting at a desk in the office just outside the study door looked up and a ready, possibly phony, smile lit up her warm brown eyes. She had big brown poofy hair that didn't move when she nodded.

"You must be Mr. Llewellyn's granddaughter—Olivia, is it? Dr. Conklin told me to expect you." She got up, came around the desk, and took Olivia's hand. She smelled perfumey like Margaret Mary and was pretty in a less brassy way. The heels on her shoes weren't as high, but they clicked as she took off down the hall, leading her at a brisk pace, girdled in God-fearing piety.

"Dr. Conklin's still out on his hospital rounds." Olivia nodded hard, covering her disappointment. "But he told me to take you over to the Kindergarten room..." Olivia made a mental note to remind God of all she was being put through. Besides, she usually had an afternoon snack. Her stomach gurgled to remind her. "...to put you to work straightening out the blocks."

Oh fine. Playing with blocks, and the preacher isn't even here. It must be some kind of test

They left the main building and walked down a covered sidewalk to the Educational Building. The whir of a floor machine echoed down the hall as they stepped inside. They passed Olivia's Sunday School classroom and went all the way to the far end of the hall. A Hispanic man was sweeping a buffer back and forth across the hallway floor nearby. Inside the Kindergarten room, a dusky woman was cleaning fingerprints off the windows with a squeegee. A housekeeping cart stocked with cleaning supplies stood in the middle of the room. The children's low tables were heaped with blocks and books.

The poofy-haired office lady let go of Olivia's hand and spoke to the cleaning woman in a raised voice, "Constanzia, I've brought you another... some more new help...mas ayuda!"

The woman turned an indifferent look upon Olivia, then regarded the office lady with a blank stare. The office lady fluttered and said even louder, "Este es Olivia!" She gestured at the blocks. "Para ayuda usted." She clopped over to the low shelves and retrieved a cardboard box and made elaborate motions to show Olivia what she wanted done.

Olivia's dry, "I get it. No need for sign language on my account" silenced her.

The office lady tittered at her error, and about that time Olivia's stomach growled even louder. Even the cleaning woman heard it. She said, "Tiene hambre," and pointed with her squeegee.

She was missing a couple of front teeth.

Olivia wished she was at Grandmother's, or anyplace besides here. It was all pointless. It wasn't going to do any good. Picking up blocks while starving to death wasn't going to bring her family back.

"I should have thought," the office lady said. "Children are always hungry after school! We have cookies in the kitchen, left over from yesterday's Fellowship Hour."

She snatched up Olivia's hand and back they went, clattering past the cleaning man's noisy buffer and scuffing up his polished hall. *Jesus better be watching this*, Olivia thought grimly. *I ought to collect big for all the aggravation.*

Inside the main building again, they took a right turn into an enormous stainless steel kitchen that smelled as if it had been coated in dirty dishwater. It reminded her of the school cafeteria. The office lady produced a plate of cookies and a glass of juice then left again, remembering aloud that she'd left the office phone untended.

Olivia climbed up onto a stool at the counter and stuffed in a cookie. It was oatmeal and raisin. Not bad. She took a gulp of the juice and set the glass down with a clank that echoed all over the big room. Well, what could you expect from Jesus's kitchen? *Heaven's kitchen had better be better than this.* It was no wonder Momma wanted to be grass instead.

She looked around at the big impersonal room and remembered the time Momma threatened to get a job in the school cafeteria to help out with finances. What sacrifices Momma made to keep things going.

The next bite of cookie stuck in her throat.

She left half of the juice in her haste to get out of that cavernous place, pocketing the rest of the cookies for later. There was nothing to do but go back to the Kindergarten room and get started on her job so she could get out of that grunge-pit. Even the preacher would never know all the stupid stuff she was having to do.

The Educational Building hallway was completely silent; the cleaning man and his buffer had vanished. She heard it again, far away, upstairs. She tiptoed to the end of the hallway, dreading to face the gap-toothed women who didn't speak English. But the classroom was empty. The cleaning cart was gone.

The light had been left on. The cardboard box remained on the little table beside the blocks and books. Olivia stood over the box and arranged a stack of green blocks in one of its corners, noting satisfaction in bringing about order, so long as there was no one to conclude mistakenly that she was playing with them.

Outside the room, a door opened. She heard the sound of traffic before it closed again. *It must be the door at this end of the hall,* she thought, but before she turned to see, the preacher said, "Ah! Here you are!"

He closed the classroom door behind him and reached up to smooth his hair in place, a gesture so like Daddy that her heart leaped. He smiled, showing the flash of dazzling teeth. She grinned back, dizzy in the presence of greatness. He walked over and put a hand under her chin. It felt cool and slightly damp.

"What a pretty sight! It's the first time I've ever seen you smile. Isn't it wonderful to rejoice in the joy of the Lord?"

Olivia felt her face flush. Nobody ever called her pretty, and she had grave doubts that she really was. She said, just to have something to say, "Momma used to call me tacky." At once she regretted revealing such a thing. Otherwise, he might not have noticed.

He frowned, took her by the shoulders and peered into her face. His dark-flecked eyes narrowed in amusement. She thought Daddy's were blue—or were they grey? In her panic she couldn't remember.

"No! Your mother wouldn't say such a thing! A pretty little thing like you?"

Her eyes watered, giving her away. She looked off quickly toward the windows. What was happening? She had great disgust for herself. She nodded rigorously, recalling the day outside Momma's room when she heard Arthur tell Momma how tacky they *all* were, and the other time when Momma told Daddy the same thing. But she should never have betrayed Momma to the preacher. She felt deep shame at such a betrayal. She pulled away, returning to her box of bricks. She was almost finished, thank God.

The preacher followed and perched on the corner of the little table, so close that she could smell the after-shave and cinnamon breath. He scooped up the remaining blocks in one enormous fistful and dumped them into the box, then pushed it aside. Words poured out of him like cream. "Jesus loves you, honey. He wants you to be happy all the time."

She shifted from one foot to the other and ran her finger along the edge of the table, feeling goofy. Even though Donnie would think it was a weenie thing to do, she had to ask. "He listens to prayers, doesn't he?"

"Absolutely!" He slapped his knee for emphasis. "The Lord said, 'When thou prayest, enter into thy closet, and when thou has shut the door, pray to thy Father... and He will reward thee openly.'"

Aha. So that was what she'd been doing wrong. Now she knew. She grinned, anxious now to get home and try it out. "I gotta go," she said, but he caught her hand.

"And just so you'll remember, I'll tell you again. Your little smiling face is a beautiful sight. You *are* a pretty girl, honey, when you smile." He tugged on her hand. "Now give us a hug."

With very little reluctance, she put her arms around his neck. "That's a girl, God love you." He held her close, kissed her cheek, and patted her on the lower back. It felt good.

When she left him, she reached into her pocket. The cookies were in crumbles. But her back still tingled. To quell her random anxious musings, she threw out a challenge: maybe if God would hurry up and answer her prayer, she wouldn't be coming back anymore.

31

For good measure, all week Olivia prayed both morning and evening behind her closed closet door, knees bared to cold boards, buoyed by expectations of an early reunion with Daddy and Arthur. By midweek, when nothing had happened, she quit turning on the light, so that when she knelt in the dark corner behind overcoat tails and forgotten galoshes, the mere rustle of a cleaning bag in the musty silence sent shivers up her neck. Shapes like upside-down bats hovered over her tabernacle, whose incense was moth crystals, recalling the farm where they spent their last summer together.

Her devotion was rewarded at the Saturday breakfast table, when Granddaddy squeezed open his little coin pure and extracted an extra dollar. He laid it beside her plate and said with gruff offhandedness, "I've decided to raise your allowance, in view of what a good girl you've been."

She felt her blood surge, too swift, like an oncoming truck, as if Donnie's blood or his spirit possessed her. Momma wanted them to be good only reluctantly. For a moment she forgot her new piety and blurted out hotly, "By whose standards?"

He jerked up with narrowed eyes; she was shocked to see past the black pupils to something beyond and before her time, as if he were seeing someone else in her place. He snapped out, "By the standards of the one who pays the bills around here, missy!" He cleared his throat and started over. "By the standards we live by in this household, that I fought for overseas. The standards of the Lord!"

But she had already sunk back into the clutching religiosity which the Lord exacted for those who wanted answers to their prayers. Donnie and Arthur would just have to understand her position. With genuine humility she touched the dollar with one finger. "I'm trying," she said, keeping her head low.

He appeared satisfied, and Grandmother grunted her approval. Sometimes when Grandmother spoke, she sounded like Momma, cajoling Daddy into noticing them.

"I saw Ruby Mullens at Prayer Meeting. She was very pleased with the way Olivia pitched in Monday, straightening up in the Kindergarten room." You'd think Olivia had descended with marshalled forces of thousands for a sweeping police action of the area.

"Who's Ruby Mullens? Is she the office lady with blimpy hair?"

"The preacher's secretary. Conscientious little soul. Looks after Dr. Conklin like a bantam hen. If she didn't, he'd work himself to death, poor kind-hearted man." She motioned for Olivia to clear the breakfast dishes and asked pointedly, "Don't you have something else to say to Granddaddy?"

Olivia gulped, thankful that she could busy herself with the dishes, and through a set jaw mumbled, "Thank you."

"Thank you what?" Grandmother said.

"Thank you *sir*." Mock courtesy escaped through clamped teeth. She turned on the sink water full force. The money was nice; she would add it to her growing cache hoarded for the hour of her escape.

The Lord needn't think He could substitute crumbs for what she'd prayed for. Maybe there was something else she should be doing. She would ask the preacher one more time. Her spirits lifted at the thought. Grandmother was right: he was a kind man, the kindest she knew.

The following morning after church service, as Dr. Conklin stood at the door shaking hands with the congregants, Olivia got into line beside Grandmother. While waiting her turn, she watched his handsome Daddy-face break into a fresh smile as he grasped each new hand, bending to hear a compliment for a white-haired woman and standing tall to exchange quips with a rough-hewn man. *Just like Daddy; working the crowd.* She felt a small stab of envy, even though she herself happened to be very special to the preacher. Surely everyone must know that.

When she reached him, she tugged on his hand, pulling his down so she could talk close to his ear. "I did like you said. I prayed in my closet."

"Fine, fine! Good for you!" He sounded jovial, but the glazed sweep of the crowd behind her never reached the top of her head. He patted her shoulder and straightened to greet Grandmother. But Olivia yanked twice at his robe.

"All I got was a raise in my allowance."

Grandmother pushed her into the foyer. "Mustn't bother the preacher, hon. He's very busy."

The clock in the foyer said twelve-fifteen. She counted ahead: it would be twenty-seven hours before she could ask him again. Her throat constricted; her lip quivered. But no: Jesus had already seen her cry once, and it didn't faze Him one bit. She'd be damned if she'd ever give Him that satisfaction again.

She slogged through the rest of the day under a cloud of hovering desperation. She slept poorly that night. Soon after she finally drifted off, she dreamed of Daddy, handsome Daddy, sharing a rare affectionate moment. She sat on his lap, feeling safe and happy while he cuddled her close. Then she noticed he wasn't Daddy, but Uncle Cas. When she looked again, his usual grin had vanished. His featured were masked in corpse-like composure; his well-manicured hand had become a clutching claw: she was in the grips of a dark griffin. In her terror, she wet the bed; the warm liquid woke her. She jumped up and ran to the bathroom, trailing a trickle all the way, then she spent the next hour mopping up the evidence of her transgression. There was no way to dry the bed, so at dawn she made it up neatly and hoped that over a few days' time it would dry by itself before Grandmother noticed.

At breakfast, when she reminded them that this was her day to work at the church, two pink spots appeared on Grandmother's morning face, which otherwise was the color of a caliche bluff. Her faded blue eyes, protected and precise behind little round reading glasses, raked over Olivia's clothes. She said in cold distaste, "Surely you don't plan to wear that!"

Olivia looked down and shrugged, shifting an invisible burden on her back. She wore her favorite pink corduroy jeans.

Grandmother set her cup down with a clatter. "You *know* how the preacher feels about women in trousers, Faye—I mean Olivia."

Ordinarily Olivia would have protested that she was not yet a woman, but she remembered the wet bed and decided not to make waves. She left the room without stomping and changed into her plaid skirt, even hanging up her jeans to that Grandmother would have no excuse to poke around in her room. She also even kissed them both goodbye although such a sudden surge of obedience and affection might alert Grandmother to her guilty secret.

The damp bed was soon forgotten and so was the visit to the church, as she went through the school day with that determined stoic intensity reserved for perpetual outsiders. When the dismissal bell rang, she remembered her intention to speak with Dr. Conklin about speeding up the praying process. Her optimism and resolve rose like a swift little tide. She shrugged on her jacket and hurried down the street to the church, noticing how the dormant trees sprang up and arched like skeletal claws over her head. *Like griffin claws.* Still, their dry branches possessed a peculiar life, a watching presence, which Momma would have noticed.

A cold mist was falling, but she didn't bother to put up the hood of her jacket. She trotted the whole three blocks. The copper-spired church materialized like a haunted castle: an appropriate repository for dying gods on crosses and a fitting sanctuary for ghosts, holy or otherwise.

Once inside, she slowed, aware of the squeak of her wet soles against the polished floor, hoping she was raising the dead, or at least the Lord. When she reached the preacher's outer office, the brown-haired lady named Ruby Mullens glanced up and offered the barest embryo of a smile.

"Help yourself to a snack in the kitchen on your way. You remember how to get there, don't you?" Without waiting for an answer, she went back to her work.

"I need to see the preacher," Olivia said, heart pounding.

Mrs. Mullens' smile did not waver, but a cool veil crossed the warmth as she said what Olivia took for disapproval, "He's out on his rounds."

Betrayal struck her like a belly blow. The Lord was not making this easy. She took a determined step closer; her question was almost a challenge. "Do you know anything about praying?"

Mrs. Mullen' prim red mouth twitched. "I might know a thing or two. What do you want to know?"

"I did like the preacher said. I went in the closet and shut the door. But God didn't answer my prayer."

"I see." The woman looked thoughtful. She motioned for Olivia to draw closer. "Maybe what you asked for wasn't the Lord's will. Did you remember to say, 'Nevertheless, not my will but Thine be done'?"

Nobody had mentioned that. Another loophole! There were too many rules, and somebody was always adding to them. It was like a money-back guarantee with too much fine print you couldn't read. She snorted. "Why wouldn't it be His will for my family to be put back together?"

"Is that what you wished for?" The woman softened; Olivia recognized the signs. If the situation weren't so vital, she could play this woman like a violin. But not now. Mrs. Mullens leaned on her elbows chummily. "Y'know, sometimes the Lord answers our prayers in ways we don't understand."

Oh brother. She saw it coming like an avalanche: the big con. She had heard Daddy use this same tone, trying to weasel out of some promise, sweeping away all hope in a tumble of words. She should have known. She wasn't in the mood for any more kiss-ass talk. She whipped around and headed for the door, forcing her tongue, leaden as stone, to move.

"Yeah, well, thanks anyway. I got to get to work." She spoke with pointed insolence.

The sting of her eyes abated in the breezeway's damp air. She tried to look on the bright side. The Lord *had* rewarded her openly like the preacher said: he *had* given her more allowance, at least. She would find out how much a bus ticket to Galveston cost, and she would save up and be done with this groveling in the closet, if that was the best the Lord could manage.

The cleaning man was entering the elevator with his buffer as she entered the Educational Building. He gave the floor a meaningful look, and she saw behind her faint damp footprints. She continued with careful tiptoes until the elevator door closed. Then she stomped on down the hall, hoping Jesus was noting with great dismay the scuff marks.

The Kindergarten room was empty; the blinds had been drawn and the books put away. But the cardboard box stood on the table beside the blocks. She was expected, then, and Constanzia had left work for her to do. She felt along the wall for the light switch, but her fingers froze when a voice spoke out of the gloom. "Here's my girl!"

Her heart jumped with relief. He sat in the shadowy alcove to the left, in a rocker near the piano. He reached out, and she went and placed her hand in his. Everything would be all right now; he would tell her what to do to speed up the process.

With tenderness he drew her onto his lap and patted her knee. He pulled off her damp jacket and tossed it on the piano stool. Self-consciously she smoothed her damp hair.

"I've been sitting her communing with the Lord and listening to the water drip off the eaves." He held her close and was quiet for a minute. "Hear it?"

She nodded hard; she wanted to hear it, but her breathing was so loud. He hadn't forgotten her after all, not like Daddy.

"What were you trying to tell me yesterday, honey?" He squeezed her knee as if to encourage her to talk.

For a moment it didn't seem so important. But then of course, it was. She said, "I prayed in the closet like you said."

"Good girl!" He gave her a tighter squeeze and murmured, "What a fine, pretty young lady you are! God's little stray lamb, Lord love you!"

The words swamped her with a longing like an unstoppable undertow in her blood. She leaned against him in gratitude, sucked in by her need. His whispers into her hair sent tickles to her ear. "What would you like to ask, my little lamb?"

She went on, pulling up like a swimmer fighting the ocean's drag. "Don't you figure God wants my family put back together?"

One hand clamped her close while the other patted her. "That's a big question, my darling child...."

The preacher stopped short, and his hand shot in a swift move to the arm of the chair. Olivia heard the scuff of a heel just before the lights went on and a dark hand dropped from the switch to the woman's side. Constanzia had taken one step into the room, but she quickly shuffled backward into the hall.

The pastor's voice became a sort purr: "Dear Lord, help this precious child to know Thy will and to serve Thee with gladness..." He droned on for some time. Olivia glanced behind her and, seeing his tight-closed eyes, realized he was praying. She ducked her head, folded her hands and waited. But she was aware of the cleaning woman's hovering presence just outside, and she didn't understand her own stab of guilt.

At length the preacher said "Amen" and gave her a gentle shove to her feet. She was surprised at the grim lines of irritation at the corners of his mouth and knew that she was to blame for taking up too much of his time. He stood and strode briskly across the room, clearing his throat, instructing her in a clipped, businesslike way.

"Continue as you have been, child. Work hard, pray without ceasing, serve the Lord with gladness, that your joy might be full." He left the room, nodding in surprise at Constanzia, as if he hadn't known she was there. Olivia should have told him, she supposed, but she was not sure why.

With a nagging sense of shame, she avoided looking toward the woman. Instead, she went direct.ly to the table to put the blocks away.

She heard the preacher take a few steps down the hall, then she heard him coming back. For some reason, the cleaning woman was still standing just outside the door.

He leaned past her and stuck his head around the jamb, looking stern and preacherly. "I happened to think: there's a book in my study that might answer your question about the right way to pray. Do you want to drop by to see it when you're finished here?"

She had a secret sense of collusion mingled with renewed optimism, as if they were putting one over on the unsuspecting cleaning lady. The fact was, he would not dash her hopes like Daddy. Things would get better, now that she was on the winning side, now that she had been baptized and had an ally. She recalled Momma telling them, after Daddy left, "People have been conquered by isolation. It's deadly." That word *deadly* echoed in her memory. She would not be conquered now, because she had a friend. Meanwhile, she would try to recall the meaning of Momma's Aristotle words for future use.

When Momma first began to teach Arthur the words, Olivia had been only three. For a bright boy of seven, Arthur seemed to have a great deal of trouble mastering them, which surprised Olivia, who quickly knew them by heart. Donnie took her aside and cautioned, "Play stupid! Don't you get it? Every time Arthur pretends he can't remember, Momma rewards him when he finally gets them right. If she finds out you know them already, you won't *ever* get a reward."

For several years, she and Donnie had pretended to struggle over the four words and their meanings, thinking they could never, ever forget them. But pain had closed a door on many of Momma's words, so that they were recalled only with great reluctance. Now she needed to remember one in particular.

Fortitude. It meant never wavering. There was more, about courage and forbearance and endurance. Keeping on. "It has a quality of stubbornness about it," Momma had said.

She would never waver. She would keep stubborn faith. She hurried to finish her work, then made her way quickly down the gloomy hall to the main building. There was no sign of Constanzia. It was later than she realized; this had better not take long, or she would be late for supper.

The poofy-haired lady was not at her desk, but the preacher's door was open, which she took as an invitation to enter. Dr. Conklin sat at his desk, reading. At her timid knock, he looked up as if he was surprised to see her. "Come in and close the door, so we won't be disturbed."

She did as she was told, noting a chill, like a cold hand upon her neck. Probably hunger. He said, "Turn the lock, dear," and she thought about it then remembered for some odd reason the wet bed, and only pretended to lock the door. But when she turned and saw him smiling, holding out his hand, inviting her with a buttery, "Come here, my beautiful little girl," she was sucked into a charismatic field as if by a magnet. Still, she stopped short of his reach, held back by a lingering reticence until he urged her on.

"Take off your coat, child." He pulled her forward and removed her jacket, laying it on the desk.

She looked around the room, searching the desk top in particular. "So where's the book?"

He gave her a gentle pull, settling her onto his lap, and pointed to the Bible. "Haven't you guessed by now, honey? The answer to every problem is in this book." He smoothed her hair before handing her the oversized book. On the front was the picture of Jesus with several sheep.

"This is a special children's Bible. Open it."

The book was large and unwieldy, but he didn't offer to help her hold it. "Turn to page two-sixty-four and read to me from the sixteenth chapter of John."

While she balanced the book and tried to find the page, he pulled her closer and patted her, whispering, "That's my smart girl, pretty little lamb." It was hard to find the page because he would not sit still, but kept shifting beneath her, moving this way and that.

At last she found the right page. He said, "Oh my Jesus! Read it out loud! Pay attention to the words and nothing else. Oh sweet Jesus!"

With heightened expectancy, she sought the verses and began haltingly to read, "Verily, verily, I say unto you, Whatsoever ye shall ask the Father in my name, He will give it to you...."

He continued to squirm, making reading almost impossible. She tried to hold herself erect and find her place, reminding herself of how important it was to get the words fixed in her mind.

"Hitherto have you asked nothing in my name: ask and ye shall receive, that your joy may be full..."

He had forgotten about her. She pushed erect to stay focused on the words, while his black pupils were glassy and remote, and his lips were parted in what must be a prayer, "Oh dear God..."

Then, in a quick burst, the door flew open and he threw her hurtling to the floor, grazing her head on the corner of his desk as she fell onto her hands and knees. Her temple seared in pain as she crouched on the floor. Mired in shame, she looked up only long enough to see the looming figure of Ruby Mullens filling the doorway. The woman's blazing eyes took in the scene and hurled daggers of loathing toward Olivia. She spat out only two words: "Get out!"

As Olivia scrambled for her coat, she glanced at the preacher, holding the big book in his lap. No longer a titan, he seemed suddenly old and shrunken, whipped by savage cravings. He wouldn't meet her eyes, but stared at the darksome woman with cold terror.

Olivia pushed past the office lady and tried to run down the hallway toward the waning sunlight. But her steps were as leaden as her mortified heart, as if they were sunken in her deep humiliation; as if she had been sucked into a quagmire from which there was no possible escape.

32

She stumbled out of the church and raced toward home, struggling into her jacket, stunned as much by the woman's menacing glare as by her dismissal. She panted against the misty air, trying to blot out her humiliation at being caught in the strange prayer and then being shoved so violently to the floor. Her knees still burned where they skidded across the textured carpet, and the chill air bit into the raw skin.

The magic secret words were vital. But her head throbbed like brains oozing out. She remembered nothing but his praying then throwing her to the floor. Nobody had ever treated her like that before.

Maybe the words would be in the Bible that Grandmother had given her when she was baptized. She had to slow down because her side hurt. She tugged her jacket closer against the mist and noticed the bleak leaden sky for the first time.

It was uniformly gray. Out on the buttes and bluffs rimming the town to the west, white was accumulating in the highest crevices. A cold wet speck hit her cheek, and then another. The chill cut into her bare legs and snaked up her skirt. She should have worn her pink cords, but Grandmother said the preacher didn't like—

The preacher, holding the book; the woman, condemning her with an accusing finger. Her heart squeezed against her devastation. Why had she done it, why hadn't she prevented it? Like with Uncle Cas, when she was very small. She could barely remember.

Snow was now sifting down in clumpy bits, straight down, dropping through the slatey trees as if to cover everything as silently as possible: hide the terrible deed. Car headlights came on along the thoroughfare. People scurried past her moving quickly. Ahead at the convenience store, several people loaded firewood into open car trunks. Across the street beyond it, at the doughnut shop, two parked police cars were already layered with a dusting of snow. She hurried across at the light, past the shop's window, peering in at the table where the policemen sat over mugs of coffee and jelly doughnuts. The sweet odor of pastries wafted out. Despite her acute agitation or perhaps because of it, she was ravenous. Hunger almost drove her inside, but she feared shame would show on her face. The officers might take one look and know she was guilty of something. She gulped a breath, but her throat closed off against the flinty cold.

No, she would hurry home and look for the magic words. Then she would go into the closet and pray and hope Jesus wouldn't be so pissed that he refused to help her altogether. She had to be more careful to keep people from getting so mad. She had to be better.

She tried to open the front door quietly, intending to head for the kitchen and hit the fridge. But Grandmother met her in the front hall with a look of cold despite. Her straight-stiff arms ended in clenched fists held tightly at her sides, as if it was all she could do to control herself. Her lips barely parted. "Just march straight to your room and wait for your grandfather."

Olivia's heart pounded even worse. She swallowed, remembering the wet bed, and knew Grandmother must have found it. She went to her room and shut the door. Her bed was still made, not too neatly, just the way she had left it. She felt the spread; it didn't feel damp yet. Maybe she was mistaken.

She took her new Bible off the shelf and went into the closet, into air sluggish with the odor of old shoes. The hanging clothes obscured the light so that she couldn't read the pages unless she stood directly under the light. The book was awkward to hold and flip through while standing. She tried to remember where to find the secret words, which were somewhere near the back. With a sinking sensation, she saw hundreds of words on every page. Her anxiety mounted as she flipped through the pages, hoping the right words would stand out.

The back door slammed. She heard Grandmother clip down the hall to meet Granddaddy. She put the book down and crept to the back wall of the closet, hoping to hear what Grandmother would tell him about the wet bed.

Grandmother said, "We've got a crisis on our hands, and you're the one who's going to have to handle it."

Olivia figured that meant a spanking. She thought about where she could hide.

"I won't ever be able to hold up my head in this town again! Ruby Mullens called—"

Her head began to buzz so that she could hardly hear. So it wasn't the bed; it was the awful thing with the preacher.

"Remember that Hawkins girl about six months ago? Well, it's happened again, the identical thing. Only this time it's Olivia."

"Olivia! Are you sure?"

"Ruby saw her!" Grandmother's voice broke with hysteria. "I don't understand it. She's been baptized."

Grandfather roared out in a rage. "She's a tool of Satan, just like the other one, trying to bring him down! Once a Catholic, always a Catholic! By God, I won't have it!" He stamped down the hall and crashed Olivia's door open. "Slattern, slut, she-devil, get out here!" He was gasping, spewing hard, thrashing like a wild bull.

She was afraid not to open the closet door. But as soon as she touched the knob, he wrenched it out of her hand, slung upon the door and caught her arm in a grip that almost tore it from its socket. He slung her across the floor, screaming, "Witch! Harlot! Have you people no values at all? Just as tainted as your mother! Have you no shame?"

As he drew off his belt, she began to wail before he ever hit her. "Please don't! I'm sorry! I won't ever do it again!"

The leather cut into her legs with such fire she knew she would die. He screams became shriller with each blow. She writhed, trying to pull free of his grasp, but he did not let up. He rambled wildly, making no sense: "My brother didn't die in Korea to protect the likes of you *or* your mother!"

She felt urine gush down her legs, but she couldn't stop it. The sight infuriated him all the more. He let out a roar of disgust as he struck her ever more savagely. "Now look what you've done!"

When she tried to draw into a ball, he slashed her across the back, on the arms, even on the head, until finally Grandmother drew him away.

"That's enough, Hank. You'll have a heart attack."

Still flailing his belt, he dropped her arm and backed away, panting and pointing with contempt at the puddle on the floor, his face purple with rage. "Clean that up, you filthy whore!"

He allowed Grandmother to lead him out, slamming the door behind them, and said, 'Where's the key? Lock the bitch in until I decide what to do with her! By God, we will not have another Faye on our hands!"

Olivia felt her arm to see if it was broken. Granddaddy was saying, "I've got to get to Prayer Meeting, no matter what. Hold my head up somehow."

"Are you going to leave me with this? What am I supposed to do?"

"Call that Catholic bunch. They'll just have to take her."

Grandmother interrupted with an impatient snort. "How can I? The grandmother died, remember? I don't even know who..."

Olivia crawled across the floor and leaned against the door, stifling sobs with both hands.

"Died? When?" He sounded as if he was in the bathroom.

"I told you. You never listen to anything I say. One of that bunch phoned. I sent a sympathy card, for the boy's sake."

Grandfather's voice was low. "You didn't tell the girl..."

"I saw no reason to. But now...the worthless father locked up and no telling what they did with the boy. Well, somebody's just going to have to step in. I'm done with that harlot."

Olivia was too stunned to move. So the white-haired grandmother was dead. She examined the great oozing welts on her legs and wondered if the pulsing pain would kill her. But she couldn't die yet. She had to get away before Granddaddy came back and beat her more when he saw that she hadn't cleaned up the stain. Because she would *never* clean it up.

She wouldn't die, either; she had to find Arthur. Peggy was dead and Arthur was all alone somewhere. Where could he be? She had no address, not even for Daddy, since Grandmother had hidden his letter. But she'd had two Christmas cards from the others.

She crawled to the bureau and inched open the bottom drawer, stifling her need to groan. Underneath the clothes lay her money cache and a small packet of letters and cards. She crept to the bed where she'd dropped her jacket, stuffing letters in one pocket and money in the other, then tiptoed to the window and raised it, hardly noticing the zots of snow. The latch on the screen gave way easily, as if she were meant to open it, as if Momma might have loosened it years before, in case she should ever need it. With the greatest stealth, she climbed over the sill and dropped into the darkening snowfall.

33

As she dropped to the ground, the letters spilled out of her pocket. She scooped them up and shook off the snow, then reached under her skirt to tuck them into the waistband of her underpants. It would have been a good idea to change into dry ones before she left. But no matter; they would dry in time.

Anyway, the added discomfort of cold wet pants lent an added dramatic element to her martyrdom. She thought with grim satisfaction that she wouldn't have it any other way. Surely this counted as Momma's fortitude.

The money was still safe in her other pocket, but she decided to move it as well, so she layered her right loafer with bills. It hurt to bend over, to strain against the belt marks that cut into her thighs. *Fortitude*, she reminded herself.

As she stepped from the shelter of the house, the full wallop of the icy wind hit her, stunning her breathless. It sounded like a convoy of trucks. She should have put on her cords and heavy coat; should have thought about mittens and ear muffs. But she didn't have far to go; she already had a plan, whispered into her brain by Donnie. She had assumed his skin; she would be Donnie *for* him.

The plan hinged on the policemen still being at the doughnut shop. She began to run, conscious of the cold against her bruised legs, cursing the overcast sky that had trapped the gloaming light, so that it was far lighter than it had any right to be. Someone might see her, someone coming home for supper, someone who knew her grandparents. But soon her mind turned to more urgent matters: fine-tuning her story before she reached the doughnut shop.

The policemen were just leaving as she crossed the street. This was even better, because they wouldn't notice the welts on her legs in the twilight. As they reached their cars, she galloped up panting and planted herself between them She pitched her voice high and innocent, like children always sounded in movies made by adults. Like Donnie always did.

"Please sirs, can you help me get home? I'm lost."

One officer, who was short and square and held himself like a gamecock, backed up and reached for the door handle on his squad car. But the taller thinner officer leaned over and said, "Sure, kid. Do you know where you live?"

"Galveston."

That brought the other officer over. "Galveston! What're you doing up here, kid?"

"I don't know where 'here' is." Sounding young and doofusy.

The men looked at each other over her head, and the chuffy one said, "Is she kidding?"

The thin one said, "You're in Abilene, kid. How'd you get here?"

"Long story. My baby sitter brought me with her to see her boyfriend. Then she got mad and put me out of the car and drove off. My mom's out of town. She doesn't even know I'm missing yet."

The story sounded convincing to her, but the chubby man seemed skeptical. "Yeah? So what's your name and address?"

"Faye Ahern. We live at—" She panicked, unable to think of an address; sorry she'd mentioned Momma's name. She leaned against the squad car. "It's hard to think when you're freezing!"

The thin officer sounded more sympathetic; in fact, she fancied that he looked worried. He said quietly, "Maybe she's hungry." He touched her shoulder with one finger, gingerly, as if she might be contaminated. "You're not fixin' to pass out, are you, kid?"

"Well…" She looked longingly toward the shop, weighing the danger of going inside. "I haven't eaten all day."

The fat officer told the thin one, "Take her inside and get her something while I check in."

But the thin one seemed reluctant to shoulder such a financial responsibility. "I may need reinforcements in there…like cash."

They all went into the shop, deserted now except for two men at the counter and the Korean waitress. The odor of coffee and warm pastry was heavenly! The box-jawed officer who she could now see was older and more experienced-looking, slid into a booth and motioned for her to sit across from him. But she said, "I need to use the rest room." He wrinkled his nose and grimaced meaningfully in the direction of her skirt. "Appears to me like it's already too late." As she turned to go, he said, "Why don't you take off your jacket, kid. Be comfortable."

She had expected that, but she had nothing to hide now. They wouldn't find anything in the pockets to disprove her story, and she knew for certain they would examine them while she was gone.

She hurried to the john, relieved to find it vacant. She locked the door and dug the letters out of her underpants. And electric hand dryer was attached to the wall beside the sink, and she was seized by inspiration. She pulled off the wet underpants, draped them over the dryer and pressed the button. While her underpants were drying, she shuffled through the letters until she found Uncle Cas's card and memorized the address. When the machine shut off, she felt of her underpants and found them still damp, so she punched the button again.

The pants didn't dry, but they were at least warm, and the air had lent them a distinct pungency. She put them on and replaced the packet of letters, smoothing her skirt so they didn't show. Then she went back to the booth, glancing through the plate glass windows for signs of life outside. But dark had finally fallen, so all she could see was her own reflection, transparent as a negative, but still impenetrable. She slid in beside the thin officer, where her food had been placed. She was pleased to note two sausage kolaches, a chocolate doughnut, and a glass of milk.

There was no need to pretend to be ravenous; she grabbed a kolache and stuffed it into her mouth whole, feeling close to tears.

The older officer, holding his radio to his ear, cupped the mouthpiece to warn her, "Easy, kid. Don't make yourself sick." He was still trying to sound gruff.

The younger man lifted his head and sniffed the air. He had the beginnings of blond stubble at his jawline. "What's that funny smell? Do you smell it, Arl?"

"Don't ask," Arl said, rolling his eyes toward Olivia, who ignored him and slurped at her milk. He waited for her to catch her breath, then said, "Okay kid, what's the name again?"

"Faye Ahern." She regretted not having been more inventive. She added, "My mom's name is Margaret Mary Ahern."

Arl repeated it into his radio phone, then said, "Address?"

Panic crept up her throat like a cold hand. She stopped in mid-chew and waited for inspiration, finally opting for stupidity. "I never can remember my number." She scrooched down into the booth, trying to appear younger and smaller than she was.

The officer next to her rubbed his stubble and muttered, "Wish I could identify that smell."

"Believe me, Deon, you don't want to know." The older man returned to his phone and listened. "Dispatcher says there's no listing for a Margaret Mary Ahern." Olivia, wondering if her aunt was dead too, pretended to be preoccupied with eating.

After a minute of two, Deon said, "Now what's going on?"

"They're calling CPS. Looks like everybody's out to supper."

Deon consulted his watch. "Won't be but one woman on at this hour, anyway."

"What's CPS?" Olivia, hoping to appear mildly disinterested, spoke around a mouthful of kolache.

Art frowned, regarding her as if she were a piece of gum stuck to his shoe. "Children's Protective Services.' He turned off the phone and laid it down. "Well this is one helluva note! Nobody answers."

Olivia made her eyes large and round, a technique perfected by Donnie when they were very young. "Then why don't you just call my daddy to come and get me?"

"Just like that! All the way from Galveston at this hour."

"Oh, he's not in Galveston. He's in Fort Worth. Didn't I tell you? Caswell Ahern, Fourteen-ten Pecan Avenue. My folks are, like, divorced."

The two looked to one another for guidance. With the worn-out air of one trained to confront bank robbers instead of lost urchins in wet pants, Arl said, "Might work. He could be here in a couple of hours, and CPS may be closed for the night. Maybe somebody called in sick or something." He eyed her again and said, "I know I sure as hell would!"

Deon was definitely edgy. Like a trapped fugitive, he had moved farther into the corner of the booth and was shielding one side of his face with his hand, avoiding at all costs looking her way. "Give it a shot. Why do these things always happen after hours, when there's not a damn soul on duty where they're supposed to be?"

Arl began punching buttons and grumbling, "There'll be almighty hell to pay if we're not reimbursed by Accounting." He slipped out of the booth and turned his back to them. Olivia, remaining nonchalant, strained to hear, but the food stuck in her throat, and her insides fluttered like a cage full of wild birds. She had to swallow a few times to make the bite go down. It tasted like straw.

Arl was talking to someone. Then he turned and eyed her with steely disgust, his glare boring down on her like the advance of a semi. He said to Deon, "I don't know what the f— is going on: This guy doesn't even *have* any kids."

For a split second, she felt her hopes drop like a rock into a well. But then she remembered the plan, and she jumped up yelling, "That makes me *so mad*! Daddy *always* does this whenever he gets a new girlfriend!" She ran over and grabbed the phone from the astonished Arl before he could stop her. "Just let me talk to him!"

She took a deep breath, summoning every bit of fury that had been accumulating since Donnie's death. "Daddy, you've *got* to come for me *right now*, and I *mean* it! I'm *all alone*!"

The man sounded as if he meant to hang up. "Look kid, I don't know who you are, but—"

"Olivia!" She looked around at the officers, covering the mouthpiece and explaining to them, "That's the name of my baby-sitter." She saw the men studying her bruised legs for the first time. Deon mumbled something to Arl.

"Olivia?" Uncle Cas's voice rose, and she surged with relief, wiping away quick tears. "I didn't recognize your voice. What's going on? Did he say he was an Abilene police officer?"

"If you don't come quick, they're going to take me to Children's Protective Services."

"But what about your grandparents?"

She turned away, hunching over the phone, and whispered, "Dead!"

"Dead? Both of them? But how?"

"Fire." She had her back to the officers, but it was imperative to change the subject fast. "I need to get to Galveston right away. They want you to take me to Margaret Mary's, to keep me from having to go to an orphans' home."

There was a strained silence. Someone at the counter dropped a spoon; the clatter made Olivia jump. She thought maybe Cas had hung up. Finally he said, "You mean tonight? Sweetie, I can't just—"

She began to whine in earnest, felling solid ground. "If you don't. they'll turn me over to…And I'm all by myself in the world and it's snowing, and I don't even have a coat!"

"Oh for God's sake! No coat, even? Okay, I'll come. But I have an important meeting tomorrow...Well, we'll work something out. Margaret Mary does know you're coming, doesn't she?"

"Come right this minute. I'll be at the police station. But hurry!" She broke the connection and handed the phone back to Arl, smiling as sweetly as she knew how.

"My daddy's coming after me. He's leaving right away. He'll pick me up at the station." She knew he would. She had something on him from a long time back, and now she thought she knew what it was.

In the coin toss to determine who would deliver her to the station and fill out the paper work, Arl lost. During her ride in his squad car, she calculated how long she would have to wait for Cas. She was certain he would start out immediately from Fort Worth. There was something about her relationship with him, something she couldn't quite remember— although while she was on the preacher's lap she almost could—that bound her to him in a special way, gave her power over him. She had only to fix an eye on him to cause him to squirm. She figured he would be in Abilene before Grandmother ever bother to check on her and discover she was gone.

At the station, Arl turned her over to a plump and pleasantly gruff dusky woman named Odessa Baines, who wore a navy uniform and had a sprinkle of freckles on her cheeks. Her voice resonated with the deep timbres of the Deep South. She had frizzy orange hair. Olivia had an affinity for orange hair, because Momma's hair had a bronze tinge in the sunlight, and Margaret Mary's had once been blatantly tangerine.

Her grandparents had carefully shielded her from people of other races since the day she brought Reginald Taliaferro home with her from school. She was especially drawn to him because he pronounced his name "Tolliver" but spelled it weird, and Momma had taught them to prize originality. But Grandmother sent him home at once, then sat her down and described the characteristics of people she should never bring into the house again.

Against Olivia's objections, Odessa Baines led her onto the elevator and punched Three. "I have to wait by the front door so my...my daddy will know where to find me," she said, trying to free her hand from the woman's iron grip.

But Odessa possessed the same resistance to manipulation that all females seemed born with. She clamped Olivia's hand more firmly and in a cheery guttural sing-song assured her, "This ain't going to be no Kodak moment, girl. No hurry. He's got to sign you out. He'll find you. If he's coming all the way from Fort Worth, he ain't likely to leave without you."

With a no-nonsense tug, she led Olivia off the elevator and through a door that said Children's Protective Services on the glass. She indicated a couple of folding chairs near a metal file box beside her desk. Noting with disappointment that there was no place to lie down, Olivia muttered "No frills here!" and slumped onto one chair, suddenly bone weary. The metal seat was cold; the hand dryer hadn't completely done its work on her underpants.

Odessa Baines sat at her desk, adjusted her computer screen and said, "Anyway, your dad'll have to fill out some forms before you're outa here."

Olivia shot up wide awake, thinking hard. Sometimes when she thought hard, she swung her legs with great vigor. Odessa Baines looked up and frowned. When she wasn't smiling, she had a face like cow poop, all plump folds and wrinkles.

"What's the matter with your legs, girl?"

Olivia had forgotten about the welts. She stopped swinging and tucked her feet under the chair, pulling her skirt down as far as it would go. "Nothing."

"Somebody been hittin' you?"

Olivia shook her head in stout denial, then remembered. "Baby sitter, the old witch!" Moisture stung her eyes. She batted them fast and looked at the clock over the door. If what Arl and Deon said was accurate, Uncle Cas ought to show up at about nine o'clock.

"Yeah? Hmm. We'll get to her in a minute!" The woman poised over her keyboard. "Let's get the preliminaries out of the way. What's your full name, girl?"

"...Twyla. Twyla...Taliaferro."

"Hold it. I thought Arliss said it was Faye something."

Olivia gaped, exhibiting disbelief. "Faye! What kind of dorky name is that?"

Odessa narrowed her eyes down to a glittery slit. "Didn't you tell him your name is Faye?"

"Gaw! Faye!" Olivia snorted. "No wonder my daddy didn't know what Arl was talking about! Look: it was snowing. My teeth were chattering." She dismissed the subject quickly and, reviving another of Donnie's tricks, let out an exaggerated yawn and looked around. "Is there any place to crash? I didn't get much sleep last night."

"This ain't the Holiday Inn, honey. Maybe you can pull up that other chair and stretch out." Odessa picked up the phone. "I got to check on this name business."

Olivia busied herself arranging chairs. "Arl can't hear worth beans," she grumbled. "No offense, but the guy's a coma case. Got poochy pecs like a soft girl. He oughta work out."

"Yeah, well, anybody ever tell you you got one smart mouth on you? Not any wonder somebody done taken a razor strop to you and dumped you." Odessa turned back to the phone. "Is Arliss still down there? Get me Arliss. He's s'posed to be down there making out a report."

She let out a mild oath and hung up. "He got called out for back-up. But I'm checking on this soon as he comes in, so you better not be messing with me, hear? I've heard it all, girl. Heard it a bazillion times, by kids that'd make you look retarded. So you better be giving me the straight of it." She turned her back to the screen, and Olivia lay down quickly across the two metal chairs, cupping her jacket under her cheek for a pillow. "Okay, what's your story, girl? Gimme that name again? You spell it with a 'Y' or an 'I'?"

Granddaddy's breath always got deep and even when he dropped off in his recliner in front of the TV. Olivia imitated it, pretending not to hear the woman.

"Hey girl! You listening?"

She kept breathing deeply until the woman gave up and turned to something else. Relief flooded her like a warm bath. But it was hard to stay awake, breathing so deeply, and she began to drift off despite her best intentions to stay awake.

Just before sleep overtook her, Momma's morose face loomed up, the way she looked after she lost the baby, the way she looked when Donnie died. Momma had sighed and told them she needed to learn from the dead, like the African Asante, who were invaded by the Danes and British but never had the concept of victimization. "They have a unique relationship between the unborn, the living and the dead...and enlightened ideas about wealth and time and motion, too. They wouldn't take this as a loss; they would *use* it. But we have to handle things the best way we can. It's too bad we can't draw on the wisdom of the dead."

Sometime later she woke with a start and looked at the clock: it was ten after nine. Odessa Baines was nowhere in sight. She jumped up, grabbed her jacket, ran out the door, and collided head-on with Odessa's solid middle.

"Now where you think you're running to? The Boston Marathon?"

Olivia had no intention of blowing it now. "Where's the rest room? Gotta go bad!" Pity was, it was the truth.

"End of the hall on the right. But you come straight back, hear?"

Olivia galloped to the john and did her business as quickly as possible. *Please don't let me miss him* was all she could think. She inched open the rest room door and peered into the hall. Odessa was standing in front of the C PS door talking to an officer. Directly across the hall she saw a door marked Stairway. She sent up another prayer that Odessa wouldn't turn around while she scurried across into the stairwell.

She passed no one on the two long flights down. When she entered the lobby, she made herself as inconspicuous as possible, avoiding all eye contact as she headed past several officers near the front door.

The night was piercing cold. Ice on the parking lot glittered like glass, but at least the snow and sleet had stopped falling. The building's façade offered some protection from the biting wind. Olivia's breath froze. Clutching her jacket, she huddled against the wall just out of range of the security camera and the entrance lights. If Cas didn't come soon, she would turn to ice. Her toes and fingers were already numb, and her nose ran so constantly she had to keep wiping it on her sleeve.

But she was right about him. In no more than ten minutes, she spied his blue BMW turning into the parking area. She slithered across the slippery lot, waving frantically. As soon as he slid to a stop, she yanked open the door and jumped in. "If you know what's good for you, you'll haul ass!"

He didn't gun it as she hoped, but accelerated only slightly, maintaining a controlled forward speed out of the lot. His heavy ski sweater looked like one of Daddy's; he even smelled like Daddy. She swallowed back the sudden wash of relief, but she couldn't unclench her fists.

He examined her with a worried look. "What's the deal? Did you trash the place?"

"Nothing like that. Just keep moving."

He let up on the accelerator. "Wait a minute. Am I going to be in some kind of trouble? Aren't they waiting for me back there?"

Her patience gave out. "Oh sure! They're like, 'Oh goody, here he comes! Pass out the party hats!' She snorted in disgust. "Go back if you want to. You'll only have to fill out about forty million forms. You'll be up all night signing stuff, and then your name'll be plastered all over their computer system. I figure you'll make it back to Fort Worth sometime next month."

He looked dubious, but he drove on, entering the expressway entrance ramp. "Just so long as they don't put out an APB."

"Like they know what to look for!" She tightened her seatbelt and settled back. "You know what your problem is? You're always full of guilt. Did you mom feed it to you in your oatmeal?"

"You got that right. Guilt was one of our seven basic food groups."

"Four. Now there's only four."

As they reached the outskirts, Cas picked up speed and blew out a relieved breath. He reached to pat her shoulder but stopped short of touching her. "Tough luck about your grandparents, Liv."

She'd almost forgotten. "Yeah. Do we have to talk about it?"

Again she pretended drowsiness and was soon asleep. He roused her a couple of times at truck stops that had buzzing lights, where she trooped off on wobbly legs to the rest room, elated by the realization that she would soon be with Arthur.

Twice during the night drive she saw shooting stars cut though the cold black sky and considered it a good omen. So the deal really worked like the preacher said: going into the closet and shutting the door.

Or more likely, Donnie had heard her.

34

It was two hours before daylight and they were crossing the causeway over the flat, calm waters of Galveston Bay, having traversed both state and season overnight, when it occurred to Cas that Margaret Mary had recently moved and he hadn't brought along her new address. Olivia, awake since they passed through Houston, tasted the green salt-marsh air with anticipation and took this as a fortuitous moment to break the news.

"Guess that's why the police couldn't reach her," she said.

In the darkened car his voice rose to a semi-hysterical pitch. "Are you telling me she doesn't even know we're coming?"

She backed down quickly. "They were trying to call. Probably they got her by now."

Cas gunned the car and whipped onto a feeder as they reached the end of the causeway. He was muttering to himself, "Isn't there anyplace that stays open all night anymore?"

Olivia was hungry and she needed to pee again. "How about someplace to eat?" She reared up and pointed toward a lighted sign ahead. "Is that a Denny's?"

"No, but it'll do." He headed for the restaurant attached to the front of an all-night truck-stop. She went into the restaurant and headed for the rest room, leaving him to fish out his phone and searched for his sister's cell number. The place smelled of disinfectant, and the commode water ran all the time. She used the last of the tissue and didn't wash her hands because it looked as if someone had thrown up in the sink.

When she came out of the john, Uncle Cas was sitting in a booth by the front windows. A large waitress in tight jeans was taking his order. Olivia slid in across from him and ordered pancakes and chocolate milk while he pretended to gag. His eyes were sunken in and his cheeks were covered with stubble. He didn't look much like Daddy after all.

"You could use a shave," she said.

"You could use a bath…guess we both could." He wallowed his tongue around and added, "And a toothbrush."

The waitress brought his coffee. He took a big swig and sighed. "She's not answering her cell, and Information doesn't have a land number for her. Guess it's unlisted."

Olivia felt a surge of alarm. "So what do we do?"

He looked at his Rolex, so glittery against his tan. The hairs on his wrist were bleached a golden white. "Too early to call Kristi. After we eat, I guess I'll wake her up and ask her to look in my address book. I think I made a note of her hew address when I got her Christmas card."

"I thought last time it was Barb. Is Kristi my newest aunt?"

He shot her a glare. "Not exactly, miss smart-ass." He took another swig and studied his cup. "There aren't going to be anymore aunts."

She thought about making a crack about her many not-quite relatives but decided to give him a rest until their food came. When it did arrive, she dug into her pancakes with great concentration. When they were gone, she felt better, and she remembered why she had come.

"If Grandmother Peggy is dead, where's Arthur? Will we see him when it's morning?"

"I'm not sure." He laid down his fork and leaned on his forearms, looking entirely too grave to suit Olivia. "I don't keep up with family things. Margaret Mary and her sisters always know what's happening." He hesitated. "You…know about your dad, I guess.'

She felt a shudder of dread. "Which thing do you mean?"

"About the appeal. He waived it. So you know where he is."

She had only the vaguest idea what that meant, except that she already knew he was in prison. "Oh sure." She finished off her chocolate milk and watched as he waggled his cup at the waitress for a refill. Olivia couldn't picture Daddy behind bars: proud, arrogant Daddy. She slid down against the back of the booth until the table was at eye level and said without much conviction, "Daddy wouldn't do anything wrong, no matter what they say."

He didn't argue with her immediately, as she had hoped. She waited until the waitress had filled his cup and left, then said, "It's about the maps, isn't it? I mean, it's not about Donnie, is it?"

He took several sips as if he hadn't heard. Finally he said, "It's the maps. That's what Llano claimed. Quent wouldn't tell the court it was all a set-up; that Llano fed him phony maps to pass onto Weldon, whose company paid him under the table for. So when the cops found the evidence in your dad's study, Llano had to pretend your dad stole them."

She wasn't interested so much, except that he was lost to her, maybe forever. "Will he be in prison the rest of my life?"

His chuckle churned into a crackly tobacco cough. "Hardly! I imagine he'll be up for parole shortly." He stood and slapped a tip on the table. "You can wait here while I call Kristi."

She sat up, feeling better, and began to swing her legs. Things weren't so bad. Arthur must be staying with Margaret Mary now. They could all live together in her house until Daddy got out of prison, and then they could get a house and find Josephine.

She watched Uncle Cas pay the check, noting the soft bulge where his polo shirt met his belt. Uncle Cas was losing it, but he wasn't totally lame yet. His tan was dark and rich, still.

She swung her legs fast while he stepped outside to phone. Presently he taped on the window and motioned for her to come. He was already in the BMW with the motor running by the time she got outside. She settled in beside him and said, "So? Did you get her?"

He backed out and headed toward the on-ramp. It was still dark; a pre-dawn fog had crawled across the road. He said, "She looked up Margaret Mary's address from the Christmas card. There was no phone number, but at least we know where she lives." He switched on the dash clock light. "She's probably not up yet. Maybe I'll pass by the old home-place first... see if it's still standing."

They drove down Broadway, its oleander-lined esplanade now bearing sentinels of bare stalks, and took a right into the old silk stocking district, which looked the same as it had the last time she was there. Probably much as it must have looked even when Daddy grew up there. The sky dithered between purple and pink: light enough that she could see the house plainly as they approached. They parked in front, and she could tell the place was deserted: tall weeds overgrew the front yard, and the house was even more hollow-eyed and drastically in need of paint. When they came before for her grandfather's funeral, it had been yellow with white trim, but now gray boards showed through.

They got out of the car, but Uncle Cas cautioned her not to climb the steps after he noticed several porch boards had fallen through. The door hung on rusted hinges. There was a faint smell of damp. She was amazed. "How did it het in such bad shape so soon?" She felt impoverished, deprived of her heritage.

They went back to the car. Uncle Cas's head sank and he sighed deeply as if somebody had died again. He said, "It's been going to pot ever since Dad got sick. In this salty sea air, you have to paint constantly or everything rots. With no man around..." His glance slid quickly away.

"But I thought Daddy was here. And Arthur..."

He turned on the ignition. "I don't know. I didn't actually come down here after Dad died."

Her mouth flew open. "Not even for Grandmother's funeral?"

He squirmed and finally said, "There wasn't any need, really. Mom was gone; she wouldn't know the difference. I'm not much for funerals, anyway. I knew the girls would take care of things." He paused. "Anyway, I was sick."

She waited. Cas turned onto Broadway again and circled back toward a new part of town. The street lights were beginning to flicker. Some went off, but when a patch of fog drifted in from the water, they came on again. She said, "What about Daddy? Was he here for the funeral?"

"I doubt it. He'd refused a plea bargain. He's not much for funerals, either."

"So it was just Arthur." *Arthur: the scapegoat. All alone at the funeral.*

They used to make fun of him, she and Donnie. They had schemed against him, willing him to fail as often as not in whatever he attempted. With their special brand of cruelty, they had pitted themselves against him while he manfully struggled on alone. Always alone.

She remembered how Arthur always took things to heart, much more than she and Donnie. He was too touchy for his own good. How had he managed, off down here on this foggy island with a strange old woman he didn't know?

How, after finally coming, maybe, to entrust himself to his new grandmother, had he coped when she died? Had she died like Momma, lingering on in a tangle of tubes tended by bustling attendants whose eyes refused to meet his? Had Arthur stood at her side at the end, watching blips on a machine like Momma's? Had he waited for a crisp efficient nurse to unwrap the pressure cuff, pull out the tubes and usher him into the hall? Had he been the only one there?

Or had she died suddenly without warning, at home in her sleep? Had he woken late one morning, wondering why there was no smell of coffee; had he gone to her room and found her still in her bed, a trail of vomit stringing from her mouth? Or had he found her on the bathroom floor, glassy-eyed, like a corpse in a TV mystery? Had he felt the gorge rising and run from the room in horror? Who had comforted him; who had taken him in?

More puzzling still, who had notified her other grandparents in Abilene? Had Arthur done it, expecting Olivia to come at once, wondering why he heard nothing from her? Had he stood beside the open grave as the priest sent Grandmother Ahern's spirit off to Heaven, had he turned, hopeful, at the sound of tires crunching on the gravel drive; had he looked forward to hugging his sister for once; had his face darkened when he saw that it wasn't Livvie at all? Had he believed all this time that she had known, that she didn't care?

Margaret Mary's townhouse was the third from the corner. They climbed the six steps to the front entry, closed off by a black iron gate. Cas pushed the door bell, and they heard Margaret Mary's husky voice through the intercom, "Yes?"

"It's Cas. With Olivia."

A buzzer sounded, releasing the gate lock. They stepped inside the gate and waited for her to come. It seemed to take a long time for her to open the door. She wore a robe over her pajamas, and she was yanking huge rollers out of her hair as she looked from one to the other.

"What are you guys doing here?" She finger-combed through her hair, then pointed to Olivia's legs. "What happened to you?"

Cas noticed the belt marks on her legs for the first time. "There's been a fire. It's a long story. Apparently the police didn't reach you."

Olivia followed them into the front room, which had a new smell of chrome and Herculon. It was two stories high with a balcony overhanding one side. Maybe Arthur was upstairs. The first dawn light poured into the high windows. The carpet and walls were white; even the sofa was white and long and inviting. She plopped down with an enormous sigh. She had made it. Safe!

Cas dropped into a chair while Margaret Mary stood over him, still open-mouthed with astonishment. She asked, "Police? What about the fire? My God, Olivia honey, are those burns?"

Cas sprawled out with his legs stretched before him. He said, "I don't know much about it. Abilene police phoned me to come get Olivia. Apparently she was the only one to get out."

"You mean the Llewellyns are—"

"Dead!" Olivia said with finality.

Her aunt rushed over and knelt, clutching her close. "Oh you poor little…How did it--?"

Olivia wriggled free. "If you don't mind, I don't want to talk about it."

Cas felt the whiskers on his face. "Yeah, we've had a rough night. I need to crash for a few hours and then get back home." He looked around. "Nice place. Is there a spare room?"

"Not a bedroom. There's only my bedroom, but—"

"Then I'll have to borrow it for about four hours. Could you go out and get us a few things? I'll need a clean shirt and some underwear, and the kid is going to need a passel of stuff." He fished out his money clip and tossed her some bills. "From the smell of her, I'd suggest you trash everything she's wearing.

Things were beginning to dawn on Margaret Mary, whose eyes had grown wide and fearful. Vestiges of yesterday's mascara clung to her lashes. Olivia was near enough to see the tiny red vessels in the whites of her eyes. Margaret Mary looked from her brother to her niece and said, "You're— not planning to leave her *here*?"

Olivia studied the gallery overhead. Her aunt had said there was only one bedroom. "Where does Arthur sleep?"

"Arthur?" Margaret Mary's voice broke in a croak.

Cas was saying, "That's what the Abilene cop told me to do; pick up Olivia and bring her here."

Margaret Mary leaned against the wall, staring at him in shocked disbelief. "But *why?*" She looked at Olivia again and said, "Arthur? Sleep here? No, he never has."

Olivia began to get the sick feeling that Arthur was nowhere around. Tears welled up and her chin began to quiver despite all she could do. Margaret Mary came and sat beside her and put an arm around her. This time Olivia didn't resist. She leaned against her aunt and sobbed.

Margaret Mary held her close and said, "Oh my gosh, you poor kid! Just don't worry, angel; of course you can stay here! At least until…." She turned to Cas. "Call Kathleen and Frances. They'll know what to do."

Cas stood and wobbled, shaking his head. "Later. I'm beat." He reached down to pat Olivia and squinted at his sister. "What happened to your eyebrows? Didn't you used to have eyebrows?"

"Don't be smart. I haven't done my face yet."

"There was nothing wrong with your old eyebrows."

"There was everything wrong. They were in the wrong place."

"Or your hair, either, for that matter. Nothing wrong with the hair you grew up with."

Margaret Mary was growing testy. "That's enough, Mr. Porcelain Caps, whose life is now a lounge act from Vegas. Now get off my case!" She released Olivia and glanced at the chrome wall clock. "Guess I'll have to phone in sick." She picked up Olivia's feet and removed her shoes, then laid her feet on the couch. "Stretch out here, darlin'. I'll bring you an afghan. Soon as the stores open, I'll get you something clean to wear."

She turned to Cas. "Have you eaten?"

"Yes, but I'll need a second breakfast in about four hours, to fuel me for the trip home."

Olivia was already drowsing when Margaret Mary brought a fluffy white throw to tuck around her. She opened her eyes a slit and asked, "Margaret Mary? Where's Arthur?"

"Go to sleep," Margaret Mary said with only the barest hesitation. "We'll talk about it later."

35

Olivia woke, sinews complaining, to the rustle of shopping bags. A blond sun streamed in the vast two-story windows, checkering walls and floor with huge crosshatches. She heard her aunt drop a paper bag onto the kitchen counter before she came into the front room, plopped into a chair and kicked off her heels. She began rummaging in another bag labeled Walmart, pulling out a man's shirt and a package of underwear. Then she noticed Olivia watching and grinned. The grin transformed her hard, painted features to girlishness.

"Oh good. You're awake. I hope to God I bought the right size. I looked in your jacket and saw size ten. But everything I got for you looks huge. Maybe we can go shopping again later for a few more things." She shrugged off her coat to reveal a black jumpsuit with gold scrollwork trim.

She tossed the bag onto the end of the sofa and said, "I'll take Cas's shirt upstairs and see if I can roust him out of bed. Meantime, you can take a quick bath. There's a john down that way, and a new toothbrush in the drawer." She pointed to a door at the end of a short hall off the front room.

Olivia peered into the bag. No cord jeans. As long as she lived, she'd probably have another pair of pink cords like her favorites that she'd left behind. But they were a small price to pay to get to Arthur and Daddy. She fished around and found some socks, underpants, jeans, and a sweatshirt that said Party Animal. Dorky, but passable.

Margaret Mary, wearing somewhat lower heels, clattered back down the stairs and headed for the kitchen, rustling bags, running water, slapping something into the microwave and beeping buttons. She called around the corner, "Better hustle with the bath, babe. I'll have Border Breakfasts heated up soon."

Overhead, Cas came out of the bedroom and leaned over the gallery rail. His stubble had grown in four hours. He said, "*Walmart*? You actually got me a shirt from *Walmart*?"

His sister stomped out of the kitchen holding a spatula, her long hair bristling wilder than ever. "Look, bucko: you told me to wake you in four hours: that's ten o'clock. Now what other store is open before ten, I'd like to know? Plus, you said have breakfast ready when you got up. What do you think I am, a freaking magician?" She stalked into the kitchen and came out again immediately, eyes flashing.

"And anyway, what's so damn terrible about that shirt, I'd like to know? No designer label? God! You've always been such an insecure little prick! You and Quentin!"

But he was already running the water upstairs. She seemed to remember Olivia and shrugged. "Pardon the French. If you want any hot water, you'd better beat feet to the other john, kiddo."

Olivia was better motivated by the smell of sausage in the microwave. She grabbed up the new clothes and hurried down the hall to the bath. Her aunt called after her, "God, your legs! Those don't look like burns!"

She quickly shut and locked the bathroom door. She flipped on the light and saw that the wallpaper was bronze with black stripes, and the fixtures were black. "Cool!" she said, turning the tub water on full blast and hurriedly stripping off her clothes. The packet of letters fell to the floor, reminding her about her money. She took off her shoe and found it was safe, too.

A bottle of bubble bath on the tub's edge summoned up Momma's dictum that a good soak actually washes the soul. She poured only a small amount into the water, afraid Margaret Mary would miss it. Gingerly she lowered herself into the bath, wincing as its warmth touched her legs.

When she finished her leisurely soak, she dried her legs carefully so as not to disturb the fragile wounds. As she feared, the rough jeans rubbed against them and made it almost impossible to walk naturally. She put the letters and money in her back pockets and pulled the sweatshirt well down over them.

Cas and Margaret Mary were talking in the dining alcove off the front room; maybe they'd be too busy to notice her stiff walk. Since she had forgotten to bring the clean socks, she padded in barefoot with shoes in hand, rummaged in the bag for the socks, then settled on the couch to put them on. Nobody paid any attention to her. She noted that grownups often talked as if kids were too stupid to hear.

Margaret Mary was saying, "So who's the new squeeze? Another pickup from the singles' bar?"

"A psychotherapist, smart-ass," he said between bites. "And I didn't meet her in a bar; I met her at Group."

"You mean you're dating your therapist? Isn't that verboten?"

"Probably not. It happens all the time. But she's not my therapist. She was just a member of the group. Only she dropped out."

"Cured? Oh I forgot: nobody's ever cured in one of those things. It's just non-stop yak for years until your money runs out."

Cas didn't answer. Olivia could see his jaw jutting. It was smooth: he had shaved off the stubble, so that he looked more like Daddy again.

After a long tense moment, she said, "Sorry. I'm just overcome by... events."

"You never say cured," he said crossly. "That implies somebody's sick."

"Right. Analysis is a way of life. So tell me about...what's her name? Kristi?"

"There's nothing to tell. She's in a different group now, that more nearly matches her paradigm: Adult Children of Co-Dependent Step-Parents. It's better that we're not in the same group, so we can each examine our own reality and resolve our individual issues without peer pressure."

"So in this never-ending round of group musical chairs, what's the group you're in now?"

He hesitated, as if he was trying to decide whether it would do any good to try to converse with a moron. Olivia knew the look well. He said, "DFA: Dysfunctional Families Anonymous."

She let her fork clatter to her plate. "I resent that! Anyway, how can that be? You're not a family; you're just one man."

"Don't be a bitch. It's family of origin."

"That's right, call me names. You know what you need? You ought to join Spoiled Brats Anonymous, you little prick!"

Olivia surmised from the rigid hunch of Uncle Cas's shoulders that he was pissed. It was like Daddy and Momma all over again. She took her time tying her shoes, figuring there was no need to barge in on a fight.

Finally he seemed to regain his composure and with it, the initiative. He looked up and met her gaze with a challenge. "You know, you really shouldn't talk like that in front of a kid."

"I'm sorry. I wasn't making fun of you."

"You were trivializing."

"I didn't mean to. Look, let's skip it." She got up to pour more coffee. "Have you ever noticed we get along fine when there's just two of us, but if even one other family member is present, no matter who—"

"I know," he said.

"Speaking of which, before you woke up, I phoned Frances and Kathleen…" She seemed to remember. "Olivia! I meant to have a look at your legs when you got out of the bath."

Cas turned, saw Olivia's wet head, and frowned. "You mean you have a second bathroom downstairs and no second bedroom?"

"Oh there's a *room* down here, but I don't use it as a bedroom."

He got up and headed for the hall. "I thought so. You are one piece of work, Mother Superior. I *knew* this place looked larger than that."

She rushed after him, grabbing for his arm. "Don't go in there. It's a mess."

But he had already opened the door. Olivia got up to look, too.

Margaret Mary said, "It's my work-out room. I've got a cross trainer and an excercycle…"

A couple of exercise machines covered with sheets were pushed against the wall. The room was bare of furniture except for a low table in the center. Cas went in and leaned over the table, studying the several objects lying on it. He picked up one small item. "What's this?"

"Put it down. You don't understand."

Olivia moved closer so she could see what appeared to be a small roundish figurine.

He turned it over. "Is this some kind of…"

She sounded resigned. "It's a Willendorf goddess replica, if you must know. I got it through a catalog."

He pointed at the floor. "And what's the significance of this?" Olivia noticed a strip of braided purple yarn circling the floor close to the walls.

Margaret Mary took the figuring from him and returned it to the table, then she ushered them both out and back down the hall. "Okay, I'll tell you. But you have to put aside your prejudices and preconceived notions. This was to be my exercise room, but now it's my rituals room… for Wicca."

He grinned. "Just can't get entirely away from religion, can you?"

"I have to believe in *something*, or life would be too grisly. You think your precious group isn't your congregation?"

He shrugged. "I'm cool with that. Does this mean you've given up all hope of finding a man and settled for a coven?"

"I'm not in a coven. I just do it by myself. I don't need bunches of 'peers' around to 'validate' me, like some people I know. Besides, 'finding a man,' as you so crudely put it, has nothing to do with feeding my spirit." The edge returned to her voice briefly, then she became more gentle and nudged Olivia toward a chair at the kitchen table. "Sit down, babe, and have some sausage. You like Border Breakfasts? It's the quickest thing I could think of, but I could make something else."

Olivia nodded and watched with satisfaction as her aunt piled food onto her plate. She looked from one of them to the other. "So what's Wicca?"

"A very ancient practice." Her aunt sounded hurried and defensive. "It's all about honoring nature and the Earth."

Olivia brightened. "Oh yeah! Momma must've been that!"

Cal said, "Your mom was just an aging flower child." Then he saw her face. "Not aging. I didn't mean that. Let's just say that your parents were kissed by the Sixties and never got over it."

She looked up at her aunt's bright painted mouth, now slightly smudged. "Were you kissed by the Sixties too?"

Cas answered for her. "Your aunt and I were too young to know what the Sixties were about. To which I might add, thank God." He turned to his sister, commanding, like Granddaddy Llewellyn. "Maybe Kathleen and Frances have some extra furniture. Or you can call Abbey Rents and get a bed over her for that room."

"I don't know why I should be the one—"Margaret Mary cut her own thought short. She buttered a tortilla with quick angry swipes.

"You're the logical one. You have fewer responsibilities. Besides, you're the one the police have been trying to reach."

They all ate in a stifling silence. Olivia's heart was beginning to pick up its pace. She didn't want to be stuck here if Arthur wasn't around. It seemed as good a time as any to ask. "Nobody has told me yet, where *is* Arthur, anyway?"

Uncle Cas nodded at his sister, deferring to her. She took her time chewing and swallowing before she said, "He's in a sort of hospital right now. In Austin."

Hospitals were where people went to die…but then, *she* had been in a hospital once, and *she* was okay. Maybe Austin was just far, far away. Maybe that was it.

"How'd he get there? Did a dog bite him?"

"He…isn't exactly sick." Margaret Mary picked busily at her food, keeping mascaraed lashes lowered. Then her face brightened, and she looked up, as if she'd just remembered the right answer. "It's like your Uncle Cas and his girlfriend: it's just sitting around, just a lot of talking and stuff."

Cas was about to interrupt when she hurried on. "Arthur's just been depressed, you know, sad. Very, very sad. Your dad didn't know what else to do with him…Your dad was traveling a lot, with the trial and all. There wasn't any *continuity* to Arthur's life. Your grandmother was sick, so your dad thought it was best to…send him away. Especially since Arthur was… well, fairly hostile at the time."

Olivia was trying to figure it out. "You mean he wasn't here when Grandmother died?"

"Oh yes, he was here. Your Aunt Kathleen and Uncle Mike went up to Austin and checked him out. He stayed with them until…after. Then he really wanted to go back, get the old synapses firing again. So they took him back."

Cas broke in. "Back to the State Hospital of his own accord? Get real! This kid's too smart to buy that."

Margaret Mary shrugged. "What can I say? It's true. Anyway, what else was there to do? But it gets even more bizarre. I don't understand it. He's now taking instruction in the Church from a priest up at the State Hospital." She leaned toward him with her lips curled in a sour grin. "Arthur wants to become a frigging Catholic!"

Cas reared back and chuckled, shaking his head. "That's our mom! Probably badgered the poor kid until the day she lost consciousness."

At the mention of their mother, Margaret Mary got up to clear the dishes, as if she couldn't sit still. "She must've kept it up from the grave, because he didn't until after she died."

"Do you think they brainwashed him in the loony—" He stopped short. Olivia bit into her tortilla and pretended not to hear, but she boiled with indignation.

"It was actually pathetic, in view of the fact that neither of Mom's sons saw fit to attend her funeral: Arthur claimed he was impressed by how

Catholic families rally around in a crisis. He's always so analytical: said Catholic men were so dependable, such good fathers." She laughed. The sound was not a happy one.

Cas said, "Mike's a good man. Arthur was doubtless treated very well at Kathleen and Mike's. It probably made him wistful for what he never had."

Margaret Mary turned on the water full force. Olivia was having difficulty swallowing her food. Her aunt was muttering so low that Olivia could hardly hear her above the running water. "It's not about religion at all. Poor little bastard! He's had such a rotten…"

She looked over at Olivia then turned off the water. She stood drumming her long fingernails on the cabinet, shaking her head slowly. Her hair was stiff and frizzy, so that the whole mass moved at once. Finally she said, "I guess I could get a rollaway. But there's my job, my friends, my social life, my—my rituals. There'd have to be school for her…"

"It wouldn't be for long. Anyway, Quentin will be out soon. He can get a housekeeper. It's his responsibility, after all."

This was not time to shrink into the shadows. Olivia piped up. "I want to go where Arthur is! When's Arthur coming home?"

Margaret Mary faced Cas, their gazes meeting over Olivia's head. He was too grave to suit Olivia. "But there's also that."

Her huge silver earrings clanked noisily with each vehement shake of her head. "Oh no! I can't! I absolutely refuse! I have a life, Caswell; I cannot take all this on!"

He got up and went over to the sink to give her a brotherly hug. She tried to hold him off with an elbow, but he pulled her close, bumping her against his side and squeezing repeatedly as if by sheer force he could convince her. "Hang cool, Meg. Just deal with one thing at a time. Today it's just you and Livvie. How hard can that be?"

Olivia shook off the familiar feeling of rejection. They needn't bother arguing. She wasn't planning to hang around. As soon as she figured out how to get to Austin, she'd be out of here, keeping one step of everybody, even the Llewellyns. In case they even cared.

36

Before Uncle Cas left to return to Fort Worth, he assured Olivia that he wouldn't be going anywhere near Austin. She had planned to hide out in the back seat and hitch a ride if he were. To allay her disappointment, he suggested that she write to Arthur, so she borrowed a pencil and paper from Margaret Mary as soon as he left.

But it was several hours before she had time to write. There were expeditions to the rental store, a couple of clothing stores, and a sandwich shop for a late lunch. They were both weary when they reached home and needed a nap. Since Olivia's furniture was due to be delivered, Margaret Mary took the sofa so as to hear the doorbell, while Olivia went upstairs. She planned to write Arthur before she went to sleep, but she dropped off before she had written a word.

She woke to the sound of voices which she was almost positive did not belong to deliverymen, because some of them were feminine. She stepped out of her aunt's bedroom to the gallery and peeked through the rails onto the living room below. Several people were sitting around; she figured they must be The Aunts, because they were speaking in low tones, probably about her. Two men, sipping drinks, took no active part in the conversation: The Uncles, no doubt, both still in their dark business uniforms, both well-groomed, lean-faced, and tanned, younger than Daddy.

She went back into the bedroom and switched on the lamp, even though the late afternoon sun sifted generously through the blinds. She sat at the desk and took her time with Arthur's letter before she went downstairs to face the roomful of strangers. They probably figured they were deciding her fate, but they could stuff it.

Armed with her letter, she took a determined deep breath and walked straight to Margaret Mary, ignoring the others as if they didn't exist. She handed her the sheet of paper and said, "I need this mailed right away."

Her aunt said, "Aren't you going to say hello to Aunt Francie and Uncle Hig, Aunt Kathleen and Uncle Mike?"

The Aunts squealed in phony delight and jumped up to hug her. *What a crock.* At least The Uncles didn't dry to bullshit her. They waited until The Aunts had calmed down. Neither got up or tried to hug her, although both smiled pleasantly. She barely gave them a glance and wouldn't have recognized them if she met them outside this room. They were nothing to her. Nobody was going to make any decisions about her except Daddy, and there was no use investing time getting to know more relatives.

Margaret Mary looked at the letter and said in a strained voice, "Livvie, go into the kitchen and get yourself something to drink." But Olivia knew the drill.

As she left the room, she turned only enough to see the letter pass to Aunt Francie. Olivia, with skills honed from years of practice, banged around the kitchen loud enough to put them off guard, but not so noisily that she couldn't heat.

Margaret Mary said, "You see where this is leading? I can't do this, not both of them!"

Uncle Hig said, "Who's the executor of the Llewellyn estate? Didn't Faye have a sister?"

"Forget it," Margaret Mary said. "At Faye's funeral they treated me like...well, like I had lice. No one spoke to me. I wasn't even invited back to the house. Wasn't allowed to get anywhere close to the children. Besides, the sister has some kind of debilitating pancreas thing. Anyway, it's not the money."

Uncle Mike broke in. "Arthur's not a bad kid...Honey maybe *we* could—"

Aunt Kathleen interrupted. "Oh no! Not on your life! He's too near our own girls' ages. It wouldn't be a healthy arrangement.

Margaret Mary lowered her voice. "Anyway, you read it." Olivia rattled the ice tray to reassure her to go on. "She wants them to be together."

Francie said, "It's Quentin's responsibility. He should..."

Kathleen said, "Shouldn't he be out by now, Hig?"

"I heard he refused to apply for parole," Hig said.

"Can he do that?" Kathleen rang out in astonishment. "Why would he do such a thing?"

Margaret Mary said, "Probably depressed. He carries that extra load of guilt reserved for the oldest son. He's punishing himself before God gets the chance."

Hig said, "Guilt is a luxury not available to a family man." He turned to his brother-in-law. "Could you make some inquiries tomorrow, find out his status?"

Mike sounded reluctant. "I suppose I could."

"What do you have in mind?" Francie asked her husband.

Hig said, "I think it's time Quentin faced his family responsibilities squarely, and there's no better place to confront him than where he can't possibly walk away."

Margaret Mary filled in her him. "Confront him...with his children, you mean."

Olivia brightened, deciding The Uncles might be worth cultivating. She took a slurp of soda and left her glass on the counter before she joined them in the living room.

"Where's my letter?" She looked from one to the other of them, enjoying thrir sudden discomfort. Uncle Mike handed it to her. She noticed his hand had freckles like Donnie's.

"Here you go. Hope you don't mind my reading it. It's a fine letter."

Olivia read it over, just to make sure nobody had changed anything:

"Dear Arthur,

"I am finally in Galveston but you're not here. I came to get our family put back together again. I am never going to live with our other grandparents again. They are too mean and strict, especially Granddaddy whipping me with a belt. I came to Galveston to be with you forever. Are you coming here or do you want me to come there? And then we will go get Daddy.

"Love, Olivia

"P.S. Grandmother didn't tell me about Peggy being dead or I would of come."

She handed it back to Margaret Mary. "If you mail it now, when will he get it?"

"Day after tomorrow," she said. "I notice you didn't tell him about the fire or what happened to your other grandparents."

Olivia gulped. "Oh yeah....Well, I didn't want to make him sad."

201

"Probably very wise," she said.

Uncle Mike rose and took the letter from his sister-in-law. "Get me the name and number of his counselor, if you still have it."

She nodded and went upstairs. Olivia glanced at Kathleen and was surprised to see her glaring at her husband. Affecting innocence, she said, "Are you mad at Uncle Mike?"

Kathleen recovered her composure but didn't take her eyes off her husband. "No, sweetie, I just think your Uncle Mike may be getting involved in something that's none of his affair."

Francie spoke up. "It's all of our affair, whether we like it or not. We can't leave our sister to muddle through this alone. Anyway, as the next oldest, Mike's the head of the family now that Dad's dead and Quentin is…"

"Mike's an in-law!" Kathleen protested. "He shouldn't have to shoulder that burden."

Margaret Mary, returning from her room, laughed. "Would you have Caswell do it?" She handed Mike an envelope and a slip of paper.

Hig said, "Don't be so hard on your baby brother. He did go for Olivia, after all. Drove all night on a moment's notice."

"And proceeded to dump—" Margaret Mary stopped abruptly and turned to Olivia while the others shifted uncomfortably. "How about some pizza, kid?"

Olivia shrugged, feeling heat behind her eyes. "Fine by me." She swallowed and changed the subject. "Did my bed get here?"

"Not yet. Par for the course. Deliverymen are never…."

At that moment the doorbell sounded. Olivia ran to the window and saw the rental company truck parked at the curb. It was almost dusk. A whole day had been wasted, and she was no nearer to finding Arthur and Daddy.

"They're here!" She hurried to fling open the door.

The others rose to leave, and Francie gave Margaret Mary a hug that hiked her jumpsuit belt up in back. "Don't worry, little sis. We're in this together."

"I hope so!" She straightened the tight jumpsuit, looking flushed and very young. "My boss won't tolerate many more days like today."

Mike directed the delivery men to the spare room and said over his shoulder, "Warn him that someday soon you'll have to go to Huntsville."

Huntsville, where Daddy was in prison?

She exploded. "Why me, in God's name? *You're* the lawyer!"

"Don't misunderstand. I'll go." He looked around. "We could all go, overwhelm him with numbers. But the only one he'd listen to is Olivia."

Olivia knew she was missing something important. She remembered how Ramona could tell when something good was about to happen by the tone of their voices, how she'd run in circles wagging her tail. She felt the same now. Things would be all right. With everyone helping, nothing could possibly go wrong.

Her aunt brought her gently to earth the next day by saying, "You have to realize that Arthur may not be well enough to come home."

"Arthur's well." Olivia was sitting in the middle of her aunt's bed, watching her get ready for work. Maybe living with her could be almost as good as with Momma. But she didn't believe it for a minute.

It had been decided that Olivia would not enroll in school until after the trip, and that while Margaret Mary was at work, she would spend her days in the care of Kathleen's and Mike's housekeeper. To avoid a delay of several weeks while Mike would be out of the country, the trip to Huntsville had to be undertaken on the following weekend if Mike could get the paperwork ready.

The three left Friday morning and drove about three hours to Huntsville, north of Houston. The prison farm, a complex of white frame houses that didn't look like a prison, sat on an expanse of plowed prairie just off the highway east of the main prison. Uncle Mike found the right building as if he'd been there before. He had explained that Quentin was not housed behind "The Walls" with the hardened criminals, but in a special unit for white-collar convicts. These prisoners were given the privilege of caring for the prison farm.

Olivia and Margaret Mary waited in the car until Mike, pink-faced from a sudden warm spell, came for them, shedding his suit coat and loosening his tie as he walked. He patted his briefcase and said, "All taken care of. I had to pull rabbits out of a hat to manage it." He pointed them to an entrance on the right of the nearest building. "You can go in without me."

An attendant came for them too soon, for Olivia realized with welling panic that she wasn't prepared, hadn't thought what to say. They were ushered into a small room lit to blistering brightness, where the only furniture was a small metal table divided by a transparent partition. Only one chair faced the partition, but Margaret Mary sat down and pulled Olivia onto her lap. Glad for her aunt's reassuring squeeze, Olivia steeled herself to look at Daddy when he was led in by a uniformed attendant. As if they weren't there, he sat down and examined the surface of the table for a while.

He was thinner than she remembered. His face was overrun with ruts. His temples were balding, and the rest of his hair, cut very short, had turned quite gray. His skin, always sheened with tan, had a dry weathered look, appropriate for the farmer he had become. His hands played restlessly with the table edge, his nails jagged and split, knuckles grimy and calloused. Occasionally he brought his hands together, working his fingers against his knuckles, kneading their roughness. She watched the movement, avoiding more than just a glance at his eyes, which seemed vague and removed. It was a look she remembered when he and Momma had an argument, when he had retreated a safe distance into himself.

He was the first to speak, sounding gruff and disconcerted. "It's like seeing Faye!" He reached to touch her before the plastic barrier stopped him.

She forgot her timidity. "Daddy," she blurted out through a sob, "I want to hug you! I want you out of here!"

It set him roaring with laughter, so that the nearby guard stirred uneasily under the blaze of lights. Olivia sank against her aunt in disappointment.

Margaret Mary shifted Olivia's weight. "I'm sure Mike has explained what we want to do, Quentin: provide these children with a home. Temporarily. Ultimately, it's not our responsibility. For their sake, we'll step in and help until you get out and can do the right thing by them."

Olivia interrupted, bubbling with plans. "We can have a real home and never have to move!" Like always, the moment she saw him, she had forgiven him everything.

Her aunt had taken on a stern nunnish manner that Olivia regretted; she didn't want to discourage Daddy from coming home. "Quentin, is it true you've come up for parole and refused to go for review?"

He jerked his head, turning a stoic profile to them. His Adam's apple was a sharp protrusion. He said curtly, sounding like the old Daddy, "It wasn't quite like that. Once Frank knows I'm free, I'll be on new assignment, no telling where."

Her tone was shot through with exasperation. "I can't believe this baloney! Quit living with your illusions, Quentin. There's no job to go back to; whatever you were doing, that's over! You'll be lucky to find work in a gas station."

He lowered his voice, eyes moving from side to side as if sweeping for mines. "Frank fired me only because it suited our purposes at the time." He leaned back with a conspiratorial smile. "I'm something of a hero in the industry. We put one over on the competition."

Olivia quit listening, caught in her devastation at his casual sloughing her aside. He rambled on as if she weren't there.

"Do you think it was a coincidence that I was located so close to Weldon? He had to believe I was no longer with Llano, that I had lifted valuable maps from them. But the maps were fake, you see, drawn up especially to throw Texoil off the scent. And the beauty of it was that he *paid* me to deliver them!"

She shook her head in disgust. "That wasn't your story on the stand."

He waved her off, eyes glittering with drive again. "You'd never understand."

Margaret Mary lost patience. "So you were just too full of scruples to put your family first, right? You abandoned them to keep the con going."

He assumed a tired tone as if he were addressing an imbecile. "You can't understand how important this is. This is so much bigger than any one person. You obviously can't think in the millions, and you'll never understand corporate manipulations. These things happen all the time. There's no shame in being involved in espionage. Nobody feels obliged to abide by things they believe are asinine. The important thing is to maintain the *company's* integrity. Thousands of stockholders are affected...."

Margaret Mary pushed Olivia off her lap and stood abruptly to leave. "Prison hasn't taught you a goddam thing, Quentin. You're still the arrogant prick you've always been!"

"Don't curse. It isn't becoming in a woman." He sat there, a weathered and graying convict, making pronouncements of authority, just like always.

Olivia swallowed hard, not understanding how things could have gone wrong so quickly. Margaret Mary grabbed her hand and pulled her out of the visitors' room.

Before the door closed, she turned for one last look at Daddy, but he had already risen. He was joking with the guard as if they had never come. In something of his cocksure camaraderie she saw a shadow of the old Daddy, working the crowd, whatever it took. It occurred to her that in her family there were always shadows of something, some other life. More than that, really: it seemed even the shadows had shadows.

37

Olivia's first visit with Daddy in over two years had rendered her limp, wrung-out with unanswered questions. She recognized traits she'd dismissed before: the single-minded devotion to career, the obsessive game of one against others, the thinly-veiled pleasure he derived from his own hatreds.

Once the three of them were back in Uncle Mike's car on their way to Austin, she easily feigned exhaustion. After several exaggerated yawns, she settled back and made the loud and regular breathing sounds of deep sleep.

For a while the adults muted their tones: his sharp and hers apologetic, so that she couldn't hear over the engine's roar. As the miles crept by, they lost caution and as Mike's impatient voice rose in anger, she caught, "... to say nothing of the disgrace he's brought on the whole family!" Olivia tightened her fists, instinctive ready to defend Daddy.

Margaret Mary's voice broke, and the catch on her handbag snapped. She blew her nose noisily, as if to make a point. "There's plenty of disgrace to go around. What about Cas? What about me? All my life I've had an uncanny knack for turning gold into flax."

"So you've both had a little trouble finding yourselves."

"We *killed* Mom!"

"Baloney! If anybody killed your mother..." He trailed off.

"Don't be afraid to say it: womanizing. Dad's running around caused me to decide to enter an order, and that was probably why Quentin studied for the priesthood. We tried to strike a bargain with God to reform Dad."

Olivia sucked in her breath and waited. The question was, had it worked for Margaret Mary?

"...and Cas turned out just like him! I'll never understand. How could one son be so much like a father who made him so miserable?"

"Nobody killed your mother, not even Quentin."

"They all loved money and position instead of people," she said. "You think that wouldn't kill any mother?"

"She was a tough old bird who lived out her allotted days."

"God was merciful, taking her before she found out Quentin had pleaded guilty to theft." She chuckled. "There I go again: me, of all people, talking about God and mercy."

"Doesn't surprise me," he said quickly. "Leaving the order doesn't make you a heathen."

"It was a lapse, figure of speech, force of habit—no pun intended. I really am left with no faith whatsoever. Or rather, 'my faith is like a starless dawn.' If our deity were less a god of progress and more a god of process… like Shiva. What is progress, anyway?"

When he didn't answer, she plunged on. "Monotheism is the culprit. It's just not symbolic of how things are."

"Oh, I don't know. What about Einstein and his Unified Field theory?"

They drove in silence until, with a hint of stubborn persistence, he said, "It's an act of Christian charity to take in your brother's children."

She snorted. "I doubt if very much charity is *ever* Christian… discounting yours, of course, doing all this legal work for someone you can barely tolerate."

He didn't deny it. "I can pave the way for him, but no one except a court can force him to assume his responsibilities."

The engine hummed along, almost lulling Olivia to sleep, until she heard her aunt say, "The last time I heard from Faye, even knowing she was dying, she was still battling religion. She told me if she had her life to live over, she'd keep her mouth shut more. Said she'd 'be more humble and reticent,' is how she put it. Why, do you suppose?"

He laughed. "You consider those Christian traits?"

"Well, you know: 'Blessed are the friggin' meek.'"

They arrived in Austin by mid-afternoon, but there was no time to stop for a drink. They drove directly out North Guadalupe to the State Hospital, a pleasant collection of old and new buildings resembling a college set on a large plot of land shaded by ancient pecan trees. Mike pulled in at the first building, an old stone edifice with a long flight of steps leading to solid double doors, over which was carved the date 1879. Compared to the new buildings, it looked like a poor but venerable relative. Mike said it was the administration building.

He got out, explaining that he would present the papers which Quentin had signed. He directed his sister-in-law toward a tall contemporary building down the drive.

"Take the car and go on down to see Arthur. He's expecting you." He looked into the back seat and flashed his big Irish grin at Olivia. "But you, young lady, will be a complete surprise!"

Margaret Mary drove to the indicated building and parked in the gravel lot under the shade of a huge oak. Overhead, a noisy flock of grackles scolded them. Olivia considered hurling a piece of gravel at them but thought better of it on the chance that God was watching. She's missed out on what Margaret Mary said about whether her deal with God worked. Maybe her own deal was still working. Hadn't she gotten herself baptized and prayed in the closet? Still, with all the people in the world, God must've made hundreds of other deals.

Inside, a burly attendant led them to a sitting room with a large mirror on the wall. Her aunt stood before it and straightened her hair, then leaned down and whispered, "Don't scratch yourself or pick your nose. That might be a two-way mirror."

When Arthur was ushered in, Olivia gasped in surprise. At fifteen, he was as tall as a man and handsome in a pasty-faced way. He looked so like Daddy that her heart turned over. There was something too of Donnie, in his high intelligent brow. She had the strangest sensation of nested images, like looking into a mirror at a mirror, on back into oblivion.

Mostly, he looked like Daddy, except that he was hunched over, apologetic for his height, or maybe stooped from multiple small cripplings. He kept his head lowered, only darting looks at them. He couldn't quite manage a smile, even when he saw her.

She hung back while Margaret Mary, one foot lifted behind with her high-heeled shoe dangling, hugged him awkwardly and went on in a saccharin falsetto about how tall he had grown. Still bubbling, she said, "Look who I've brought!" and beckoned Olivia forward.

Olivia approached him slowly, as if he were a feral creature she didn't want to frighten. The attendant still hovered nearby, as if Arthur might bolt at any minute and attack her. Her hand shook, something Arthur obviously noticed, for he relaxed and watched her hand travel up his sleeve and come to rest on his chest. The attendant and Margaret Mary backed discretely away.

His top shirt button was undone, and she was surprised to see a lone scraggly black hair. His arms hung limp, oversized wrist bones protruding from flopping sleeves. She reached up for his cheek, the blameless face of her dear brother. Slowly he lifted a vacant gaze to hers. His eyes, once so darkly blue, had faded. The fragile skin around them was almost blue; in fact, a tiny blue vein pulsed below one eye.

She swallowed twice. "Arthur? Say something. It's me, Livvie."

Only a flicker of the old Arthur glinted through. When she thought she couldn't stand the silence any longer, he spoke in a voice cracked from disuse. "Like Momma. You look like Momma."

She thought of the drab, dragged-out woman who had sat out on the stump in the midday sun waiting for mail from Daddy; thought of the brave fierce soul kneeling beside a grave, explaining with such earnestness about Donnie and Mother Earth. She thought about the tube-laced wraith in the ICU smelling of death, croaking through cracked lips, "Remember how we used to sing." Still, she wanted desperately to be like Momma; wanted to make Arthur sing again.

She put her arms around his waist and squeezed tightly. He hardly noticed; she wasn't connecting, but she would not be put off. She took his hand in both of hers and jerked hard, pulling him down so that she could kiss his cheek. His face was cold, like Momma's death-hand.

Very near tears, she wailed, "Come back, Arthur. We need to be a family again!"

It seemed too much for him to take in. He said again in wonder, "You look like Momma." He shook his head slowly and added, "The same things keep happening over and over and over."

Another man wearing a stethoscope around his neck had come in and was speaking to Margaret Mary, telling her it was all right to take Arthur out on the grounds. Margaret Mary stood very tall, sucking in her stomach and fiddling with her blouse button, shifting from side to side, probably figuring she looked sexy when really she looked as if she needed to pee.

The doctor was smiling at Margaret Mary, saying, "He has shown no recent signs of being a threat to himself or anyone else. He's been well enough for some time to go home, only he had nowhere to go, no one to take responsibility. Since he's under-aged...."

Their aunt eventually followed them outside, somehow having allowed the doctor to slip the noose. They found a bench in the shade at the side of the building, where they could keep watch for Uncle Mike. When they were settled with Arthur in the middle, he looked questioningly at his aunt.

"So what's the deal?" He sounded, at last, like the old Arthur.

Olivia piped up, "We can live with Margaret Mary, and Uncle Mike's going to get Daddy out, and we can get a house and be a family again."

His pale eyes showed a flicker of interest before they shut her out. He folded his arms across this chest. They stared out across the green expanse where people strolled or lay on the lawn under the ancient trees. Olivia couldn't tell if they were patients or staff or visitors. His heavy sigh rose from some private despond.

Margaret Mary said, "Something wrong?"

He appeared to be grappling with a decision. "It's a welfare state within these grounds, a great leveler. You can't tell staff from patient. If you want to work, they'll give you a job cleaning apartments in the doctors' building, or bricking around a boiler, or working in the pea-shelling plant where they bring the vegetables from the hospital farm. I worked there until it got monotonous."

He might as well be giving a commercial for a cruise. He was talking over her to Margaret Mary. "You can go in for crafts. Nobody censures what you do. If you want to play tennis and there are already four on the court, you can grab a racquet and join them anyway. Nobody complains. Nobody *thinks* in here. They have dances...and style goes. If you want to sing, you can." He turned toward Olivia, "But I don't want to sing."

"You haven't sung since Momma died," she said.

His gaze slid away to the grounds. "They have a good library. I've been reading Shakespeare." He turned to Olivia again and said in wonder, "There's an Olivia in *Twelfth Night*. She lost *her* brother, too...See? The same things keep happening over and over."

He frowned, pondering his own thoughts before continuing. "If we hadn't been so smart, we would've been happier. People who aren't inquisitive get along better. Maybe Donnie..." He shifted quickly and said to his aunt, "Sometime you ought to come over to the canteen and see the paintings. Know why they're so good? Because nobody judged them. Creativity thrives here."

Olivia was thinking about Daddy, and apparently so was Arthur. He said, "Maybe prison is like this place. Could be it's better than being on the outside. Freud says people are extremely reluctant to give up what gives them pleasure."

Margaret Mary said, "Are you saying you don't want to leave here?"

He frowned, considering. "You don't have to protect yourself here, don't have to lie. Lying is a tool of the unempowered out there. When the powerful lie, that's called betrayal. Maybe Momma was the smart one; she lived in a state of abject vulnerability. She used to say the universe was her protection."

What a crock, Olivia thought. *And the universe let her down.* A warm tear tricked into the crease by her nose.

Nobody said anything except the noisy grackles, whose chatter escalated to fill the silence. Olivia studied the stone arches of a building across the way, with their repeating design of sun and shade, sun and shade, falling on the veranda wall beyond. Over and over, sun and shade, sun and shade, clear to the corner of the building, beyond which she couldn't see.

From out on the lawn, a mock tussle between two young men rolling on the grass distracted her, until quite suddenly the two got up and raced off out of sight. They were only pretending to fight. Maybe they were patients pretending to be visitors, or maybe they were doctors…except that *surely* doctors never pretended. It was hard to know what was real in that place.

Arthur sighed. "Then there's my instruction."

Margaret Mary's head shot up, but she quickly recovered her nonchalance. "Your religious instruction?"

"This is something I want to do—have ever since I stayed with Aunt Kathleen and Uncle Mike. I saw how they treated each other, so different."

"Maybe you should've known your 'good' Catholic grandfather," she said in a dry voice.

"I have a sponsor, a couple from the local parish. The first Sunday of Lent I was brought into the church and accepted as a catacumen. But I have to continue my instruction."

Margaret Mary cleared her throat. "They know you're a patient here, don't they?"

"Yes. They work with lots of people here."

"And that you're under age?"

"I don't know what you mean by that. I'm fifteen. Is that okay with you?"

Olivia could see the effort it took for her aunt to nod so enthusiastically. Great wisps of bleached hair shook loose, and when she brushed them back, damp roots appeared from the beads of perspiration at her hairline.

In her best sporting heroic manner, she forced a robust, "Sure! That's fine by me. You can continue all that from my place. It'll work out just the same."

Olivia shook her head in contempt. The woman had so much to learn about using her wits, things she should have been born knowing. It was hard to believe she was related.

His thin features twisted into a quizzical tartary grin. When he shrugged, it was noticeable that his collar was much too large for his scrawny neck. At the sight of his bony clavicle, Olivia was swamped with pity. He said, "Oh sure! Like *you're* going to oversee my Catholic instruction!"

"I never said that. Look: if you're doing this for yourself and not just as an act of rebellion against Quentin…."

Olivia looked back toward where Uncle Mike should be coming, but he was nowhere in sight yet. She was tired and hot, and knotted with mounting panic about where this talk was leading. Certain things were sacred, and Arthur was picking at them, trying to tear them down.

Tears welled up and she heard her own fury burst out at a startled Arthur. "What's the *matter* with everybody? Can't anybody listen to *me* for a change? What about *me*? I need a home and a family! I need *you*, Arthur. Don't you need me at all?"

Then inspiration struck, and she said, "*Surely* you don't plan to turn sixteen in this place!"

Bingo.

38

They returned to Galveston the next day in a restrained silence, which Olivia tried only sporadically to break. As they left the bosomy beauty of the hill country for the flat coastal plain, Arthur's countenance grew ever more sullen. But once they crossed the causeway over the lazy lapping dazzle of bay water, he suddenly came to life, delivering a typical glum assessment, "Living on an island breeds insular attitudes. That's the big problem."

The usual primal serenity evoked by the smell of seawater waned as they turned south into the wind, and the sound of hard-driven waves of the Gulf knuckling the granite rocks below the seawall registered with Olivia as dread. Everything teemed with flux: intermittently the warm March sun disappeared behind clouds shifting low and grey. As they passed the first of several cemeteries, she remembered Cas's comment about island dwellers being unable to avoid confronting their graveyards. She had expected to be happy with Arthur home, but instead she felt uneasy and faintly nauseous. Arthur, almost sixteen, had changed.

Margaret Mary had been instructed to check in at the University of Texas Health Science Center to get Arthur plugged into out-patient therapy support. She skipped work on Monday morning to present his papers at the appropriate office in the psychiatric wing. Then she drove them to register them both in school. High school convened thirty minutes before elementary school, so Arthur was delivered first. When she saw that the parking lot was filled, she pulled into the front loading zone and stopped at the curb. With apprehension, Olivia got out with the others.

As they approached the school entrance, a sour campus policeman limped up to intercept them and barked, "You'll have to move that vehicle. No parking in a fire lane at any time."

Margaret Mary did not smile, did not suck in her stomach, or wiggle or shift from side to side as she had done with the dishy doctor. Olivia watched her shrink and become shy and colorless as a wren. Her quavering voice sounded like a whiney child. "But there's no place else to park and I have to register this boy for classes."

"The boy can't enter by the front door," he barked, never looking in Arthur's direction. "He pointed a one-jointed forefinger toward the side door. "He has to go through that metal detector like everybody else. And you're not allowed to leave a car at the curb unattended under any circumstances!"

She froze and took it all in before she drew up and looked down her nose past his mutilated finger. "Did you say metal detector? Like, for *weapons?*" Without waiting for an answer, she grasped both children by their arms and jerked them around toward the car, saying loud enough for the policeman to hear, "This is obviously not the place for us!"

Olivia, leaning over the back seat, felt an exhilarating sense of hope. "Does this mean we're not going to school?"

"Arthur's not going *there*, that's for damn sure!"

From his seat in front, Arthur remained passive, but his shoulders straightened. Olivia watched the backs of his ears for any sign of a grin.

Margaret Mary said, "Your school won't be like that, Liv." Olivia leaned back to sulk as they drove toward her imprisonment. Margaret Mary turned to Arthur. "I don't know how we'll manage tuition, but you're going to have to go to Jesuit High School, like it or not. I'm sure with Mike's pull, we can get you in."

Arthur shrugged. A siren warned them to the side of the street. Margaret Mary waited until an ambulance had raced past them before she continued.

"Maybe if everyone pitches in each month until Quentin gets out…"

Arthur pointed toward the elementary school directly ahead. "Hey! That's where the ambulance stopped."

Margaret Mary slammed on her brakes, rolled down the window, and yelled at some children running toward the flashing ambulance lights. "What's happening?" When no one paid any attention, she eased the car forward, but the street swarmed with onlookers who ignored her honking horn. Two women dragging reluctant children bore toward them down the middle of the street, coming from the direction of the school. Margaret Mary tried again. "Is somebody hurt?" she called to them.

"Knife fight in the school yard," one woman said, scarcely looking up. "We're getting out of here!"

Margaret Mary put her head on the steering wheel. Olivia watched as the small body of a child was loaded into the ambulance.

"He's not dead," she said. "I saw him waving."

Arthur said, "It's not a he. It's a girl. She's got on nerdy pink tennis shoes."

Margaret Mary raised her head but seemed lost. They watched the scene until the ambulance pulled away and the street cleared, leaving only a knot of the curious standing at the curb rehashing the event. She sighed. "That's two for two. I must've missed the handbook that covers this." She turned the car back toward home.

Olivia said, "So does this mean I'm not going to school either?"

Her aunt's laugh was more of a snort. "Are you kidding? I can imagine how long you'd last on the playground with that mouth of yours!"

"So am I going to Jesuit school, too?"

"That's a boys' high school. You'll go to St. Anne's, where at least they don't go in for strip-searches, unless it's changed since I was there. I can't believe I'm doing this to you guys. But hey, I never promised to be Mega Mom. Anyway, you'll both get a good grounding in the three S's, that's for damn—darn sure."

"Which are?" Arthur asked.

"Sanctimony, Sacrifice, and Sin, as I recall."

Arthur said, "Mom told us the Kalahari bushmen don't even have a word for sin."

"Neither did the Greeks or Romans," their aunt said. "That's because their gods were very big on excesses.

"Once a woman named Anne Hutchinson was tried for her so-called sins, and her defense was that God's will couldn't possibly be circumvented by mere humans, so there couldn't be such a thing as sin."

"Did she win her case?" Arthur asked.

"Probably not. Maybe she shouldn't have won. God, we need *some* kind of standards. We're a people reduced to our mindless appetites."

Olivia noticed with relief that they were nearing the townhouse, so she thought it safe to ask with a note of regret, "Aren't we going to the Catholic schools now?"

"Hell—mercy no! We can't just show up. First I'll need to fish your aunts for tuition, and we have to apply formally with some references…"

Olivia grinned and gave a little bounce on the back seat, breathing in the salt breeze, hearing the happy squawks of gulls and roseate spoonbills.

Now she and Arthur could stay home and play computer games while Margaret Mary went to work. Maybe they would squeeze in several days of freedom during the delay.

A strange car was parked under wagging palms in the drive, blocking the garage entrance. "Shi—oot!" Margaret Mary said. Arthur looked around at Olivia and smirked. Their presence was taking a toll on their aunt's vocabulary.

A tall man built like a bullet with a slight paunch met them at the door with a hand towel thrown over his shoulder. For a heart-stopping moment, Olivia thought it might be Daddy, but the man was too broad-shouldered, and his head was too pointy and only scattered with fuzz. He appeared only mildly surprised to see Arthur and Olivia.

He tried to kiss Margaret Mary, but she eluded him and said, "What are you doing here?"

"Glad to see you, too," he said. He was standing in the foyer in his stocking feet, looking completely at home.

"I mean, you're not due back for another week."

"Wrong, rosebud. You've lost track. I'm due back today."

She shuffled past him into the front room and dropped onto the couch. "Oh yeah. I forgot. I've been...." She indicated the children. "Well, you can see."

The man stuck out his hand to Arthur. He had protruding lizard eyes with thick lids. "Hi Arthur. Glad you're—good to see you, man." He turned to Olivia. "I'm Gary. You must be Livvie."

She shrank from his outstretched hand. Any touch without warmth was suspect.

Margaret said to Arthur, "Would you take Olivia back to your room for a while? Gary and I need to discuss some things."

The spare room, first designated as Olivia's, had lately become Arthur's, and she had been moved upstairs to share Margaret Mary's room. She followed Arthur down the hall and shut his door, then leaned against it to listen out of habit. Arthur flopped down onto the bed and said, "Don't do that."

Olivia shushed him with a finger to her lips. "I'm trying to find out what the deal is."

"The deal is, while Gary's been gone, you hogged his space."

"You mean he *lives* here?"

"This is where he stays when he shows up in town. He's in the awl bidness in Oklahoma, which means he's about halfway up the food chain from inorganic matter."

She wasn't certain whether he referred to Gary or Daddy. "How do you know so much?"

He folded his hands behind his head, studying the ceiling, a cynical curl tightening the corner of his mouth. "He used to show up at family gatherings before Peggy died. I figured the old broad was afraid he was staying over here. She wouldn't come right out and ask. She was *so* fake!"

She motioned for him to be quiet while she turned the knob and eased the door open a crack. Gary was saying, "So where does this leave me?"

"I don't know. Guess you'll have to cast around for another trophy," Margaret Mary said.

"What the hell's that supposed to mean?"

"Every time I meet one of your friends, they go, 'Oh you're the ex-nun.' It's like the only thing you're ever told them about me."

"That's not true."

"It's like, oh she must be hot to trot, virgin territory!"

"That's not true."

"Tell me this:" Her tone was hot and rising. "Must we *always* be identified by our trauma? Like, 'Oh she's the divorcee.' Or 'She's the one coming off drug treatment.' I know what you jerks say. You sit around and mull over your chances of getting a little piece—"

"My God, this is crap! No wonder Freud was baffled."

"Why? It's very simple. All women want is to be cherished. They don't want to fight like hell and be expected to make up in bed, I'll tell you that for damn sure!"

Arthur rose and shut the door. He pulled Olivia away and plunked her into a chair. Olivia noticed his red ears and briefly wondered why. She had heard nothing significant, and by now she had a good handle on what was pertinent to their welfare.

"Is he the boyfriend?" she asked.

Arthur sneered and returned to the bed. "Naw, he's the pizza delivery man."

"Well, you never know. He doesn't look so great to me. I mean, like, he's got minimal hair and a beer gut."

"When you get to be her age, you can't be choosey."

She figured Daddy's youngest sister must be at least thirty and decided that her outlook must be very bleak indeed. "Isn't she too old to get married, anyway?"

"Not if she can hook somebody. Lots of geriatrics get married."

With alarm, she thought about Daddy: surely he would never marry. Anyway, if he came to live with Margaret Mary too, the problem would be solved. Neither of them would have to get married.

She said, "I'm not ever going to get married."

He rolled over, turning his back to her. Since he had been home, she couldn't think of a safe subject. She thought of Momma's explanation about how the family changed while Daddy was gone; how it was like the geese formation whose leader cuts through the air currents for the others for a while, then drops to the rear to coast on the airflow made by the activity of te rest. How the flock reorganizes in mid-flight and another bird takes the lead. Arthur wasn't ready to be lead goose, nor, apparently, was Margaret Mary. Daddy could never be counted on for long. Then she thought of a solution and brightened.

"Maybe Daddy could marry Josephine, if we could find her."

He turned over, laughing. "Jesus! Why the crap would he want to marry Josephine?"

"So we'd have a lead goose. So we could have a whole family without Margaret Mary. Than Gary could move back in and be her boyfriend again."

"Dad wouldn't ever marry Josephine, you dork."

"Why not?" By now she had forgiven Josephine everything.

"Because she's an Indian." After he said it he squirmed and bopped his pillow a couple of times. "Anyway, even if being an Indian's okay, she's fat. A real porker."

She tried to remember what Josephine looked like and conceded that possibly she was truly fat. "But she's nice anyway," she said stubbornly, close to tears which she was unable to justify. "And she loves us."

He sounded somewhat penitent but held onto a dark, belligerent scowl. "Anyway, people don't marry fat women, and that's just how it is."

It was a fact of which she had been unaware and could not dispute. She filed it away for future reference, recalling only briefly Daddy's kneading fingers against the fleshy butt of the dusky au pair they'd had when they were very young.

"Besides," he went on, "your idea of family is like out of a Sixties sit-com. Now they're made out of scraps and scum that ought to be scraped off. Who needs it?"

She fell silent, straining to hear more of the quarrel, but it appeared to be over. She stayed in Arthur's room even after Gary slammed out of the house. A heavy weight lodged in her chest as she wondered when life would ever be back to normal again. She wanted nothing more than to go upstairs and climb into Margaret Mary's bed and hide under the covers and never wake up.

39

Arthur attended his catechism class one evening the following week, but Olivia didn't wait up for him to return. The Arthur of now was not the Arthur she had conjured up during their two-year separation. He had grown up; rather, he had grown old. She took pride in her easy communication with elders, but Arthur was different. She could find no key to making connection with him.

When she heard him come home, she got out of bed and went out onto the upper gallery, sitting close to the railing so she could look down as her aunt greeted him. He was neatly dressed in the remnants of two almost identical navy suits, donations from Uncle Hig.

Margaret Mary was lying on the couch reading, but she quickly sat up and moved over, patting the cushion beside her in invitation. "How'd it go, sport?"

He ignored the invitation and went into the kitchen, commenting in passing, "Potty-training."

She chuckled and called, "Having second thoughts?"

He returned with a soda and flopped into a chair opposite. "You'd like that, wouldn't you?"

"Hey, it's no skin off my nose what you want to join, so long as it's not the Mafia."

He took a drink and thought a while. "I wish it weren't so damn much like therapy. I've had enough of that self-absorbed crap. It's like being taught to ride a tricycle when nobody needs lessons." He leaned forward with fresh earnestness. "Will you be straight with me?"

She squirmed but said, "Shoot."

"Why did you quit being a nun? Was it because of sleaze religion?"

Her laugh contained an element of relief. "Precisely which sleaze are you referring to? Televangelists?"

"Or neon billboards, or Jesus bumper stickers, or the sign on a wrecked, 'Yahweh's Wrecker Service: The God Squad.'"

She shook her head. "Nothing as distasteful as that, although maybe we don't pay enough attention to fundamentalists, Every time extremists have gained power in history, we've had tyranny. I left because they were trying to make something so simple into something so complicated. And because—" She grinned broadly as if she'd just thought of it. "To quote Dante, 'Better to reign in hell than serve in heaven.'"

"You weren't afraid of sacrificing your salvation? Isn't that what religion is all about?"

"Quite the opposite. I figure wherever there's danger, that's where your salvation is."

Olivia could see his lips moving, repeating it. She leaned back and watched him as he mulled it over, becoming so engrossed that his next question seemed to catch her off guard.

"Is that why my dad quit the priesthood?"

"I don't know if I have the right to tell you." She was so serious that Olivia held her breath, afraid she wouldn't say more. "The truth is, *you* were in the works. It was one of your father's finest hours. Made your grandparents on both sides madder'n hell."

Olivia tried to decipher his expression; it registered surprise, even shock.

Margaret Mary said, "In the South religion seeps under every door, regardless. But if you're trying to atone for Quentin's ---"

"No!" He used the semi-snarl that discussions about their father often evoked, but he quickly regained his composure. "Even though religion is something for the old to grab onto, it has brushed against my sleeve more than once—even before….Donnie. I figured it was all stop-gap, to keep from facing life as a tragedy. But I couldn't let it go."

"You're like Jacob, wrestling with the angel, hanging on and waiting for the blessing."

He sounded old and wise. Had trauma made him that way? Olivia wondered. "I wanted there to be *something:* a psychic shudder, some kind of epiphany, some mystery. But don't confuse me with someone with faith in anything except evil. Walter Benjamin called it an angel, the angel of history, about one single catastrophe that kept piling up wreckage and hurling it at his feet…."

She nodded eagerly. "It seems everybody's got a Big Bang in their life, like the beginning of everything, you know, that just keeps on resonating forever after. I see Donnie's death as the Big Bang in your family that started everything: the divorce, your mother's sickness…."

As she spoke, he began to fidget, his movements became jerky. Suddenly he slammed the can down on the table and jumped up in an explosion that set Olivia's heart banging.

"Like hell! *He* started it! It was his lies, his schemes, his ambition that caused everything! *He* was the catastrophe. *He* killed Donnie and Momma!" He was trembling from head to foot. Olivia could see fiery rims around his eyes.

Margaret Mary jumped up and touched his arm, but he jerked away. "Easy, Arthur dear. You're right. You're right. I was wrong. I was wrong." She said it over and over. She rubbed his back with a circular motion and gradually turned him toward his room, speaking in a soothing monotone while he continued to shudder and shake. He had quit shouting and allowed himself to be led away.

Olivia, sickened by the outburst, felt too heavy to move. She rested her head against a baluster and waited, listening for some other sound from down the dark hall.

When Margaret Mary returned, she glanced up and saw Olivia leaning there. Quickly she bounded up the stairs, took Olivia by the arms and lifted her to her feet. Like Arthur, Olivia allowed herself to be led away to her room. Margaret Mary closed the bedroom door and gently pushed Olivia toward the bed. After she had tucked the covers snugly around her, she sat on the bed, looking scraggly and disheveled. The short tendrils around her face that frizzed when they got damp had escaped and flew about like stray wool from a hamster cage. Still, she spoke softly, with no hint of concern, pushing the fuzz aside with an unconscious swipe. Olivia felt her own heart slow its racing.

"We must be patient with Arthur. He's been through so many changes…you, too, of course. But in case you haven't noticed, males just don't adjust as readily as females."

Olivia wanted to believe her, but she thought of Momma, always lying across the bed snarfling and carrying on before every move, while Daddy didn't seem to mind half as much.

"I think our adaptability is tied to the phases of the moon," her aunt went on chummily. "Our biological makeup equips us to cope with change. I'll explain when you're older."

"Daddy 'copes,'" Olivia said stubbornly, guessing at the meaning of the word.

"Oh, men aren't always helpless. My grandfather was a farmer, very attuned to the seasons. Farming's a noble way to live. He was an honorable man, able to handle whatever the elements dealt him. You can't help a horse to foal or work in the soil and be rigid or mean-spirited."

Olivia remembered Momma digging in the dirt, and k new it was so. In those days, Daddy never dug in the dirt. But now that he had been on a prison farm, he would be different.

She snuggled deeper into her pillow and asked drowsily, "When will my daddy be out?"

"Soon. I've been meaning to tell you, babe."

40

Olivia, occupied with strenuous end-of-school work at St. Anne's, followed by summer school make-up classes, had no time to dwell on when Daddy would finally be home. One July evening as Arthur returned from Mass, she felt suddenly expectant, as if this might be the special day. She and Margaret Mary were nibbling at their supper, trying to make it last until Arthur finally arrived, took his seat opposite them, and filled his plate.

At this range, in the artificial overhead light, Olivia could detect the blue tinge around his eye sockets, so like Daddy's. With a pang of longing, she was struck again by how many ways he resembled Daddy. Now the astonishing shadow of a mustache showed on his upper lip, compounding the resemblance. She realized that he must be shaving by now. She had allowed this passage to adulthood to slip by unremarked. She detected the unmistakable odor of cigarette smoke and glanced quickly at Margaret Mary, but her aunt only frowned into her iced tea glass.

Since the evening of his outburst, Margaret Mary had quit discussing his religious training, his father, or anything of consequence with either of them. Their lives had moved along on a steady monotonous track for too long, and the niggling devil in Olivia that demanded excitement was growing restless. She finished off her milk with a loud smack, swiped her mouth with the back of her hand and turned to her aunt.

"What's the word on Daddy? Thought you said he was supposed to get out."

Arthur's fork was poised midway to his mouth, expectant tongue a flat pallet, a landing strip. He glanced up with guarded interest. His chin jut barely concealed a challenge. Olivia shivered, noted his shoulders tense, saw their aunt cut her eyes toward him before she began buttering another roll with vicious lashes. Her voice was a bare mumble. "Yeah, well…"

Her reticence created an electric reaction in Olivia and Arthur, who exchanged quick glances. Arthur's paralysis was broken. The fork clattered to his plate, causing the other two to start, then stiffen at the raw gravel of his voice.

"What's this about? Nobody mentioned it to me."

Olivia noted that he didn't refer to their father by name.

Margaret Mary put down her roll and leaned across in an exaggerated show of concern. Her mouth curled in the suggestion of a smile so that, despite the crosshatch of lines around her eyes, she appeared almost girlish. A girlish mini-skirted nun. She toyed with the loops of gold chains where they met at the vee of her blouse, like counting beads on a rosary. "A while back you asked me why I quit the convent, but you never asked why I became a nun in the first place. I'd have thought you'd be curious."

He said, "What's that got to do with—"

"Patience. I'm going to tell you. I went into the order as a sort of deal with God. See, my dad—your granddad—was doing some hurtful things I didn't like, and not doing other things."

Struck with sudden interest, Olivia broke in. "What other things?"

"Let's just say he wasn't carrying his load as head of the family, at least some of the time. Let's say he was unreliable. We never knew when we could depend on him."

Arthur said to Olivia. "Sound familiar?"

Their aunt went on. "I got the idea that if I sacrificed myself in religious service, God would shape up our father."

"Did it work?" Olivia's curiosity ran to personal reasons.

With a wry grin, Margaret Mary picked at a crumb on the table, then gave it a contemptuous flick. "In the immortal words of Woody Allen, I found God to be basically an underachiever. My father, after spending everything they'd saved for their old age, died in a VA hospital from a rotten liver. And I decided that I hadn't entered into a covenant with God for the right reasons. I also realized that, if there is a God, He holds all the cards and makes no deals. And he plays cut-throat poker."

It wasn't what Olivia wanted to hear. She slumped back in her chair as Arthur mumbled, "I told you once before that my conversion has nothing to do with Dad, if that's what you're driving at."

"I'm only pointing out that the nut doesn't fall very far from the tree. As it happens, you dad's already out, but...."

The news was electrifying. Olivia jumped up and squealed, "Daddy's out!"

Their aunt rushed on. "Mike has been working on this for months. He got him out some time ago."

Olivia sank back, devastated by the walloping blow. "Then where is he?"

"I don't know. I keep expecting…"

From the pit of a dark gloom, Olivia watched as from a distance as Arthur got up abruptly and went to his room. From a far flitting corner of her memory, she heard Momma say to Daddy, "I've put my soul into this house, trying to put down our roots. But it means nothing to you. Less than nothing." A fat tear plopped onto her plate with a noticeable ping.

Her aunt said, "Oh Jeez, I hate this. But honey, you had to know sooner or later."

From the hour of her parents' final separation, again the tragic voice of her mother challenged, *"I am less than nothing to you."*

As if bidden, the doorbell rang, and Olivia's spirits leaped. It had to be Daddy! She ran into the foyer, where she could see the shape of a man through the glass panels. She yelled, "Daddy! Daddy!" But faced with meeting him alone, she did not throw open the door. Instead, she ran down the hall and burst into Arthur's room. "He's here! Daddy's come!"

Arthur rose from his bed and followed her into the hall, where they both waited, caught breathless in anticipation and dread. It was so quiet she could hear the dim bleat of a foghorn offshore.

But as Margaret Mary opened the door, they could see it was only Gary, forcing a lizard-eyed grin. He caught her hand and said, "Babe, we've got to talk. I've been miserable." He glanced past her and saw the children in the hall. "Can't we go someplace else"

Margaret Mary sent a pleading glance to Arthur, who said, "Sure, take a break. I'll watch Livvie."

Margaret Mary shot him a grateful grin, grabbed her purse, and stepped into an enveloping fog. Under the diffuse orange halo of the porch light, she paused to offer an obligatory, "Sure you'll be okay?"

A pause before a thunderclap. Then: "Don't be insulting."

Olivia grinned. She recognized the old insolent Arthur, the one she knew how to deal with.

But once they were gone, he turned back to his room without even looking at Olivia. When she started to follow him, he said, "Go entertain yourself, squirt. I'm going to bed."

She revived her famous whine and caught hold of his belt, staying close behind so he couldn't shut his door on her, "You're supposed to baby-sit me. And if you don't, I'll…."

He wrenched free and fell across the bed. In the darkened room, his voice took on fresh menace. "You'll what? Tell on me? You know I could snap you in two like a toothpick?" He rolled over and leaned up on one elbow. "Do you know what today is?"

She recalled that several days ago he had circled an item in the paper about a golf tournament in Galveston, noting that it would be on Arthur's sixteenth birthday.

"Oh gosh, this is it, isn't it? The big day? And nobody remembered." Then she rallied. "No really, I remembered, but your present that I ordered didn't get here yet."

"Save the bullshit," he said. "I already got the best present I could have. Masterson's dead."

Olivia felt her heart jump a beat. She crawled up alongside him on the bed. "Quit joking. Anyway, how would you know?"

"Remember how good I used to be at throwing a baseball? In the closet I found this." He produced a golf ball from under his pillow. "It was like my jinn, my birthday jinn, sent it to me to use as a killing machine."

She thought how pleased Momma would be that Arthur believed in jinns. Still, his manner was troubling. He was still propped up on one elbow. She could see his handsome profile in the moonlight. He appeared more serene than she ever imagined he could be, but his tone was strong with animation. "I knew Masterson would come for the tournament, so I went down and hung out in the trees along the fairway. When he sliced one into the woods, I saw my chance."

He turned toward her, but she could only see the outline of his head in the dark. It was enough that they were sharing a moment, like the three of them used to do, whispering in the dark, plotting, figuring things out. Sometimes they would manufacture scenarios, things they wished would happen.

"I knew I'd be lucky enough to nail him on the first try, and I did: whacked him right between the eyes! He twisted as he fell and looked at me. I could tell he recognized me and thought I was Dad."

She couldn't jeopardize the moment by voicing doubts. Now she was too overcome with gratitude for this moment of intimacy to protest. They both knew it was a fantasy. Still, maybe this time it was dangerous. She said, "Cut it out. Get over it. If that had happened, it would be in the newspapers."

"You don't know how the oil business works to this day, do you? The Company couldn't afford to let the stockholders know. They're pretending he's still alive. Only I know better."

Chills overtook her and she shook, not because she believed him, but because *he* believed it. She tried to move away, but he flung an arm across her, pinning her close. It was his idea of comfort. He whispered, "Don't worry, Livvie. It's over now. We can't take on the whole corporate system."

She had believed he was doing so well. He was so much like Daddy after all: letting his fantasies take over. The weight of his arm was a reminder of her heavy responsibility to hold things together. No one must suspect that he was not well, or they would send him back. She remembered Momma saying, after one of her hospital bouts, "In the end, all our battles are solitary ones." Then Momma had noticed their stricken faces and added, "But our triumphs are group efforts. Our noble times are our overcomings." Now she could think of nothing to say.

Arthur removed his arm and rolled over onto his stomach, growling, "You don't have to sleep here. I don't even want you to. Although I could force you if I really wanted to."

She was so stunned that she could only jump to her feet and camouflage her retreat with a show of contempt. "Oh sure you could, Godzilla! Anyway, who needs you? Rent a movie, birthday boy!" She stomped out, banging the door behind her, then leaning against it to shake for a while.

Except for the soft squish of her sneakers, the house was eerily quiet. She couldn't even hear the foghorn. She meant to go up to Margaret Mary's bedroom, but the cavernous dark at the top of the stairs appeared too ominous. Instead, she settled on the far end of the living room couch, arranging a fort of pillows around her and manning the TV remote as her only weapon.

Eventually the unremitting noise of an old war movie lulled her into uneasy sleep. A German U-boat from the movie became, in her fitful dream-state, an ugly monster emerging for a primal bog. On the opposite bank of the black pool of blood stood her father, still wearing his impeccable gray suit and shiny shoes. From that vantage, he tried to conquer the monster by pointing a stern finger and hurling threats and insults. The monster shrank back and disappeared under the slime, where he remained just out of sight. But Daddy had no trophy to prove victory;

the great menace still lurked under the surface. Someone must dive into the mire and grab the beast with bare hands, must tear off his hide and wear it as proof of victory, and as protection against future calamity. She knew what she had always known: that Daddy was never going to do it. Someone else would have to be the lead goose. Arthur, having reached sixteen, had gone to find his fame, so it was up to her to save them. But she couldn't do it alone; she needed the help of all her ancestors for such an undertaking. And she didn't know how to find them.

She searched fitfully for them until an unmistakable sound filtered in, galvanizing her into instant wide-awake alert.

It was Daddy's voice, yelling from somewhere nearby. He hadn't forgotten Arthur's sixteenth birthday after all.

41

As if what had gone before with Gary had been a rehearsal for this moment; as if, as Arthur had said, patterns kept repeating themselves, Olivia didn't rush to throw open the door. Instead, as she had the last time, she ran down the hall to tell Arthur. She burst into his room and flipped the light switch. He still lay face down on his bed, dressed in his navy suit. Maybe he had been asleep.

"Daddy's really here! He remembered your birthday and came!'" She was breathless in the telling of it, above the banging and Daddy's insistent yelling.

"Yeah sure," Arthur said, but all the same, he sat up groggily on the side of the bed, rubbing his forehead as if he didn't know where he was.

Even from beyond the front door, Daddy sounded strange, slurring his words in his rage. His anger was meant for his sister. "Open the goddam door, Margaret Mary! I know you're in there!" It sounded as if he might be kicking the door.

Olivia made a decision not to wait for Arthur this time. She said, "I'm going to let him in."

As she left his room, Arthur muttered something about the same things happening over and over.

When he said it, and he seemed to say it often, the truth of it shot to a deep core, the part of her that recognized things without having to examine them. It called up an echo of what Momma used to say about people being able to know if something was true if they stood very still and didn't try to think too hard about it. The thing that was happening over and over wasn't about Gary coming to the door before. It had to do with Daddy, from a long time ago. But she didn't have time to stand still and not think so as to know what it was. She ran to the door, unlocked it, and threw it open.

Daddy was in a pitiable state: unshaven, dirty, stinking of booze, his striped silk tie stained and crooked. He leaned against the jamb, barely able to stand. His eyes were boozy red from rage and from crying. He never stopped crying.

He lurched in, dogged with purpose, feeling in his back pocket for a handkerchief, wiping his nose in snorts, still yelling at Margaret Mary. "What in hell have you done with my car?"

It took him a few minutes to get his bearings. He looked around wildly, yelling, "Where is she?" before he focused a bleary gaze upon Olivia for the first time. He seemed surprised. "What're *you* doing here?" It sounded like a challenge.

She had already launched herself toward his arms. His question was like a ball bat between the eyes. The impact of it stunned her in mid-launch. Almost knocking her backward, out of breath. He hadn't come for her, hadn't come for Arthur's birthday. But she mustn't allow him to believe she had expected him. It was a lifetime habit, hiding disappointment from him, never admitting to dashed hopes. Her chest contracted with the effort to affect nonchalance, and she required a very deep breath before she could answer. It seemed to help put things into perspective. After all, here was Daddy, same as always. She should have expected this. In an instant, there was nothing to forgive.

He didn't wait to hear her answer. He stalked through to the dining area windows looking out onto the back patio and demanded, "Has she got my car?"

He turned and saw Arthur, who had just appeared at the corner of the living room entrance. Arthur, knees sagging slightly, looked ill-equipped for confrontation; he had the appearance of someone just wakened for battle who had forgotten to strap on his weapon. The sight of him seemed to sober Daddy to a degree—not to the extent of acknowledging him, but of offering, at least, an explanation. "I went to the homeplace for my car. The house is boarded up. What have they done with it?"

Arthur swallowed and said in a papery voice, "Mike and Kathleen took it to their place. They were afraid vandals might trash it."

Daddy wobbled uncertainly and faltered toward the living room couch. His words were flat with the effort of manipulating a fat, dry tongue that seemed to get in his way. "Feel sick. I need some---"

Arthur looked at Olivia. "We could make coffee. There's instant."

Relieved to have something to do, she hurried to the kitchen ahead of Arthur. She dug into the pantry the coffee while Arthur filled a mug with hot water. He allowed Olivia to carry the cup into the living room, but Daddy hardly noticed either of them. He was still talking, addressing an empty room. He sat with his elbows on his knees, looking at the floor, telling them the whole sorry story before they even got there to hear. She tried to hand him the coffee, but he ignored her. She set it on the table and backed away. He must be talking to them; there was nobody else.

"Llano's got a new building, did you know? Masterson had to put up a new phallus after Shell built a taller one than his. The FAA asked him to shorten it a few feet because it interfered with the landing pattern at the airport, but he refused: then his wouldn't be the tallest. Can you beat that sonofabitch?"

Olivia eased in beside Arthur in a chair facing Daddy and held onto Arthur's wrist to calm them both. She said, "Is that where you've been? To see Masterson?"

Daddy's bitter laugh ended in a rattly cough. He wiped his mouth and eyes with the handkerchief, but it didn't do any good: water kept coursing down his cheeks. He said, "He wouldn't see me. Nobody would see me, not even those pompous middle-men behind their security locks and barred reception rooms. I couldn't even get on the elevator in the lobby! I'm the Company pariah. Isn't that a sorry-assed laugh! I was supposed to be the hero: fixed them up with Weldon, fed him phony maps so Llano could snap up some leases cheap, took the rap so they could maintain their contact with him."

She already knew it, of course, had known it since that night with Fayedell, but the sharp pain almost blinded her. "You took the rap. You're not talking about the maps, are you? You mean you...protected Weldon because you didn't want anybody to know *he hit Donnie!*"

His body contorted with a convulsive sob. "He didn't mean to. He meant to hit his own kid. Oh my God, my God!"

Olivia forced her tongue to work. "Then what?"

He appeared almost unable to go on, but she could tell that he wanted them to know. He seemed to force himself to confess. "The kids had sneaked into my study and taken a map. They heard us coming and hid in the window seat. We'd had something to drink. Weldon gets a little crazy when he drinks. We yelled at the kids to come out, and Donnie popped up—The little guy was always so good—" He broke off into fresh heaving sobs.

She steeled herself to hear through an enveloping fog. She was fading in and out, able to see, not wanting to see, the whole scene. A monumental anguish tore through her.

"The kids started to climb out of the window seat. There was no harm done. Weldon didn't need to do it. He threw a punch at his own kid, threw all his weight behind it. But Fayedell feinted like an old pro—like she had dodged his fists before. Donnie was right behind her. I saw his head pop back in a funny way, heard the crack. He looked so surprised....Nobody'd ever hit him before; he didn't know how to duck like she did. His eyes were on the ceiling...Maybe he was already seeing Heaven."

He put his head in his hands and heaved and shuddered in unspeakable anguish, then held it up again, shaking it back and forth as if to throw off the visions in his head, wailing, "Oh my God, my God!"

Arthur, who had sat impassively listening, pulled his wrist free from Olivia's grasp. He said evenly, as if the question were of no real importance, "Why did you go to prison for stealing the maps? Why didn't you tell the judge the truth?" His voice rose only a degree. "Why did you break Momma's heart?"

Daddy blew his nose noisily. "I had to. Masterson insisted. We'd worked so hard to set up this deal; he needed Weldon. My livelihood was at stake, my whole career."

He gazed up at Arthur with a telling directness. He no longer appeared to be drunk. "Besides, I felt I deserved to go. I wanted to go, to atone somehow for...what happened to Donnie. I wanted to make it right, to pay...and pay. Can you understand that?"

It was monstrous. Olivia put her hands over her ears and cried out, "You left us alone so that *you* could feel better? What about us? What about Momma? So now Momma is dead and Arthur—"

Daddy gagged, grabbed his mouth and rushed into the hall, looking for the bathroom. Arthur jumped to his feet and stalked behind him while she waited, shuddering, listening to Daddy wretch and sputter. Finally she could not discipline her mind not to leap back to that unspeakable scene at the window seat. Donnie, trusting Donnie: he'd never expect a fist. She didn't think she could bear her grief. Her body wasn't big enough to contain it.

Down the hall everything was quiet. The quiet jolted her back with the sense that something was not quite right.

She rushed to the bathroom door and saw Daddy kneeling in front of the toilet. His feet thrashed to right himself; his arms flailed to reach over his head. His head was hidden by the rim of the bowl, and Arthur's foot was pressed on the back of Daddy's neck. Arthur's pants leg was wet to the knee.

She screamed, "Arthur! Stop! Let him go!" She shoved all her weight against him, beating him with her fists, trying to pull Daddy's head free of the surface of the vomit, but the more she struggled, the harder Arthur pushed against Daddy's neck.

Arthur was rigid calm. "He has a little more paying yet to do, now that I'm sixteen." She had heard it before: the double voice, one several octaves lower, like the Devil's chilling terrible rumble. She had heard it when Momma was dying.

Daddy's hand found Arthur's ankle and clamped around it, while he continued to try to gain his footing. Olivia danced around them, pushing here, pulling there, not knowing how to part them. It occurred to her that Daddy was stronger than Arthur; it was only a matter of time before he would break free, and then Daddy would win and Arthur would lose. Maybe he would kill Arthur. Even if he didn't, he would know Arthur was sick. He'd send Arthur away again, then Daddy would leave.

"Help me, Livvie!" It was Arthur. She didn't know what to do. She leaned against Arthur's back, clasped her arms around him and held on tight, figuring she was hindering them both.

But as if Daddy heard Arthur's words, heard the double voice, and realized their significance, he stopped struggling and slumped to one side. It was as if he quit breathing intentionally. Now she could hear Arthur's panting and nothing more.

Arthur reached down and pulled their father's head free of the water by his hair. Blood oozed from the corner of Daddy's mouth. His eyes were rolled up so that only the yellows showed; his face was a cyanotic blue. For one moment, the eyes rolled down, but he was not looking at anything earthly, certainly not anything heavenly. It was a very intimate, private moment with death that she seemed to be participating in from a distance. She could only think about Momma's quote from Henry James: "So here it is at last, the distinguished thing!"

A groan of anguish escaped her as Arthur dropped Daddy's head back into the toilet and backed her out of the room. He gazed down at her with the frantic eyes of a wounded animal and said, almost pleading, "Now things won't keep happening over and over again. Momma and Donnie won't have to wait for him anymore, now that I'm sixteen."

After her first screeching cry, the sight had rendered her mute with horror. She kept opening her mouth to scream again, but not even a strangled sound came out. Her sorrow had no more tongue. It was the same sort of nightmare she'd had after Donnie, and after Momma, when she tried to scream out in her sleep against unspeakable terrors and couldn't make a sound.

Her brain lay heavy, like a deflated blimp, crowding down against her brow, hooding her vision. But her hearing was acute, and what she heard was the terrible grinding of the universe. It was a deep rumble like the echo of Arthur's second voice, and it was inescapable. She tottered and caught Arthur's arm like a life rope. He led her back to his room and lay down beside her, shaking and holding her fiercely.

She had come to know how much the dead matter. The dead mattered most of all. They took on new life, like worms in her brain. Now Daddy's absence would have meaning that his absences never had before. Daddy himself would have meaning.

In time they both stopped shaking enough for her to wriggle free and dial 911. At the sound of her voice, Arthur roused and asked with great calm, "Did I kill him?"

"No!" she said fiercely. "It was like the Masterson deal: all in your head, in *both* our heads." She would leave him out of it, would close his door and meet the ER guys by herself.

They would surely see that Daddy had drowned in his own vomit, that a small girl couldn't have pulled him free; nobody could ever pull Daddy free. She couldn't risk losing Arthur again. Surely now that he had reached sixteen, all his dreams about his life would come true. Besides, somehow she had begun believing in his dreams too; they were her dreams now.

Later she would try to find Josephine, who dwelled safely with Momma and Donnie in her belly or in her mind's closet. She would find Josephine so they could be normal again. Just because something was futile was no reason to give up on it. She had to hold the family together.

Anyway, there was no escaping being lead goose. Everybody has to take a turn eventually.

PART II

MAKING DO

42

Ten years later

The paralysis of grief had carried Olivia through the first year after Daddy's death but had lessened in time. There was her schoolwork and Arthur to tend to. He had returned to a catatonic state where he seemed more dead than alive. He had been placed in a private sanitarium not too far from the medical center because it was too dangerous to leave him at home unattended.

Following high school and graduation from a local college, she longed to be reunited with Arthur, who had over time regained a semblance of normal functioning. With Uncle Mike's help, she checked him out of the sanitarium and instructed him to help her pack their few belongings. She bade goodbye to Margaret Mary, Frances and Hig, and Kathleen and Mike, promising to write soon. They left in less than a week, with Daddy's ashes in the trunk of the car which had been her graduation gift from The Aunts.

She allowed instinct to choose their destination and found that they were heading toward the big Thicket of deep East Texas. Common sense warned her not to commit their nest egg from Peggy Ahern's and her father's estates to purchase property until her grief was behind her. But the secluded little cabin canopied under towering pines near Coldspring was well under market value. It came complete with the former owner's meager furnishings and two Labradors who themselves were grieving for their deceased master. She overrode caution and instructed Arthur to sign a check for the entire price. They were still left with more than half their principal. The interest from that, plus their mother's small estate, might be enough to live on if they lived very simply—for about a month. What was she thinking? At the moment Olivia could not envision ever being able to work outside the home, but supplementing their income was inevitable. She would have to find work in Coldspring.

She led Arthur to a rocker on the shaded porch and introduced him to Boudreaux and Lena, the two labs. The love-starved dogs approached him shyly. He appeared not to notice them for the longest time, until Lena let out a groan of impatience. His abstract gaze fell upon her and he absently dropped his hand to his side. That was all the invitation the dogs needed. They vied to lick his hand, and Arthur responded with a single word: "Ramona." Satisfied the dogs would be gentle with Arthur and he with them, Olivia began to unpack the car.

She put Daddy's ashes on a shelf in the shed, figuring that one day she might be able to scatter them under the trees. For the present she must devote herself to bringing Arthur around again. She looked over the yard at the tangled mass of myrtle, yaupon and laurel knit together by the vine of muscadine grape, the whole overlaid by tall pines, and said with satisfaction, "Momma would approve of this. She was a great hand for letting nature do the healing."

The cabin consisted of one big room that served as living area and kitchen; one bedroom and bath downstairs, and a loft accessible by ladder from the front room. She decided to give Arthur the bedroom and to sleep on the couch in the living room. She didn't want to let Arthur out of her sight; did not want him to go wandering in the middle of the night.

She looked in the cabinets and discovered that either the former owner had starved to death or that someone had taken any canned goods that had remained. There was a large sackful of dogfood; obviously someone had been feeding the dogs since the owner died. Olivia had brought only a few provisions and had counted on being able to get by for a day or two without having to search out a general store. But she hadn't even enough on hand to prepare an adequate supper.

She picked up her purse and went out onto the porch. She took Arthur gently by the arm. "Come on, dear; we have to go shopping."

To her surprise, he resisted. Without looking up, he said, "You go."

"What? And leave you here all by yourself?"

The dogs continued to circle around his feet. He was actually watching them, she realized with a surge of hope. He said, "Not by myself."

He wanted her to trust him. She sighed and agreed. "No, not by yourself."

She assured him that she would be right back, then tore out down the backroad toward the main road to Coldspring. There was a small gas station at the crossroads. She decided to stop and check out their supplies and to settle for whatever they had.

The sole attendant was a woman probably in her mid-thirties. The startling white hair and colorless eyes attested that she was albino, although judicious use of cosmetics had minimized the pinkish tinge of her skin and eyelids. Her features were regular but pinched, as if stunted by malnutrition or maybe too many cigarettes. She grinned, revealing a mouthful of sharp of teeth as Olivia came in.

"You must be the new owner of Claudie's place." She spoke in a slow sweet drawl. "I'm Willie Virginia Osborn. Guess we're your nearest neighbors."

Olivia introduced herself and learned that the woman, her parents and sisters lived in a trailer house behind the store.

"Sure we've got groceries, girl," she said in answer to Olivia's question. "You don't think we'd let you drive clear to Coldspring for a carton of milk, do you?"

She indicated a cooler in back, where Olivia found a few dairy products and lunch meats as well as eggs. On the shelf were a few canned goods, bread, cookies and the inevitable dogfood.

"Those dogs are mighty happy to have somebody to belong to, I expect," the Osborn woman said. "My sister Gladdie has been feeding them when she thinks about it. 'Course, they wouldn't starve anyway. They're pretty good cooners. Daddy said we positively could not have one more dog, or we would've probably taken them in. Not that they'd have stayed. They would've run off by sundown, gone on back to Claudie's."

"I'm glad they're there. My brother is…loves dogs. They'll be great company."

A flicker of interest sparked in the pale eyes. "Just you and your brother all there is, I hear. Is he…full grown?"

Olivia figured that eligible men might be scarce in San Jacinto County. "Yes, but he has been ill for a long time. That's the main reason we're here: to let him recuperate in peace and quiet."

She paid for the groceries and left hurriedly to discourage further questions. Besides, she worried about having left Arthur there alone.

He was sitting where she left him. He didn't look up until she reached the porch steps. Then he raised his blank eyes as if he didn't recognize her. But his toneless voice belied that. "It's you."

She tried to sound light. "Yes. I found food! We eat!" She threw open the screen door, marched to the small primitive kitchen area and began unloading the groceries onto the rough cabinet. She would have to scrub it as soon as she had time. Everything would have to be scrubbed. She'd have to do all the things she'd always avoided.

She leaned against the counter and squeezed back tears. "Oh God, it's too much. I can't do this. I can't."

The crickets began to chirp as dusk fell. Still she stood there and cried. But no one was coming to console her. Arthur would sit out there and starve before he would come. If she didn't turn on the lights, the house would soon be dark. If she didn't put sheets on the bed, Arthur would have to sleep on the mattress. It was all for her to do alone.

Being lead goose wasn't all it was cracked up to be.

The dark night of their father's death rose fresh in her mind, as it still did every time she let down her guard for an instant. *How long, lord?* She squeezed her eyes tightly shut, but the image of Daddy's upturned death-face remained as vivid as it had ten years before. She pressed against her eye sockets, shaking her head violently.

She had barely managed to live through it once. She couldn't keep living through it for the rest of her days. She sank to the floor and sobbed aloud, heaving in shudders. Who would minister to her? She was the sick one. Arthur was blessedly amnesiac about that night. She could not stop it from playing and replaying in her mind.

The room grew completely dark. The dogs began to scratch on the screen, demanding to be fed. She lifted her cheek from the linoleum floor and brushed grit from her face. She must remember to mop the floor tomorrow. Arthur must be famished. But then, he would never know. He never asked for food, hadn't since…. She had to remind him to eat; often had to spoon-feed him. Otherwise, he might get so weak he couldn't walk. Then what would she do? She dragged herself to her feet and opened the lunch meat. He would have to settle for a sandwich tonight.

Tomorrow she would make a big pan of lasagna. Maybe they would have a glass of beer, if Willie Virginia Osborn had any for sale. It would be their first full day in their new home, their new life. She would think of some way to make it special. The days after that? She couldn't even imagine. What had she been thinking, holing up in this desolate place?

43

Two days later Olivia loaded Arthur into the car and drove into town, justifying the excursion because the trip would be good for him. The truth, she admitted to herself, was that she would go berserk if she didn't get away from that dismal cabin. Her spirits lifted when they hit the highway, and even Arthur became more animated as they neared Coldspring.

She parked at the curb near the center of town, and they walked to the local café for a burger. Just the sound of voices was salubrious, but she longed for someone to talk to her. Other customers paid them no mind, presuming they were travelers just passing through. She wished for someone to engage them in conversation. During her college days, talking to other students, while maintaining a safe distance, had been her salvation.

After lunch, she took Arthur by the arm for a stroll window-shopping at the local merchants'. When they passed the hardware store, she stopped to read the hand-lettered sign taped to the glass: Part-Time Help Wanted. A thrill shot up her back. It wouldn't hurt to inquire, she figured. But she hesitated to expose a prospective employer to Arthur. She led him back to the car and instructed him to wait there while she ran an errand in the hardware store. He had no curiosity and meekly complied.

She hurried back to the store, peered in the window and saw no customers. *Good.* As she opened the door, a tiny bell tinkled overhead. *Good.* She liked the place already.

A middle-aged man appeared from behind the curtain to the back room. "Can I help you?"

"I came about your sign," she said, more timid than she'd intended. She took a bold step forward and extended her hand. "Hi. I'm Olivia Ahern, a new resident. I could use a part-time job."

His face lit in relief. She noted he had great teeth: pricey orthodontist work, she figured. He looked her over critically eye. "I need someone on weekends, mostly, when I have to be out of town."

Out of town fishing, she figured. "Weekends are okay by me."

He indicated the tall shelves and rolling ladder on one side of the store. "It requires some climbing, and lifting gallons of paint, sometimes."

"I'm up for that," she said.

"Hourly pay."

She grinned. "You can't discourage me."

Again the flash of teeth and a shrug. "Guess I'll quit trying." He stuck out his hand again. "My name is Rod Benson. Can you start Saturday?"

So soon? At her hesitation, he added, "Just a couple of hours the first time, to get acquainted with the stock and your duties."

Doable. She would stop at Osborn's store and ask Willie Virginia if she or Gladdie could look in on Arthur Saturday morning.

She left the store humming. Although Arthur showed no interest in the reason for her absence, she told him, "I just got a job."

"Uh huh."

"I'm going to stop and ask the people at Crossroads Store if they'll come by to keep an eye on you while I'm gone."

"Or I could go there," he said. "They have a horseshoe pitching yard."

Better yet. He could use the exercise.

44

Olivia nestled into her new job and knew immediately that it was what she had always wanted to do. She liked her boss, who didn't seem as lackluster as she had first thought. She had learned that his grandfather had established this store before Rod was born. His father, like hers, was a company man. Rod was, she assumed, not married.

Arthur didn't seem to mind her absence. After the first week or two he began to look forward to spending Saturday afternoons at Osborn's pitching horseshoes with the men or helping the sisters in Crossroads Store. Olivia noted with satisfaction that he began to acquire an animation he had never possessed, even in childhood,

She had not had time to get to know the members of the Osborn family; did not know if any others besides Willie Virginia were also albino. So she listened with genuine interest, sitting beside him after work, as he recounted tales of Mr. Osborn's war adventures and of the various Osborn girls' many marriages and divorces.

"So they've all been married more than once? And all bounced back home again?" she asked.

"All but Willie Virginia. She's the oldest."

"She's never been married?"

His reticence should have alerted her. "She lived with someone once in Nacogdoches while she was going to Stephen F. Austin."

"So she's college educated. And running a gas station."

"Well...she went only one year. A little less. She...got pregnant." He leaned over the rocker arm to pick up a book from the porch floor.

Sensing his reluctance to reveal all that he knew, Olivia couldn't let it rest. "So where's the child? Living at Crossroads Store?...presuming she had the baby."

He pulled his gaze from the book. "She had him all right. But he ran away."

"Ran away! How old was this kid, anyway?"

He shrugged. "About ten, I guess. Maybe twelve or thirteen."

Olivia did some mental calculations. "My gosh, that would make Willie Virginia about...thirty."

"Thirty-nine," he said.

Olivia laughed. "You can't mean it. And here I thought she was about your age.'

He returned to his book, but she noted his heavy breathing. She tweaked him in the ribs and teased, "You're not getting a crush on an older woman, are you?"

The vehement denial she anticipated did not come. Arthur's gaze remained steadfastly on the book, but she watched a flush rise to his cheeks. She was more than stunned; she felt real alarm. Arthur was entirely too vulnerable. She should never have left him alone. She knew she must say something; must keep talking, talking, deflecting the threat, shooing this danger away. She began a stammering ramble, anything to divert him.

"It's only natural for you to be attracted to her. She's practically the only female you've seen besides me in ages. But of course we both know that being attracted to somebody's pretty face or by...well, just being in proximity to somebody with, um, rising sap, you might say...of course, not that there's anything wrong with...It's perfectly natural, is what I'm trying to say. But not with the wrong person."

She stopped, out of breath, and waited. Arthur still did not look up. She said, "Arthur?"

When he finally raised his head, his eyes shone with a defiant glint. He said, "Willie Virginia wants me to help her find him."

She took a swelling breath of relief. "Her son? Oh well, I think that's great. Good idea. But where would you look?"

He shrugged. "Wherever she thinks he might be."

"How long has he been gone?"

"About two years, I think."

"Two years! But he could be anywhere by now. He could be dead!"

Arthur seemed genuinely distressed; she hadn't meant to distress him. "I know," he said. "Poor kid all alone out there somewhere. Anything could have happened to him. He ran away to look for his daddy."

She understood his empathy for the boy and even felt a measure of it herself. Did half the population of the world long for a lost daddy? Of course Arthur would have to go. She would have to trust Willie Virginia to take care of him. Olivia would speak to her, of course. At least she could be assured that Arthur's interest in the woman centered on her lost son and not her sexual charms. He could so easily be crushed by a premature liaison with an older, experienced woman. Anyway, Olivia could not imagine Arthur ever wanting to leave his sister, not after all they had gone through to be together. They were only just now finding one another.

She left the porch rocker and went into the house to fix super. She caught a glimpse of Arthur's unmade bed through his open door. She smiled in mock dismay; Arthur must really be undergoing a metamorphosis. Up until now he had been overly meticulous; he had never left his bed unmade before. Then she recalled seeing him make it that morning. He must've had a nap since....

But if he had spent the afternoon at the Osborns'...

She crossed over to his room and began automatically spreading his bed, smoothing the sheet, when her hand encountered something damp... and sticky. She jerked her palm back, heart thumping against her chest. Now she examined the bed more carefully: both pillows were indented. She leaned down and sniffed at the nearest one, burying her face in it. She would know Arthur's scent anywhere.

This was definitely not it.

45

6:00 p.m.

At closing time Rod phoned his mother that he'd be late for supper, late giving his dad a bath. His one employee hadn't shown up for work that day, and he needed to check on her. He had neglected to get her phone number when he hired her., but he knew approximately where she lived, about a half-hour outside of town past the Crossroads Store.

Tight-chested call home: Rod objected to reporting in after decades of independence. He had left home and married twenty years earlier, before so many corporate casualties littered the landscape, while his father was still bloated with middle-management hubris and the delusion of his indispensability. Before the old man, shucked off under the guise of "early retirement," had skulked back to East Texas to lick his wounds and pretend he had come home to manage Granddad's store because the place had gone to pot since the old gentleman developed senile dementia.

And before Rod's father suffered the stroke that had rendered him shrunken and one-sided, unable even to propel his spidery body to the john: a vegetable body imprisoning red-rimmed rage. A sun-dried tomato.

Rod felt uneasy urgency to get to Olivia's; she'd never missed work before. A reliable girl—Jillian would chide him for calling her a girl, even though from the vantage of forty-one, twenty-three didn't seem like a woman. Most of the time.

Never missed a day. He worked to control his thready, shallow breaths as he drove out Main Street heading west, wondering what he would actually blurt out when he got there.

Wondering what he would find: the brother, Olivia's brother. Odd duck. Off-kilter. Maybe dangerous. Strange how differently two people could react to the same tragedy: one wraps up in a cocoon of insanity; one develops a wacked-out view of disaster as comedic and possibly even redeeming. She wore blinders, maybe. Neither sibling took the classic route of mainlining Guadalajara gamma dust; that was something, at least.

Olivia never brought the brother into the store. Even when she came in to apply for work, a skittish breathless little person of rather elegant proportions, the brother waited outside in the little black Kia parked at the curb.

What would he say, what excuse would he give for driving all the way out in the country just to check on her? *Just passing by and thought I'd...* No, he would rehearse something impersonal, just as he'd rehearsed his call to his mother.

Tight-chested, gut-wrenching call, because the obligation ran only in one direction. Resentment at having to justify hiring Olivia in the first place. *What does she know about hardware?*

As much as I did, he could have reminded his mother, but there was no need to touch tender surfaces. He'd come home to help, he'd told them; to run the store and lift Dad onto the toilet, into the tub, into the wheelchair. Anyway, the store's books needed his organized mind; the stock, his precise attention to detail. He'd come to get them in order because he was constitutionally noble.

Not because Jillian had left him and he had no one else. Not because his own future in the field of Third World Literature had evaporated after the Board of Regents voted to eliminate his department. Not because he had consistently failed to reach tenure. Not because, after unemployment benefits ran out, child-support payment were out of the question. Not because when Jillian remarried and gave him the choice of jail or signing papers allowing her new husband to adopt young Roddie, he had given up all rights to his only child. Not because he no longer had a life.

And this is why I sojourn here/Alone and palely loitering.

It was dusk. Street lights flickered on. He nodded to the druggist, just locking up for the night, and tried to put the sound of his mother's voice out of his mind.

I hope to heaven, Rod, you're not becoming besotted by a girl almost young enough to be your daughter. It wasn't the first time she'd said it. He had denied it, stopped short of accusing her of jealousy, avoided pointing out the similarity of his own situation when she said of Olivia's brother, *What kind of man lives with his sister? What's wrong with him, anyway? He doesn't even have a job!*

Her brother wasn't well, Olivia had told him in thin, fragile bytes, her glance sliding toward the store's glass front and the car at the curb. He had watched her small pinched face, large fierce eyes daring him to refuse her a job.

His mother voiced no surprise that Olivia hadn't shown up for work that morning. *She watched PBS Frontline last night, about that oil company thing. You know good and well the Quentin Ahern he mentioned was her father. She can't face anybody; it's as simple as that.*

No need to argue that the expose on corporate espionage might be about some other Ahern, or that Olivia probably hadn't seen it anyway, or that scarcely anyone in the community knew her name or cared. Still, he had a vague unease that Olivia's absence and the business about her father were related, if only tangentially. Now he waited with impatience at Coldspring's only traffic light, revving his engine, causing the few stragglers left on the sidewalk to turn and stare in curiosity.

Don't throw yourself at this girl, son. Even if she weren't too young, she's not your kind.

Oh, but she was exactly his kind: corporate kid educated on the run between well-kept suburban communities, reared by anxious mothers, live-ins, au-pairs, and far-ranging fathers striving for one more rung. Understanding even in primary school that a horizontal promotion was the kiss of death. Another kid born already owing her soul to the Company store.

Reared fluent in the language of war, Jillian had once said with great contempt—for her father was a doctor and thus in her mind exempt from the barbarities of the business world, even though he was part of what was euphemistically referred to as *the health care industry*—"Did you ever notice the language of the business page is the vernacular of battle? The corporate strategy is the tactic of combat: keep your adversary off-balance. And who's the adversary? The entire world!"

And the victims? Strewn everywhere. Scrape the carcasses from the corporate parking lots like so much road kill. Deposit them in the compost heap of small-town America, or in retirement condos on top of a nuclear dump site out on the plains where real estate's still a bargain. Maybe in time somebody will take root. But not Rod. Not here. Even though the turf of academia had proven no less riddled with casualties from skirmishes of adversaries locked in mortal combat for tenure.

Arthur's been sick. Eyes darting toward the waiting victim at the curb. One of the many civilian wounded of the corporate wars. Rod recognized a fellow vet when he saw one. And with a jolt of pain he saw his own six-year-old son as well. No. No longer six: an eight-year-old appendage attached to a new Jewish family.

I knew Jillian would leave sooner or later. Mixed marriages never work. His mother's voice had wrung with triumph. He thought Jillian had left because she wanted to resume her career, wanted the stability of a permanent address. But now she had a new baby. What had she wanted that he couldn't provide? What the hell do any of them want, Sigmund?

Arthur's not well. Anxious little bird hands, little freckled hands, clasping, unclasping. Graceful hands, for all that: a musician's hands. Another of the walking wounded, eyes darting, musical hands comforting one another, clasping, unclasping.

The light changed and he jolted forward so suddenly that he killed the engine. *Damn!* He ground on the ignition, pumping the accelerator like a madman. The engine turned over and took off like a bomb, startling nearby drivers. *Get a grip, man. You're hot-rodding like a teenager.*

What does a girl like that know about hardware? His mother had said it almost nightly for a month. *As much as Dad did,* he told her over and over; *as much as I did. She can baby-sit the store so I can come home a take Dad to the john without having to lock up in the middle of the day.*

She had harrumphed and said he probably only wanted to get away so he could hang out at the Hop, that Fifties coffee shop and drive-in throwback that was Coldspring's only claim to fame. There was too much truth in her accusation to deny it, even though he would never screw up the courage to join the GOBs for morning coffee: chair legs scraping over to make room for one more around the two tables they had already pushed together, cigarette smoke boiling up, phlegm-loosening coughs punctuating the laughter at the same old jibes. No nuclear magnetic resonator to capture C-cells in dying color around Coldspring: those were reserved for Corporate America. Out There. On the other side of Interstate 59.

He could never do it; he wasn't one of them. The skirmish skills of academia were of no use here. Never mind that his grandfather had built the only hardware store in town; that his dad had grown up here. Rod had never spent more than a few days in the summers in Coldspring, and after high school he never came back except for funerals. *Such a blessing,* everyone said when both grandparents died in the same month. *The old gentleman couldn't have managed without her.*

Then, inquisitive looks at Rod and the inevitable question: *And where's that pretty little wife?* They knew, they knew; people know these things. They enjoyed watching him squirm. *Serves him right for marrying a Jew,* they wanted to say.

No, he didn't belong with the crowd at the Hop. Except for the rattling coughs, the place grew quiet whenever he went in—like Blundgen: *a shepherd in a soldier's coat,* so he'd begun using the drive-up window. What the hell.

I hope you're not getting involved with that little girl, she'd said over the phone. Bands tightening around the chest. Age had already thrown up an inseparable barrier.

Would you like to go to dinner? He had asked, but the specter of Justice Thomas loomed and he added, *Your brother, too, of course.* But again she'd told him, *My brother isn't well.*

What did they live on in that shanty in the woods? She'd been born in Sands' Point, Long Island, where he graduated from high school. The same year, it turned out—but he didn't tell her that. They'd both been transferred soon after.

He's been sick. But he didn't look sick this very afternoon, sitting behind the wheel in Willie Virginia Osborn's faded green pickup, parked at the curb. Rod had recognized the frizzy-haired albino from Crossroads Store. At the time, he'd even considered asking, "Don't you live out there close to the Aherns?"

Crossroads Store was located at the turnoff to Olivia's place. Rod thought it was peculiar, Willie Virginia driving all the way into town to buy a tarp and some rope and a five-gallon gas tank from him, things he would've thought she could have gotten at Crossroads Store, But then, he'd never been inside the place; maybe they didn't keep much stock besides a few canned goods and some live bait. Yet he could've asked, "Have you seen Olivia?"

With only passing curiosity he'd watched the Osborn woman, of the watery pin-point pupils of someone who's recently snorted a line of Sausalito Sin, as she tossed the purchases in the back of the truck and got in on the passenger side, puffing on the ever-present cigarillo. He's almost dismissed her already until the pickup backed out and jerked into forward gear, as if the driver were an amateur.

Come to think of it—with a start that churned his gut—he'd never seen Olivia's brother behind the wheel before.

This afternoon Rod had sensed rather than seen the animation of the man behind the wheel. Still, it was only a matter of seconds; he could have been mistaken.

6:10 p.m.

He rounded the bend at the city limits and veered to miss an old pickup with a Shit Happens bumper sticker, gunning out of the service station beyond the curve. It was Willie Virginia again, this time at the wheel, driving like a wild woman, spitting gravel from the oversized tires, shrouding the city limits sign in a cloud of dust. Beside her, tossing off a Shiner Bock and keeping time on the dash to the primal throb of the radio's heavy metal, was Olivia's brother Arthur. He sure as hell didn't look sick. High, perhaps. Maybe out of control. Stir-fried neurons, maybe. But not sick.

Could be she had never said, *He's been sick*. Maybe she'd said, *He's not well*. With a blind rush of apprehension, Rod realized the two were not necessarily the same.

My God, what if they've done something to Olivia?

46

Willie Virginia's faded green pickup tore out of the gas station and was almost out of sight in a matter of seconds. It must be doing eighty. No way that could be safe, a rattletrap like that.

What was up? Maybe nothing. Maybe he'd become so accustomed to life reduced to a slow crawl that anything faster made him jumpy.

As Rod passed the station, he looked at his own gauge: below a quarter of a tank, but plenty to get to Olivia's and back. Couldn't be more than ten miles to the crossroads and about five after that. Thirty miles round trip max.

Still, he edged on the brakes and whipped into the station at the last minute. Something else was operating here, a higher intuition impelling him Vague *what ifs* niggled their way in, the kind that used to drive him crackers back in the days with Jillian.

Better throw a six-pack of Evian in the trunk. What if we had car trouble on a lonely road?

At least keep your shorts handy. What if where was a fire?

What if the plane crashed and nobody could find the silver? I need to call the folks and tell them where we hid it.

He'd teased her that it was the ghost of Jewish motherhood, making a virtue of disaster, but he'd noticed in the last few years that his parents had begun covering all their bases in the same way, so that any alteration in routine called for tedious preparation.

What if....He couldn't bring himself to speculate under what circumstances he would need a full tank just to drive out to Olivia Ahern's and back. But the nameless fear persisted.

Wouldn't take more than three or four minutes more, anyway.

The pump gauge clicked its labored way by reluctant tenths. He equated them with miles separating him from the pickup rocketing toward the crossroads bearing Willie Virginia and Arthur. Arthur: of the unbalanced mind, although Olivia had reiterated the fact of his special genius: *Arthur's a megawig. He studied astronomy and philosophy and stuff before he was a teenager. He was trying to figure out what life is supposed to be about.*

Prior to today, Rod had felt great sympathy for the boy Arthur must have been, whose relationship with his father must've paralleled Rod's own with his dad. Despite the dozen years' difference in their ages, he and Arthur must have had similar childhoods. But something must have happened. When Rod had asked Olivia if her folks still lived in Texas, she'd looked quickly away and croaked, *There are no parents.*

So. No ongoing family obligations. No pretended fealty to Northland Petroleum, from whence the retirement check. But Llano Petroleum must have had a similar retirement package. If her parents were both dead, she and Arthur must have a fairly decent income.

Face it. Jillian's disdain for company loyalty fed on Rod's continuing clashes with his father. *Your dad was a fathering washout. Not because he was a bad person, but because he was married to the Company.* It was her trump card in her campaign, the ongoing denigration of Rod's devotion to his profession. Now he could dispel his bitterness against that very university which betrayed him: repaid his conscientiousness with a pink slip.

He couldn't wait for the tank to fill. He stopped when the charges registered an even ten.

6:16 p.m.

Back on the road, pushing the Blazer for all it would safely do. His orderly mind scouted through the events of the past few months. He could pinpoint nothing specific to justify his mounting panic. It might be an a amalgam of small things, incidental remarks by Olivia about her past, or her reluctance to leave Arthur alone in the evenings, or his own observations of Arthur's change from circuit overload to all systems charged, or his impression that the albino woman was operating on a flatten-any-obstacle agenda.

He was a rational man, not given to acting upon intuitive flashes; yet he was obviously being governed by something besides empirical evidence. Certainly it could not be fondness for the girl, elegant thighs notwithstanding.

He was fond of her, yes, but not flummoxed by any means. He even considered her a mild irritant and often thought that taking her on may have been a mistake, because she had complicated his life, his barely tolerable life. Olivia and her problems, which she refused to recognize as problems, occupied too much of his thoughts. She was like a wad of Double Bubble stuck to his shoe.

Even now he was driving too fast. He forced himself to let up on the accelerator and found himself gritting his teeth with the effort.

The first day when she came into the store—why hadn't he just told her no? The truth, he had to admit, was that he couldn't take his eyes off her. Her eyes, much too large for her face, reminded him of those waifs that some painter made famous. At times hers were almost electric blue. It wasn't a sexual attraction. Actually, at the time he'd had no idea she was more than a teenager. He wondered if she had ever even set foot in a hardware store before.

Yet he couldn't bring himself to turn her away. There were no other jobs in Coldspring, he was sure. If he hadn't hired her, who would?

So now he felt responsible for her. She had turned out to be a dependable, conscientious worker. She wouldn't just not show up without sending word. The brother could've delivered a message if she was ill...

His stomach clenched in a knot. Visions of the albino woman rose like a specter. What was wrong with that woman? She must be fifteen years older than Arthur. They couldn't be a couple, surely. He had heard rumors....What did they say about Willie Virginia? That she was violent? Berserk? Crazy? That she'd been locked up a time or two? *Why didn't I pay closer attention?*

...when he was in the Hop, pretending not to hear what the GOBs were saying, when he was thinking about himself and his intolerable life, instead of what the men were saying about Willie Virginia Osborn. About how she'd just as soon run over you as....

47

Headlights coming toward him: a truck, eighteen-wheeler from Conroe. Not many along this road at this hour. Good thing, too. The road was too narrow, visibility too bad. Trees overhung the road so low in places that big vehicles were forced to drive in the center.

Still, a little traffic was better than none, in case he had to hitch a ride. What if he had engine trouble or a flat? Since they started putting tires on with pneumatic lug wrenches, he couldn't possibly change one.

Jesus! I sound like Jillian, with her effing what if's.

Why the hell couldn't that girl get a phone? There were limits to the extent of acceptable eccentricity. She was a throw-back to the Sixties, an era she considered ancient history. She was, in fact, going for the throw-back record. She and the ever-looming brother, whose quirks she shrugged off: *He knows he's been semi radically ozoned for years, but he doesn't back away from it. In fact, he wears his overload like a merit badge.*

Flip on the radio, catch the tail end of the news out of Houston. Catch the weather report. Need rain. Grass is dry. No time to water the lawn; too much to do, hauling the old man in and out of bed, baby sitting while Mom gets out of the house for a break.

So much to do. Maybe he ought to turn around, forget about Olivia. To hell with her. Any responsible employee wouldn't called if she wasn't coming to work.

Only Olivia *was* responsible.

Why're you here, in this place? he'd asked, and she's snapped back, *So you think we'd be better off out there in Bush-land? You really think we're the type?* It was always *we*; always including the brother.

She had perched on the edge of his desk and said, *Let me FAX you a bulletin: you're lucky to have such roots. It's a trip working in the same store your grandfather established!*

It isn't how it seems, he'd told her. *I hardly knew my granddad. My dad left home after college to work for a gas pipeline company. Lived thousands of miles from here most of the time.*

She was soft-spoken, wistful. *At least you knew them. I never laid eyes on our dad's parents, and Arthur never knew our mom's. At least you had the good sense to come home. At least there was a home to come to.*

Rod switched channels in his head to the running argument he'd had with Jillian ever since she left: rebutting accusations she'd flung at him so effortlessly.

We didn't have the big network of family ties to fall back on. When something happens, there's no safety net.

But Jill wasn't listening; she was still talking: *Maybe it's not you so much; maybe it's the life. I look at women who've been at this a little longer, and they've got migraines or mastectomies or drinking problems. Their kids are in drug programs or homes for unwed mothers.*

What about me? he would've said. *Don't you think I've got problems? What choices did I have?* Or maybe he did say that.

You see? You're not listening to me. When I begin a sentence, I can feel your impatience for me to get to the end of it.

Just living for ourselves doesn't work. We've tried it for two generations and see where it has led: in a complete circle.

Rod, you're not listening to me!

Look at Mexico: the people live every day of their lives with their forebears and their progeny, with a sense of history. It's what he shouldn't said, but he didn't know it back then. Olivia had taught him. There. Before she can answer, switch channels again. Let Mom deal with Jillian for a change:

I must have warned you a thousand times it wouldn't work. Jews stick together like sardines. You'll never be anything but an outsider to those people.

Wait a minute. Mom's not talking to Jillian. Switch channels again. Back to Olivia.

It's not halcyon heaven, he'd told her, *being close to your folks after you're grown. It has its down side. There's no room to maneuver.*

You mean like taking care of your dad.

That wasn't what I meant, but—well, that, too.

I'd give anything to be taking care of my dad, to be living with both my folks and taking care of them. They say, you know, that when you're about nine or ten years old, you make a promise to yourself about what you're going to do when you grow up. And you spend the rest of your life either trying to keep that promise, or else being punished by the ten-year-old kid you broke your promise to. Nothing is so sacred as that promise.

So? Do you remember your promise?

She nodded vigorously. *I promised, if it was the last thing I ever did, to get our family back together again under one roof.*

He knew a little about her family by then, and all he could think of to say was: *Oh say. I'm sorry.*

Don't be. Listen; I don't suffer. Arthur taught me that suffering isn't inevitable. He's always believed that everybody finds a way around suffering. It may be mainlining ampules of Armenian alpha acid, or it may be fundamentalist religion or snake-handling. Arthur's way is just to disappear.

What do you mean? Run away?

Arthur flatlines it. His body is here, but the essential Arthur drifts away. She recovered and added quickly, *Or he used to. Arthur is much better than he used to be.*

She hopped off his desk and swung in a circle, a girl once more. *Anyway, my idea of heaven would be to have a huge family all under one roof—several generations—and to live in a town where everybody knows everything there is to know about you.*

Don't you think that would be stifling, inhibiting?

Might be good if we were inhibited. Might keep us from repeating the same mistakes our folks made. But think how well you would be defined. *You'd have no doubt about who you were; you'd know your place in the clan. You'd have* a place.

He'd watched her dancing like a sprite around the old uneven wooden floor. When he first took over, he'd intended to cover the floor with vinyl as soon as he could afford it. But now he'd grown used to its pleasant creaks, to the odor of layers of floor oil, to the rich mellow texture of its grain.

He said to himself, just figuring it out, *Nothing we're taught by society turns out to be so.*

Good! she said. *So maybe there are fairies and elves and magic after all.* She stopped before a calendar on the wall depicting a mist-shrouded lake. *Did you ever come upon a lake where the fog hovered so low you couldn't see the treetops, and get the eerie feeling that at any moment a giant might step out of the mist?*

He dropped into his childhood with alarming speed and knew precisely the combination of dread and anticipation that had accompanied his encounters with fog. But he laughed her off and went back to examining his books. *You're a case, kid. Let me get back to the real world.*

Flip off the radio. Forgot to listen to the weather report, anyway. From the looks of the sky, no chance of rain tonight.

6:25 p.m.

Dusk in the piney woods. Country road lined by a thick stand of towering pine and oak. Lights of Coldspring flickering on behind him. Not many lights, except on the first Saturday night of the month. At home, Mom would be trying to spoon-feed Dad in his bed, and he would be croaking orders in a voice like the teeth on an adze, sputtering, dribbling food down the tea towel she had tied around his neck. Still outraged, still profoundly taken aback to learn of his mortality. *All we are is incidental music to fill the frame,* he would tell them with great astonishment; but no one would be able to understand him. Mom invariably pretended that she knew, and she frequently interpreted his grunts to Rod, but the interpretations only elicited louder grunts, meaning he'd said nothing of the sort.

I'll tell you what I want: It was Jill again. *I want to he held and heard. Is that asking so much?*

Or was it Olivia?

Nothing is so sacred as the promise made to oneself. He tried to remember where he was when he was nine: California. He'd seen sequoia for the first time, majestic and deep-rooted and absolutely serene. He had decided that he would like to be a tree. Later, he developed "loftier" ambitions.

But by then, he was no longer nine.

Olivia, dancing around, envisioning giants stepping out of the mist. *I'll tell you what I want…is that asking so much?* With a start, he saw his father's face, saw plainly his stroked-out father mouthing the very words, Jillian's words.

Maybe he should turn around. Surely his parents needed him more than Olivia. Nothing was wrong with Olivia. Yes, he'd turn around and go on home. Find a side-road, someplace to turn around. Forget Olivia.

Blow it off. Go home and eat pot roast. Carry Dad to the toilet. Run his bath water, undress him, put the soiled pajamas in the hamper, holding them gingerly between the tips of thumb and forefinger. Test the water with an elbow. Lift the spindly carcass weighing no more than a good-sized alley cat into the water, duck the flailing arms, cautioning over and over, *Steady, Pop. Easy, Pop.*

Yes he needed to go back. Side road coming up fast. Ease up on the gas, Rod. Foot up, Rod. Off the gas pedal, man. Aw effing goof-up; look what you've done: you missed the freaking turn!

His foot was frozen to the pedal. He was being sucked inexorably toward the crossroad as if it were a vortex.

48

Olivia could not wait until supper was over, could not hold off the welling panic. She made the excuse that she'd forgotten to gas the car and left him sitting at the kitchen table while she barreled down to Crossroads Store, heart pounding hard.

Anyhow, she couldn't trust herself to be alone with him yet, could not think what to say. She dared not confront him about the bed, because he would resent her intrusion on his privacy. Yet she knew that unless she left immediately, she would blurt out, "Why? Why?" in spite of herself.

Crossroads Store was closed for the day. She drove around back to their mobile home, screeching to a stop a few feet from the door. Gladdie Osborn and several others peered out the windows, but it was Willie Virginia who opened the door and came down the steps toward her. Olivia noted that the albino woman possessed a certain animal grace when she walked. She wore her shirt unbuttoned a couple of buttons more than necessary, and her sharp, thin features possessed a hungry look that a naïve man like Arthur might find appealing.

Willie Virginia leaned beside the car window and grinned, but the flash of her gaze was steely and unrelenting. "Something you need?"

"Get in the car," Olivia hadn't meant it to sound like a command. When the woman showed no signs of having heard, she added in a softer, confiding tone, "I've got something to tell you."

Willie Virginia didn't budge. "I can hear okay from here."

Olivia plunged on without knowing how to begin, but hoping to elicit the woman's sympathy. "Arthur's had a very hard life. Much harder than you can imagine."

"So?" The woman shrugged and looked away. In the gathering dusk Olivia could see a less-than-perfect profile: Willie Virginia had a small bulb at the tip of her nose, and her chin was too prominent, like the sharpness of an Appalachian's: like someone with no teeth.

"He has been so mistreated," Olivia said. "Abandoned, really. He lost his whole family, except me, and it...broke him. He's been in a mental hospital for years."

Willie Virginia still looked the other way. Finally she said, "Has he cornered the market on mistreatment?"

Olivia was pleading now. "He's very vulnerable. He can be hurt so easily. Any little trauma could send him into a tailspin."

Again, Willie Virginia said, "So?"

Exasperated, Olivia almost shouted, "So leave him alone, for God's sake!"

The woman turned very slowly toward Olivia. Night had closed in, but Olivia could feel her eyes boring in. It was impossible to misinterpret the iron-steady resolve in her voice. "You think he's the only one who carries around a bucket of shit. You think anybody could hurt him even if they tried. Arthur's like me. After a while you get impervious."

"Don't you believe it," Olivia hissed through clenched teeth. "Arthur can easily be devastated by you. He isn't able to cope with a relationship."

Willie Virginia's laugh rang like the clang of two pan lids. "God! Who said anything about a relationship! I only gave the kid an initiation, and brother did he need it!" She leaned closer into the car window, and Olivia caught a whiff of tobacco breath. Or maybe weed. "Or didn't you know that the poor little bastard was a virgin?"

Olivia's temples throbbed as she attempted to blot out the images Willie Virginia's words elicited. She had never allowed herself to think about his sex life; in her mind, she had not even allowed him to have one. Arthur was hers. He didn't need anyone else. Relieved that darkness masked her instant tears, she swallowed to regain control. "I can see that he's a play toy to you, but we can't allow it. Do you understand? If you try to see him again, I'll...take him away from here."

"What does Arthur say about that?"

Her hand trembled as she reached for the ignition. "I make the decisions for both of us."

She backed out quickly, catching Willie Virginia's smug grin in the headlights as she gunned onto the road. Willie Virginia did not believe her; she had no intention of leaving Arthur alone again. She should have known better. She would have to work on it from Arthur's end, and she would have to be extremely cautious.

He was sitting on the front porch. As she got out of the car, he said, "Did you get it?"

She was caught off guard. "Get what?"

"Did you gas the car?"

"Oh. No. They were closed. I…tried to get Willie Virginia to open up for me, but she can be very hateful sometimes. I'm sure you've noticed that about her. I…don't think she can be trusted. She has two personalities, one for you and one for me. She's very two-faced."

He didn't answer. She walked uneasily past him into the house and went into the kitchen to finish preparing dessert. She had left before she served it. In a minute she heard th screen door, heard him shuffle toward the kitchen. She didn't look up when he came in but pretended to be busy making coffee.

He said, "Did you go to talk about me?"

She clattered a spoon against the pot. "What do you mean? I went for gas. Why should I talk about you?"

There was a pause before he turned to go. "Never mind."

"No really. I'm not sure what you're driving at. Why should I talk about you to Willie Virginia? I don't tell our business to anybody. Our life is very private, Arthur. That woman is an outsider. She'll always be an outsider."

He stopped in the doorway but didn't turn around. She noted that his hair curled down over his collar in back. He seemed to be studying a spot on the floor, as if he were about to say something more, but he only shuffled away.

She finished preparing their dessert: a frozen peach pie with a dollop of Cool Whip, then decided it looked too uninspired. She got down a bottle of Zinfandel she'd been saving for a special occasion, wishing for some stemware. What had become of all of Momma's nice things? Probably Grandmother had taken them; maybe she had been saving them for when Olivia married.

She poured the wine into two jelly glasses and served the dessert with ceremony on the living room coffee table. Arthur, on the sofa, looked up with a faint smile. She said as off-handedly and light-heartedly as she could, "I feel like celebrating tonight."

"What's the occasion?"

Her mind raced for a story. "I've waited until now to tell you the good news. We've…been offered a fabulous price for this house. Can you imagine?" Sensing his disbelief, she stumbled on. "It happened today while I was…at the post office. A man just walked up and wanted to buy it, just like that! It's just too good a deal to pass up." She raised her glass with trembling fingers, waved it in salute and took a large gulp. Funny how after the first lie, the next ones got easier.

He stared at her blankly. "I didn't know you were trying to sell it."

She drained the glass and shrugged gaily. "I wasn't. That's what makes the whole thing so unbelievable! Someone wants to buy it, and the price is so fantastic."

"How much?"

"Huh?"

"How much?"

She jumped up to get the bottle and sloshed wine over the side of her glass as she tried to refill it. "Oh look at me! What a mess!" She giggled and ran back for the kitchen towel.

"How much?"

She settled back down on the couch and thought hard. "I figured it out. I think it's about twice as much as we paid."

"You think?"

"Yes, that's about right. Taking our for realtor's fees or whatever. Eat your pie. What's the matter? Don't you like this wine?"

He picked up his fork and stared at it, as if he couldn't remember what to do with it. He said, "I thought you liked it here."

"I do! Love it, love it, love it. But not all that much. Sometimes I think we made a hasty mistake to move so far from civilization, you know? We should go someplace where we can go to shows and concerts, stuff like that. Someplace where you could get more intellectual stimulation and eventually find work if you want it."

"Someplace away from Willie Virginia, you mean?"

She looked as incredulous as she could manage. "Now what on earth could Willie Virginia have to do with anything? She is nothing but an ignorant old middle-aged country bumpkin who means nothing to us."

She waited for him to react. He poked his fork into his pie. She said, "Don't you agree?"

He took several bites without showing any indication that he had heard her. She lifted her glass again and said, "Anyway, here's to our good fortune!" and clinked her glass against his.

He didn't drink or change his expression. She couldn't read his thoughts. "Does this mean we're moving?" he said.

"It means more than that," she said. "It means we'll be rich! We can live anyplace we want."

Uneasily she acknowledged the reality that, unless she could actually sell the property, they would be hard-pressed for cash very soon. But if she could only get Arthur away from here, she could take a full-time job, any job…maybe go back to Galveston, do whatever it took to keep Arthur safe. Eventually, when she had to confess the truth, he would forgive her. He would know she did it for his welfare.

He said, "Is that what you want, to move away?"

"Oh yes! More than anything. I'd like to go to Houston. We could have a good life there. It's close enough to The Aunts that we could be with family for Christmas, and…."

"Yes." He took a first sip of the wine. It seemed to her that his mood had lightened. They finished dessert on an almost festive note.

Long into the night after he had gone to bed, she worked feverishly packing dishes and linens into plastic garbage bags, paper bags, whatever she could find. There was no time to waste. She would not leave his side until she had moved him away from the threat. She would not go to the hardware store the next morning; she'd work straight through the night until everything was done, until they were in the car and safely down the road, away from Willie Virginia forever.

Toward morning, exhausted, she collapsed on the couch to rest for a minute. But sleep claimed her immediately. She slept dreamlessly until the heat of mid-morning made her restless. Then she became aware of the odor of sausage and coffee, and she knew that Arthur was already u and preparing breakfast.

But the kitchen was vacant. Her own breakfast sat at her place on the table. Arthur's dishes—he must've had to rescue them from the plastic garbage bag where she had placed them the night before—had been washed and returned to the cabinet.

She called to him. "Arthur? Thanks for breakfast." But he didn't answer. She went to his bedroom: the bed was made. He would be sitting on the porch, then.

He was not on the porch, and more ominous was the fact that the dogs were nowhere in sight. The dogs went where Arthur went. So he had probably hiked all the way down to Crossroads Store to see Willie Virginia.

She would not allow it; *could not* allow that woman to poison his mind! She raced into the house and got the car keys and left immediately to intercept him.

The position of the sun overhead brought a gasp of dread. In all likelihood, Arthur had been up for hours. How could she have allowed it to happen?

As she rounded the curve near the crossroad, she spotted the dogs flopped in the shade of the station's overhang: a sure sign that Arthur would be inside. She was too late: "Dear God, what will I say?" she said aloud. It didn't matter. It was too late for politeness, too late for games. She would simply get Arthur and they would leave. Maybe they wouldn't even go back home for their things.

She leaped out of the Kia and stormed into the station. Arthur was sitting in the chair behind the cash register holding Willie Virginia on his lap. The woman could not hide a triumphant sneer. Choked with rage, Olivia had no control over the tremor in her voice. She couldn't help screaming out her rage. She rushed up and tore at Willie Virginia's arm, flinging her to the floor.

"Get off, you bitch!" Olivia yelled, but Arthur was on his feet pulling her away, pining her arms to her sides.

"Stop it, Livvie! You're making a scene." His tone modulated to tenderness as he turned to the albino woman. "Are you all right, babe?"

Willie Virginia was on her knees, glaring but still triumphant. She took a signal from Arthur and rose and banged out of the store, leaving Olivia alone with her brother.

"We've got to get out of here," she said.

"Olivia, I'm not going."

She didn't want to hear it. She pulled at his arms, trying to drag him out, angry that she could do nothing to control the desperate tears streaking down her cheeks. "Don't say that.!"

"I'm going to marry Willie Virginia."

The blood left her head. There was buzzing in her ears. She thought she might faint. *You what?*

"I didn't know what to do until I found out about the sale. Now we don't have to be dependent on each other. There'll be plenty of money for both of us. I didn't know you wanted to leave until last night. Now we can both have what we want: You can go to Houston and Willie Virginia and I can travel around in her truck, go up to Fort Worth and look for her son."

She leaned against him, hearing his words through a gray fog that swept her into merciful unconsciousness. Her life was over. Passing out was the only thing she could think of to do.'

6:29 p.m.

The sun was creeping near the pine tops, making driving easier. Most of the time Rod no longer had to squint into the glare. He consulted the odometer and decided he must be nearing Crossroads Store. He couldn't be sure, but he had the sense that she lived north of the intersection.

Crossroads Store hove into view around the next long curve. He could see the sign out front lit by a single halogen spotlight, already burning in the waning daylight. The sensible thing to do would be to stop and ask directions. Jillian would feign shock: among her litany of his conjugal failings, she accused him of blind driving for hours in the wrong direction rather than stop for directions.

Funny he should think of it now, how he and Jillian had been hundreds of miles from either of their families when the break came. There was no one nearby to talk them out of walking away, no one to shame them for not thinking more of their son's welfare. No one to account to.

Rod's own parents hovered in his consciousness as somebody he could blame for his neuroses, but there was little support they could offer when crises appeared. He'd seldom confided in them, anyway. Even when his father was a healthy strapping man, he hadn't been approachable. Work occupied even the weekends, when he invariably brought home a full briefcase. In the matter of the divorce, when Rod finally screwed up courage to tell them, both parents looked at each other as if to say, *Didn't we warn him?*

The spotlight on Crossroads Store sign went off just as he pulled in, and he realized that the lights inside the store were off as well. He jumped out of the Blazer and hurried to the door, hoping to catch old man Osborn before he locked up for the night. He peered through the screen over the Nehi sign but could see no one inside. Old man Osborn must've already gone out the back to the mobile home anchored behind, where he lived with five or six offspring. Rod did not have the nerve to face the whole mob. He could find Olivia's place on his own.

He backed the Blazer out and turned north onto the crossroad. Among the several disreputable vehicles parked behind the store was the pickup that Willie Virginia had driven to his hardware store a short while ago. The sun had now dipped completely behind the treetops, but the peripheral gleam from his headlights caught the shape of a shadowy figure stowing something in the pickup bed. Rod braked and turned into the yard, his headlights capturing the shocking white of the albino woman's hair framing her startled face. She had a cigarillo in her mouth. Arthur was nowhere in sight. Rod leaned out and called, "I'm looking for the Ahern place. Is it up this way?"

She didn't remove the cigarillo, just shook her white head and pointed in the opposite direction: south. He whipped the car around and dug off.

49

As Arthur drove her back to the house, Olivia wrestled with her conscience. She had one cudgel left in her arsenal to defend them both against this assault by Willie Virginia. She could tell Arthur the truth: she could tell him how crazy he was. She could tell him about what he'd claimed to have done to Mr. Masterson. She could tell him what he did to Daddy.

He stopped in the front yard and turned off the engine. "You'll be all right now?" He sounded it as if he didn't plan to stay.

"I feel weak." She felt of her damp forehead and decided she wasn't exaggerating.

He came around to her side of the car and helped her out, handing her the car keys as he took her arm. So maybe he planned to stay after all. The dogs, who had chased them all the way home, greeted them with panting excitement, circling them and nudging them with wet noses.

"Why don't you lie down on my bed for a change?" he said, bending to fondle the dogs before he helped her up the steps. As they entered the front room, he looked around at the sacks and boxes stacked against the wall.

"I see you're all packed. I didn't notice them when I left this morning, or I would've loaded them into the car for you." He picked up a couple of the nearest sacks. "I'll just do it now."

Olivia dropped onto the couch and said, "Arthur, don't" much more sharply than she meant to. She patted the seat beside her. "Come and sit with me for a minute."

When he had perched on the edge of a cushion, she sighed and said, "There's no place to go."

"Huh?"

"No place. There's no house sale. I...was trying to save you from Willie Virginia."

He put his hands resolutely on his knees as if he might get up and leave without another word, but he seemed to reconsider. Finally he said, "Livvie, we've been trying to create an artificial something here."

"Don't!" she said. She made up her mind and rushed on before she could change it. "Arthur, there's something I've got to tell you, about you and Daddy, about that night...." Her voice trailed off as he took her hand, squeezing it a trifle harder than necessary. If she lost her momentum, she might never be able to tell him. But his words, unnaturally commanding and insistent, cut her off.

"I've never talked much about my time in Galveston, with Peggy. Maybe I ought to have told you what I learned from all that. In a nutshell, it was that Dr. Freud is full of shit."

"What? What are you talking about?"

"All this cult of analysis, using up precious time digging into the past and meanwhile losing the present moment. Peggy was so busy thinking about what had happened years ago that she lost her whole life. We could all see it happening, but we couldn't prevent it."

Olivia knew it was true. "You're saying I do that?"

"You want us to be a family like in the old days. First place, we were never that family, thanks to Dad. We *aspired* to be that family, but we never were. I'm saying you're living in a fantasy world, and you're trying to force me into it with you."

There was no good answer. "Then what should I do?" she asked.

"I guess, if you haven't sold this place, you'll have to live here. Willie Virginia and I will go on up to Fort Worth and poke around, see if we can get a line on her son. We might even hook up with Uncle Cas. When we run out of money, I guess we'll come back here. This house is half mine. Only we may need to take the couch, if you don't mind."

"If you don't live in the past, I would think you didn't plan for the future, either."

"Yeah, well, maybe we'll get flattened by a semi."

She gave an involuntary sob. "I couldn't stand it if something happened to you."

He stood abruptly and strode toward the door. "Maybe that's the best reason I can think of for leaving: so you'll get busy and find somebody else to pin your hopes on. But I'm warning you, you'll be disappointed again."

"You...make it sound as if I'm...a leech or something."

He didn't answer. He went out onto the porch and she called, "Where are you going?"

"Going to walk back down to the crossroads, find out when we're leaving."

She rushed to the screen and called after him. "She's an ignorant country woman, Arthur. You're so brilliant! You're wasting yourself on her! Arthur!"

He never looked around.

She turned back to the room and surveyed the mess. The sackful of books had tumped over and spilled onto the bare wooden floor. She kicked the books aside and picked up the nearest bag of groceries and took them back into the kitchen. Her breakfast plate was still on the table. She ran a sink full of sudsy water and began washing up. When she had finished, she turned her attention to the stove and cleaned all the burners, then washed the refrigerator shelves before she returned the condiments to them. One by one she emptied the sacks she had packed the night before and put everything away. She worked all afternoon.

When the sun dipped behind the pines, she fixed the dogs their supper dishes and wait for them to come home. Then she would sit in Arthur's rocker and scratch their ears, the way he usually did.

The night closed in and soon stars would wink in the openings between the pine branches. Fireflies flashed across the yard, and night creatures began their clicking songs. A bullfrog bayed down in the gully, and tiny tree frogs chirped somewhere overhead. The old rocker gently creaked back and forth, almost without her effort. The creaking of a rocker is in tune with the music of the spheres, Momma used to say.

How could she keep from thinking about the past?

She considered going inside to fix Arthur some supper but decided she would just sit there and wait until he showed up. Or not.

When it became evident that he wasn't coming, Olivia went into the kitchen and did what she had thought about so often: she turned on the gas in the oven, pulled up a chair before it and stuck her head into the oven.

50

No urgency, then. The two had not been going to Olivia's. She was probably all right, then. Except that she hadn't shown up for work; hadn't tried to phone.

In his rear view mirror Rod saw a car—was it the pickup?—back out of the Crossroads yard and gun off north.

My brother doesn't work. He's not well, Olivia had told him in a bare murmur, then she'd lowered her eyes, so somber and cavernous, so almost violet that they looked bruised sometimes. She had turned back to rearranging tubes of solder on the shelf, warning him to question no further.

***

At that instant, Olivia heard Willie Virginia's pickup rattle to a stop outside. *I knew he would come.*

She rushed to the front in time to unlatch the screen for Arthur.

"I've come for the couch," he said. "We want to get on the road."

"You mean tonight?" she said. Olivia could see the glow of Willie Virginia's cigarillo through the truck's windshield. It pulsed as if she were taking quick restless puffs. She rushed outside with Arthur following.

He said, "She says if we don't leave while we've got our nerve, one of us will change our minds."

Olivia's voice rose to a hysterical pitch, causing the dogs to circle and bark with nervous excitement. "You were going to sneak in here and leave again without even telling me goodbye?"

"I told you goodbye earlier. No need to tour the ruins all over again, Liv."

Olivia began bawling openly. "My God, Arthur, don't you have any feelings for me at all? Your only family? Doesn't family mean anything to you?"

Willie Virginia climbed out of the pickup, talking around the cigarillo that clung to her lower lip. "Oh for Pete's sake! Put a cork in it! Arthur, get whatever you need in a hurry. I gotta go in and pee."

She took off for the house while Olivia continued to harangue at Arthur, to plead, shame, cajole. Arthur pursed his lips tightly and headed for the pickup without another word, with Olivia following, still blubbering—until she remembered.

She turned to yell out just as Willie Virginia reached the front door. "Wait! Don't go in there with that lighted—"

The explosion blew Willie Virginia all the way out into the yard.

51

The impact drove both Olivia and Arthur to their knees. The initial noise temporarily deafened her. The house went up in a flash of light before her eyes, and when the reverberations from the explosion died down, she could hear Willie Virginia's screams.

She scrambled to where the woman lay, half naked, hair smoldering, her clothes still afire in places. Light from the burning house illuminated Willie Virginia's face. It was glistening black and oozing, the features impossible to make out.

Olivia batted the fire from what remained of the woman's clothes and screamed for Arthur. "She's hurt bad! We've got to get her to a hospital." She looked around and saw him still kneeling on the ground, both hands covering one eye. "Oh my God, Arthur, are you hurt?" She ran to him and tried to pull his hands away from his face, but he rigidly refused to budge. He seemed to be in a trance.

"Arthur? Arthur! You've got to help me move Willie Virginia." She shook his shoulders, but he seemed not to notice. As usual, she would have to do it alone.

Olivia considered the Kia and realized it was out as a vehicle for transporting them all to the hospital. Besides, she didn't know how much gas she had. She would have to manage to get the two of them into the pickup by herself.

She lowered the tailgate and tried to shut out Willie Virginia's moans while she assessed the situation. The truck bed was packed for their trip, complete with sleeping bags. She arranged the two suitcases and ice chest along either side and rolled out both sleeping bags, one atop the other, down the middle of the truck bed, so that Willie Virginia would be wedged in, unable to roll around and injure herself any worse during the ride.

She ran back to the house and got Willie Virginia under the arms, hardening herself to her screams, and labored to drag her out to the truck.

Arthur staggered onto the porch and fell to his knees. The dogs Boudreaux and Lena, who had run into the woods when the explosion occurred, made a timid reappearance, circling her as if to help, then running to Arthur to lick his hands and face, then scampering back to the women each time Willie Virginia cried out again. Somehow, panting and grunting aloud, straining until she thought she would burst a blood vessel in her temple, Olivia hoisted the injured woman up onto the tailgate. Then she climbed into the truck bed and dragged her onto the bedrolls.

She returned for Arthur, took a firm hold of his arm and commanded, "Get up, Arthur! We have to go!"

Obediently he rose, and as he took his hands away from his face, she saw that one eyelid was swollen and glistening, as if it had been struck by a piece of burning debris. She led him to the passenger side and told him, "You'll be all right. The doctor will fix you up." She couldn't speak in the gentle tone she usually reserved for him; it was necessary to yell over the roar of the fire and noise of the dogs.

She patted both animals and told them. "Stay here. I'll get Gladdie to feed you." She got behind the wheel, buckled Arthur in, and took off toward the crossroad. She could hear Willie Virginia's screams of agony from inside the cab. It would take more medicine than she could fine in Coldspring to save her.

At Crossroads Store, she turned and headed west toward Conroe medical center. From there, Willie Virginia could be life-flighted to Houston, if necessary.

As she spun around the corner, she saw a Blazer approaching the intersection from dead ahead. She recognized the vehicle, recognized the driver.

"Now what's he doing out here?" She spoke out loud, but not to Arthur, who usually communicated very little when he lapsed back into catatonia.

But he startled her by answering, "Looking for you."

"For me? How do you know?"

"Willie Virginia," he said.

Ah. Willie Virginia again. Always Willie Virginia. She must've sent Rod off in the wrong direction. Nothing but trouble, Willie was.

She consulted the speedometer, saw that she was doing eighty, and eased up on the accelerator. No sense in killing them all, driving so fast in this old heap. No telling what kind of tires it had. A blowout at this speed would throw them off the road. Besides, the trip would be less bumpy for Willie Virginia if she slowed down a little.

From the back, Willie Virginia's screams had subsided. Olivia took that as a good sign, one way or the other.

52

6:38 p.m.

The Blazer plunged deeper down the narrow road that cut through the pines, curving occasionally around a small scraped-off piece of farmland with a dismal shack set close to the road. He could tell by the odd washing machine or worn-out sofa on the front porch, or the auto parts strewn in the yards that none of these was the Ahern place. He looked at the odometer. How far had he come since the crossroad? What had Olivia told him?

About five miles from the crossroad. Was that what she'd said? Or: *Five miles* north *of the crossroad.* But he was heading south.

A few more miles. A little farther. He would clock his odometer for three more miles, and then...

It was the faint perception of orange that ate its way into his consciousness. A glow in his rear view mirror, the gloaming orange of a sundown. He realized that with all the turns in the road, he must've become disoriented: he had thought west was to his right. Instead, it must be behind him

***

6:40 p.m.

Headlights on bright, cutting a swath through the black. Twilight well past. Deep of evening now, almost starless. And still the sky behind him glowed, pulsed, lighting up the forest.

***

6:45 p.m.

No sense going any farther. The steel railings of a bridge caught the headlights. Must be the bridge across the creek at the county line.

Olivia didn't live outside of the county, he was certain. Willie Mae had deliberately misled him out of sheer orneriness, most likely.

Rod backed and filled, making a careful turnaround on the narrow road that was banked by deep ditches mired in swamp water. Maybe he ought to head on home. He'd told his mother not to wait supper for him, but he knew she wouldn't eat without him. It was part of her control over him, another insidious way to keep him beholden.

He'd tried to confront her about it one evening after he'd had a couple of drinks; tried to remind her he was a 41-year-old man with a child of his own. *You'll always be my boy,* she'd said, with just the right degree of catch in her voice. He had no life. She had sucked the life out of him until there was nothing left.

Until Olivia.

Her hair was long, her foot was light,/And her eyes were wild—

Her presence had reintroduced the harmonics of possibility. Since she had come, he felt existentially alive again, able to experience things once more. It was like springtime. The sap was running. It was like scratch and sniff: there was hidden perfume again.

It happened gradually after she began working at the store. He noticed with shock that whenever he said anything, she stopped whatever she was doing and listened. Not politely; really listened. It was a heady experience, exhilarating, like wild stallions galloping through his blood.

There was a ladder on rollers in the store that allowed access to the high shelves. He'd been in his office one day when Old Man Carpenter came in. Rod heard him ask Olivia for a large can of spackling. Minutes later he heard her calling, "Mr. Benson?" then "Rod?" with an element of panic. He dropped his pen and rushed out to find her halfway up the ladder in her flat-soled sandals, clinging to a gallon can of spackling.

"It's too heavy," she said. "I don't think I can get down with this."

He climbed up behind her and reached around her to take the can. His chest grazed her tight-jeaned rump; he allowed the contact to continue a fraction longer than was necessary. He climbed down, put the can on the counter, nodded to Old Man Carpenter, and went back to his office, leaving her to ring up the sale. When the bell on the front door tinkled, he waited, getting his breath under control. He knew she would come.

She stood in the doorway waiting. For several long minutes he kept his eyes on his books, waiting for her to say something. Finally she did.

"Maybe I ought to quit."

He searched for how to answer. He could have tried to explain: *It's been over two years since my divorce.* But that was beside the point. How could he describe what her being there had done? *It's being pressed into the margins, not staying in the congealed center. It's being out in the dangerous edges. It's like being in prison and tapping on the wall for a thousand days, then one day someone taps back.*

He only said, still not looking up. "I hope you'll reconsider. I need the help. You could just call me whenever somebody wants something off the high shelves." Knowing that was not what she meant.

She didn't say anything. His hand shook as he took a swig of his coffee. It was cold.

He said, "Heavy stuff like that ought not to be up that high, anyway." His heart was thumping.

"No," she said finally.

"Maybe I could rearrange the stock over the weekend," he hurried on, encouraged. "Put all the gallons down where they'd be easy to get.'

She said, "I wouldn't want to put you to so much trouble."

"It ought to be done anyway. One of these days it'll be too much for me, too." He swallowed and looked her squarely in the eyes. "I'm forty-one, you know." *Not a threat to you,* he wanted to say. *Just a harmless old man. Getting on up there.*

The front bell tinkled and she went out to wait on a customer. At least she hadn't winced when he told her his age. In a minute she peeked in again, apologetic. "Sprocket wrench?"

He started to get up and get it for her but checked himself in time. "All we've got are over on the left wall. Let him find it himself. That's what I usually do."

He would foster the Old Man thing, regain her confidence. He would take great care never to do anything else to offend her. He couldn't imagine going back to the way it was before she came.

His mother, too: he had to get her off his back. She was quick to suspect The Worst. She groused because he no longer came home for lunch on First Saturdays, when the outdoor market and musicians filled the town square. Olivia worked until 5:00 on those Saturdays, to help out with the extra drop-in business that seldom materialized, the business he told his mom he was needed to service. Actually, on those days he would beat the crowd to the Hop for take-out burgers so the two of them could be on hand to handle the onslaught that conceivably could show up. It was his one legitimate meal of the month alone with Olivia.

The April first Saturday featured bluegrass bands from as far away as Iowa. Rod and Olivia decided to eat near the front window so they could watch and hear the bands. To see over the heads of the crowd on the sidewalk, they climbed up and sat cross-legged on the countertop.

As she bit into her burger, he saw that she was biting into the wrapper as well. He reached over and pulled the paper away from the bun and then recognized it as an intimate act. She shot him a warning look and he shrugged.

"What can I say? Once a father, always a father."

She accepted that and let it pass. She took another bite and concentrated on the music, talking with her mouth full. "Arthur would appreciate this. He used to play guitar. Had aspirations of being a musician once."

Rod perked up. "So did I! Hey, maybe he'd like to get together sometime, jam a little, see what we could come up with."

She looked dubious. "I don't know..."

He pulled back immediately. "Naw, I'm sure he wouldn't want to fool around with anybody in the codger age bracket. We probably don't even know the same music."

She took a swig of her soda then tapped his knee with the corner of the can. "Look: you can tone down the Old Codger bit. Nobody's going to accuse you of being the Clarence Thomas of the hardware set."

He flushed, unaware that he'd been so transparent.

"Besides, being old is no big deal. I used to be enamored of a man who was way over than that." She dipped a fry into the little cup of ketchup and brandished it around before popping it into her mouth. Eating seemed to put her in an expansive mood.

She chomped on another fry and gazed out the storefront over the top of the insulation display, nodding, remembering. "He even had a paunch. Paunches are very sexy, actually. He had this little pone of fat over his kidney that just begged for biting."

He strangled on his soda and had to stop and cough for a while.

"You all right, Rod? I didn't embarrass you, did I? What kind of name is Rod, anyway? Short for Rodney?"

"Rodman," he said through tears of strangulation. "Family name. My mom's a genealogy freak."

"Good God! How Freudian! Why not just come on out and name the poor kid Phallusman or Penisman?"

He dissolved into sputtering fits of laughter. "You are a case! Where'd you get that smart mouth? Give you a full belly and you get completely zoned!"

She grinned. "Maybe I take after my mom. She was something of an eccentric."

"And Arthur? Is he eccentric, too?"

She sobered at once and turned her gaze back to the window. "Arthur's been…not well."

6:52 p.m.

He was nearing the crossroad, time to make a decision. Should he forget it and go home to supper? He'd become accustomed to having an early dinner. His mother tried to stick to his favorites, and she'd promised pot roast tonight. It was like returning to the womb. Maybe he would just go on home.

Anyway, he owed it to the old man, helpless old sonofabitch. No, by God, he didn't owe the bastard a damn thing! *Where were you whenever I got hurt? Off in Aberdeen? Remember when I broke my arm playing ball and you didn't even notice the cast when you came home?*

Oh sure, the college thing. Hell, Rod got that tuition crap crammed up his nose every time he turned around. *I wish the sonofabitch had let me paint houses for a living; I wouldn't be any worse off now.*

Barreling toward him, stirring up a cloud that fogged the headlights, was what looked like Willie Mae's pickup. But it didn't turn in at Crossroads Store. Instead, it passed the store and turned right, spinning almost out of control, spewing gravel across the road, then careened west on the road that led toward Cleveland and Conroe.

6:53 p.m.

Past the Crossroads Store again, past the trailer home with its retinue of old cars. The radiance in the sky ahead brought to mind Stephen Hero's *Claritas: the luminous silent stasis of esthetic pleasure.* Olivia, too, called up esthetic pleasure, maybe even luminosity, but certainly not silence and definitely not stasis. She was too unsettling to fit Joyce's definition; better the luminous noisy metastasis of esthetic torment.

Visions moiling, tires jouncing along dry ruts—*Jesus H. Christ, hurry!*

The turnoffs fretting the road offered the final opportunities to change course. Rod's unreasoning conviction grew that if he didn't turn back now, his life would be altered for all time. But at the mere thought of Olivia in peril, his resolve scattered like autumn leaves—*And the pale queen of Autumn casts her leaves*—blown away by the fresh wind of her memory, a blinding visitation.

The sky pulsed. *I am caught in a blinding shaft of animal magnetism.*

Her breath, thin and shallow: *He's not well.* Dear God, what had she meant?

He lived, he now realized, in a perpetual shiver of expectancy for Saturdays. He listened to her smart mouth with a frisson of awe and disbelief.

While there's time, open the reliquary, examine the treasures one more time, find the justification for this insanity.

On top of the heap must lie the remnants of his shattered marriage. The union that had once amazed him. He had never known he could love one person so much. But very quickly he realized that Jillian did not, could not live in his world. Although she was not particularly devout, she was married to her ancient tribal faith. But that was a secondary union: her first bond was with her father. She had mentally seduced him and been mentally seduced by him. It was disgusting.

That led to the current problems. The brother, Olivia's brother, wired or drifty, either way, a nascent menace to himself and to Olivia.

But she was resilient, tough as a boot. *There's no honor in the oil business. You know they put down a well that tests high, then they lie about it and cap it and hold it for years while they pick up all the surrounding leases for a pittance.* That offended her, the perfidy of her father's profession.

Guess I shocked you with the bit about me and the preacher, huh? So what—am I fired? For all her bravado, she remained committed to the notion of the virtue of physical virginity.

Virginity, he had told her, *is sacred only because it is a state of openness to the infinite,* to which she'd asked, *Are you talking God, or what?* She had a pagan need to live for some higher purpose, to believe in magic, in guardian angels, perhaps, in good fairies. She had an unshakable conviction, despite all evidence to the contrary, that good would prevail.

What you did was pretty lean, she told him in awe, wistful, *coming home to help your dad.*

He'd protested, *It isn't as altruistic as it seems,* but she didn't choose to believe him. He tried to dissuade her. *You make me out better than I am: you ascribe to me nobler motives than I'm capable of.* She'd answered, *Isn't that what people are supposed to do for each other?*

That had brought a stab of pain, because a few years ago, he had believed that he and Jillian were destined to have such a relationship: to admire each other deeply, to finish each other's thoughts, to by-God *stand up for each other!* But in any contest between Rod and Jillian's father, there was no question whose corner Jillian would be in. That realization had rendered him bereft.

Olivia had told him, *I know about dealing at any cost. I know about groveling, about having your whole life go down the dumper for no good reason. I know about crude buyers, too, passing off new crude for old oil that has no price cap*—This, in defense of Arthur's withdrawal—*These men were part of our lives growing up. They were in and out of our house. They were Arthur's real role models. They were also big contributors to Bush's campaign.*

Lulled by her flippancy, bloated with the pleasure of her vivacious proximity, Rod had ignored the obvious: She had emerged into adulthood through a system of infinite veins of corruption. She must've been badly bruised, but she was strong. She had refused to be beaten down by circumstances; she had already survived the venal ethics of that corrupt era when, in the almighty name of capitalism, everything was fair, especially war. How much worse could it ever be?

Maybe, whatever madness Arthur and Willie Virginia were embroiled in, Olivia, through the strength of her own quirkiness, her own guilelessness, would persevere. She had an earnest quality of innate goodness that attracted genies of protection. *She cannot be hurt; she cannot die.* God, what is this fixation on death?

There *is* a comic vision of reality; Olivia was not the only one to be doggedly determined to see it: it was apparent from Dickens to Melville to Orwell. *Why can't I adopt it? Why must I see the dark side?*

6:59 p.m.

Yes, it was definitely fire ahead, streaking up to the sky in jagged fingers like lightning traveling backward. Someone's house had gone up in a flash, blinding the night with crackling, crashing flames, groaning as it devoured the crumbling timbers. Already he could see the black skeletal upright supports; could see clear through the house, like an X-Ray. No use to call the fire department. Nothing could possibly be left unconsumed.

Except that now the entire forest was threatened.

He looked at his odometer. He'd gone exactly five miles from Crossroads Store. And Olivia's little black Kia was parked in front of the wreckage—empty.

53

Rod jumped out of the Blazer before it stopped rolling and ran toward the burning house. It was a conflagration: as if a fire bomb had gone off. A roaring, crackling inferno that shot furious red tongues up past the tops of the tallest trees. It throbbed with life and blistering heat.

There had been only two people in Willie Virginia's pickup as it spun around the crossroads, hauling west. What was left of Olivia was inside the blazing house.

He screamed out, "Olivia! My God, Olivia!" Knowing no one could possibly be alive to answer.

Intense heat forced him backward and a crashing beam sent sparks flying. He held up his arms to shield his face and felt the sting of a live spark burning a hole through his shirt sleeve. He beat out the smoldering cloth and backed still farther away, falling to his knees, gasping for breath. Heat and remorse brought tears to his eyes. He put his head against the ground and heaved, trying to find comfort in the earth, crying out over and over, "Oh God, oh God, Olivia, oh my God!"

Sparks shot skyward and arced back, fizzling, like his life, not like the life he could have had—like the academic life of dislocation, intermittent striving and relocation—boards spitting, sap fizzing—like the moving, the treks with realtors through dozens of "executive estates," tract houses built on spec in "upwardly mobile" communities—crackling, heat whistling through disintegrating timbers like his disintegrating life. Long tedious weekends with Jillian and their son when they tried half-heartedly to find common ground, when he could not have imagined this kind of disaster, when he pulled himself back repeatedly from thoughts and plans about his work, his precious work, inter-departmental politics, strategies for a bigger slice of grant money, presenting papers to make a name—heat, the heat of the Devil himself, whistling, deafening heat—not like the infrequent sweaty, boiling, stifling nights when he'd tried to cajole some passion in the king-sized bed that had been disassembled and moved across country so often that the frame screw threads were stripped so that the vicious thing squeaked and wove like a drunk derelict every time he turned over. Wove like Jillian after her second gin. Squeaked like the sound of nail upon wood wrenching itself free and crashing to the smoking floor.

Olivia, my love! Did you suffer? Oh my dear God.

Now, sparks spewed up and over, or shot up and up until they faded from sight, not like the life he could have had with Olivia if he could have forgotten that she was twenty-three, if he could have broken free from the sense of duty that held him in a choke-hold, stifling as the acrid billow from the little house: Herculon fibers were melting and poisoning the forest. If he could have hired someone to lift his dad onto the toilet and wipe his backside, hoist him into the tub, dry his shriveled nether parts and listen to his thick frozen-tongued complaints. It wasn't meant to be this way, A man doesn't work hard all his life to end up like this.

He coughed but felt no relief from the sting in his throat; heat had seared his esophagus and rendered it raw. Through watery slits he tried to get his bearings and locate his car, fearing he might have left it too close.

Everything was so clear not: If he had stood up to his mother *I can't keep this up, no matter what sacrifices he made for me. I have to have a life.* If he had faced the old man: *You can't expect to dress in street clothes if you can't do it yourself. There's no need to keep up appearances. There's no one left to impress,*

No one left.

The inferno beating on the top of his head pushed him back even farther. He groveled against the ground. Even that was warm to the touch. As if the voice were somewhere in the distance, he heard himself begging, "Don't, Olivia! Oh my God, don't die!"

He could have thrown himself at his mother's feet, or at his father's bedside, and begged them to excuse him from this burden. *And while you're at it, absolve me from guilt*—choking on the smoke and the guilt, smoke infiltrating and permeating the forest thick as remorse—*better still, back up our lives and start over. Leave off the messages about busting my butt to get to the top of everything.*

Because ultimately it all comes crashing down in flames.

But no. His rage that shot up like sparks in unguarded sleep was carefully damped upon waking. He was unsuitable for a fresh-faced urchin like Olivia. No, not fresh-faced but dewy. Like the dew that collects on an ancient plowshare, long used and abused and then cast aside. She was old, older than the earth, its molten core forging all elements into itself.

He pressed his cheek against the ground and screamed out his rage. He was not a sensitive man: upbringing and circumstances had militated against sensitivity. But he came into her circle like a man breaking through a magnetic field that held her tragedy pressed to her: he entered the field and it weighted upon him like gravity, like the force that sucks all elements into a vortex. Like the whistling black fire that seemed to be around him, that he wished would sweep him into the black hole with her.

But it was too late. It no longer mattered but it would always matter. Olivia was no more. No more dancing around the store, envisioning giants stepping out of the mists. No more brandishing a French fry and teasing him about his name.

He heard his own scream: "It *does* matter!" He lifted his head, crawled to his feet and staggered to the Blazer, realizing if he didn't get out now, he would be trapped in the escalating forest fire. Pine needles ignited easily. Flames would devastate the land and obliterate all proof that Arthur had destroyed his sister in the fire. Rob must survive to give witness of this terrible crime.

He rammed the Blazer into gear and looked at the dash clock. It was 7:21. They were a good twenty minutes ahead of him already.

54

He wheeled in behind the Crossroads Store, reached the trailer in half a dozen leaps and called out, "Open up! Fire! Fire!" as he banged on the door. The youngest sister Gladdie Osborn, wearing a long T-shirt and apparently nothing else, opened the door a crack. Smells of fried ham and sounds of the television and of clanging pots poured out around her.

"Call the fire department! There's a fire up at the Ahern place!"

"So that's what we heard." Gladdie turned back into the room but did not give an inch in the doorway. "Did you hear that, Daddy? That bang must've been up at the Ahern place. Some kind of explosion, maybe."

Rod could see the old man's stolid back through the crack. He sat in front of the television is a fog of smoke. A can of Shiner beer rested on the vinyl arm of his recliner. To his daughter's announcement he made only a grunt, then aimed the remote at the television, turning up the volume.

Again Rob said "I've got to use the phone! We need to get the fire trucks out here—"

"Store's closed," the old man hollered without turning around.

The girl faced Rod with an apologetic shrug. "The phone's in the store, see."

Rod advanced up the steps and pushed her aside so he could stick his head inside. "If you don't get some help out here, that fire's liable to burn down the whole damn forest, and this place along with it!" His outburst brought people running in from every room.

Mrs. Osborn came in from the kitchen and peered out the window facing the road. "I see the glow from here," she said. She motioned to Gladdie. "Go on up to the store. And give the man a quarter if he needs it."

"A quarter?" Rod asked as they ran across the yard to the back of the store. Barefooted, she minced, tender-footed across the gravel, and he had to stop and wait for her.

"Pay phone," she explained as she unlocked the door.

He called the fire department and then dialed his mother, who masked her exasperation as concern.

"Thank heavens you finally called! We've been frantic with worry! And of course, Rod, your father's bladder is ready to burst. I don't know how you could be so…"

"Put him on the bedpan. It doesn't take a brain surgeon. I won't be coming home." He was surprised how easy it was to say, and how light he felt: Atlas after dropping the world. Tersely he explained about the fire and then added, "I'm the only one who saw who did this, and I'm going after them."

"Oh don't try to act the big hero. It doesn't suit you. Leave that for the police."

"There's no time to argue, Mom. I'll talk to you tomorrow." It was his first time to hang up on her, ever. *Maybe,* he thought. *Maybe I'll call her tomorrow.*

He turned away free—and faced Gladdie Osborn, who was perched on a stool behind the counter, her bare legs crossed and swinging with carefree suggestion. She was in the process of lighting a cigarette. Rod pushed past her and stalked toward the door, resisting the urge to fan the smoke away, not even tempted to look at her. "Thanks," he said.

She hoped off the stool and followed him. "S'pose anybody was hurt?"

He grimaced to himself. The others hadn't even thought to ask. "No way of knowing," he said. "Fire's too hot. Place is too far gone."

"You see anything of a pickup? The one my sister drives?"

He lied. "Haven't seen a soul."

"I heard you say you saw who started the fire.'

He jumped into the Blazer and ground on the ignition. "Forget it," he called, slamming the door. Then he thought better of it and rolled down the window. "I was talking about something else." He realized he was shaking all over.

But she had already forgotten it anyway. She had picked her bare-footed way across the graveled yard to the edge of the road, to have a look at the flush of the sky five miles away.

Rod gunned past her and wheeled toward the crossroad, at once buoyed, despite the tragedy, by the exhilaration of the avenger invigorated by the hunt. "Damn, I should've bought a candy bar," he said, suddenly ravenous. He looked at the clock. It was 7:40. He pushed the Blazer to do a hundred.

55

There is no way a Blazer can do a hundred over all these hills on this convex road. No way to see ahead through the swampy night, no way to see around the curves.

No way a man can sign over the rights to his son, his namesake, to another man. No way to do it and live.

No way a human being can keep on sacrificing for a paralyzed vegetable indefinitely, even if that vegetable stares out through eye sockets red-rimmed with rage.

No way a man can watch someone he loves—yes, by God, loves—be consumed by fire and not move the earth to find her killers and destroy them.

No way in hell to catch them, when they had a forty-minute head start, hauling ass as fast as that old pickup would take them.

We'll still call him James Rodman Benson, Jillian had told him. *We'll just add Gold to the end. So he can still be Rodman the Fourth if he wants to be, but for legal purposes, he'll be James Gold. We'll keep your last name as part of his given name. In fact, Stanley likes to call him "Ben" instead of "Jamie." Ben Gold has a nice sound.*

No way under God's heaven that a man who's been without a job for over two years can continue paying child support. No way he can avoid signing away his rights, acquiescing to the adoption by Jillian's new husband so that both children can be bar mitzvahed with the same surname. No way to keep from giving up all claim to his precious son, his only child, his Presbyterian namesake.

I don't know what's your beef, Jillian had said. *At least now you won't be hauled into court for being in arrears. Seems like if you really had Jamie's best interest at heart, you'd be glad for him.*

Glad, she said: No way.

No way a man can dwell on the pain without his chest bursting. No way.

8:10 p.m.

No way to wipe out the sight of that burning house, Olivia's pyre, to shut out the thoughts, to keep from imagining Olivia's horrible death: her screams that no one was around to hear. Little Olivia, bearing up the world's weight—Arthur's perpetual sickness—on her narrow girl-shoulders.

No way to say now what he should have told her, what he wanted to tell her. Impossible to see now through the tears.

Impossible to see. Impossible to catch up with that fiend Arthur. Impossible to survive with this unbearable pain.

Impossible to hold the car on the road at this speed.

Impossible to make the curve.

56

No time:
> *"The game is done, I've won, I've won,"*
> *Quoth she and whistles thrice.*

Rod was conscious when the trucker reached him but lost consciousness before the ambulance arrived. The Blazer had left the road and nosed into a deep watery ditch, flipping onto its side as it hit the far bank. He was aware of a burning pain in his right arm—he hadn't been wearing his seat belt and was thrown across the cab against the passenger door—but he did not know the extent of his other injuries.

From time to time voices spoke to him, reassuring him, asking him where it hurt, asking if he could move. He thought he recognized his father's authoritative rumble, warning him not to move, but he was under the impression that he himself was nine years old. He wanted to hug his father around the knees, but his arms were too heavy to move.

He felt something sticky on his forehead where it rested against the door handle. When it occurred to him that it might be blood, he thought his mother cradled him in her arms and patted him on the back until he fell asleep again.

> *She took me to her elfin great*
> *...And there she lulled me asleep.*

Jillian was there, too, looking the way she did when they were in college, pushing her wispy red hair behind her ear with the long silver nail of her forefinger, teasing him, running a pink tongue across her even white teeth. He wanted to be alone with her, wanted to go off somewhere quiet where he could lie beside her and throw one leg possessively across her and rest against her. He wanted to bury his face in her hair that always smelled like Vidal Sassoon. Then he was nine years old again.

The sound of sirens brought him back to the present disaster, but when they lifted him out of the Blazer, the pain was so excruciating that he blacked out. He heard someone scream, heard someone moan, and he wondered if it was his voice that he heard. He realized that he must be dying.

Someone—his mother?—slipped a mask over his mouth and nose. He felt a slight prick and then he was playing racquet-ball with his dad, then with his fourth-grade classmate. Flashing lights, sirens, more faces from elementary school. Off one gurney onto another. Voices, many voices, his high school basketball coach, his grandmother. A cold table, lights, a machine overhead, deft hands, a rubber apron. Maybe an autopsy. *Wait! Not again!* Again, the unfamiliar voice, moaning. Another prick. Darkness.

Bright lights, people speaking in hushed tones: his superiors at the University. Today they were working him over, tearing him apart, torturing him. It would go on forever. He was in Hades.

Forgive me, son, for signing those papers, for giving you up. Forgive me for failing you. Failure as a father, paralyzed father. Father father father father: funny meaningless word. Senseless. Cents-less father.

Tubes restraining him. Head throbbing. Something else holding him. Rail. Rails on both sides. A bed. Another bed to the right. He tried to turn his head to see. A man in the bed, sitting up, reading a magazine. Arthur.

Voices again, women's voices. His mother, putting a cuff around his arm, pumping it tight, squeezing his arm. His mother's voice: "He's coming around. You awake, Mr. Benson?"

Two women talking: his mother and Jillian. No, not Jillian's voice. "You've got your hands full, nursing two." The other voice, close by, connected to a hand that was holding his. "I don't mind. It's what I like."

He was not at home. He was not at work. He was not in the Blazer, rushing after Arthur, not lying in a ditch, moaning.

He was in a hospital bed, where people he didn't know were treating his body as if it were theirs; someone he didn't know was holding his hand. He forced his eyes open to see.

Her lips were red, her looks were free,
Her locks were yellow as gold.
Olivia.

57

Several times when Rod woke—he wasn't sure whether the intervals were punctuated by hours or by days—she was sleeping in a recliner. On occasion he opened his eyes to see her reading, or combing her hair at the mirror, or moving to the side of the other bed in the room. Gradually he became accustomed to the idea of her presence, and to the idea that she was not a result of a Demerol-induced fog. When he was at last able to speak, it was her name he spoke, hearing his own raspy voice with surprise.

"Olivia." It was not a question, but a summation: a sermon.

She had been looking out into the sunlight, so that he saw only her silhouette against the windows, her hair a baby-fine halo, a radiance. Olivia: the luminous noisy metastasis of esthetic pleasure. He knew her by heart, as he had known her voice chiming though his stupor. It hung there still in the back of his brain, reverberating like a long-remembered tune.

She came to him grinning and took his hand. "Surprised? Quite a coincidence, all of us ending up here, huh? Or *not*."

He mumbled, "Coincidence is the best form of intention."

Quite naturally, as if she did it every day, she bent and kissed his bandaged forehead. "God! You guys think you can just chill and keep on living this cocktail and canapé life forever! You think I have nothing to do but baby-sit you both?" With a nod she indicated the other bed.

Rod shifted so he could see Arthur, propped up in the other bed, looking at a magazine with his one unbandaged eye. Olivia frowned, reached over and turned the magazine right-side up. Arthur's face remained unchanged.

With no attempt to lower her voice, she said, "Arthur's in his catatonic state. But we'll keep *that* from the doctors, because they'd do their godawful best to bring him out of it. If we keep quiet about it, they'll never know the difference: they spend so little time in here."

Rod realized he must still be quite confused. He seemed to have missed something altogether. He did not feel inclined to ask appropriate questions, to be filled in on how they all managed to wind up here together; it would take much effort to bring himself up-to-date. It would be easier to jump directly into the present with both feet, enter the race at mid-point and run along like hell with the rest of them—and try to sort it out on his own as he went along.

He asked, "But doesn't he need psychiatric treatment?"

She shook her head. "This is Arthur's way of coping. He was getting much better, but the explosion set him back again. Give him time; he'll be okay."

Rod shut his eyes, tired with the whole idea, and she said, "I know what you're thinking: that I want to keep him this way to protect him from Willie Virginia."

Who the hell was Willie Virginia? Oh yes, the Crossroads Store. The albino woman. The one who had been in the hardware store today getting camping supplies. Was that yesterday? She'd had Arthur in the pickup, and she'd deliberately given Rod wrong directions to get to Olivia. They were going to kill Olivia....

He said, "Where...is Willie Virginia?"

"They took her to Galveston, to the burn center there, once we got her past the triage nurse from hell—You're in Conroe Regional Hospital, by the way. They figure with skin grafts she'll make it, in about a bazillion years. So see, she's no threat. She won't be taking *anybody* to Fort Worth anytime soon." She was holding his hand. She patted his cheek with her other hand. "How're you feeling?"

He hurt all over. He tried to shift again and felt a sharp pain in his abdomen that made him wince and groan aloud.

She said, "Guess that answers my question. You have a ruptured spleen, among other things. I can't figure out how that happened. Weren't you wearing your seat belt?"

He could see the cast on his right leg and left arm and could feel the head bandage that reached down as far as his eyebrows. "What did I do to my head?"

"Slight concussion and a small gash. You were damn lucky. You have some stitches there." She grinned. "You're no prize. You'd better settle while you can. I don't think anybody else'll have you now. Even the nurses think you're a pain in the butt. They don't wear those goofy little caps anymore, did you know? But they still stand when a doctor enters the room. Pretty barbaric, huh?"

He tried to take it in. Maybe he hadn't understood what she was suggesting. He said. "My mom…"

"I phoned her. She was hysterical at first, but I got her calmed down. She calls me about four times a day to check on you. We've gotten to be buddies, practically."

"He closed his eyes again. Olivia was alive. He was alive. But maybe he was too beat to be anything but depressed. She babbled on, the voice in his head that he had been listening to for hours. She was talking about his dad, his mom, calling her "Margaret" as if they'd known each other for years. Could so much have happened overnight?

"What time is it?" he asked, not opening his eyes.

"It's about three. Three o'clock Tuesday. You missed most of Sunday and Monday. They kept you pretty busy Saturday night and Sunday and yesterday, patching you here and there.'

He didn't remember anything with clarity after about eight on Saturday. She was still saying the things she'd been saying for hours, it seemed.

"Before you turn me down, I know you came looking for me. You're all bashed up right now because you came looking for me."

He made the barest of shrugs, feeling foolish, and decided not to try to justify.

"Look at it this way," she said. "You have what I need, and I, apparently, have what you need."

He still had his eyes closed. "What do I need?"

"A wife, maybe." She waited for a moment and added, "I could have a child, too."

As if anyone could replace Jamie. Besides, he didn't want to think about going through all that crap again. His head was throbbing. He needed a pain pill. And a pillow that wasn't stuffed with discarded gallstones.

She said, "Don't you want to know what I need?"

She held his one good hand. He couldn't even ring for the nurse. So he said, "What?"

"Well, it's not nail boutiques and sushi bars."

"What, then?"

"Roots. Several generations under one roof." Before he could protest, she added, "Someone I can take care of; we can all take care of each other."

He heard the echo of Jillian telling him, *What I want is so simple: someone to hold me and hear me.* But he hadn't believed her, any more than he believed Olivia now. His mouth was so dry. He needed water and all she did was talk. His tongue clicked against the roof of his mouth with every word. "You're talking about living in that house, all four of us together."

"No. I'm talking all *five*. Because I won't ever be without Arthur again. And Arthur needs his dogs. So that's seven."

He'd forgotten the dogs, running in frantic circles at the site of the fire. "Are the dogs okay?"

"I phoned Gladdie. She's feeding them. They're very resourceful, though. They've learned to fill up on mail order catalogs during tough times. Good fiber content."

Belatedly she noticed his dry mouth and brought the bent straw to his lips. He took several grateful gulps before he said, "My dad is paralyzed. If you think I'm a lot of trouble now...."

"Good. We can all help. Arthur will be a big help in lifting him. Margaret worries a lot about how hard it's been on you, having to do it all alone."

He was surprised to learn of his mother's concern for his welfare. He said, "You think you know her, from a few phone calls, but you don't. You don't know my life—it gets old."

"Look, we're not talking perfect here. We're talking about a bunch of people who need each other."

He felt very tired. Yes, he needed relief. He would just as soon lie in this bed forever as to face going back to that house, to lifting his father, to consoling his mother. Olivia was still tlking: a desperate little edge had crept into her voice.

"You're thinking you don't dare trust your dad to a mental case. But I know Arthur: he'll be fine. He's very intelligent, practically a genius. He knows how much reality is healthy for him, and so when his peace of mind is threatened, he just retreats."

It sounded so eminently sensible. "Arthur's no wus," he said.

"Damn right. It's how he copes. Momma would consider catatonia perfectly natural, for Arthur."

He must be pumped full of Halcyon. She made good sense.

They lapsed into silence while each waited for the other to broach the most important topic at hand. Sounds of the hospital took over: the forced cheerfulness of nurses in the corridor, the voice of the pager on the public address system, the beeps of monitoring equipment in a nearby room. He couldn't bring himself to utter a word.

At last she blurted out, "I know you must care about me or you wouldn't have gone out to look for me. And when I called the Osborns to tell them about Willie Virginia, Gladdie said you thought I was dead, said you were going after my killers with blood in your eye. That may not be love, but at least it's something!"

He swallowed, feeling transparent. She went on. "I don't even care about sex so much...."

He had to laugh, a careful, painful chuckle. "What, do you think I'm in the bone yard?"

"I know better than that. Remember I told you I've been with a man—in a way--older than you, only now that I look back, I see he never listened to me. You listen to me. And you've already told me it doesn't matter about the...virginity thing."

He'd never allowed such a fantasy to creep in until now. If only she would let him sleep, he might give way to it. She waited for him to answer, and when he did not, she said, "And the other thing is, no matter what happens, no matter what you do, I will never, never leave you." And he knew it was so.

He'd all but forgotten about the pains in his head, spleen, arm, leg. He was losing an argument he was too weak to hold. "My God, I'd have more dependents than King Lear! We would be the dysfunctional family beside which all others would pale: a man with a wife half his age, a stroked-out father, a martyred mother, a catatonic brother with an ominous past, and two seventy-five pound dogs who eat mail-order catalogs. What more?" He had risen off the pillow several inches but quickly fell back in exhaustion, knowing the answer to his own question; the ghosts of Donnie and of Olivia's parents, even the ghost of the essence of the sane Arthur.

She shrugged. "What can I say? You want normal?"

"It would be nice."

"Hockey puck! People are always saying what they're going to do when things get back to normal. Well, take a good look." She held her arms out wide. "This is as normal as it gets. Look: evolution started with the Big Bang and a couple of gasses: helium and hydrogen, maybe. Since then for billions of years things have been evolving from the simple to the more complex. You can't fight evolution."

With all the strength he could muster, which was very little, he protested, "But you don't know my mother. She's been playing the victim for so long."

"Baloney! She *is* the victim!" she said indignantly. Then a light came into her eyes. "And I know just what she needs—just what our family will need to round it out: a housekeeper. Somebody really simpatico. Someone of your mom's generation that she can talk to and who's like an ally.

"And I know the ideal person! Name's Josephine. She's not forty miles from Coldspring at this very minute, back on the reservation after serving some time in...oh but Josephine took good care of our family.

"She's only got one teeny problem that crops up if she gets upset. She sets fires sometimes. But you're going to love her!"

The End
(Thank you, Jack)

Books by Guida Jackson

Fiction

Passing Through
The Body in the Smokehouse
Subtractions
Death by Chicken
Cybergasm
Hitting It Big

Non-Fiction

Women Who Ruled
Women Rulers Throughout the Ages
Encyclopedia of Traditional Epics
Traditional Epics: An Oxford Literary Companion
Encyclopedia of Literary Epics
Women Leaders of Africa and Asia
Women Leaders of Europe and the Western Hemisphere
The Patchwork Mind
Through the Cumberland Gap
Virginia Diaspora
Heart to Hearth
Legacy of the Texas Plains
The Literature of Cultures in Crisis
Evolution of the Literary voice in Emerging Cultures
African Women Write
Fall from Innocence, with Jackie Pelham

Plays

The Lamentable Affair of the Vicar's Wife
Nothing Like Nigel
Showdown at Nosegay Cottage
The Man from Tegucigalpa
Heaven or Hell
Queen Julia is Peculiar
Nibelungenlied

Printed in the United States
By Bookmasters